Progeny

K.M. Hardy

Picaty Press —Tooele, Utah
ISBN: 978-1-7367346-3-6
Library of Congress Control Number: 2021924327
Title: *Progeny*
Author: K.M. Hardy
Digital distribution | 2021
Paperback | 2021

This is a work of fiction. The characters, names, incidents, places, and dialogue are products of the author's imagination, and are not to be construed as real.

This is a work of fiction. The characters, names, incidents, places, and dialogue are products of the author's imagination, and are not to be construed as real.

Dedication

iii

For my wonderful husband and kids, my mom, and my Gran.

And special thanks to MC for inspiring a new and fun to write character, I hope you like her.

Chapter One

December 21, 2021

Chief Anthony Humbar of the Cleveland, Ohio PD walked leisurely down the stairs to get some breakfast. From the smells of vanilla and sugar, it was obvious that his wife, Candice, had fresh muffins coming out of the oven. Considering she was a big-time meal planner and not a fan of getting up super early, fresh muffins meant she was going to ask something of him. He chuckled, straightened his tie, and walked into the kitchen. Sure enough, he was greeted with a fresh cup of coffee, blueberry muffins, two over-easy eggs, and a slice of bacon waiting for him at the breakfast table.

"Good morning, honey," Candice said cheerfully, greeting him with a kiss.

"Good morning, sweetheart," he smiled slyly. Walking over to the table, he mused aloud, "Mmmm... eggs, bacon, blueberry muffins. What do you want?"

His wife chuckled and replied, "I want to repaint the office next weekend."

After thirty years of marriage, he knew she wouldn't waste any time beating around the bush with her requests. Her tactics still made him laugh out loud, nonetheless. "And when you say the office, you mean the *whole* office, right?"

"Yes, but it's only one color this time, I promise. I've already got the paint and supplies ready to go; it shouldn't take us longer than half a day—a whole day, tops."

Humbar groaned; he was hoping to spend the first weekend of 2022 watching the Cleveland Browns go up against the Pittsburg Steelers. It had been a great season so far, but he'd only been able to watch the games after they'd been recorded. Christmas weekend would be no exception: That day was dedicated to family. New Year's Day he hoped to finally catch a game live, but when Candice put her mind to something, there was no changing it. Feigning major disappointment, he teasingly grumbled, "Yes, dear."

"Thank you, honey," she teased back a grumble. Kissing his forehead, she turned to get her own plate of food.

Humbar had barely taken a bite of a warm, delicious blueberry muffin when his phone started ringing. He grumbled for real and answered, "Chief Humbar, Cleveland PD."

"Oh no, I interrupted breakfast, didn't I?" answered a woman's voice.

It had been years since they'd spoken, but Humbar knew the voice of his old partner Dana Evanston like the back of his hand. Chuckling, he answered, "Dana? Well, this is a surprise. How's the Columbus office treating you?"

"Same as always. Listen, I've got a body off 71 near Chesterville, and I want you to come down and take a look, please."

"What for? I haven't worked homicide for almost fifteen years."

"Trust me, Anthony, you really need to see it for yourself."

Judging by the graveness of her reply, he knew this was no small matter. Looking at the clock, which read 7:01 a.m., he knew the traffic would be bad. "Alright, it'll take me about an hour to get there."

"Use your lights," Dana answered before hanging up on him.

Humbar did as he was told and blared his siren the whole way to Chesterville, but the weather did nothing to help his travel. It had been snowing almost every day for two weeks now, and he practically had to dig his car out this morning before he could even get on the highway. *At least the roads are plowed,* he thought to himself. An hour passed before he could tell he was getting close to the crime scene. The traffic began to get heavy; spectators during the morning commute were slowing down, trying to catch a glimpse of what all the fuss was about far off the side of the highway. Finally, he broke through the last of the cars, went off the road and onto the makeshift path through the snow. Several other vehicles were parked just before the tree line, their lights and sirens on. He looked around and took note of his surroundings: The road was lined with thick trees and forests for miles. Although the heavy blanket of snow made it difficult, he could see glimpses of public officials working diligently, collecting any and all evidence they could find in the forest. He walked over, doing his best to stay out of everyone's way.

Wading through the dozens of civil servants, he didn't have to wander too long before Humbar saw Dana walking towards him. It had been fifteen years since they worked their last case together, and while he may have put a couple pounds on around the middle, she hadn't changed one bit: With rusty blonde hair cut shoulder length and a black suit hidden away under her thick, maroon coat, she looked like she belonged in a court room and not out in the sticks.

"You made good time," she said in her own friendly way. "The body's over here."

Yup, she hasn't changed at all, Humbar chuckled to himself. He followed her through the rabble and the trees until they came to an open field. The snow continued to fall, but it was white as far as the eye could see. A few yards out stood the usual circle of forensics experts surrounding something that was partially buried in the snow, which he assumed was the body. His suspicions were confirmed as they got closer. Lying peacefully in the snow was a young woman with a white peony on her chest. The victim looked young, possibly in her early thirties, pretty, naked, and impeccably clean from head to toe. It was as if someone had bathed her before dumping her, and the purple-blue bruises scattered sparsely along her body stood out against the pearly white snow. Her lips were blue, and her eyes shut, but the color that surrounded her eyelids was just as abnormal. Humbar's blood started to run cold before Dana donned a pair of gloves, knelt down, and pointed to the left side of the woman's chest, just above the breast.

"Look here," she said somberly. "It's a needle mark, 16 gauge."

Humbar knelt next to his old partner and took a closer inspection of where she was pointing. Sure enough, positioned right over the victim's heart, was a deep, red, ugly mark that no doubt was made from a large, thick needle. The skin surrounding it was bruised and purple, and the veins were clearly visible through the skin. Although he already knew there was no point, he looked to the coroner and asked, "Was it the cold or poison that killed her?"

"Definitely poison. She's been dead for hours before somebody moved her out here. The cold has only enhanced everything, including preserving her body."

Dana stood up and began walking deeper into the field. Humbar wasted no time in joining her. When they were far enough away to not be overheard, she said quietly, "Look around, Anthony: It's practically deserted but still off the main road. It's open, but it's surrounded by trees. It's winter...and the flower. I'm not wrong, am I?"

"No, you're not," Humbar nodded. "I honestly thought it was over, we haven't seen anything like this in almost fifteen years."

"We *both* assumed he was dead. It turns out he was just hibernating again."

Turning back to look at the body of the girl one last time, Humbar shuddered. "Dear God...he's back."

"Yeah, he is. So, what are we going to do about it?"

"I want this son-of-a-bitch once and for all, and I know a guy that can help."

***

Back in Cleveland, about ten minutes away from Lake Erie harbor, near the Irishtown Bend, was an apartment complex that was situated on the bridge over the Cuyahoga River. The apartments weren't anything particularly special. They housed many singles and families of the low-median salary range. But on the first floor, in a two-bedroom unit, was the apartment that served as home to Sampson Angus McKay: a Scottish immigrant who had come to America nearly fifteen years before. With twenty-five years of differing law enforcement positions under his belt, from being a Constable to an IA Detective and then a Hostage Negotiator, he was now a permanent asset of the Cleveland, Ohio FBI office and the leader of the Special Investigative Task Force. The position allowed him to live as an official citizen of the United States, as well as be closer to his family: Meredith Staton, his ex-wife, with whom he shared an amicable relationship post-divorce, and their sixteen-year-old son Oliver.

It was 8:30 a.m., and Sam had just finished making a rather large breakfast of eggs, bacon, and pancakes. He was a big guy, coming in at six and a half feet tall, and could easily eat a lot, but even he knew he'd made enough to feed an entire army. Or at least enough for a ravenous teenage boy.

"Oliver! Move yer heide!" Sam called over his shoulder but was met with silence. He continued preparing two plates.

A few minutes later, just as he was getting ready to call his son again, the sleepy teenager emerged from his bedroom looking more dead than alive. Oliver fumbled to the table and whined, "Dad, it's Christmas break! I don't have school for the rest of the year; why do I have to get up so early?"

"Because yer mother'll kill me if ye eat nothin' bu' poptarts an' cereal three meals a day, an' I've made enough pancakes t' carry ye t' lunch if I'm lucky." Setting the plates down on the table, Sam turned around to pour himself a cup of coffee before joining the boy.

"Ooh, I thought I smelled pancakes. Chocolate chip?"

"We've go' syrup, we donnea need chocolate chips, too."

"Whatever," Oliver mumbled and rolled his eyes before greedily digging into the enormous plate of food. Before Sam could tell him to take a breather, half the plate was already gone.

Sam chuckled. "While I'm a' work, I'd like ye t' a' least vacuum an' make yer bed before ye spend the rest of the day in front of the telly."

"Actually, my friend Bryce is going to pick me up later. We're going to play Smash Brothers at his house."

"When?"

"Like eleven-ish."

"An' who's goin' t' be there?"

Oliver rolled his eyes, "Come on, Dad, Mom's done this with me dozens of times before. I know the drill: No drugs or drinking, and I'm too young to have sex but, just in case, I've got a condom in my wallet."

Sam narrowed his eyes. "So there will be girls there. Will there be any parents?"

"Bryce's mom and dad work all day. Look, I promise it's just video games and pizza, nothing else."

Although Sam wanted to chuckle, he kept his face calm and stoic as he continued his parental figure duties. "First, tell me abou' the girl."

Oliver's eyes widened in alarm. "What? What girl?"

"There's gonna' be girls a' this party, an' obviously ye like one of 'em if ye've admitted t' keepin' a condom in yer pocket. So, before I say yes, I wanna' know who she is."

Sam's abilities to discern the teeniest details from his son always threw the boy for a loop; the teenager looked absolutely flabbergasted, and Sam couldn't hold back his amusement any longer. It appeared in the form of a snort.

Oliver looked at his hands in embarrassment before mumbling his answer. "Karliegh Branders."

He was so quiet; Sam almost missed the name. "Ye meet her a' school?"

"Yeah, we have pre-cal and home economics together."

"Well? Wha's she like?"

Finally, the boy smiled, "Really hot."

Sam narrowed his eyes, doing his best to convey how much he disliked Oliver's choice of words. "Wha' else do ye know abou' her?"

"She's big into volleyball; she's the outside hitter for the school team. And I think she likes the color...turquoise?"

"Have ye talked t' her outside of class?"

"No."

Sam took another bite of his breakfast and continued. "Well, I wouldnea jus' say 'ye're hot' t' a girl ye hardly know."

"Well, duh! I don't want her to think I'm a creepy stalker-dude! We already have a few of those at school."

Sam chuckled again. "Are any of her friends comin'?"

"Yeah, a couple."

"Then here's wha' ye do: Ask one of them wha' her favorite soda is an' bring her one. Then, try t' take a seat near her. Bu', if under any circumstances, she donnea feel comfortable an' moves away, ye donnea push it."

"I know, Dad. Mom's gone over the consent speech with me, too."

"Well, I haven't. So I want t' be sure ye know the meanin' of the word."

Once again, Oliver rolled his eyes and answered, "No means no. A woman has the right to say 'no' at *any* time, and I always listen to her."

"Exactly," Sam nodded. "I's nice knowin' ye are listenin' to yer mother an' me. Alrigh', make yer bed an' vacuum, an' ye can go. Lock up an' keep yer phone on, an' ye answer when I call, aye?"

"Got it," Oliver smiled. "Thanks, Dad. And can I just say, these last couple of weeks living with you have been a lot more fun than being alone at Mom's."

Although Sam prided the compliment, he quickly rushed to Meredith's defense. "Give yer mother a break, Oliver. Since Staton Homes has taken off, she's been verra busy."

"I know, and I'm glad her business is doing good. She's really happy. I'm just saying, it's been way too quiet at her house. At least you call me to tell me when you'll be late."

Polishing off the last of his food, Sam deposited his dishes into the sink and answered, "I'll be sure t' mention tha' to her. Now, donnea forget: vacuum an' yer bed. When do ye think ye'll be comin' home?"

"Probably late, maybe around ten."

Sam gawked. "Ye'll be playin a video game fer eleven hours? How is tha' possible?"

"Don't knock Super Mario Smash Brothers, Dad."

Even though Sam couldn't begin to understand the youth's obsession with a game he'd barely heard of, he let the matter go and grabbed his coat. "Fine, have fun. Answer me when I call."

"I will," Oliver answered, his mouth full of another bite of pancakes.

"I love ye."

"Mhmm, lub you doo."

Satisfied that the boy was situated for the day, Sam headed out the door to work: Cleveland, Ohio's FBI office. It didn't take him very long to get there, which was a bit of a surprise given the weather: snow for days and days. Not that it bothered him; he really liked the winters in Cleveland as they reminded him of his home in Scotland: the quaint village of Rosneath on the western shore of Gare Loch in the vicinity of Helensburgh. Most of the weather throughout the year consisted of rain, but when it got colder, there would be sleet and ice and, occasionally, snow. Ohio's weather conditions were similar to Rosneath's, but the white blanket of snow just felt more like home, even if it was a pain to drive in.

Before long, he was parked and walking in through the front doors of the FBI. Just as he scanned his badge and passed through the body scans, he caught sight of his old friend and colleague Anthony Humbar sitting on a nearby visitors' bench. Sam's curiosity was piqued when Humbar started towards him, carrying a box.

"Humbar? How are ye, big man?"

"I wish I was better," the portly man answered. "I need your help."

Sensing the urgency, Sam wasted no time in ushering him to an open room where they could talk privately. He had barely shut the door before Humbar had five case files from the box out and laying opened on the table.

"Wha's all this?"

"Cases of rape and murder of the most heinous nature, dating back as far as 1982, where I first saw one as a beat cop. And this—" Humbar pulled out a sixth case file and handed it to Sam "—is the most recent victim: Chloe Hale. Her body was discovered this morning near Chesterville buried in three feet of snow. The Columbus coroner is still thawing her out before he can officially declare the time of death and the cause, but I don't need to wait for the answers to know it's the same guy as these other cases."

"How do ye know tha? I's pretty sparse, the numbar of victims. No' exactly the typical pa'ern of a serial."

"Yeah, I know, but the method is exactly the same: Death by an injection directly to the heart, and that's only one of the similarities."

Sam picked up a file and skimmed over the contents. "Any pa'erns in the choice of victims? How abou' when an' where he attacks?"

"No, nothing like that. None of these women looked anything alike, and they were of completely different age, financial, and social groups. Two of them had a history of running away; two were reported missing by their significant others, and one had been living on the streets. The last case was in 2006, Joyce Shingle, one of the missing persons. After ten years without seeing anything...I honestly assumed this guy had either died or was arrested for something else, and *somebody* had to have gotten a DNA match on him. But when I saw the body of that poor girl this morning...I know it's him, Sam. And in forty years, I haven't been able to catch him. I need you to help me do it."

Sam didn't need to be told twice. Despite knowing he would need the official okay from his boss, Director Belinda Copper, he was determined to help Humbar stop his serial killer. "Aye, ye got it. I donnea suppose ye've go' a suspect?"

"The only thing I can give you is the name that the media gifted him with: The Christmas Angel."

Chapter Two

Sam walked with determination to Copper's office; he didn't really expect her to fight with him. In the two years he'd known her, Belinda had proven anything but predictable. Weaving through the hallways of the third floor, he finally came to the door at the end of the hall and knocked.

"Come in," answered the cheery voice of Copper's right-hand man, Agent Evan Dower.

Sam walked in with Humbar right behind him.

"Good morning, Agent McKay!" Dower answered with a smile.

"Mornin'. Is she in?"

"She's finishing up a report before a meeting with the Attorney General this afternoon. She asked not to be disturbed."

"I's important," Sam urged.

"Okay," Dower answered in a sing-song tone. It usually didn't take much for Sam to convince the young man to make exceptions for him, as the agent had made no secret about his admiration and slight infatuation. His puppy dog behavior didn't bother Sam; instead, he found it amusing and was always able to use it to his advantage when he needed to. "Agent McKay and a plus one are here to see you, ma'am. He says it's urgent."

"Send them in," came her usual, level reply.

Sam walked through the next door with Humbar right behind him. Director Belinda Copper was, as always, sitting stoically behind her desk going over dozens of reports and files. With her shoulder-length snowy white hair, maroon lipstick to compliment her porcelain skin, and irritated cat-like demeanor, anyone could sense that she was a force to be reckoned with. Sam could attest to that. In the short years since they met, he had come to deeply respect his superior, and not just because she was a bit older than him. Copper's methods weren't questionable, but definitely intriguing. There had been plenty of times Sam had no trouble expressing his disapproval of her decisions, and while his voice easily rose to make the point, she would forever remain calm and indifferent, which tended to infuriate him. Still, he couldn't help but admire her for that ability.

When she didn't look up, Sam cleared his throat and said, "Ma'am."

Continuing her work, she answered, "Yes, McKay?"

"Ma'am, this is Chief Anthony Humbar, my old friend from the Cleveland PD."

"It's a pleasure, ma'am," Humbar said.

"What can we do for you, Chief?"

"Ma'am, what do you know about the serial killer known as 'The Christmas Angel?'"

He had the Director's attention; Sam watched with interest as she looked up from her stack of paperwork, set the pen down, and met Humbar's eyes. "The serial killer who kidnaps and rapes his victims, kills them with a homemade poison, and leaves their bodies in random, secluded areas with a single white peony left on their chests? That Christmas Angel?"

Humbar, visibly unnerved, nodded. "Yes, ma'am."

"The last case found was reported in 2006, wasn't it?"

"Until this mornin'," Sam answered. Handing over the very skimpy file belonging to Chloe Hale, he allowed himself to take a seat and gestured for Humbar to do the same as Copper skimmed through the contents.

"Yes, it would appear to be the same M.O. as previous cases. Do you have any theories on why he's been missing in action for fifteen years?"

"Not yet, ma'am," Humbar answered her. "But, if this son-of-a-bitch really is back, then you know we don't have much time before this gets cold."

"Our resources are yours, Chief Humbar. Agent McKay's team will, with your permission, take over the case and begin immediately, with your assistance. When you have a suspect, you will be supplied with the manpower to stop him."

"Thank you, ma'am. Thank you so much."

Copper handed the file back to Sam and gave her final words. "Good luck."

Sam knew by her tone that was the end of the conversation. Taking back the file, he and Humbar left the office and quickly made their way to the third floor on the other side of the building, where

Sam's team had their own abode as the Special Investigative Task Force.

The trio (Julie, Rivera, and Simon) were, as usual, bickering about something in their own sibling-like way. Derrick Rivera, Sam's partner and the designated 'big brother' of the group, was going toe-to-toe with the others. What he lacked in height from the rest of the group, his Latin heritage more than made up for in his passionate arguments.

"You've made some out-there claims before, but this is by far the stupidest thing I've ever heard," Rivera said with an eye roll.

Simon Abler, the incredibly young computer genius, was laughing and egging the fight on with his sarcastic, witty replies. African American and almost as tall as his superior, Simon was an incredible valuable asset to the team. But, unlike the others, he was incapable of being intimidating to anyone because of his age and the thick-rimmed glasses he chose to wear. At least that was what Sam had determined about the young man.

"I'm telling you, the CIA is only saying they 'released' the UFO footage because they don't want to admit that they got hacked." Simon puffed up his chest proudly and smiled. "How else is the 'most secure agency in the world' going to keep up the façade that they're untouchable? By taking credit for somebody else's work. They just used the press to frame it. That was their intention because the world was going crazy anyway. They might as well add a new crisis to twenty-first century bingo."

And off the sidelines, while occasionally throwing in a retort that would keep the argument going, was the fiery redhead, Julie Russell. She was definitely the sister of the group, as the other two would quickly put anyone who even looked at her the wrong way in their place. Not that she needed their help; the woman had more guts and gumption than anyone Sam had ever met, which she had proven time and time again since her time in SWAT. Nothing could tear this unit apart, not even themselves. They were a family.

"And if they find out that *you're* the one that hacked them, your ass is grass, Simon," Julie chuckled and took a sip of her coffee.

"You know, it insults me that you still think they'd even be able to find me," Simon answered.

"Hey, *we* did," Rivera smirked. "You're not as untouchable as you think, kid."

"And you're not as tough as you think, meat-sicle!"

As Sam got closer to them, they must have sensed how important their assignment was as they immediately stopped their squabbling and stood to attention. "Conference room, now," he grunted.

After a quick nod and quiet 'hello' to the police chief, everyone followed and immediately took their seats as the older gentleman began to pull out every case file from the enormous box.

"Alrigh' everyone," Sam started, "we're racin' against the clock on this one, so pay attention. Humbar, tell us everythin' ye know."

His old friend nodded and cleared his throat. "Have any of you heard of 'The Christmas Angel?'"

Julie and Simon looked at one another with puzzled expressions while Rivera nodded. "Serial rapist, I first heard about him at Quantico in 2003. The last known case was a few years after that, and nobody has seen anything of him since."

"Well, they have now. The body of Chloe Hale was discovered early this morning off of 71, three miles west of Chesterville—" his phone suddenly pinged with a text, interrupting him. Humbar looked at the screen and sighed, "And the coroner just confirmed the bloodwork: She was killed with a poison consisting of bleach, hydrochloric acid, and sodium hydroxide."

Simon was the next to speak. "He kills them with cleaning chemicals?"

"Using a needle directly to the heart, yes."

"How many women has he killed?"

"Six, that we know of."

"So, you think there are more bodies of women out there somewhere?" Simon shuddered.

Humbar nodded. "I don't have anything that proves it, but I definitely believe it. The number of women that run away or go missing or even live on the streets...it's unbelievable."

"Were you able to figure out how he'd get these women without anybody seeing?" Julie asked.

"Only just, and it was from the coroner reports. Every one of them had fresh contusions on the back of their heads, which suggested that he would knock them unconscious so they wouldn't struggle during the kidnapping. None of the contusions have even been close to alike, so the coroner determined he would just use whatever was convenient. And considering there were absolutely no witnesses, and no one ever came forward saying they saw something odd, the best we could figure was he'd lure them somehow and then knock them out. Kind of like Ted Bundy."

"Does he have a victimology pattern like Bundy?" Julie asked again.

"Not a thing: No type, no area he favors, none of these women ever worked in the same circles. There wasn't even a pattern to where he would kidnap these women. Believe me, we've tried to find one even with only five victims. The only thing we can say for sure is that he kidnaps these girls at a random time through the year, sometimes as early as spring or as late as fall. Then he rapes them and waits until there's snow before he kills them and dumps their bodies."

"That's weird," said Simon. "What's so significant about winter?"

"Maybe he gets too cold and can't get it up," Julie said, the malice in her voice undeniable.

"Could be," Rivera nodded his agreement. "Have any head-hunters been over this?"

"Not any that have gotten back to me; I asked for help, but they never came through. The victims were deemed too far apart for it to be considered an urgent case, and there were other serial killers still killing that needed to be found immediately."

Sam picked up one of the older case files and looked through its contents. "Tell us abou' the crime scenes ye've been to. Anythin' ye can remember."

Humbar's face paled, but he swallowed and answered, "The first time I saw this was in 1982. I was the first on the scene after the call. Some poor kid was driving home with his girlfriend and had run out of gas on Shepherd Lane, but he had a spare can in the trunk. He said he got out to refill the car when he saw something off to the side of the road and went to go see what it was. As soon as he realized it was a body, he hurried and filled up and drove to the nearest gas station to call the police. My partner and I followed him to the spot. I remember the snow had just barely started falling, but any footprints left behind were already covered and untraceable. The victim was lying on her back, completely naked, her hands resting at her sides, and positioned right over her heart was a white flower that I had never seen before....Her name was Gail, Gail Rodney. She was only eighteen and had run away from home. I knew right then and there that somebody had planned to kill her and went to extreme lengths to stage her the way he did. But what could I do? The detectives took over the case, and I went on with my job.

"The next time was in 1994. I had just made Detective in Homicide. My partner Dana, who coincidentally informed me of the newest victim this morning, and I were called out to Cuyahoga Heights and had to take some little dirt path deep into the hills. Some industry guys were scouting out an area for a factory or some such when they found the body of a woman that had been living on the streets for years. We couldn't figure out who she was; she's the only Jane Doe in these files. It had been over ten years since I'd seen the work of the Angel, but seeing this poor woman naked with that damn flower on her chest and the snow falling on her was too familiar. So, on a hunch, my partner and I set to work calling every department in Ohio asking if they'd seen any cases similar to this. We found out that his area wasn't only limited to Cleveland. I found out that there had been two other cases in Athens and Hilliard, Betsy Ringer and Annie Fall. And the last one we found was in 2006 in Jackson about twenty miles from the state line, Joyce Shingle. I called every agency in Ohio for the next ten years asking if they'd seen any more of him, but he'd just disappeared...sooner or later, you can convince yourself that a nightmare is over. But look at the good that did."

Everyone was quiet; Humbar took a shuddering breath and sat down at the table with them. He looked as though just telling the story had physically taken its toll. Not that anyone doubted it; it was clear that his encounters with these victims had done more than haunt him.

Sam broke the silence. "Di' ye have any leads a'tall?"

"Oh, we had lots of leads. We figured he had to have some sort of connection to the medical field, given he likes to use needles and industrial-grade cleaning supplies as his weapon. So, we decided to use the press to our advantage after victim number four, Annie, and warn the public about walking alone, to use a buddy system, as well as report anyone standing near their vehicles who might be acting suspicious, or anyone that may have medical training that was acting peculiar."

"Those are pretty wide parameters," Rivera noted.

"Yeah, you're telling me; but I had five dead women and absolutely nothing to go on. We had to do something. Thousands of people called the tip line reporting their weird neighbor or uncle. We chased down every single one of them. Two of them seemed like pretty good candidates: Larry Tanner and Carl Gebbs. Larry Tanner served time for aggravated robbery in the 80s, but he was on house arrest for a misdemeanor when Joyce was found. Carl Gebbs was a registered nurse with a few complaints filed against him, but he was paralyzed from the waist down and confined to a wheelchair since the summer of 1995. I checked on them this morning, just to be sure, and Tanner has since gone back to prison. Gebbs died two years ago."

"Wha' abou' physical evidence?" Sam asked. "Anythin' a' all tha' suggested where he was keepin' these women? Somethin' we can use t' do a geographical search with?"

"We could only *wish* he had left some dirt on them for forensic soil analysis, but each and every girl was cleaned before they were dumped. Thoroughly."

"You said he raped them," Julie continued. "Were any seminal fluids collected from the bodies? Pubic hair follicles, spit, anything at all that didn't belong to the victims?"

Humbar shook his head, but everyone noticed the shiver. Taking a deep breath, he answered, "Before he dumps these women, he washes their genitals with the same poison he uses to kill them with. Any physical evidence he might leave behind gets eaten by the acids, if it's not destroyed from the time of decay. It's been impossible to get a DNA profile on anything. I told you, he cleaned them all thoroughly."

"Jeeze," Simon whispered, the horror in his voice unmistakable. "We're dealing with a psychopathic ghost."

Sam could tell the young man had only voiced what everyone else was thinking by the way the room fell into a deep silence. He ignored it and continued with his questions. "The name is interestin'. Why is he called 'The Christmas Angel?'"

"After we found Jane Doe, somehow the way this bastard kills was leaked to a reporter," Humbar answered, the annoyance he felt very clear. "Jake Varnce. He's the one who named him. Believe me, we tore him apart for it, but he wouldn't give us anything. Finally, I asked him why he picked Christmas Angel, and he said it's because of the timing, when he kills the women. Always right around the holidays."

"Good God," Julie said with disdain. "Reporters make me sick."

"Di' he have an alibi?" Sam continued.

"Yeah, but just to be sure, I convinced my chief to put a watch on him. Hell, I spent every spare minute of my time watching him. Other than his disgusting dramatic flare, he appeared to be innocent of these murders."

"I don't know if I would say *completely* innocent," Simon (who had been typing furiously on his laptop) said. "It looks like he wrote another article about the Angel in 2018 with an interview from 'an anonymous source.'"

Everyone was on alert, but Humbar spoke first. "Why would an 'anonymous source' want to talk to him about The Christmas Angel fifteen years later… unless the source is the Angel himself?"

"What does the article say, Simon?" Julie asked.

"Nothing really incriminating to whomever the source is. The article was published in a psychological journal, not public newspaper. It could have been an interview with a fanatical psychologist of the Angel."

"Even still, this source might be helpful to us," Rivera said. "We should press Varnce for a name."

"Good luck," Humbar sighed. "He filed a restraining order against our department once he became a suspect. I imagine he'll do something similar to you guys."

Sam looked back down at the case file he held. Glancing at the photos of Betsy Ringer, he paid most of his attention to the details outlined in the report. Not that he doubted anything his old friend had told him, he just knew that sometimes a new perspective could catch things that might otherwise be missed. But nothing stood out to him as wrong or otherwise incorrect, so he set the file on the table again and stood up.

"Alrigh', I want everyone t' forget everythin' tha' was just discussed here."

While his team knew to trust his instructions, Humbar looked up in shock. Sam continued before he could question his methods.

"Fer now, we're goin' t' look a' this with fresh eyes: We'll go t' the scene where Chloe Hale's body was found, order a new autopsy, interview her friends an' family fer any peculiar behavior or people in her life, all of it. We treat this case as if it's the first time this man has attacked someone. I donnea want any assumptions made on this." He then turned to Simon and instructed, "I want ye t' find out if any more cases like this have been reported outside of Ohio since 1982, an' then I want ye t' start findin' an' enterin' any cases tha' havenea been reported int' the system. Once tha's done, then I want ye t' cross reference all of them, lookin' fer a pattern. Everythin' ge's re-done, understood?"

"You got it, boss," Simon answered before looking at the files on the table. "Ugh...have I mentioned how much I hate paper?"

Ignoring him, Sam turned back to Humbar. "Call yer ol' partner, Dana, was it? Have her meet us a' the scene, we'll need all the help we can ge'."

"She's already insisted she be on board for this," the Chief nodded.

"Remembar everyone, assume absolutely nothin'. If we look a' this with a new perspective, we migh' jus' stop this man."

"We're right there with you, Sam," Rivera answered.

"On it, boss," Julie added.

"Good, dress warmly, an' le's ge' goin'."

***

An hour away from the city, about three miles west of Chesterville, the car belonging to Chief Anthony Humbar and an SUV carrying Sam, Rivera, and Julie pulled off of the main road and parked before the tree line. There were plenty of other cars and vans (including various news trucks) still parked there. The forensics teams were still combing the area dutifully for any and all microscopic clues they could find. As Humbar led the trio through the brush to the site, Sam took note of everything around him: You couldn't see through the trees to the open field they were headed to, which would make it easy for the killer to hide and never be seen from the road. He looked down at the snow-covered ground: There were plenty of footprints everywhere, most of them already saturated with mud from the constant walking done by the teams. But Sam couldn't see any evidence markers next to any of them, which told him they had yet to find a footprint, if there even was one to find amidst the white. And when they finally came to the open field, Sam could see around him for miles: This was obviously farmland that was off for the season, judging by its expansiveness and the large house and barn in the distance. The snow was much deeper where it hadn't been disturbed. Sam's coat did the job of keeping his top half warm, and he was glad he had listened to his gut and put on thermal underwear before dressing this morning, as the air was already bitter and cutting.

"Who found the body?" Sam asked.

"The farmer that lives over yonder—" Humbar pointed to the house in the east, "—he said he just got a new pup that he's training, and the little thing just took off running through the snow, so he had to follow him out here. Poor thing was damn near frozen by the time he found it, but it was whining and digging at something. The farmer assumed it found a dead rabbit but called the police when he figured out it was a body."

"This snow is at least two feet deep," Julie uttered as she trudged through the drifts. "If that dog hadn't found her today, she probably wouldn't have been discovered until the spring."

"Yeah, and by then we'd be another year too late. Thank God for animals and their instincts." Humbar stopped just short of a large, pitched canopy that stood over the scene, surrounded by the official yellow tape.

A woman who appeared middle-aged and of a sour disposition stood on the other side of it but quickly walked around to the group.

"This the guy, Anthony?" she asked.

Sam could tell she was referring to him by the way she looked him over, as though she was appraising his value.

Humbar nodded and made the introductions. "Dana Evanston, this is Sam McKay."

"Pleasure, ma'am," Sam offered his hand.

She gave him a quick, very strong handshake but almost immediately tore her hand, and her attention, away from the trio and back to the dug-up scene. "You're all filled in on who we're dealing with, right?"

"Yes, ma'am," Julie answered. She opened her mouth as if to say more, but the Lieutenant interrupted with her next question.

"And you've been over the files already? Think you can just come out here, and all the answers will be right in front of us?"

"They're not here to take over, Dana. We're going to be there when we catch him," Humbar said soothingly.

"*If* we catch him this time," she stated plainly, making a point that she was less than optimistic. "But you said your buddy here is one of the best. I trust you, Ace. Okay, agents, go ahead and work your magic. Tell us what we don't see."

Sam wasn't sure how to feel about their new associate: Her prickly and patronizing attitude was very off-putting, but the few things he noticed about her told him how passionate she was about her work, which made him a little more forgiving. She kept her hair professionally done at all times, which told him she was the type of woman who was ready for anything at a moment's notice, much like Meredith. But the redness of her nose and cheeks and the dampness on her slacks legs also told him she'd been out in this weather for hours. She didn't seem like the type to stand still in one place, so he could only assume she had been scouring the area for anything at all. He decided to let her attitude lie for the moment, but behind him he could tell that Julie and Rivera were already not so keen to work with her.

Stepping over the crime scene tape, Sam snapped on a pair of rubber gloves and knelt down inside of the dugout area. The body had already been moved, but the position it was left in had been carefully preserved thanks to the tent. It was just like the ones he had seen in the files: The victim had been posed lying on her back, her hands at her sides. Next to the outline of the body were some drag marks; he couldn't be certain, but he would guess that the man laid down the girl's body and moved her until she was positioned a certain way. He looked outside of the canopy, past Humbar and the Lieutenant, and out to the sky: there were still clouds, heavily laden with unfallen snow, but a tiny glint of sunshine still shone through to the east.

"She was facin' northeast, or thereabouts," he noted.

"Yeah, so what does that mean?" Dana said.

"Nothing yet, Lieutenant," Rivera answered her. "He's just calling out everything he's noticing. He does that sometimes."

Sam hardly heard them as he continued to look around the site: There were roughly four feet of cleared snow surrounding where the body had been, so he carefully examined every inch of it, looking for anything that might stand out as abnormal. There were some extremely shallow dents in the ground that could have been made by footprints, and he pointed to them. "Have yer men seen these?"

"Yes," Dana answered. "And they've been carefully digging in the direction they're going looking for a solid footprint to cast, but the snow's thickness was successful in masking any marks he might have made."

Sighing, Sam stood up and took off his gloves. "Maybe, bu' an expert'll tell ye tha' this means he's abou' average height an' weight. An' tha's only the start. We'll have one of our men come ou' an' see wha' he can tell us abou' this man's build."

"So we're looking for an average guy of average weight, huh? That really narrows it down, thanks." Dana continued to jeer, but quickly went quiet when Humbar gave her a look that suggested she stop the condescending retorts.

"As far as I can tell, there's nothin' else t' see here, an' nobody has found anythin' of interest nearby. Perhaps interviewin' the family'll tell us more."

Sam didn't wait for another remark from the sour Lieutenant as he easily hiked his feet over the tape and started back for the SUV. Julie and Rivera were right behind him.

Chapter Three

While Humbar and Dana escorted Chloe Hale's body to the Cleveland office, Sam and the others headed to the house of the closest known relatives: the parents. Chloe's parents—Aaron and Constance Hale –lived in an elegant red brick house deep in the suburbs of Elyria. With the forest of Elywood Park practically sitting in the backyard, Sam almost wanted to go search the trees before the talk, but Mr. Hale answered the door and ushered the team inside before he could get the chance. He focused on the task at hand.

Aaron Hale was an average man who had little whisps of grey glinting in his mousy-brown hair. His manner of dress told Sam he was an office worker of some sort, and the den in the corner of the home housing a computer and desk only confirmed the theory. Other than his sharp wardrobe, nothing about him was memorable. Constance Hale was very much the same: a lovely woman wearing a yellow blouse and light grey slacks, with her hair pulled into a ponytail. Both were of middle age, but the redness of their eyes made them look older and more exhausted. Their home and presence had a non-threatening, peaceful aura. Two completely average, good-natured people struck with tragedy of the worse kind: the loss of their child in the most brutal fashion. Sam's heart ached for them, but he kept his face stoic and business-like as Rivera led the interview.

"Thank you for meeting with us, Mr. and Mrs. Hale. I'm Agent Derrick Rivera of the FBI, this is Julie Russell and Sam McKay. We are very sorry for your loss."

The two parents nodded but didn't say a word.

"We need to ask you some questions about Chloe, if you don't mind. When was the last time you saw her?"

"November 15th," Mrs. Hale choked out, "she left for work that morning. She'd been staying here for about a week. Her apartment was having a problem with the pipes and wasn't livable until it was fixed."

"Where does she work?"

"She's a dental assistant for Packer Family Dentistry; it's downtown. She usually worked all day until closing time, but she recently went to half-day shifts so she could study for dental school."

"Do you know if she got to work that day?" Julie asked gently.

Mrs. Hale nodded. "When she didn't come home and wasn't picking up her cellphone, I called Dr. Packer and asked if she was still there. He said she'd left around one in the afternoon, and he hadn't seen her since."

"Did she ever go anywhere else after work?"

"Sometimes she went to the library to study. Not the one near her office, the one north of the turnpike. She liked the feel of it there, it was more open."

"And they hadn't seen her either?"

"No, I even drove up there to show them a picture and ask for myself after we...reported her..." Mrs. Hale suddenly dropped her face in her hands and began to sob.

Mr. Hale wrapped his arm around her and continued where she'd left off. "After we reported her missing, we went everywhere we knew she would go and looked for ourselves. No one had seen her."

Rivera spoke next. "What about places that she wouldn't normally go to? Did she ever have places she liked to go with friends or people that were interested in her?"

"Chloe hadn't been seeing anybody since she and Liam broke up, but that was three months ago."

"Liam who?" Julie asked.

"Liam Norris, they met at college and were together for a few years. Honestly, it was shock when she told us they weren't together anymore."

"Do you know why she broke up with him?"

"She didn't really want to talk about it, but I got the feeling she was upset about it. Liam doesn't seem like the type to cheat, though."

"Do you know where we might be able to find him?"

The both of them shook their heads, "Chloe and Liam lived together for almost a year, but he moved out when they broke up."

While Sam listened to the interview, he looked around at the walls of the Hale's home and took note of everything he saw: Awards from a 5th grade spelling bee all the way to college graduation announcements hung on the walls, intermingled with photos of Chloe, her parents, a young man, and some other people whom he could only assume were uncles and grandparents. The Hales not only appeared to be a tightly knit family, but also a successful one. One large photo had his attention: Mr. and Mrs. Hale stood in the center, and on the right was Chloe with her arm wrapped around her mother, and on the other side, under the arm of Mr. Hale, was the young man in some of the other pictures. Sam pointed to the photo and asked, "Who's the young man in tha' photo?"

"That's our son Mitch, Chloe's older brother," Mrs. Hale answered.

"He an' Chloe had a good relationship?"

"As far as brother and sister go, yes. They'd have their moments, just like any siblings would, but they loved each other."

"Does Mitch live here a' home?"

"No, he's got his own house in Olmsted Falls."

"Wha' does he do fer a livin'?"

"He works for Beauvoir Assistance Center as a nurse."

The detail of Mitch's chosen profession had Sam's attention. Keeping his calm façade intact, he pressed further, "Mr. an' Mrs. Hale, is there anythin' abou' yer son tha' ye can think of tha' migh' help us? Fer example, has he ever been in any kind of trouble or had a...'prodigal son' period?"

"What are you suggesting, agent?" Mr. Hale answered rather defensively. "You think our son kidnapped, raped, and murdered his own sister?"

"Mr. Hale—" Rivera quickly jumped in "—the statistics of kidnapping cases for both children and adults show that the kidnappers are usually family members or people well known to the victims. Agent McKay isn't suggesting anything, but we just want to be thorough. And trust me when I say that it's better for you to tell us any information you can think of than for us to find out on our own. It would only mean more trouble for you and for Mitch. We just want to find the person responsible for what happened to Chloe, and we want to quickly rule out anyone who wasn't responsible. You have my word."

Rivera's answered didn't appear to appease Mr. Hale that much, but Mrs. Hale stopped her sobbing and answered. "We unofficially adopted Mitch after three years of foster care when he was ten. His mother was addicted to cocaine and couldn't care for him; childcare services took him away and placed him with us. His mother would cause the usual trouble of trying to get him back, insisting she could get clean if she had him, but it never happened. Mitch reacted just as you would expect any child in those circumstances to react: Troubled, confused, lashing out, but he'd never done anything that got the police involved."

"Wha' *di'* he do?" Sam asked.

"Every time she would call us demanding to know where her son was, it would only upset him. He'd lock himself in his room, wouldn't eat; only once did he get so angry that he broke a mirror—but he's never hurt any of us! When we finally got our number changed, the phone calls stopped, and he started to get better."

"How old was Chloe when ye took 'im in?"

"She had just turned three, five when we decided that he was our son."

"Has he ever talked abou' re-connectin' with his mother?"

Mr. Hale answered. "He would mention it once or twice when he was a teenager, but we didn't really encourage it. Any time that woman got involved, he would turn into a mess. Mitch needed a stable, loving home environment, not the strung-out junkie who gave birth to him. But he hasn't talked about it since he was sixteen. We thought he'd moved on."

"No child jus' 'moves on' from their parents, bad or no'," Sam replied. "Do ye know her name?"

"Gillian Usgord. You can never forget the name of someone that harasses you for years."

"We'll be sure to look into her," Julie said. "Is there anything else you can think of that we should know? About anything at all: Chloe, Mitch, any strange people you might have noticed?"

The parents shook their head.

"Well, if you do think of anything, please give us a shout," Rivera said as he pulled out a card from his wallet and handed it to them. "Thank you for your time, Mr. And Mrs. Hale."

While the wife nodded a reply, the husband was more than grateful that the painful interview was over. He very quickly led the trio to the front door and practically slammed it shut once they were out.

"Nice family," Julie noted. "Though I get the feeling they baby the son a bit too much."

"Why? Because they were trying to give him a good home instead of a shitty one?" Rivera asked, somewhat perturbed.

"I'm just saying they were very defensive about him and his behavior; you can't help but wonder if there's more they aren't telling us."

"Jules, troubled kids do actually stop being troubled, under the right circumstances. If it weren't for them, Mitch probably would be strung out just like his mom, if not dead on the streets. Instead, he's a nurse, and he has his own house. That's what I call good parenting."

"Whatever."

"Our opinion doesnea matter," Sam said as they got to their SUV. "He's still a person of interest, an' so is the ex-boyfriend Liam. Ask Simon t' find out where we can find the biological mother an' Mr. Norris while we go pay Mitch a visit a' Beauvoir Assistance Center."

The nursing home where Mitch worked was about ten minutes east of Olmsted Falls in a very relaxing, open area far away from crowded streets and cities. Despite the thick layer of snow on the ground, there were a few residents, dressed head-to-toe in warm clothing, walking about the grounds in groups of four or five while a staff member walked with them in case someone fell. It appeared very pleasant and peaceful, and the inside of the building even more so: The walls were a soothing beige color, and various paintings of seashores and landscapes were hung along the walls and hallways. Beauvoir Assistance Center felt more like a hotel than a nursing home. The staff at the front desk were incredibly friendly and were quick to call Nurse Hale once they were asked. Within moments, a young man dressed in scrubs, overlaid with a thick coat, and donning a face mask came walking around the corner towards the trio of agents. The rims of his eyes were red and puffy, and once he pulled the mask down, it was easy to tell it was the same young man from the Hale family photos.

"I'm Mitch Hale, can I help you?" He asked, a slight break to his voice.

"Mr. Hale, I'm Agent McKay of the FBI, an' these are Agents Russell an' Rivera."

Almost as soon as Sam had introduced themselves, the young man's expression turned from friendly to downcast. "I've been expecting you. Fran, I'm going to be a few minutes, can you ask Ben to delay lunch for me?"

"No problem, honey," the receptionist answered understandingly.

"Agents, please follow me," Mitch said as he led them down a hallway. After passing a few open sitting rooms, they came to a set of double doors, and the young man opened them for Sam and the others. It didn't take the tables and chairs to tell it was the cafeteria he'd led them to as, very quickly, the smell of chicken soup, bread, and apple pie filled the air. Mitch led them through the empty room to a table sitting at the back, far away from the staff in the kitchens and any eavesdropping ears. "This is the most private spot we'll have in the building. You're here about Chloe, aren't you?"

Sam nodded, "Her body was found this mornin'."

"Yeah, I just got a message from my mom," Mitch sniffled, but quickly wiped his eyes. "I was on my way home when you got here."

"We're very sorry, Mr. Hale," Rivera said kindly. "We can't imagine what you're going through."

"Were you and your sister pretty close?" Julie asked, hardly giving any time for Rivera's words to be heard.

"She was my baby sister, agent. We fought, argued; heck, we even wanted to kill each other sometimes. But when we were in school, some jerk thought he could cop a feel when she was alone in the hallway, and I gave him a bloody nose for it. Of course, we were close."

"Where were you when she went missing?" Rivera asked.

"I was here; most of my time is spent here. I remember the night she was kidnapped; I was present for the transition of one of my patients, Mrs. Gail Werner. Once my shift was over, I went straight home. Mom called me to ask if I'd seen or heard from Chloe that day, but I hadn't. I keep my phone on silent when I'm working."

"We didn't say she was kidnapped," Julie said pointedly.

Mitch Hale turned to look at her and answered, "She's dead, Agent Russell. You don't have to be a genius to guess what happened. Besides, like I told the cops when they first came to talk to us, she'd never run away from home a day in her life; why the hell would she start now?"

Julie's face remained emotionless. She also didn't answer.

Sam took the opportunity to get away from the awkward moment and change the subject. "Wha' do ye know abou' her boyfriend, Liam?"

"Only that they broke up a while ago; she didn't want to talk about why. She was pretty upset about it, though. I even offered to find him and help her key his car, if it would make her feel better, but she kept saying it wasn't worth it, and she would move on."

"Do ye know where we can find 'im?"

"I know he was working as a carpenter's assistant when they broke up, but Liam took a lot of odd jobs."

"Did he give you the 'deadbeat boyfriend' vibe?" Rivera asked.

"Funny enough, no. He went to college to be a consultant of some kind, but with last year's events, there was a hiring freeze, and a ton of downsizing everywhere. He's not a loser, but he does what he can."

"And you're certain Chloe never gave you any indication of why they broke up?"

"Not once," Mitch shook his head. "Hold on, you guys don't think that Liam did this?"

"We're checkin' everythin'," Sam answered. "Includin' old boyfriends."

"Look, Liam broke my sister's heart, but he would never, ever hurt her. He cared about her too much."

"How do ye know?"

"I just do," Mitch insisted, "I mean, they were together for two years and lived with each other for one."

"We'll still need to check out his alibi," Julie answered. "And, just for the hell of it, where were you last night from 7:00 to 11:30?"

"Here, agent. And then I went straight home at the end of my shift at ten. I've got a mortgage and a dog to feed. I'll have Fran get you my logs."

"Can anyone confirm you were home from 10:00 to 11:30?"

"Other than Cooper, I live alone. Why don't you ask my neighbors if they saw me?"

"We'll do tha'," Sam interrupted, thereby quickly ending the vicious back and forth. Handing Mitch a card, he followed up with,

"Thank ye, an' we're verra sorry abou' yer loss. If ye can think of anythin' a' all, please call this numbar."

Mitch nodded, pocketed the card, and walked away from the table before anyone could say another word to him.

Rivera's phone suddenly pinged with a text alert. "Simon's got a living address for Liam Norris, and says his current means of income is for a gutter cleaning service on Bagley Road; it's about twenty minutes from here."

"Then le's go see wha' the ex has t' say abou' his girlfriend, an' le's try t' be polite abou' the fact tha' he may be grievin'," Sam cast a warning look at Julie. She met his stare in equal annoyed measure before she turned away and made for the doors.

Rivera went ahead and called Liam's place of work to make sure their next suspect wasn't out on a job somewhere. Thankfully, he wasn't, so he gave instructions to have Liam wait at the building. A short drive later, the SUV pulled into the parking lot of a small metal building that looked more like an oversized shed than a warehouse. A young man with dark brown hair cropped short was standing in front of the building. He appeared to be waiting for them. When Sam, Julie, and Rivera exited the car and walked forward, the young man offered his hand.

"I'm Liam Norris. I understand you're looking to talk to me?"

Sam shook it, as did Rivera, but Julie simply nodded.

"Aye, we're Agents McKay, Rivera, an' Russell of the FBI. We'd like t' talk t' ye abou' Chloe Hale."

Liam's eyes widened in surprise. "The FBI? Does that mean you found Chloe? Is she okay?"

"You knew she was missing?" Rivera asked.

"Well, yeah, her mom called me and asked if I'd seen her when she didn't come home for a couple of days. Chloe hasn't spoken to me since we broke up. Seriously, is she alright? What happened to her?"

"She's dead," Julie answered quickly. "Her body was found in a field this morning."

Sam turned to shoot her another stern look, but Julie was watching the ex-boyfriend and carefully avoiding any silent warnings Sam was trying to convey.

Liam's already widened eyes suddenly grew wider, and tears began to brim at the corners. "D-dead? What do you mean? How?

When? What the hell happened to her?! Who would want to kill Chloe?!"

"We thought you might be able to tell us," Julie answered, leaving the implication clear.

Liam appeared to have missed her double meaning as he continued to bemoan, "Oh my god...Chloe can't be dead, she just can't be..."

"If you were so crazy for her, then why did you break up with her?" Julie continued. "We got the impression from her family that you broke her heart."

"I didn't break up with her; she broke up with me!" Liam answered emphatically; the wobble in his voice was unmistakable. He took a deep breath and answered, "But the truth is, she just did what I didn't have the guts to do."

"Okay," Rivera jumped in. "Why don't you start from the beginning and tell us why you wanted to break up with her? Were things just not good for a long time?"

"No, nothing like that. Things were great. Chloe wasn't just my girlfriend; she was also one of the guys to hang with. That's one of the things that drew me to her in the first place—how cool and chill she was. It's just...we had gotten to that point where we were starting to realize that we both wanted different things from life. I'm still trying to get my life off the ground; she was preparing to go to dental school, but marriage and a family were also on her mind...we just couldn't really find a way to make both of our dreams work. I spent months making myself sick trying to think of how I could make her see that we should probably take a break...but she cut through all of the red tape."

"Where were you the night she was kidnapped?"

"I was at a bar in West View with some friends. I told the cops this when she first went missing."

"And what about last night?" Julie asked.

Liam snapped his head back up again, this time there was anger in his eyes. "Why? You think I'm the one that killed her? Are you psycho?"

"We're jus' tryin' t' be thorough," Sam answered quickly. "An' tha' means rulin' out anybody tha' had nothin' t' do with her death."

"Fine, I was at home packing."

"Packin'? Fer wha'?"

"I've got an interview with a firm in New York in a few days."

"So, you pack for it three days ahead of time?" Julie asked incredulously.

"I was excited; I wanted to be prepared. Look, I'm sure you don't believe me, but I would never hurt Chloe. I love her. I love her whole family."

"Okay," Rivera said. "Can you think of anyone in Chloe's life that seemed suspicious or off? Even before you broke up?"

A tear had escaped from Liam's right eye. He quickly wiped it away and sniffled, "Nobody comes to mind. Everybody loved Chloe. She never had a bad thing to say about anybody; she worked hard at her job; her boss even promised her an opening when she graduated from dental school."

"Are ye sure the two of ye were never followed or noticed anybody tha' seemed t' hang around the two of ye too much? Maybe an odd neighbor a' the apartment?"

"No, nothing like that. The only neighbors we really knew lived next door to us, but they moved out about a month before I did. That apartment was vacant when I left, though, so if anybody did move in, I couldn't tell you their name."

"Alrigh', thank ye for yer time." Sam handed another business card to Liam and immediately turned back to the car, but not before grabbing Julie's elbow and pulling her along with him. Rivera was right behind them, and as soon as the ex-boyfriend retreated into the oversized shed, Sam wasted no time in towering over Julie. "Wha' the hell is yer problem?"

"I'm just being thorough," she answered. "He was already planning to break up with her but was too chicken to do it? Come on, he's obviously hiding something."

"We donnea punish people before we have a reason, Russell," Sam growled her surname, which caused her to look up at him defiantly. "We're usin' fresh eyes, bu' no' drawin' fresh blood withou' cause. Ye got it?"

Julie yanked her arm out of his grasp and nodded curtly. "Fine."

Rivera's phone text alert broke the tension. "Simon says the last known record for Gillian Usgord was in 2011 from her parole officer, but she hasn't been seen nor heard from since. She's probably homeless or OD'd by now."

Sam sighed. "Alrigh', then le's see if Chloe Hale's body has anythin' t' tell us."

Chapter Four

Thanks to Humbar and his old partner, Chloe Hale's body had already been moved to FBI headquarters. When Sam and the others arrived back at the building, the two police-officers were sitting at the front, waiting for them. Lieutenant Evanston appeared to be calm and patient as she obviously remained unhopeful, but Humbar made no effort to hide his anxiousness to move along to the second coroner report. Sam agreed with him and immediately led the way to the coroner's lab.

The lead coroner, Dr. Judd Bicks, was put on the case personally, given the nature of the crimes. Plain looking with larger than average eyes, his lack of a bedside manner and blunt delivery made him one of Sam's least favorite people to work with. But there was no denying the man's thoroughness in his examinations. They had barely walked through the door and saw the cold, still body of Chloe Hale on the table, when the doctor began to barrage them with the facts, as he was already finished with his examination and waiting for them. "Chloe Hale: twenty-five, malnourished but not starved, and killed with an injection of bleach, hydrochloric acid, and sodium hydroxide directly to the heart with a 16 gauge needle."

"Just like the others," Dana stated plainly. "Did you finish with the rape kit?"

"Do you want the nitty-gritty or—"

"Could you be a *little* bit more respectful, please?" Humbar growled. "This girl has been brutalized."

Sam grunted his agreement.

Dr. Bicks didn't appear to have heard either of them as he continued with his results. "She was raped, beaten, and raped again. Any foreign DNA I might have been able to collect was destroyed with a washing done to her genitals of the same solution he poisoned her with. There are bruises, cuts, and scars all along her body, but those have been spritzed with the solution, too. The best I can tell you is that he used either his fists or whatever object was closest to him whenever he'd hit her, but I couldn't find any definitive marks to tell you what kind of object was used. It could've been anything from a boot to a flashlight."

"I donnea suppose ye found anythin' of interest under her fingernails, did ye? Somethin' tha' we migh' be able t' use to help identify her attacker?"

"Your guy took the time to make sure he didn't leave anything behind."

"You said she was malnourished but not starved," Rivera continued. "Was there anything in her stomach that could tell us something?"

"From what the lab can tell she had a cheeseburger, but there were different levels of digestion on virtually every particle. Your guy would bring her one fast food meal and then she'd have to ration it out herself to avoid starvation, but she was still starving. There were high levels of fatty and amino acids in her blood plasma. Not even a 2,000-calorie cheeseburger can stop your body from being hungry, if you're not eating often enough. But as far as anything peculiar goes, nothing in her stomach stood out."

"And you couldn't find anything at all to help us at least figure out where she was being held?" Humbar asked.

"I did find some trace samples of dirt under her toenails. She probably picked it up when your guy dragged her for the dumping. I've sent what I could get to an expert who might be able to narrow it down. But unless the composition comes up as something obscure like the coral pink sand dunes, I wouldn't hold out too much hope for any answers there."

"How long will it take for the results?"

"A few weeks at least."

"Great, so we've got nothing again." the Lieutenant muttered.

"Glad to be of help," Dr. Bicks answered uncaringly; he turned around to a second body sitting on the next slab and didn't bother to see the group out of his morgue.

As the five of them headed for the elevators, Dana said, "I got the missing persons report for Chloe. Her last known location was at a Food Mart the day she was kidnapped, but no-one has been able to find her car, despite the BOLO for a yellow Nissan Sentra."

"Well, that's great," Julie said. "We're dealing with a guy who really cleans up after himself. It's like he makes these women completely disappear when he takes them. Then they suddenly reappear again, starved and sparkling clean."

"Don't forget the flower," Rivera added. "What did you say it was, Humbar?"

"A white peony, always a white peony."

"What's the significance of that?"

"A colleague mentioned in passing that white peonies mean regret and apology," Dana answered for Humbar.

"Okay, then that means he's showing remorse for hurting these girls. That tells us a bit more."

"Yeah, and they're rare. Hardly any flower shops carry them, and they're impossible to find in the winter."

"So, you've checked out florists both local and out of town?"

"Of course, we have," Humbar answered. "And not one of them sells these things during the winter."

"It could be that he grows them," Julie volunteered.

Back on the third floor where Sam's team was stationed, Simon had obviously been busy, judging by the mess of scattered paper all along the desks. The young man looked very pale and horrified. Julie reached him first and put her hand on his shoulder.

"Hey, you okay?"

Simon gulped, "I...I don't even know where to start...but I think I'll start by telling you this guy hasn't just been terrorizing Ohio. Guys...his work has been found in Utah, Oregon, Montana, South Dakota, Michigan..."

Rivera had already started moving and suddenly appeared with a large map of the United States and thumb tacks. Pinning the map on the largest wall, he put a thumb tack in every spot where Simon told him a body had been found, including all over Ohio. By the time he was finished, a long line of fifteen thumb tacks stretched across the top of the map from the East to the West.

"Jesus Christ," Humbar shuddered. "He's been terrorizing the entire north of the country."

"Perhaps more," Sam grunted. He turned back to Simon and continued, "I want ye t' reach out t' every agency an' ask abou' these cases. We had some tha' havenea been recorded yet, others are sure to as well."

"I thought the same thing, and I'm already on it, boss. As soon as I saw his penchant for traveling, I compiled a list of every agency in the country's phone number, and holy crap, are there a lot! I just finished with everyone in Alabama before you guys got here, but so far nobody down south has seen anything of this sort."

"It might be safe to assume that he favors the colder, snowy states," Julie said. "Should we just stick to the northern ones for now?"

"No, I donnea want t' give this bassard the chance t' trick us. We assume nothin' an' check everywhere."

Simon had already began dialing the next phone number; Humbar and the Lieutenant cleared their throats, causing Sam to turn around and give them his full attention.

"I know you said to look at this with fresh eyes, Sam, but it might be helpful to go over some of the older cases again," Humbar said.

"We can help you there," Dana nodded emphatically. "We know everything about this guy like the back of our hands."

"Which is why Rivera an' *I'll* be reviewin' the cases, an' ye two'll be helpin' Julie an' Simon reach out t' see where else this man has been."

"What?!" Dana barked, and Sam was shocked to have finally gotten a passionate response from her. "Now see here, pal! We're more than just desk jockeys! We know this son of a bitch!"

"Ye also have been too close t' this case fer too long; yer vision is narrowed," Sam growled right back at her. Standing up straight, he asserted his height advantage over Humbar's old partner before he continued. "If we're gonna' catch him, we gotta' look a' everythin', an' no' jus' wha' we think we know. He's invisible, so we gotta look a' the invisible. Now, I've tol' ye how ye can help, so go help."

Humbar nearly had to drag Dana away, but eventually the stern woman settled down in her temporary desk and picked up a phone to make her way through the list of phone numbers Simon handed her.

Meanwhile, Rivera had already begun setting up in the conference room: A projector screen shone onto the large, white wall behind them with the fifteen known cases so far. Sam looked at every name on the files shining on the board. He clenched his fist and took a deep breath, trying to control the rage he felt welling up inside of him. He'd only been on this case for six hours so far, and the number of victims had tripled. And, as Humbar suspected, there was most likely more. Shaking himself out of his moment, Sam joined Rivera at the table. His younger, and shorter, partner was already busy scouring every detail and rapidly making notes, but Sam couldn't concentrate. At least not until he had the question that had been plaguing him since that morning answered.

"We donnea have good odds on this one, do we?"

Rivera didn't look up, but he sternly shook his head. "Nope, we don't."

Sam sighed, "I was afraid ye migh' say tha'."

Sam and Rivera read, re-read, and followed up on every piece of evidence collected in every single file before them. As thorough as they combed through everything, they were only able to confirm the three connecting factors between the victims: Every one of the women had gone missing at random times before they were found; their bodies were discovered during the winter season; and all of them were lying on their backs with their hands at their sides with a white peony over their hearts. Next, they tried to focus on the killer; Rivera was arranging every case in order by date on the map, hoping they might at least be able to identify a traveling pattern. That proved useless, as the women were either kidnapped or reported missing from random areas far from their 'burial' sites. Hour after hour, they studied and compared, but there was not a predictable pattern to be found. By the end of the day, the team on phone duty had uncovered three more cases along the northern border of the country. It was only the first day of the investigation, and everyone was already feeling weary.

Sam, in particular, felt the familiar angry, yet nauseous, feeling in the pit of his stomach as the sheer number of dead and violated women began to haunt him. Just like Chloe Hale's body, the man they were hunting had been incredibly thorough with the others. It was beyond maddening. Not once did he look at a clock as he tried to find something, anything that would give them a direction to go on. He was reading one of the last cases discovered in Washington when Rivera tapped him on the shoulder holding a Styrofoam box and a plastic fork.

"Chicken chimichanga," his partner said as he thrust the food towards him.

Sam hadn't even noticed when Rivera left; wrinkling his nose at the offering, he grunted, "Ye know I donnea like spicy food."

"It's mild shredded chicken wrapped in dough and deep fried. Think of it as a flavored version of fried fish. We've been here for almost nine hours straight, and everybody else has already eaten."

Sam glanced out of the conference room towards Julie, Simon, Humbar, and Dana and noted how they all had empty Styrofoam containers next to them while they continued their phone calls. He hadn't eaten since breakfast with Oliver, and his stomach growled in protest when the smell hit his nostrils. Conceding, he opened his container and took a hearty bite of the giant fried log. He wasn't particularly fond of the burnt taste of spices, but it was tolerable and not altogether unpleasant. Another large bite was all he allowed himself to have before turning his attention back to the files.

Rivera sat down across the table from him. "Look, it's late and everyone is already burned out. It's time to call it and go home for the day."

"No' until we have somethin' t' go on."

"Sam, no matter how long we look at these files the details are not going to change. We all need to be at our best to get this guy, and sleep will help us do that. Sometimes, we just have to step away."

"He's exactly right, McKay," came the familiar voice of Director Belinda Copper, but Sam refused to look at her.

He picked up another case file, but the Director had suddenly appeared in his vision and gently took it from his hands. "Even I don't expect you to solve this on the first day. Go home."

Finally, he looked up at her. "This man has been runnin' free fer forty years, there has t' be somethin' here we're no' seein'. I donnea want another woman t' end up dead."

"Neither does anyone else. These women will get justice, but it needs to be done right. Starting with the well-being of the investigators. Now go home, McKay. That's an order."

Sam hated it when Copper pulled rank on him, though he knew that was the only way anyone could get him to stop doing anything. Reluctantly, he rubbed his eyes and sighed. "Verra well. Rivera, tell everyone t' go home, an' we'll meet back here in the mornin'."

Everyone packed up and were out the door within minutes of Rivera's quitting time announcement, but Sam dragged his feet. Finally, he forced himself to look at the clock and started; it was almost midnight, and not once had he texted Oliver. Yanking his phone from his pocket, he was relieved to see that the boy had thought ahead and texted about an hour before: *I figured you're really busy, but I'm heading home. Party was fun. I didn't do anything stupid.* The relief and much needed break from the case made Sam chuckle, and he suddenly felt the exhaustion from the day's draining events sink in. He locked the door to the conference room and left the office without another thought of the elusive serial killer known as the Christmas Angel.

Walking in through the door to his apartment, he was relieved to see Oliver was still awake and watching a show; he needed the back-and-forth banter with the teenager to help him clear his mind.

Sure enough, the boy didn't waste any time. "So, what happened to 'I'll text ye t' check on ye today?' Have you suddenly been overcome with trusting your only son?"

Sam smirked, "I'm sorry, i's been a long day, an' time go' away from me. How was yer party? Di' ye win a' tha' Mario...wha'ever game?"

"It's not really a game you win, Dad, but yeah, I did alright."

"An' how abou' this Karliegh? How di' tha' go?"

Though he tried to hide it, Sam caught the little smirk that pulled across the young man's face. Chuckling, he nudged him. "Tha' well, eh?"

"Her friend Janell was there, so I did what you said and found out she likes grape soda. So, when Bryce ordered the pizza, I gave him some extra money to have the guy buy some on the way over here. She seemed to like that I knew that about her and let me sit next to her all night, and we even friended each other," the boy smiled giddily.

"'Friended each other?' The hell does tha' mean?"

"On social media, Dad. Now we're friends and can follow each other on Facebook and Instagram."

Sam narrowed his eyes in confusion. "Ye dinnea ge' her numbar?"

"I don't need it; this is better," Oliver beamed. "Now I can like and comment on everything she posts, and even get to know her better, like you said."

"An' ye cannea do tha' over dinnar?"

"Geeze, Dad, you don't just ask a girl you just met to dinner. Are you nuts?"

Suddenly Sam's head hurt even more; he decided to make himself a cup of tea to help before turning in for the evening. While he put the kettle over the heat, he grumbled, "I donnea know when the politics of teenagers datin' changed, bu' tha' jus' seems ridiculous."

Oliver laughed and jeered at him. "Welcome to the new world order, Dad. Boys don't just pick up girls and take them out for milkshakes anymore."

"Hey, I'm no' *tha'* old. An' i's getting late, ye should be getting t' bed soon."

"Dad, winter break, remember?"

"One more hour of telly, then tha's it."

"Deal."

The kettle started screaming, and Sam made himself a cup. Wishing his son goodnight, with a reminder of the in-place curfew, he walked down the little hallway of the apartment to his room and shut the door behind him. Even with a nice soothing cup of tea and a copy of *The Odyssey*, sleep was still hard for him to grasp. As much as he tried to distract himself, nothing could block out the images of the Angel's victims saturating the tables at work. For what felt like hours, he lay in bed stewing about what his team should do next; even after hearing Oliver turn off the television and retire for the night, he still couldn't relax. Finally, he decided it was pointless to try to sleep, and he sat up. A pen and pad of paper sat on his nightstand, and he hastened to pick them up and began scribbling down everything he could think of. By the time he had finished with the list of facts and circumstances, he had two pages of paper nearly dripping with ink. And at the top of it all was the infamous killer's name: The Christmas Angel. Sam glared at the name, almost wishing he could make it burn right off the page. But even if he could, sleep still wouldn't have come any easier that night.

***

Despite his battle with getting some sleep, Sam rolled out of bed at six a.m. and began his usual winter routine of sit-ups and pushups before jumping into the shower. He had barely turned off the water when his phone started ringing. It was Rivera.

"Di' ye find somethin'?" he grunted while awkwardly toweling himself off.

"Yeah, I just got off the phone with the footprints expert, and he wasn't too optimistic about his assessment. *But,* due to the length of the stride, he thinks the guy that dumped Chloe Hale's body had to be between 5'8"-5'10". After factoring in the packed snow screwing with the indent pressure, he says the guy is between 130-160 pounds."

"So, either skinny or jus' abou' average weight," Sam sighed. "Well, i's a start."

"I haven't even gotten to the good part yet," Rivera answered, the sarcasm in his tone made Sam pessimistic about what he had to say. "Simon apparently got bored last night and did a little hacking into Chloe Hale's life and, from what he can tell, she had absolutely no enemies whatsoever. Honestly, her only mistake was working for a dental office that had less-than-favorable reviews."

"Wha' abou' her brothar an' the ex-boyfriend?"

"Liam Norris' alibi checks out, and what he told us about not seeing Chloe for almost a year is true. At least, according to his phone records, it is. And Humbar's officers have witness statements confirming that he was home the night Chloe went missing, as well as no suspicious activity. Same for Mitch. But, according to one neighbor, they did see him get into a yelling match with a woman a few months back."

"Was i' w' Chloe?"

"No, the neighbor described this lady as older with dark hair. The argument seemed heated, though. The neighbor said they heard the phrase 'you're not my mother' and more along those lines. Maybe Mitch finally made contact with his druggie mom after all and quickly regretted it. Should we track it down?"

"Nah, we'll le' i' lie fer now." A second call started buzzing in his ear and he looked at the screen. This time it was Humbar. "I've go' t' go. Thanks."

"See you in a bit."

With the push of a button, Sam answered the other call with a "Mornin', big man."

"Sam, another body was found off 77 near Greentown this morning. It's another one of the Angel's, just like Chloe."

Sam's eyes opened wide. "Wha'? Are ye sure?"

"Yeah, a friend from Stark County Sherriff's office called me when he saw the white flower. They're already running blood tests to confirm everything else, but all of the usual clues say it's his work. Coroner has put her TOD window at last night between 9:00 p.m. and 1:00 a.m."

"Christ," Sam hissed to himself. "Alrigh', have the body moved up t' the office. We'll meet ye a' the scene in an hour."

Humbar grunted his agreement and hung up.

Sam toweled himself off enough to be barely considered dry and quickly got dressed, ignoring how his clothes were sticking to his damp body. He quietly pushed open the door to Oliver's room and saw that the sixteen-year-old boy was completely passed out in bed. Not wanting to wake him, he gently shut the door and made for the kitchen. After taking down a pack of cinnamon sugar PopTarts and folding a $20 bill behind them, he wrote a quick note to Oliver explaining that he had to leave early and to probably depend on buying himself some dinner that night before signing 'I love you, Dad' and walking out the door. A quick call back to Rivera to round up the rest of the team, and he was in the car and on his way to the next crime scene.

Considering how early it was, the road to Greentown was quick and silent; not that it mattered, as Sam had his siren on the whole way there to prevent any delay. Before long, he could see the myriad of cop cars and forensics vans on the other side of the highway and flipped a U-turn through the dirt median separating the roads to join them. Humbar and Dana were already there waiting for him, and before long, he heard another siren signaling that the rest of the team was right behind him. Once everyone was assembled, they trudged through the heavy snow, past the forensics teams to yet another dug-out site with a tent positioned over the top of a peacefully laid-out body with a flower sitting on her chest. As Sam got close enough to the body to make out a few features, he started: The girl had to be Oliver's age. What was worse, she was sickeningly thin. Although her young face haunted him, he noticed some very light drag marks next to her body; they looked similar to the ones he saw at Chloe Hale's burial site. After looking back up to the sky for a direction, he made a note that her toes and hands weren't pointed completely south, but rather, almost southwest, according to the position of the sunrise. Although he examined the surrounding ground with care, he couldn't find any noticeable indentations that could have been made by shoes. Considering how skinny this young girl was, he wasn't all together surprised.

A man Sam didn't recognize stood over the body, lifted the single white flower that barely covered her breast, and pointed to her heart. "Highway patrol was doing a routine stop when they called this in. As soon as I saw the needle mark, I thought it might be your guy."

"Yeah, you were right to call me, Lee," Humbar said somberly. "This is the Angel's work."

"But we just only found a body yesterday," Julie said, "I know you said he's probably got more bodies out there somewhere, but why would he leave another one for us to find already?"

"Because he's sending a message," Rivera answered her. "He's taunting us."

"Why?" Simon asked. "What's he trying to say? That we'll never catch him?"

"Something like that. He goes forty years without being caught, then he hibernates for fifteen of them; maybe he thought he had it out of his system. Then he gets antsy and goes back to his old habits, only now he's upping the ante."

"Aye," Sam nodded, his eyes never leaving the face of the poor dead young girl. "An' unless we find 'im soon, I suspect tha' we'll find more girls all wintar'."

Chapter Five

Sam, his team, and the two detectives were waiting out in the hallway of the morgue while Dr. Bicks finished his examination. While the others were talking and theorizing back and forth, Sam couldn't get the young lady's face out of his mind: She was so young, just a kid. A kid her age was supposed to be getting upset over whether or not she was going to a school dance, not terrorized and violated. It made him sick.

The coroner suddenly emerged from the morgue with a new file in his hands. "Well, your guy certainly doesn't discriminate. This girl was living on the streets long before she was abducted."

"How can you tell?" Dana asked.

"For one thing, Jane Doe in there is a teenager, maybe 16 or 17. She's so skinny, you can see the outline of her bones. So, either she was anorexic, and her parents didn't notice, or she could hardly find anything to eat. There are needle marks on her arms and scarring in her nasal cavity, which tells me she picked drugs over food. And your guy wasn't the first John she had sex with, either."

"Good God," Humbar shuddered. "Another teenaged prostitute. What the hell is this world coming to?"

"Di' the Angel give her the same treatment as Chloe Hale?" Sam asked.

"Yup," Bicks nodded. "A solution of bleach, hydrochloric acid, and sodium hydroxide was injected into her heart, and the same solution was found on her genitals, where there are signs of rape. Your guy cleaned up after himself again."

"For God's sake, Bicks, could you *please* stop calling him 'Our Guy'?" Julie snarled. "He's a sick bastard called 'The Christmas Angel'; call him by his name."

"I'll call him John Jacob Jingleheimer-Smith if you want me to, young lady," Bicks answered without care. "It makes no never mind to me. Anyway, she has a tattoo on her ankle of a ladybug, but other than that, I can't give you anything that might help you figure out who she is."

"Aye," Sam nodded, taking the file from his hands. "Thank ye, Bicks."

The coroner retreated into the morgue.

Everyone made their way for the elevators and then the third floor. All the while, Sam remained silent; he was trying desperately to think of what they could do next, while everyone else around him talked.

Dana was the first to speak. "Two bodies in two days. Agent Rivera is right; he's escalating."

"Which is both good and bad," Humbar muttered. "The more he kills, the more likely he is to make a mistake. How many dead girls is it going to take until we stop him?"

The elevator pinged the third floor, and Sam led the way, as everyone made for their little corner of the building.

"Well, the first thing to do is figure out who this girl is," Simon said as he sat down, opened his laptop, and let his fingers fly across the keyboard. "I'm checking the missing persons database now for teenagers with ladybug tattoos and... eight across the country fit the bill.... This girl looks like her, doesn't she?"

Simon turned his laptop around to show everyone, and Sam started when he saw the picture. The girl in the photo was chubbier and healthier looking, but it was definitely the same one who belonged to the body currently freezing in the basement.

"Lily Vanderguard," Simon continued. "Seventeen years old, reported missing by her parents from Pittsburg, Pennsylvania, on August 27th, 2021. The police searched the streets and talked to her meth dealer, Nicky Gold, but he said he hadn't seen her since he sold her some crystal August 15th. After asking some of the other streetwise addicts, the last confirmed date she was seen was August 23rd."

"Her parents waited four days before reporting her?" Rivera asked incredulously. "That sounds like a real happy family."

"According to their statements, Lily ran away pretty often, but she'd usually come back after a couple of days. Eventually they stopped reporting and just waited for her to come back. But, and this is in quotation marks by the investigating officer, the father said

'Something just felt wrong this time,' and that's why they called the police."

"The Angel really is taunting us," Julie growled. "He kidnaps a local and an out of towner, but both of the bodies end up in Ohio in two days."

"And, again, we've got nothing to give us a clue on where to start looking for him," Rivera nodded.

"We'd better talk to Lily's parents," Humbar said. "At least now they can finally know where their daughter is."

"I'll go with you and ask the questions. Sam? You've been awfully quiet. What are you thinking?"

Sam heard them talking, but he spent the whole time staring at the map with thumbtacks pushed into it (and added another one for Lily) hanging on the wall.

"I'm askin' meself why. Wha' could push the Angel t' leave another body t' be found so quickly?"

"I don't want to be the thorn in everybody's side here," Simon said sheepishly. "But is it possible that he didn't mean for the bodies to be found so quickly? I mean, they both were found by accident."

Nobody argued for a minute then Humbar spoke. "You might be right, actually. Half right, anyway. The girls that were found from 1982-2006 were close to properties that were guaranteed to be staked out at some point. Chloe's body was found on a farm. Lily's body was quite literally in the middle of nowhere. The closest thing to her is a golf course that's fifteen miles to the east. She might not have been found until who knows when, if it weren't for the officer that made the traffic stop."

"Even if you're right, Ace," Dana said, "this changes what we know about him. He's not killing once every few years. He could've been killing all winter for every winter since 1982, and it's just that nobody's found the girls yet. That only mean's he's even more dangerous than we thought, and more women are already dead. How many more are in danger?"

Sam finally stood to his full height, crossed his arms, and said rather assertively, "I know tha' these girls are matchin' up t' the Angel's MO, bu' le's no' forge' the basics of our jobs. I want ye four t' go t' Pittsburg an' see wha' ye can learn abou' Lily. Rivera an' Julie, I want ye two t' talk t' the parents. Humbar an' Dana, ye two'll collaborate with the police tha' investigated her disappearance."

"And what are you going to do?" Dana asked, the irritation in her voice evident. "Sit here and stare at the map until another thumbtack appears?"

Sam was quickly growing tired of her cynical attitude and was about to tell her to shut-up when Humbar quickly jumped in to diffuse the situation with a quiet, "Knock it off, Dana." Then Rivera, Julie, Humbar, and the Lieutenant left Sam and Simon alone.

While Simon remained quiet, knowing better than to interrupt his boss while he was thinking, Sam wouldn't have been able to hear anything he said anyway, as he stared at the faces of the girls throughout the years. Every one of them was so different, but he knew their cries for help would have been the same. He could almost hear them, and that only made the rage he felt for their murderer intensify. He continued to carefully look at every single piece of evidence on their board when his eyes fell onto one name: Jake Varnce, the reporter that christened the Angel.

"Simon, where can I find Jake Varnce these days?"

"The scummy reporter? Hang on....Varnce is not only alive and well, but he's now a lead editor for the news outlet *The Plain Dealer.*"

"There's nothin' else t' go on," Sam mumbled to himself before voicing much louder. "Perhaps I should pay a visit t' the man tha' seems t' know all abou' the Angel."

"For what? Remember what Humbar said: Varnce wouldn't give up his sources back then, he's highly unlikely to do it now. Guys like Varnce don't help the police unless they have something to gain, and unless you're willing to give Varnce an insider tip on the cases we solve from now on–which I know you're not—then we've got nothing to bargain with."

Sam already knew that Simon would voice the problem, he just didn't want to outwardly admit that Varnce helping them was a long shot. What Simon said about something to gain was correct, they had nothing to offer Varnce....*Bu' we migh' have somethin' we can take away...*

"Simon, I need ye t' hack inta' Varnce's wifi remotely an' ge' me somethin', *anythin',* I can use t' persuade him."

"Okay, sure." Simon worked his magic and within moments he was shrugging his shoulders. "Well, he's a fan of porn, but I don't see any incriminating videos in his browser history."

"Ach, if he's truly as stubborn as Humbar says, tha' won't be enough." Sam paced the floor angrily; the constant wall after wall they hit was driving him insane. "Simon, can ye tell me if ye're capable of alterin' Varnce's history t' look as though he's been engagin' in illegal activity?"

"Yeah, yeah I can. But what am I doing to him that's illegal?"

"Ye said he's a fan of porn...could ye add some less-than-desirable videos to his watchlist? The illegal an' immoral kind."

The young man's face changed from curious to worried. He looked all around himself as if to check if anyone nearby was listening before he whispered, "Boss...you want me to make Varnce out to be a pedo?"

Sam did not approve of law enforcement officers abusing their powers against the public; he'd made that point very clear during his time in Internal Affairs. But the number of dead women on the board behind him was at the forefront of his mind, and he ignored the way his gut told him what he was suggesting was wrong. *We need a lead*, he rationalized with himself. *Playin' dirty'll ge' us one.*

"No' ye'," he answered quietly, "Bu' when I go t' visit Mr. Varnce, I want ye a' the ready."

"Didn't you just tell everybody that we need to start with the basics and not just assume we're dealing with the Christmas Angel?"

"I'm coverin' all the bases," Sam answered with annoyance. "Perhaps Mr. Varnce's source migh' have somethin' useful fer us. I'm goin' t' talk t' this reporter today, an' I need all tha' I can get. Understand?"

Simon seemed to understand how serious he was, as the boy didn't give a sarcastic or funny quip. He simply nodded. "Yes, sir."

An hour later, a copy of Jake Varnce's recent browser history in his pocket, Sam walked through the front doors of *The Plain Dealer*. His badge in hand, he strode through the hallways of the news outlet without care, ready to walk through everyone he had to in order to reach his destination. A few people turned their heads to watch him, but whether it was his height or the determined look on his face that stopped them all from approaching, he didn't know or care as he made his way to Jake Varnce's office on the top floor of the building. The elevator doors opened to an enormous, and very loud, room of cubicles that had heads peeking out from the tops watching the giant Scotsman. Ignoring them, Sam walked through them all, looking at every nameplate on each door. Varnce's office was the third, and Sam didn't bother to knock as he pushed the door open.

A round-faced man with a crownlike balding head was sitting at a desk at the back of the room, a bookshelf of awards and framed magazines purposely displayed behind him. His face contorted with annoyance, he was talking on a phone with quick, domineering answers, and didn't even appear to notice anyone in his office. Sam didn't wait for an invitation and walked over to the chair on the other side of the man's desk and took a seat.

"I don't care about forty inches of snow or your cheap boots, Kullman! Don't leave until you get a comment! …Then I suggest sending Wendos for coffee and a good tent!" Varnce ended the phone call and finally turned to Sam. "Look, pal, if you're here about an unflattering article, then I suggest growing some thicker skin and taking it like a man. A big man, in your case."

Sam flashed his badge. "I'm Agent McKay of the FBI; I'm here t' ask ye a few questions abou'—"

"Listen, buddy, I don't know what the rules in Ireland are, but here in the U.S. of A. we have something called the First Amendment, and you know what it protects? Freedom of speech. As a news outlet, we have every right to follow and report everything the public needs to know."

His interruption (and the wrong nationality comment) deeply annoyed Sam, but he kept himself calm as he continued, "I'm here abou' a series of articles ye wrote surroundin' a killer called The Christmas Angel."

Varnce's face shifted from busy to curious with the raise of his dark, striking eyebrows. "Oh yeah, the serial killer that first appeared thirty-forty years ago, that's right."

"Ye're the one who named him, aren't ye?"

"Indeed, I am, and it made my career," Varnce answered with a smile; he turned around to his bookshelf and grandly gestured at the display, "Two Pulitzers, four Nationals, and a Peabody Award because of my articles on him. Only a handful of reporters in the world have achieved all this. And I owe it all to The Angel."

The man's choice of words greatly disturbed Sam, but still he kept his temper in check as he continued his questioning. "The las' article ye wrote abou' him was in 2018, which was a piece tha' included an interview with an anonymous source."

"Yes, that's right," Varnce smiled a smile that made him look like he was talking about an old family member. "It had been a long time since the Angel had struck, and I thought it might be a good idea to help with a psychology paper, with the help of an insider's opinion."

"An' who was this insider?"

Sam thought Varnce's smile was ghoulish, but it was nothing compared to his laughter. Mocking and boisterous, it equally angered and unnerved him.

"Please, pal. A reporter has an obligation to keep their sources anonymous for their own safety. And the source has the right to anonymity through our favorite amendment."

That was the final straw; Sam slammed his fists on Varnce's desk and growled. "No' if the source is the one tha' di' the killin', in which case yer precious First Amendment cannea protect 'im *or* you. Now listen, 'pal', my bein' here is really a courtesy on yer behalf. I wanted t' give ye the chance t' do the right thing before havin' my man tear apart yer systems an' findin' out fer himself."

Varnce blew an amused raspberry, "Go ahead and have your basement of eggheads try and crack our firewall; I'll keep my fingers crossed for them. What's it matter, anyway? The Angel hasn't been spotted for fifteen years and then he suddenly starts killing again? He must be dead by now."

Sam glared the man down. "Do ye really want t' try lyin' t' me? I've seen yer news trucks a' the scenes, ye know this man isnea dead."

Varnce met his glare with a nervous chuckle. "Okay, sure, my reporters told me what they found, and I put two and two together. Look, either way, you're out of luck. My source has been listed as anonymous, and you can't legally make me break that trust."

Not having any other choice, Sam withdrew the incriminating piece of paper from his pocket, unfolded it, and laid it on the table right where Varnce could see what it contained perfectly. Finally, the infuriating man's face shifted from cocky to nervous.

"W-what's this?"

"Pornographic sites ye're a regular member of."

"So?"

Sam withdrew his phone, "So, my man go' these from yer computar. An' if I call him right now, he'll add child pornography t' yer browser history as well as leak yer fetish t' the public. Do ye think ye'll ge' t' keep all those awards if this ge's out?"

Varnce started. "Now wait a minute! You can't just—"

"If my people can ge' t' yer computar t' do tha', then I can promise ye they will find yer source. No' only will yer reputation'll be ruined, bu' ye'll do jailtime. Now, if ye tell me who yer source fer the article is, then I'll make sure none of this evar happened. Bu' if ye donnea tell me, then by the end of the day this information will be sent t' yer boss an' every committee ye won awards from. Ye have ten seconds t' decide; this offer is only good until I reach the door."

Sam turned on his heel and began walking out of Varnce's office, doing everything he could to resist the urge to throw up from his ghastly threat. With every step, he grew less and less confident. Truthfully, he didn't know whether or not his team could find Varnce's source. Simon could find out anything through a computer, but even he had his limits. Varnce seemed like a smart man; perhaps he was smart enough to not even make a note of who his source was. Either way, the only card Sam had was his threat. Sam's hand had barely touched the doorknob when Varnce yelled out.

"Okay! Darrel, his name is Max Darrel!"

Sam closed his eyes and sighed; he shook the relief off his face and turned back to Varnce. "Where'd ye find 'im?"

"Actually, he found me. I got a letter saying he could give me information about The Christmas Angel and to meet him at this little place in Toronto. Normally I would assume this guy was a nutjob, but he detailed a few things that I didn't know before, like the positioning of the bodies and such. Seemed credible enough, so I made the trip. I don't remember the name of the restaurant, but I can tell you it was a dump. I met him, he gave me information and let me ask a few questions, then he left."

"Anythin' else I should know?"

"No..."

Sam narrowed his eyes.

"I'll look over my old notes and see if I can find something that might help you."

Sam retrieved a business card and threw it on Varnce's desk. "Call me when ye do."

"Yeah, yeah, sure."

Sam left his office without another word, feeling a little better about the case than he had only an hour before, despite the sick feeling in the pit of his stomach. He pulled out his phone and was just about to call Simon when he thought he saw a flash of someone familiar through the crowd of reporters and researchers. However, before he could get a better look, the person had disappeared. Although left curious, Sam decided to shrug it off and continued his phone call.

Ring... Ring... Ring...

"What's up, boss? Need me to smear the reporter?" Simon tried to answer in his usual witty tone, but Sam could hear how uncomfortable he felt underneath the façade.

"Start lookin' fer everythin' ye can abou' a man named Max Darrel in Toronto."

"Y-you actually got him to give up his source?"

"Aye," Sam grunted. "I did."

By the time Sam had returned to the office, Simon was sprinting towards him with a smile on his face; he could tell that meant good news.

"You wanted Max Darrel? Well, I found him," the young man beamed. "And I can tell you everything from his favorite toothpaste to the first girl he got laid with."

"Start with where he is an' wha' he does, Abler," Sam answered as he made his way towards the conference room.

"He's a consulting forensic psychologist for the RCMP, the Canadian equivalent to our FBI, or at least he was until three years ago."

"Wha' happened three years ago?"

"He was fired for attacking a suspect in a case he was working, and subsequently charged and acquitted. I figured you'd want to know what the case was about, so after I engaged a little hiccup in their systems and got past—"

"The point, Simon, ge' t' the point."

"Yeah, of course, boss. Well, it turns out the Christmas Angel doesn't limit his attack area only to the USA. He's been in Canada."

Sam stopped in his tracks just as he entered the conference room, making Simon bump into him. He turned around and asked, "Are ye sure?"

"I checked every case three times," Simon nodded. "It turns out our guy wasn't really hibernating, but he'd moved to a different country, and that's where he's been hunting. I got on the phone with the RCMP and asked them to send everything they have about The Christmas Angel, since he's back in our jurisdiction. Don't worry, they're cooperating and said we'll have everything by tonight."

"How many cases have they go'?"

"Six, that they know of. And the last one they saw was in 2018. So, he's only been hibernating for three years, not fifteen."

"Christ," Sam hissed. Rubbing his face, sat down at the table. "Wha' else di' ye find abou' Darrel?"

"He was recruited from the University of Montreal, where he was working as a Criminal Psychology professor. However, because of what happened while he was consulting, they haven't hired him back. It looks like his whole reputation has been ruined over this. But, right now, he's working as a freelance tutor out of his home in Laval."

"Well, a' least we were right abou' the published article belonging to a psychology fanatic. Any hints on why Darrel i' so fixated on 'im?"

"The case he was fired from, and the last known case of the Angel—the victim was his wife," Simon answered sullenly. "Angelica Darrel, 39. But her body wasn't found in a random place; it was found in his backyard. Cleaned up, laying on her back, and a white peony on her chest. No witnesses saw anybody."

Sam stiffened. "He go' personal; tha' mus' mean Darrel was getting close to him...Call Rivera an' the others an' tell 'em wha' ye know, while I go see Copper abou' escortin' Mr. Darrel t' our office."

"You got it, boss. Should I tell them to come on back?"

"No, no' ye'. I still want' know everythin' we can abou' Lily before we jus' assume the psychologist has all the answars."

Simon whipped out his phone and made the call while Sam marched to Copper's office; despite how horrible he felt about going against his own moral code for the lead, he immediately willed the guilt away.

Chapter Six

Copper didn't argue with Sam's decision to bring Dr. Max Darrel on board with their investigation, and she had Evan arrange a visa for the man within minutes of their conversation. Sam wanted to go and retrieve the psychologist himself, but Copper insisted that there were other people in the office who had that job and instructed him to get back to finding the murderer until Darrel arrived. Sam would have if Rivera and the others had been able to find out anything useful from their errand to Pennsylvania. Unfortunately, given that Lily Vanderguard had run away three months prior to when her body was found, her parents and the Pittsburg police didn't have much about her as it was.

"Well, it's no wonder Lily kept running away from home," Rivera had said over the speaker phone. "Her parents have been fighting for years because of dad's thing for young brunettes and mom's subscription to Smirnoff Daily. They were going through an even nastier divorce the last time Lily took off."

Julie's voice came next. "According to both of them, they figured that Lily would come back when she was ready, so they stopped all of their searching a month ago. Great parents."

"Pittsburg PD thought so, too," Humbar added.

"Di' ye ge' any leads a' all from the police?" Sam asked.

Dana answered next. "Other than her dealer, who had a rock-solid alibi of being held in a cell for drunk and disorderly conduct on the night she went missing, there wasn't anything else to go on. According to the investigators, Lily's teachers and peers described her as a loner; she didn't really hang out socially or do things with kids from her class. She was kicked off any and all extra-curricular activities her parents signed her up for because she'd bring drugs to the meets and give some to the other students."

"There wasnea *anythin'* they could find? Come on, *somebody* had t' have seen this girl."

"The PD said, and I quote, 'Do you have any idea the number of missing girls we get in just one week? We do what we can to find them, but the odds aren't exactly favorable.' Pittsburg gets more missing girls cases than Ohio does, Agent McKay. You can't hold that against them. I got the impression that everyone assumed Lily had OD'd behind a dumpster somewhere."

"Wha' do her parents do fer a livin'?"

"Mason Vanderguard is a big-time stockbroker, and Victoria Vanderguard is a desperate housewife," Julie answered.

Sam turned to Simon. "Stockbrokers can make enemies; di' Mason have any?"

Simon's fingers flew across his keyboard. "If he does, I don't think it's for financial reasons. The firm he works for has a pretty good investing record with minimal losses for their clients. And I can't see anything in his personal financial records that looks fishy; if he got tangled up with a bookie, he's got more than enough to cover his debts."

Sam sighed. "Then Lily really was a random vic, completely strung out on crystal."

"And that probably made her the Angel's easiest target," Julie's voice said again. Sighing, she continued, "I hope you guys had a little bit more luck than we did."

"Aye, we did. We've go' a lead comin' in from Canada. He'll be here tomorra'."

After Sam explained the situation regarding Max Darrel, they all agreed there was nothing more they could do for the day and would have to wait until the only man who had made an impression on The Christmas Angel was there to help them move forward. Sam instructed everyone to return to their homes safely, and they would meet again in the morning.

Truthfully, Sam felt he needed the afternoon off more than the others did; no matter how much he tried to justify his actions with Jake Varnce, the guilt of threatening the man's career and life kept eating away at him—so much so that he couldn't focus. He hoped an afternoon with Oliver would help him regain his composure, if not help him forget the circumstances that helped their case. As soon as he was packed up, he quickly texted the boy that he was on his way home and was surprised to learn that Meredith was there and planned to hang around for a few hours. *U better hurry Dad. Moms raging that we haven't set up Christmas stuff yet. We're going shopping now.*

The minute Sam walked through the door to his apartment, he was greeted with the smell of store-bought sugar cookies baking and the sight of a brand-new small pine tree sitting in the corner of the living room with a few shopping bags under it. Before he even got the chance to remove his coat, Meredith was already coming from around the corner of the kitchen counter with a plate of the frosted cookies; her long dark hair pulled into a bun on the top of her head, she wore a silly Christmas sweater that made Sam snort.

"Do you have any idea how hard we had to look just to get that little Charlie Brown number over there? Why haven't you made your Christmas pudding yet? Doesn't that need to age a few weeks before you can eat it? I know we'll be celebrating Christmas at the house, but you should at least have *something* around here for Oliver to get in the Christmas spirit!"

Sam wanted to be annoyed at his ex-wife's antics, but he couldn't bring himself to do anything other than chuckle. "I've been a wee bi' busy, Meredith. An' Olivar's ge'in a bit old t' be writin' t' Santa Claus, donnea ye think?"

"Maybe the writing part, but I'm never too old for presents!" The boy's voice sounded from the hallway. A moment later, he emerged from his room wearing a dark red sweater with multicolored lights and a Grinch face on it, and a scowl on his.

Sam couldn't contain his laughter and started guffawing at the site of him.

"Yeah, ha-ha-ha," Oliver answered with a roll of his eyes, then his face shifted from annoyance to a devious grin. "Just wait until you see the one she has for *you.*"

"Ach, Meredith, I'm beggin' ye—"

"Nope, no excuses. You boys brought this on yourselves: Christmas is in three days, and if anyone didn't know any better, they'd call you a bunch of Grinches for not even putting a wreath on the door. Oh yes—" she walked towards the bags positioned beneath the smallish tree and pulled out a green pine needle wreath dusted with fake snow "—I got you one to solve that problem. Now go get your sweater on. We're going to decorate this place and eat cookies while we watch *It's a Wonderful Life.*"

"And then *Scrooged,*" Oliver added pointedly, "You promised, Mom."

"Yes, yes, then we'll watch *Scrooged.* Go on, Sam, the sweater's on your bed. And dinner will be here in a few minutes."

Sam chuckled again and shook his head in amusement. Knowing it was pointless to even try arguing, he removed his coat and boots before he walked down the hallway to do as Meredith told him. His sweater was similar to Oliver's: dark red and adorned in Christmas lights but with the words "Bah Humbug" written in green instead. Slipping the sweater over his shirt, he emerged from his room a moment later and began to help the others remove all the decorations Meredith had bought from their bags and containers. Before long, the tiny Christmas tree was gleaming with multicolored lights and glass balls of all sizes. Sam, as was their family tradition since he was so tall, put a star on the top of the tree. Both Meredith and Oliver laughed loudly at how, for the first time, he had to bend over to put a star on instead of reaching up. He told them both to shut-up but laughed about the irony as well. Then dinner, Meredith's choice of Thai food, arrived, and the three of them sat around the little table in Sam's small kitchen and had a laughter-filled family dinner, followed by movies and sugar cookies. Sam was able to momentarily forget about the two girls who had been found.

After they finished *Scrooged,* Meredith allowed Oliver to remove the ugly sweater, and the boy practically sprinted to his room to change into something much more comfortable.

"You can take off your sweater, too," she said mockingly to Sam.

"Ach, I'll keep it on 'til bedtime, i's warm."

Meredith giggled. She stood up from the couch and started to pick up all the garbage and leftovers. Sam immediately did the same, but unfortunately the process of calming down from their holiday fun also allowed the thoughts of his case to creep back into the forefront of his mind. Meredith could obviously sense something was bothering him and asked innocently, "Everything okay?"

"Hmmm? Oh, aye. Jus' stuff a' work."

"I don't suppose you want to talk about it?"

"No," he answered, emphatically shaking his head.

"Alright."

During their marriage, Sam had never once troubled Meredith about the cases he'd been a part of, as he didn't want to worry her.

He intended to do the same now, but thoughts of their guest Max Darrel and his unfortunate wife forced Sam to reconsider that stance. Just this once, anyway.

He cleared his throat. "Do ye still have tha' .32 I gave ye for yer birthday ten year' ago?"

She looked up at him curiously. "It's collecting dust on a shelf in my closet, but yeah."

"Wha' abou' yer concealed permit, have ye been renewin' it every five years?"

"You know I haven't," she said incredulously. "Because you know I hate guns."

Sam sighed and shook his head in disappointment. "Tomorra', I want ye t' ge' t' the range an' get it renewed. Tell Geoff I sent ye, an' he'll rush yer paperwork through."

"Sam—"

"Please, Meredith," he answered, holding up his hand to stop her. "Jus' this once, will ye please do this? Fer me?"

He could tell that she wanted to argue with him by the look in her eyes, but he was relieved that she didn't and instead nodded her head. "Alright, I'll go first thing in the morning."

"Thank ye," he sighed. He couldn't bring himself to tell her the whole truth about why he wanted her carrying her piece around, but he felt better that she wasn't fighting him on the issue. At least now, he could relax a bit knowing that she would at least be somewhat protected.

After they cleaned up, Meredith gave Oliver and Sam a goodbye kiss each and went home. While Oliver wanted to watch a new Christmas comedy on TV, Sam decided to retire early and bid his son goodnight. Lying in bed, he waited until he got a confirmation text from Meredith that she had gotten home safely (which he knew she would do, given his odd request) before he allowed himself to fall asleep. It was still difficult to do so.

***

Once again leaving Oliver asleep in his room after a very late night, Sam went to work bright and early. The team, Humbar, and Dana arrived shortly after he did, and before the six of them could begin reviewing the cases again, Director Copper suddenly appeared from around the corner. A middle-aged disheveled man carrying a briefcase was following her. No one recognized him.

"Everyone, may I present your guest, Dr. Max Darrel, just arrived from Toronto an hour ago."

Dr. Darrel waved to all of them. "Hello, Agents. Thank you for inviting me here."

Sam stepped forward first and offered his hand. "Doctar, I'm Sampson McKay. This is Rivera, Julie Russell, Simon, an' our friends Captain Humbar an' Lieutenant Evanston joinin' us."

"It's a pleasure," he nodded to everyone before turning back to the Director. "Thank you, again, for your hospitality, ma'am."

"You're welcome, Doctor," she nodded quickly, yet politely. Before Sam could also thank her for her efforts, she continued, "I will leave you all to collaborate. Good luck."

Away she walked; Sam rolled his eyes.

Dr. Darrel chuckled, "She doesn't waste time, does she?"

"Ye have no idea," Sam grumbled. "Well, Doctar, I assume ye've been told why we've invited ye t' join our investigation?"

"Please call me Max. Yes, I was informed that you all believe I can help you...because of my late wife."

"The Angel has never changed any of his M.O. before, but he changed his pattern of drop location for you," Rivera said.

Julie stepped forward. "He killed your wife and left her in your own yard. I think it's safe to say that you were getting close to him for him to do something that personal. We'd like you to tell us everything about the last case, and why you attacked a suspect."

"Yes, of course." Max sat in one of the closest seats, opened his briefcase, and pulled out a thick manilla envelope. "Her name was Rachel Mayers; she was a 28-year-old waitress and single mother attending night classes for business management. Nothing damning was found on her body or her clothes, but her bloodwork proved to be very interesting: The ratios of bleach, hydrochloric acid, and sodium hydroxide were almost always 50%, 32%, and 18% of each, give or take a percentage or two. In Rachel's blood, the ratio was 47% bleach, 20% hydrochloric acid, and 31% sodium hydroxide, with an added 2% of pine wood oil."

"You found him because he changed the brand of cleaning stuff he used?" Simon asked.

"It was a clue, and a telling one. Up to that point, the Angel had been obsessive in his use of the chemicals for his method of poison. For him to veer away from it told me one of two things: either A) he was changing his method, which was highly unlikely, or B) wherever he bought the chemicals from had a supply and demand problem, and he had to settle on something else. In this instance, it turned out to be the latter. Thankfully, a member of the investigating team remembered a little store that sold a homemade pine-scented all-purpose cleaner. We were able to connect the cleaner to this particular convenience store. Unfortunately, the owner was an older gentleman that couldn't give us a very definitive description of the man who bought the chemicals, other than he wore sunglasses and a hooded coat, was possibly a middle-aged man, maybe older." Dr. Darrel produced a sketch from the folder, which had a picture of an unrecognizable man wearing glasses and a hooded coat just as he had said. "He couldn't remember any unusual scars or facial hair; even the coat looked like a normal coat you would see on any member of the population."

"And I suppose it would be too much to ask that he had cameras in the store?" Rivera asked.

Max shook his head. "Not a one. All we had to go on was the word of an eighty-year-old man. But he did remember seeing a white van. He didn't remember a license plate number, however."

Sam took the sketch from him and tacked it onto their board. "Alrigh', so wha' di' ye do next?"

"Well, at that point all we had to go on was the van and the initial psychological profile I had put together: The Angel obviously had access to travel, as there is no discernable pattern to his movements and the locations where he would leave his victims. Because of the crude needle wounds to the heart, I ruled out the possibility of him being a traveling nurse. More than likely he has access to needles because of a medical condition of some sort. And then, finally, where he would drop his victims suggested he would be very outdoorsy, possibly familiar with equipment that could be used for excavation or building."

"What about the use of the chemical solution on the body to erase evidence? Didn't that tell you he might have had forensic training?"

"I wondered that at first, but judging by how clean the bodies were, it was more likely he was doing that because of an obsessive-compulsive need to 'wash' his victims, rather than with a thought to erase evidence."

Julie snorted. "That doesn't make sense to me: Why else would he wash the bodies of the victims, if not to make sure nothing could be traced back to him? And what is with this flower he leaves on them?"

"It may not make sense to you, Agent...Russell," Max answered her gently. "But what he does makes perfect sense to him. The Christmas Angel hates women; this much is obvious. So, he rapes them and obsessively cleans them, but he takes the time to pose them as if they're sleeping when he drops them. The white peony further signifies his remorse for killing them. But the thing is, he's not remorseful for killing any of the victims. All these women were stand-ins for who he's really trying to kill. So, to continue, my profile suggested that he had an abusive mother that would frequently use cleaning chemicals on him for anything she deemed to be 'bad behavior,' especially anything sexual. His adolescence would have been a feeding frenzy for his mother's abusive tactics. As a result, he has a compulsive need to be a perfectionist, successful, and whenever he would meet or see a woman that reminded him even remotely of his mother, he would fly into uncontrollable rage and enact his revenge. But when he finished, he'd still go through the motions of apologizing to her, right down to the flower on her chest."

"Okay, but what significance does the winter have on his thought process?" Dana asked. "Every girl's body has always been found somewhere between late December and the end of March, at the very latest."

"It's likely that a traumatic event occurred in his personal life during those three months, which in turn, triggered him to start killing. It could be likened to an anniversary: As he gets closer to the date of his trauma, if any woman crosses his path who even remotely resembles his mother in looks, actions, or speech, she automatically becomes his intended target."

"Geeze, can anybody say twisted?" Simon mumbled. "Were you able to find any suspects that met your profile?"

"One man fit the profile like a glove: Freddy Parinski, a freelance construction manager from New York who was hired by a shipping corporation to build a new warehouse near Chedoke Park in

Hamilton. He has a history of sexual harassment and misconduct, abuse towards his employees, and he even has Type 1 diabetes."

"Did you figure out he could be the Christmas Angel before or after your wife was killed?" Humbar asked.

"I'd had my suspicions when we first talked with him; he showed classic signs of Malignant Narcissism in the form of hostility and his general anti-social tendencies. He'd never join the others for a beer after work, and he frequently berated the youngest members of the construction crew, particularly the women, if something on a project didn't meet his standards. Up to this point, we didn't have any other viable suspects, so he was our main focus. But we couldn't find anything to connect to him. So, against my recommendation, the officer leading the investigation decided to prematurely release the sketch we got from the store owner, along with the description of the white van...my wife went missing that very night, and her body was found the next week in my back yard. Parinski had managed to evade the tail we had on him during that whole time, but he had an alibi, which was confirmed. We had him picked up all the same. When we brought him in for questioning...he made a derogatory comment, and I lost my temper, which in turn, helped us lose the case.

"The van and the sketch weren't enough for a conviction: As you can see, anyone could be the man in the sketch with the right sunglasses and a hood over his head, and all the white vans on Parinski's project were accounted for during the time of my wife's murder. Plus, a neighbor came forward saying they saw somebody that looked kind of tall leaving my yard early in the morning. Parinski is 5'4". Between the circumstantial evidence and my blunder, the case against Freddy Parinski was thrown out almost as soon as it got onto a judge's desk."

"Wha' abou' the needles? Were ye able t' ge' anythin' from tha'?"

"Every prescribed needle was accounted for on his person, even the discarded ones. And not only were they they wrong size, there were absolutely no traces of Rachel Mayers' blood or the combined chemical solution on any of them."

"Freddy Parinski could still be our guy," Dana jumped in. "It's not unheard of for killers to take on a protégé, someone to take over the methods when they're gone. Or he could even have a partner."

"I've often wondered that myself," Max nodded. "But since my disgrace, not even my friends were willing to tell me anything they found. I have no idea where Parinski is now."

"Simon?" Sam grunted.

"Freddy Parinski, I'm on it," the young man smiled and turned his focus to his laptop.

"I have one question," Rivera asked. "You're obviously an expert on the Angel's behaviors, and...no offence, but with the death of your wife, you didn't exactly have anybody else left to lose. Why did you have Varnce keep you anonymous during the interview?"

Max looked down in shame. "That's a fair question, Agent, and the answer is because after my mistake with Parinski, I was considered a hinderance to the investigation, not a help. The university wouldn't hire me back, even though my credentials are still intact. A mistake like that will get even the most brilliant literature thrown in the trash. I don't care who gets the credit for catching this guy, I just want him caught. And I thought if I couldn't do it, maybe somebody else could, with my research."

"Tha's verra commendable," Sam shot Rivera a quick look of warning before he turned back to Max. "Doctar, di' ye happen t' notice anythin' peculiar abou' the way the Angel would leave his victims?"

"What do you mean?"

"The two tha' we've seen have drag marks next t' their bodies as if they...had t' be facin' a certain way before he left."

Dr. Darrel raised his hand to his chin and thought. "No, I can't say that I've noticed anything like that before. But I'll review my notes and the case files and see if I can turn up anything."

Simon suddenly stopped typing and turned his laptop around to the others. "Well, the good news is your friend Parinski finally got what was coming to him: He was sentenced to twenty-five to life for raping a colleague and has been in Rikers since September 2019. The bad news: He's had absolutely no contact with anyone other than his lawyer, probably trying to appeal the sentence."

"Well, a guy like that, I can't even imagine his mom would want to talk to him," Rivera said bluntly.

"That still doesn't totally rule him out," Dana said next. "Considering the way the Angel has travelled for the last thirty years, I'm sticking to my theory that he may not be working alone."

"Aye," Sam nodded. "I agree with ye. A' least now we know where we can find one suspect, an' if we find any proof tha' yer theory is right, then we'll pay Mr. Parinski a visit an' see wha' we can ge' out of him."

Suddenly, Humbar's phone started ringing; while he answered grunting "Chief Humbar," everyone around him stayed quiet and watched him.

"Are you absolutely sure? ...Okay, we'll be there in ten." Humbar placed his phone back in his pocket and looked to the others with sheer mortification. "Another dead girl was found on 480, just north of Oakwood."

"Oakwood?" Dana started. "But that's a pretty populated area; are they sure it's the Angel?"

"Lying down, a white flower, and a big, ugly needle mark over her heart; it looks like his work."

Max stood up from his seat. "May I accompany all of you?"

"Of course, Doctar," Sam nodded. "Ye've been the bes' lead we've had since we started this investigation. I want t' know everythin' ye see."

The seven of them filed out of the office without another word and made for the newest crime scene. As usual, the whole area was teaming with people who were doing everything they could to collect and analyze any trace evidence they could find. But everyone moved out of Sam and the others' way as they waded through towards the body, which was much closer to the highway than the other two had been. An M.E. was still examining the body of the woman, and Sam recognized a few officers from Humbar's precinct standing nearby. They all shared a quick, pleasant hello before the officers stepped away from the scene, handed everything they knew so far over to Humbar, and walked away.

"According to Gene and Dill, a driver called in early this morning during their commute to report something weird on the side of the road, and dispatch sent them to check it out. Her name is Lorraine Wyatt, she was reported missing in November of 2016."

"Five years? That's a lot longer than the Angel has ever kept his victims," Dana said.

The seven of them stood around the peacefully posed body and out of the way as the medical examiner continued to poke, prod, and otherwise check any and all nooks and crannies he could initially find before the body could be moved.

Sam looked all around her body, but couldn't seem to find any drag marks, however, there were some slight indentations in the ground just like the first body. He pointed them out to the others to confirm that the footprint expert should have a look. Then he turned his focus on Lorraine, and when he looked closer at the flower positioned over her heart, he could tell something was already amiss: It was a rose, not a peony. He didn't have very long to think about the direction of the body when the Medical Examiner suddenly muttered a low, but discernable, "Huh..."

"What? What's 'huh'?" Rivera asked.

"It's the strangest thing, and obviously will need to be confirmed with a tissue sample, but if I didn't know any better, I'd think this girl was frozen."

"There's three feet of snow everywhere; I'd be amazed if she wasn't frozen."

"No, no, I mean frozen like a store-bought turkey; I think she's been in an actual freezer."

Sam stepped forward, "How can ye tell?"

"Well, for one, parts of her skin have ice crystals on it, not snow. And for another, I nearly broke a finger off trying to collect a sample under the nails. Even if this is 12-hour rigor-mortis, her fingers would be hard to move, but they wouldn't break."

"Couldn't that mean she's been out here in the cold for a pretty long time, though?" Julie asked.

"It's possible," the M.E. nodded. "Like I said, though, I'm only speculating. A tissue sample would be more conclusive."

Everyone nodded and remained quiet while the M.E. finished his preliminary exam. Sam's focus was on the victim's face: this poor woman had obviously died in fear—her features were contorted. And her eyes were wide open, milky and blank. But the blaring evidence surrounding her couldn't be ignored.

"This isnea the work of the Christmas Angel. I's obviously a copycat."

"I'd have to agree," Max nodded. "The flower alone is a dead giveaway."

"Well, just to be sure, we better do the full markup on her," Humbar said. "She's still got the needle to the heart. We could at least make sure the poison ratios aren't the same."

"Aye, we'll have Bicks take a look a' her t' be sure, bu' I donnea think he'll be able t' tell us much." Sam stared at the woman lying in the snow and cursed under his breath. *A copycat, tha's all we need...*

Chapter Seven

"Lorraine Wyatt: age 31, living in Tremont when she was reported missing by her grandmother November 27th, 2016. She never showed up for Thanksgiving dinner." Simon continued working his magic on his laptop while everyone around him made room on the white board for the newest potential victim's information. "Dad died of cancer in 1995, and mom committed suicide in 1993. Her only family was her grandmother Mimi Smith. According to Mimi, Lorraine didn't have any enemies other than her ex-husband Trevor, whom she divorced earlier that year in January."

"Di' they have any children?" Sam asked.

"The police reports don't say anything, but hang on...according to medical records, she'd been to an obstetrician four times for pregnancy. But I've also got four E.R. visits citing miscarriage, the last one a nurse made a note of bruising found around the abdomen."

"The husband abused her and made her lose her kids," Julie snarled.

"Maybe, but I've also found records of Lorraine seeing a therapist and being on a high dose of anti-depressants, one of which has a known side effect of bleeding disorders, including easy bruising."

"And you believe that?"

"I'm just saying, the woman appeared to have issues, so maybe we shouldn't jump straight to blaming the husband yet. Especially because I can't seem to find any record on him, other than a speeding ticket from three years ago. Trevor Wyatt is a psychotherapist with his own practice; he probably recognized his wife's depressed behavior and was trying to help her."

"Did he have an alibi when she disappeared?"

Again, Simon's fingers flew across his laptop. "According to the police reports, he said he was with patients until 9:00 p.m. the night of Lorraine's disappearance, and then at a bar with friends for the rest of the night until almost 2:00 a.m. Alibis checked out, but the grandma insisted he was a danger to Lorraine. He allowed the police to search his home and his work; they didn't find any evidence that Lorraine had been near him in months."

"He could still be involved—"

"Aye, he's no' off the hook ye', Jules," Sam quickly interrupted her. "An' the details of the body are too different from the othars t' be the work of the Angel. Bu' the first thing we need t' do is tell Mrs. Smith abou' her granddaughtar an' make absolutely sure we know everythin'. Julie, Rivera, I want ye two t' talk with Bicks abou' the body: Find out if she was killed by freezin' or poisonin'. Either way, we can rule out the Angel fer this woman, an' i's a poor attempted copycat, or no'. If i's the lattar, then perhaps there'll be more we can learn, an' we're finally ge'in close t' this bassard."

Humbar stepped forward, "What do you want us to do? Go talk to the grandmother? We can work this ourselves and try to rule out if she's a victim of the Christmas Angel."

"No, I'll handle tha' meself. With the rush of this mornin', ye three—" he gestured to Max "—havenea properly talked. I want ye t' tell the Doctar everythin' abou' the cases ye've seen. Simon, ye're with me."

"You got it, boss," the young man nodded and closed his laptop.

Sam turned to Max, who was stroking his chin with his fingers and looked deep in thought. Curious, he asked, "Doctar, wha' are ye thinkin'?"

"I'm pondering more on the theory that the Christmas Angel could possibly be more than one person. Yes, Lorraine's body was dumped in a different location than the others, and yes, she's been missing for five years. If the ME is right that her body's been frozen for all that time, that's certainly an oddity for his methods. But even though the fine details are wrong, every piece of the formula of the murder appears to be the Angel's M.O. These oddities could be personal interpretation of a protégé, much like the accidental cleaning supply factor."

"Or i' could be a copycat hit made by someone t' throw us off his trail an' blame i' on a serial killer a' large again."

Julie, though already nearing the elevators with Rivera, seemed to have overheard the Doctor's thoughts and quickly shouted her opinion: "My money is still on the husband!" before the doors closed.

Max chuckled, but quickly turned his expression back to serious. "I suppose a blood sample will tell us whether or not the real Angel could have been involved with this one. If the poison ratios match up, only he would be obsessed with that detail."

"Rivera an' Julie'll tell ye the moment they know anythin'. Fer now, I need ye t' go over the cases again, please."

"Yes, of course."

Satisfied that everyone had their orders, Sam marched towards the elevators with Simon right behind him.

***

After finding the house that belonged to Mimi Smith empty, Sam and Simon learned from the eighty-five-year-old's neighbors that she would most likely be found at her church, having a group therapy session. The building itself was located near the heart of Broadway-Slavic Village; Tall and made almost entirely of red bricks, it felt like a cathedral to Sam. The inside of the building was even more so: Dark wooden pews faced a long hall with beams coming to a point over three massive stained-glass windows. Before each window was a statue of a crucifix and a white marble altar. Just beneath the center altar was a circle of a dozen folding chairs; people of various ages and ethnicities were sitting in them. But in the middle of the group, standing and talking, was an older woman with white-blonde hair and black half-moon glasses. Curious, Sam pulled Simon to the side, and the two of them stood in a shadowy corner of the church to watch them. Sam's focus was on the woman leading the session.

"Our loved ones can rest from the trials of this world, but what comfort does that give to us? We are not only the survivors; we are victims as well." Her voice was soft, but her tone was very magisterial; there was a murmur of agreement from the other participants.

"But here's the truth behind being a victim: A victim remains a victim if they continue to give the attacker power. Why? Because power is control. Can we control the anger and pain and sadness we feel towards the people who took our husbands, wives, children away from us? Of course not, we're only human. So, what is it that we can do to take power away from them?"

The group looked to each other questioningly before an older gentleman answered, "We can forgive."

"Yes, we can forgive them. I know, I know how ridiculous that sounds. How can you forgive the man or woman who took everything from you? It's inconceivable. The answer: God. None of us are spotless before God, and it is not our place to judge whether someone else's cloak is more stained than ours. 'Bear with each other and forgive one another if any of you has a grievance against someone. Forgive as the Lord forgave you.' Hate is a poison, and poison kills faster than grief ever could. Forgiveness is the antidote. Forgiveness is not an antidote that we take only once: We will always have days where we can feel the poison coursing through our blood just as strongly as the first time. Those are the days that we must call upon God for the antidote, that we must rely on his strength to cure us. Amen."

"Amen," the attendees muttered with a nod.

"Phillip, would you kindly close our session with a prayer? And ask that we all lean on God for the antidote of forgiveness in times of anger."

At that moment, Simon attempted to open his mouth and alert the group of their presence, but Sam quickly nudged him and motioned that he bow his head in respect. The group held hands, and a very soft, inaudible prayer was uttered before it was finished with a clear 'Amen.' Everyone began to disperse, and Sam finally allowed Simon to get clear of the shadows and clear his throat.

"Ahem, please excuse us for interrupting, but we're looking for Mimi Smith? We were told that we could find her here."

Sam wasn't the least bit surprised to see the leader of the therapy session, the one who had given the speech on forgiveness, raise her hand. "I'm Mimi Smith. How can I help you?"

Sam stepped forward with his badge in hand. "Mrs. Smith, I'm Agent McKay of the FBI, an' this is Agent Abler. Is there someplace we can speak t' ye in private?"

The other members looked at the old woman curiously, but she gave them all a kind smile before answering, "It's alright, everyone. I'll see you next week. Drive safely."

Although there was hesitation, eventually they all began to leave and, before long, only Sam, Simon, and Mimi were alone in the church. Now alone and facing her, Sam couldn't help but notice the interesting necklace that she was wearing; it was a flower with an intricately carved band studded with jewels surrounding it. It wasn't something he had ever seen before, but it definitely caught his attention by the way it gleamed.

"You're here about Lorraine, aren't you?" She asked in the same soft tone. "You found her body?"

Sam focused on the subject of their visit at hand again; her lack of surprise made Sam curious. "Wha' makes ye so sure tha' yer granddaughter's dead?"

"It's been five years since she went missing, Agent, and I'm an old woman. I stopped harboring any false hope that she might still be alive some time ago. Tell me the truth: She's dead, isn't she?"

Simon spoke next. "Yes, ma'am. Her body was found this morning."

Mrs. Smith took a deep breath and sat in the closest seat to her, her left hand reached up and held the pendant. "Please, can you tell me whether or not she suffered?"

Simon opened his mouth, but Sam quickly answered before he could. "We donnea think so, ma'am. I' appears tha' her death was quick."

Mrs. Smith eyed Sam for a moment, and he felt curiously uncomfortable under her gaze. Finally, she nodded. "Well, at least now I can finally lay her to rest."

"I'm afraid tha' won't be possible yet, ma'am. We're still investigatin' the circumstances surroundin' her death an' her disappearance. In fact, tha's wha' we wanted t' come an' talk t' ye abou'. Accordin' t' yer report, ye said Lorraine's ex-husband should be investigated."

"That's right, and I still believe that he was the one who kidnapped my poor Lorraine. I'm sure that he killed her, too."

Simon cleared his throat. "No offense, ma'am, but you sound very angry for someone who was just preaching about forgiveness."

"As I stated in my sermon, Agent, forgiveness is a constant antidote that we need to apply frequently. I admit that I will have to apply it again and again, now that I know for certain that my granddaughter is dead, but that doesn't make the pain and anger I feel any less potent right now."

"An' tha's perfectly understandable," Sam nodded. "Ma'am, I realize this is a difficult time fer ye, bu' may we ask ye a few questions abou' the day yer granddaughter disappeared?"

"Yes, of course. Please, have a seat."

The two of them sat down in various chairs of the circle, and Sam began his questioning. "When was the las' time ye spoke t' yer granddaughtar?"

"Two days before Thanksgiving in 2016. She wanted to bring dessert, but I insisted I had everything under control. When she didn't show up, I knew something was wrong. But the police insisted they couldn't do anything until 48 hours had passed."

"Can ye tell us why ye're convinced Mr. Wyatt is guilty?"

"I had my suspicions that something was wrong for some time after their wedding...if I'm being honest, I never really liked him in the first place. Then when she left Trevor earlier that year and came to live with me, I confronted her, and she finally told me the truth. She told me he was beating her, and she'd miscarried a baby because of it. That very night we began to prepare for a divorce. Trevor was furious; once he came to my house in the middle of the night demanding that Lorraine come back with him, but I wouldn't let him see her."

"How did you stop him?" Simon asked innocently.

Mrs. Smith looked up and smirked, "I didn't, but my old revolver did. I told him to leave at once, or I would call the police. He left and never came to my house again. After the divorce was finalized, Lorraine was starting to get on her feet again. She got a job working for Willie's Essentials. That's a little tool shop about five miles from my house. She was planning on moving out and had even started looking into some apartments around town in...August, I believe. I thought it was too soon, and I told her she could stay with me as long as she wanted, but she insisted that she was ready. She'd moved into a friend's basement apartment...a month later, she disappeared. I immediately suspected Trevor had something to do with it."

"Did you tell all this to the police?"

"Yes, but Lorraine had never called the police, no matter how many times he'd hit her, so they couldn't find a reason to look into him until she'd been officially declared missing. And even then, they told me that he was 'extremely helpful' and that there was absolutely nothing that linked Trevor to Lorraine's disappearance. They even said something about an alibi. But, if you knew Trevor, you'd know he's too smart to leave behind any sort of connection." A tear appeared at the corner of Mrs. Smith's eye, but she quickly removed her glasses to wipe it away. "But I suppose now that Lorraine's body has been found, you might be able to find this 'evidence' that is needed?"

To this question, Sam answered. "Ma'am, if ye'll permit me, ye should know tha' i' is entirely possible tha' he's no' guilty of kidnappin' yer granddaughter."

The sadness in Mrs. Smith's eyes was quickly replaced with a fiery anger that did not sit well with her kind, old face. "And he'll get away with all those years he beat my granddaughter and killed her baby?"

Sam sighed, "Aye, he migh'. Bu' ye have my word tha' we'll take a deeper look inta' Mr. Wyatt. If he is involved, I promise ye tha' I'll make him pay fer everythin' he's done."

Mrs. Smith kept her focus on Sam, as though she was searching for a lie. Finally, she nodded, appeased by Sam's oath. "Alright, I will be patient a little while longer. Agents...may I see Lorraine's body? I just need to see her for myself, to know that her suffering really is over."

Sam nodded and gently placed his hand on her shoulder. "Of course, ma'am. We'll arrange fer someone t' take ye t' her immediately. An' if ye need or can think of anythin' else, please give me a call."

Sam handed her a card with his number on it, which she took without a question. While Simon arranged for someone from the FBI to come and pick Mrs. Smith up, Sam sat with her and listened to her tell stories of her granddaughter. By the time a car had arrived, Sam had learned that Lorraine loved horses and Chinese food, and Christmas was her favorite holiday. Though the woman had kept herself calm and composed during their discussion, Sam could tell that she was on the verge of breaking and had no doubt she would lose her composure when she saw her Lorraine's body. As soon as the car was away, he told Simon to inform Rivera and Julie of Mrs. Smith and to stay with her during the identification. Then, thanks to Simon's magic fingers, they knew the location of Trevor Wyatt's business and his home, and Sam was determined to speak to him next.

In the northern part of Lakewood, on the second floor of a two-story building that had a view of Lake Erie, was the office of Dr. Trevor Wyatt, Psychotherapist. His name was printed in gold letters on the clouded glass door, and Sam could hear muffled voices on the other side of it. He already knew that he did not like the man and wanted to storm inside and demand precise answers for his whereabouts. The fact that the only thing Mr. Wyatt had against him was suspected spousal abuse stopped him from acting on his impulse. As patiently as possible, he and Simon waited in the hallway for the door to open. Thankfully, they didn't have to wait long, as it opened only a few minutes after they'd arrived.

The Doctor, an average looking man of a bulky build, was escorting a young woman out the door with a smile on his face. "You did very well today, Yazmin. We'll talk again next week, okay?"

"Thank you, Dr. Wyatt," the young lady smiled, then upon seeing Sam and Simon standing there, quickly rushed down the stairs and out of the building.

Once Sam and Simon were the only people left in the hallway, the doctor turned his attention to them and asked, "May I help you gentlemen?"

"Trevor Wyatt?" Sam asked sternly.

"Yes, I'm Dr. Wyatt."

Sam flashed his badge. "I'm Agent McKay, an' this is Agent Abler. We'd like t' ask ye a few questions."

"Of course, but can I know the subject for your questioning?"

"Yer ex-wife, Lorraine."

"What about her?"

"Her body was found this morning." Sam kept a hard stare on the man and wasn't surprised to not see a change in his behavior. Wyatt simply took a moment to process the news before standing to the side and beckoning that Sam and Simon come into his office.

The room wasn't too large, and a long couch sat facing a cushy leather chair. Other than the large window giving a view to the snowy outdoors, there wasn't as much as a painting on any of the other walls. Sam didn't like the feel of it.

"For the record, and it is in fact on record, agents, I haven't seen Lorraine since we divorced six years ago," Wyatt said simply.

"But you did know she was missing, didn't you?" Simon asked before taking a seat on the long couch.

"Yes, I heard that when her crazy grandmother sent the police over to my house to search for her. You can check the transcripts or reports, whatever it is that you do: I let them search my home and business from top to bottom but, as I told them, I hadn't seen Lorraine, and that was the first I'd heard about her disappearance."

"What makes you think that her grandmother is crazy?"

Dr. Wyatt took a seat in the plush chair across from Simon. With a shrug of his shoulders and a sigh, he answered. "First of all, Mimi was against our marriage from the start. Second, Lorraine was suffering from depression and bipolar disorder. She was seeing a colleague of mine about it, who prescribed standard anti-depressants and anti-anxiety medication while she attended therapy. Mimi has always thought the idea of being on medicine is ridiculous and wanted Lorraine to drink teas and try oils...once, she even told me that 'God can heal all things.' I tried to convince her that Lorraine needed real medical help, but she wouldn't hear any of it. She convinced Lorraine that I was forcing her to take the pills and go to therapy, until eventually Lorraine believed it. ...It grew to be too much for me, so I just buried myself in my work. Shortly after that, the steps towards divorce were being taken."

Sam didn't budge from his spot as he asked pointedly, "Wha' abou' the times Lorraine went t' the hospital fer the miscarriages?"

Wyatt turned and looked at Sam with shock. "W-what? What miscarriages? We never got pregnant."

His reaction interested Sam, but before he could continue, Simon answered. "She miscarried four times, Dr. Wyatt. You really didn't know?"

"There's no way I could have, agents...I'm sterile." The anger suddenly reappeared on Wyatt's face. "I had always suspected she started seeing someone towards the end...I guess this finally proves it. Honestly, by the end of our marriage, I was ready to get out. I couldn't handle Lorraine's grandmother interfering with our lives any longer. And now I know she wasn't the only one."

Sam stepped forward. "Then ye wouldnea mind tellin' us abou' the nigh' ye went t' Mimi's house demandin' t' see Lorraine."

Dr. Wyatt sighed. "That was a misunderstanding. I came home from work and discovered that Lorraine had just up and moved out:

No phone call, no note, she just grabbed a suitcase, packed her things, and left. I knew she had gone to her grandmother's, and I tried one last ditch attempt to tell that woman to quit meddling in our marriage and get Lorraine to come home. But when she pointed that gun at me, I knew Lorraine was already lost to her lunacy. So, I left."

"Tha' must've made ye angry."

"Of course, it did, agent. But I know when a cause is lost. I left, and I never went back again."

"Ye were verra accomodatin' t' the police the night of yer ex-wife's disappearance. So, ye won't mind us askin' again where ye were the night she went missin', will ye?"

"Not at all, I was with patients until 9:00 p.m., and then I went to a bar around the corner to celebrate a friend's birthday."

"What bar?"

"Um...Buckeye's, I think. It was either that or Two Bucks."

"You donnea remembar?"

Wyatt looked up, the annoyance he felt evident. "It was five years ago, agents. But I'm pretty sure we went to Buckeye's. And the birthday boy's name is Rick Tellman. Here, I'll get you his number, and you can ask him yourself, along with all my other friends who were there that night, just like the police did when Lorraine was reported missing." Wyatt pulled out his phone and a pen and began to write down various phone numbers in a notebook sitting next to his chair.

Sam clenched his fist at the man's careless attitude towards the woman, who was supposed to be (at one point) his dearly beloved's, death.

Simon must have sensed how angry Sam was becoming, as the young man quickly jumped in. "Um, no offense dude, but you're not exactly acting heartbroken over the news of your wife's kidnapping and death."

"Ex-wife, agent. Yes, I'm not upset. Would you be if you found out the person you were supposed to spend your life with lied to you repeatedly? I haven't given Lorraine a thought since the police came to question me. I had nothing to do with her disappearance, and I certainly didn't kill her. I have nothing to hide from you. And I have an appointment with an extremely paranoid gentleman in a few minutes, so I'd like to get you what you need and send you on your way before he gets here." Wyatt finished writing on the paper, ripped it from his little notebook, and handed it over to Sam without breaking his hard stare.

"Well, if you have nothing to hide, then you wouldn't mind if we took another look around your house, would you?"

"With a proper warrant, not at all. Was there anything else?"

"No, I think that will do it for right now. Right, boss?"

"Aye, fer now."

Knowing that getting a warrant for a five-year-old suspect would take time, Sam decided they should return to the office to see what the others had found. Part of him strongly disliked Trevor Wyatt, but the sensible part told him there was absolutely no reason to let the words of Mimi Smith be their only proof he was guilty. But, just to be certain, he would have Humbar and Dana double check the doctor's alibi later, as well as his claim to being unable to have children.

Chapter Eight

Simon, who had been clacking away furiously on his laptop since he and Sam returned to the office, finally looked up from the keyboard with a grimace. "Well, Doctor Wyatt wasn't lying about his soldiers being unable to march. I found visits to an infertility clinic in their medical history from eight years ago where there's a confirmed test of his sterility. The babies Lorraine lost weren't his."

"Tha' only gives him motive," Sam answered. "She was seein' someone an' go' pregnant, so he beat her an' then killed her when she wouldnea stop."

"Or he could be telling the truth and had nothing to do with it. He does have an airtight alibi; even the bartender confirmed his whereabouts that night."

"The more we learn abou' this couple, the more I'm convinced tha' Lorraine's no' one of the Angel's victims. There's too many differences here, an' the biggest one bein she's been missin' fer five years, an' all tha' time she's been in a freezer. If she was an Angel victim, ha' would make 'im decide t' keep her fer so long when he doesnea keep anyone else tha' long?"

Right at that moment, the elevator door opened and out came Julie and Rivera, both of whom looked worn and tired.

"Mrs. Smith just left...I've had to help a lot of families through victim identification before, but this was something completely different," Rivera sighed as he sank into his chair.

"What did she do?" Simon asked.

"What *didn't* she do is the real question," Julie answered. "First of all, she tried to pull some oils and things out of her purse to rub down on the body, but Bicks stopped her. She kept saying something about bringing peace and happiness to her granddaughter's spirit with the oils, but Bicks told her she could do that when he was done. Then she dropped to her knees and started praying right there in the morgue."

Sam didn't think Simon's eyes could get any wider, but the boy proved him wrong when he answered, "Wow."

"You can say that again," Rivera nodded. "What church is this lady apart of again?"

"I honestly got the impression she started her own thing and just borrows a building now and then."

"Oh, so she's one of *those* people."

Sam interrupted them. "Enough, have some respect fer the woman. She's no' hurtin' anyone, an' she believes she's helpin' her granddaughtar."

Even though the three of them remained silent, Sam didn't miss the condescending look that they passed to each other.

"Di' Bicks finish his examination before she arrived?"

"Yeah, barely," Julie nodded. "And you're right: This is definitely a copycat job. The bloodwork says the cleaning chemical ratios were all off. The other girls were practically starved, but Lorraine had a last meal before she died: steak, string beans, potatoes, and some red wine. Bicks also said there weren't any signs of rape or any sexual activity for weeks, but she was eight weeks pregnant when she was killed."

Sam sighed and shook his head. "Fantastic, a double homicide. Wha' abou' the M.E.'s theory tha' she'd been frozen?"

"He was right on the money," Rivera answered. "Bicks found ice crystals in her lungs, and a tissue sample confirmed that it came from an actual freezer and not the elements. All we've got to do is find the freezer she was kept in, and case closed."

A ping came from Simon's computer. "Well, the warrant to search Dr. Wyatt's home just got here, so I guess we'll go take a look at his freezer first."

"We'll handle tha'. I' looks like those three could use a break—" Sam gestured to Dr. Darrel, Humbar, and Dana. "Have them run down Dr. Wyatt's alibi again while we're gone."

"You want *me* to tell *them* to take a break from the Christmas Angel cases? Yeah, that's going to go over well."

"Jus' do it."

Sam almost took pleasure in flashing the warrant to Dr. Wyatt as he, Rivera, Julie, and a team of forensics experts entered his house and began to search every nook and cranny again. The house, much like the office, was a plain and almost sterile environment that unsettled Sam: There were no pictures on the walls, every piece of leather furniture was positioned absolutely perfectly, nothing seemed out of direct ratio to another. It didn't feel homely at all. It didn't take long to find a large chest freezer in the basement, and Sam had the very best member of the experts come and process it himself. Dr. Wyatt showed them receipts proving that he purchased the freezer three years ago—which was under their window of time when Lorraine went missing. Sam didn't care; he had the freezer processed anyway.

"He probably hid her body somewhere else until he could move it here," Julie whispered under her breath. Sam subtly nodded his agreement.

It was afternoon by the time they finished the search of the house, and Dr. Wyatt was more than perturbed. After being warned not to leave town until the evidence results came back, the Doctor simply scoffed and slammed the door in their faces.

The trio had barely gotten back to the office when Humbar and Dana informed them that, after re-checking the Doctor's alibi, it turned out to be shakier than before. The birthday boy said he thought that he saw his friend at the party, but after five years, he couldn't be exactly sure. Eventually, he admitted that Dr. Wyatt called him a day or two after the party to tell the police he was certain his friend was at the birthday party. Then, thanks to the rush Sam had put on the evidence, the swabs taken from Dr. Wyatt's freezer came back positive for epithelial tissue belonging to the late Lorraine Wyatt. All this news had the entire group, even Dr. Darrel, beaming.

"Well, at least we can say we've managed to catch one bad guy today," Julie smiled. Turning to Simon, she jeered. "I told you it was the husband; you owe me dinner."

"Yeah, yeah, fine. Pick out where you want to go, and when the boss says we're done, we'll go."

Sam, feeling good about the much-needed win, went ahead and conceded to everyone. "We'll call i' a day. We've been workin' too hard fer almost 72 hours straight. Everyone go home, celebrate, an' we'll ge' back t' the serial killar tomorra' mornin'." As everyone started packing up, he handed the documents pertaining to Lorraine Wyatt's murder over to Dana and said, "I believe yer people can handle this arrest, aye?"

Even the prickly Lieutenant had to smile. "The scum'll be behind bars before you can say 'haggis'."

While the rest of his team looked awkwardly at each other, Sam simply chuckled at her poor attempt at humor. Out of the corner of his eye, he saw Dr. Darrel not making any effort to pack up. Instead, the man retreated to the office where he, Humbar, and Dana had been going over case files together. Sam followed him.

"Doctar, I promise ye this'll still be here in the mornin'."

"Call me Max, please. And I know," the man smiled. "It's just that I haven't been able to see any of these case files since I was fired. I'm just re-familiarizing myself so I can be helpful."

"Do ye intend t' do tha' all night?"

"Probably, I do have a tendency to be unable to let things go when I get set on a path," he chuckled.

Sam snickered in return. "Aye, me too. Bu' take i' from me, Max, ye need t' take the good times an' enjoy them when ye can in this line o' work. I donnea see how fixatin' on this now'll help anyone."

Though it took a beat, Dr. Darrel conceded with a nod. "Alright, I'll let it go for tonight. Could you recommend somewhere I can find a good steak?"

Sam smiled. "We've a few, bu' my favorite place is the Cleveland Chop. As a matter of fact, I was goin' t' pick up my son an' go t' dinnar there. Would ye care t' join us?"

"Thank you, I'd be honored."

An hour later, seated at a small table in the back, Sam, Oliver, and Dr. Darrel were each enjoying their meals and conversation. While Oliver was a little suspicious upon learning that Max was a psychologist, very quickly the boy warmed up to their fellow dinner guest and had no problem talking to the gentleman. This put Sam in an even better mood. Oliver was never this animated around the psychologists he worked with since he came home from the juvenile ward. Max just had the correct approach for the teenager, and Sam sat back and listened to the two of them talk back and forth, while he enjoyed his ribeye and potatoes. As they were obligated to avoid the case in front of Oliver, the whole evening was spent getting to know one another. Just as Max learned that Sam had actually adopted Oliver when he and Meredith married, Sam learned that Max and his late wife were planning to be foster parents and had even started the paperwork before her tragic end.

"How come foster parents?" Oliver asked, his mouth full of the cheesy mashed potatoes. "Didn't you guys want your own kids?"

"Well, Angelica and I were both in the middle of grad school when we got married. Then after graduation, our careers demanded a lot of our time. Before we knew it, we were just a little too old to start having babies. We figured even if we got pregnant right away, our kid wouldn't graduate high school until we were senior citizens. So, we decided that even if we couldn't have our own children, we could at least be parents to other kids."

"Huh...so, kind of like my dad."

Sam almost choked on his glass of beer. "Wha's tha'?"

"Well, you and mom didn't have any more kids after you got married. It's just me. I think I actually asked you guys to give me a little brother once, didn't I?"

"Aye, when ye were a wee lad. I' jus' wasnea the time fer either of us. So, I guess like Max, things jus' go' away from us."

"Yeah, right up to the divorce. Max, does this make sense to you? My mom and dad got a divorce, didn't talk for a good year, and then when I got in trouble, they suddenly started getting along again."

While Sam felt very uncomfortable with the way the conversation was turning, the good Doctor simply smiled and answered. "It sounds to me like they both love you very much. That can bring even the most at-odds people together, Oliver."

"Yeah, but here's the weird part: They get along great now! We even have family dinner at least once a week, and neither of them are dating anybody else, and whenever they *are* together, they flirt with each other!"

That was enough for Sam. Setting down his beer, he shot the teenager a warning look. "Oliver—"

"What? You know you do! You even wore that stupid sweater Mom bought you the whole night a few days ago!"

Sam was about to retort when Max intervened. "Oliver, I don't think you should spend time worrying about the relationship between your parents. For one thing, that's really between the two of them. And if you spend too much time fixating on that, you'll miss out on other important stuff in your life. Don't you have other things going on? Like school? What about girls?"

There was the magic word; Oliver's face shifted from accusatory to a happy smile. "Actually, yeah there is a girl I'm interested in."

Relieved, Sam smiled. "Aye, how is I' goin' w' Karliegh?"

"Good, we've been messaging back and forth like crazy. Talking mostly about stuff around school, a little bit about college and stuff."

Sam was more than grateful that the conversation had shifted from him, and for the rest of their meal, the two grown men listened to the teenager talk about his (hopeful) girlfriend. It was almost 9:00 p.m. when they left the restaurant, and while Sam offered to drive Max to his hotel, the doctor insisted he would get a cab or an Uber and bid the two of them goodnight. Oliver continued to talk about Karliegh the whole way home, and Sam just listened. It was a good, restorative night for him. And, considering how little sleep he had been able to get for the last two nights, he decided to retire early. Sleep claimed him the moment his head hit the pillow.

***

Christmas Eve, 7:00 a.m.

Sam awoke the following morning feeling well-rested and ready to return to the difficult case awaiting him and the team. He had just started to prepare breakfast for him and Oliver when Meredith knocked on the door, holding a box from her favorite bakery and a big smile on her face as she announced, "Merry Christmas Eve!"

Sam smiled. "Merry Christmas Eve. Ye're early."

"Well, I knew you were going to rush off to work, and I didn't want you to miss out on the fresh chocolate croissants. You think you'll be late tonight?"

"Aye, mos' likely."

Oliver suddenly emerged from his room looking groggy. "Christmas break...it's supposed to be Christmas break..."

Meredith laughed. "Yeah, today it's just Christmas break; tomorrow you'll be jumping out of bed before the rest of us are awake."

"I wouldn't bet on that; I know the presents will still be under the tree whether I wake up at 7:00 a.m. or noon."

"Okay, Mr. Grinch, come have a croissant."

The three of them sat at Sam's little table and enjoyed breakfast together before Sam insisted that he needed to get going. Snatching

81

one more croissant out of Oliver's hands, he leaned down and kissed Meredith on the cheek and headed for the door.

Everyone at the office was in a happy mood, and Sam cheerfully wished everyone a good morning as they all started to get back to work looking for clues on the Christmas Angel victims, both old and new. While everyone reconvened, Sam went to the breakroom for his second cup of coffee. He found Dr. Darrel in the breakroom having his own cup, and from the dark circles under his eyes, Sam could tell that the man chose not to sleep the night before.

"Max, if my superior sees ye like this, she'll personally escort ye t' our lab fer a sedative."

"I have no doubts that she would," Max chuckled. "Thank you again for dinner last night. You have a very precocious young man on your hands."

"Aye, tha' he is," Sam chuckled. "He gets tha' from his mother."

Max nodded. "And from what I gathered from your son, she's a lovely lady."

"Aye, tha' she is."

"That divorce must have been pretty hard on all three of you, but something good must have come from it, considering your relationship has gotten so much better."

Sam eyed Dr. Darrel over the rim of his mug. "Are ye tryin' t' drag a story out of me, Doctar?"

"I'm sorry," Max laughed. "That's the habit of being a psychologist for so long."

"Well, perhaps ye could use tha' habit t' get into the mind of the Angel again."

"That's pretty much what I was doing all night. I was about to sleep when my mind started wandering to that question you had about the positioning of the bodies. I think I remember reading in Chloe Hale's report that you noticed her body was pointed northeast, and she had drag marks under her?"

"Aye, wha' abou' it?"

"Well, you made a similar note about Lily Vanderguard's body, too, didn't you? Only she was pointed in a southeast direction?"

"Aye, bu' wha' are ye getting at?"

"Well...I did profile the Angel to have an OCD complex by the way he obsessively cleans the girls, but it never occurred to me there's more to the posing than just the regret. The wheels just started turning, and the next thing I know, I'm up all night working out theories to my profile. So, I've been here since 4:00 a.m., looking back at all the photos and the files from the cases I participated in, trying to see if I could find a pattern. I think I might have found one." Max pulled a pen out of his shirt pocket and turned to a nearby table to snatch a napkin. After making a few marks, he handed the napkin to Sam.

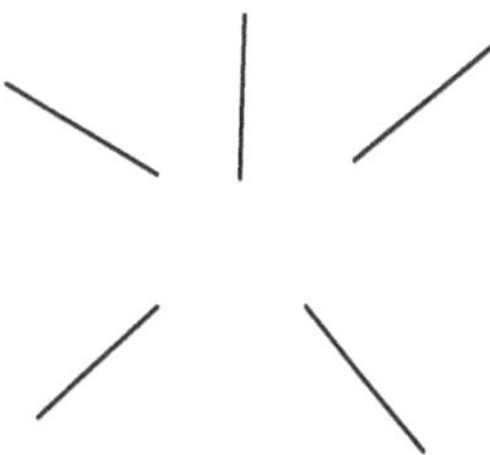

Sam furrowed his eyes. "Wha' is i'?"

"I've been wondering that myself. It could be a star, but he leaves a flower on his victims so maybe it's supposed to be a flower. ...I'm almost positive it's a star, though. The point is: I think the Angel has been purposely leaving his victims facing a certain direction that correlates with every one of these strokes until, eventually, it makes this shape."

"Why?"

"I have a theory that I'm working on... what I can tell you for certain is that something about this this shape means something to him."

"There's five strokes here, Max, an' the average amount of bodies found every wintar is two. If yer theory is right, wouldnea he be killin' five women every year t' make this shape complete?"

"I believe he would, yes. The only answer I have for that, considering how clever the Angel is, is that the bodies signifying the other strokes were never found. Every body was found purely by accident by commuters, property investigators, and patrolmen in random, decently secluded areas."

"Then how di' ye come up w' this?"

"Fortunately for us, every single body that has been discovered has matched at least one of these strokes: North, Northeast, Southeast, Southwest, and Northwest. Some of the past detectives were a little vague in their description of how the bodies were found, but I pieced the direction of each body through their descriptions."

"An' ye're absolutely sure abou' them all creatin' this shape?"

"I've spent all night making diagrams of the directions of the bodies, I'm pretty positive... like about 80% positive."

Sam couldn't deny that the theory was a little bit of a stretch, but his gut assured him that the Doctor was on to something. "Well, 80% is bettar than wha' we've go'. Alrigh', I believe ye. Bu' we've only found two bodies thus far."

"Yes, back-to-back. We all agree that the Angel is escalating; he's even leaving the bodies in more easily accessible places. So—"

"So, he's go' three more girls t' kill before the cycle's done...Christ. We bettar' tell everybody wha' ye've found."

The two of them had barely set down their coffee mugs when Simon came running into the room, the look on his face dire. "Dispatch from Hebron's PD got a call about a body off of Lancaster Road that ticks all the Angel's boxes this morning, and Humbar just got a tip about another one found near Parma Heights."

"Two of them," Max said in horror. "Are they absolutely positive they're not copycats?"

"The officers did a Google search to confirm the flower: Both girls had a white peony left on their chests."

Sam sighed. "Julie, Rivera, an' Lieutenant Evanston'll take Lancastar, an' we'll take Parma w' Humbar. Tell them t' look fer drag marks near the body; we think the Angel had t' position the bodies purposely. Tell 'em t' call me if they find 'em."

Simon nodded and ran back to tell the others.

"Sam, that's four bodies in four days," Max said, his voice low and serious.

"Aye, we've go' till midnight t' stop him from killin' the las' one."

"If he hasn't already."

Max said it first, but Sam was already thinking the same thing.

Upon arriving at the crime scene just off 480, the three men weren't the least bit surprised to see it already swarming with the media. The first response teams were doing everything they could to keep the cameras away from the scene. Sam and his two companions practically had to shove their way through, until the officers lifted the yellow tape for them. Once again, while the forensics guys were combing every inch of the perimeter, Sam's focus was on the small crowd of gathered policemen a couple hundred yards away. As soon as they were close enough, he could see the body in between them: mid-thirties, blonde, lying peacefully with her hands on her sides, sparkling clean even against the white snow, and a single white peony placed over her chest. The coroner was just starting to load her for transportation, so Sam made quick work of analyzing the scene for the newest clue Max had uncovered, while Humbar relayed the details of where the body was to be taken. Sure enough, next to her were very light scuff marks that indicated her body was moved until it fit the perfect position. Sam took a quick look around and at the sky to get his bearings. She was facing southwest.

Sam leaned over to Max and said in a hushed voice, "If the Angel's followin' a pat'ern, then this makes his third victim of the star-shape thing."

Max nodded and tapped the coroner on the shoulder. "How long has she been dead?"

"This weather's interference completely screwed up a liver temp, but I can tell you it's definitely been at least 24-36 hours. The chief examiner will narrow it down for you."

Sam already knew they wouldn't need to wait for a confirmation from Bicks. This was definitely the third body of the shape, and Sam had no doubt Rivera and Julie would be finding a fresher corpse that made stroke number four. He knew that he should immediately start looking around for more tells and clues and evidence, but the reality of what Max had discovered was setting in, and Sam could almost feel the clock ticking. The rage and desperation he felt clouded his judgement.

His phone started ringing.

"Rivera, is i' another one?"

"Everything matches up right down to the white peony, Sam. This is definitely one of the Angel's."

Sam dropped his face in his other hand and rubbed his temples. "How long has she been dead?"

"The coroner's sure she was killed less than 24 hours ago."

"Di' ye find drag marks aroun' the body?"

"Only just, the Lancaster guys did a good job of walking all over the scene before forensics got here."

"Wha' direction is the body facin'?"

"Um...I'd say northwest-ish. Yeah, Simon told us you and Dr. Darrel have a working theory. Care to share?"

"Head back t' headquarters when ye've finished w' the scene. We'll tell everyone then." Sam angrily pressed the end button on his phone and turned back to Max, "My team found numbar four."

"Goddammit," Max hissed under his breath. "It's...quarter to nine. We've got maybe fifteen hours to stop this monster."

Sam could sympathize with Max's vested interest in this case, but he could already see that the poor man was starting to lose it with how quickly the bodies were piling up. The obvious lack of sleep certainly didn't help things. Not knowing what else to do, he slapped his hand on Max's shoulder and said, "Ye found somethin' tha' none of us found before, Max. Perhaps the most important piece t' the answer. We'll stop 'im this time. Yer wife'll ge' justice."

His words seemed to soothe the doctor, as Max relaxed his shoulders and nodded his agreement. "You're right...you'd better get to doing your thing with the scene, then. We don't have a moment to lose."

There was nothing else Sam could say to help his new friend, so he did exactly as the man suggested.

Chapter Nine

Christmas Eve, 1:05 p.m.

Everyone returned from their crime scenes and headed straight for the conference room where Simon was already ready and waiting with his laptop. Sam let Max do all the talking, and the doctor's zealous presentation seemed to convince him more than ever. Truthfully, Sam was convinced too, and he was prepared to back the man up, if any of the people in the room doubted him. Thankfully, nobody did. Everyone had a look of relief on their faces to finally have a tangible, if somewhat crazy, answer to what the Christmas Angel was doing.

Dana was the first to speak, in her usual cynical tone. "This is all well and good, but it doesn't exactly help us figure out who he's targeting, and how we can stop him. The victimology is still too random."

"Yes, but it gives us a better look inside of his head. I've been thinking about this since last night and...I think the Angel is acting out some religious cult practices that he's most likely twisted to his desires."

This new revelation had Sam's attention. Before he could ask, Max continued. "We all agree that this shape closely resembles a star, right? Where have any of you seen a star associated with murder before?"

"In horror movies," Julie answered, "mostly to do with Satanic rites and exorcisms."

"Exactly," Max nodded. "I profiled that the Christmas Angel targets women that remind him in some way, big or small, of his mother—"

"It's always mama's fault," Simon interjected sarcastically.

The comment earned a light chuckle from the rest of the room, but Sam cleared his throat, which quickly settled everyone down. He encouraged the doctor to continue.

"You all know the statistics for serial killers having suffered traumatic childhood abuse being correlated with the way they choose their victims. The way he's posing these women takes it a step further. I think the Angel's mother may have been a deeply, fanatically religious woman. The methods in which he uses to kill her over and over are a direct rebellion to that. He's not only killing his mother over and over again, he's spitting in her face for everything that she believed in."

"But she's still his mother," Rivera said next. "That's why he's leaving the victims so peacefully. Maybe the white peony was her favorite flower, and that's why he uses it. Everything about his actions is a paradox: He's angry, and he's remorseful."

"As are most serial killers with abusive childhoods," Humbar added. "Okay, then we need to look into religious cults that are repulsed by this star?"

"I believe this star is a crude form of a pentacle, to be more specific," Max nodded.

Simon snorted. "The irony—this guy's nickname is just *perfect.*"

"But that doesn't exactly narrow it down," Dana jumped in again. "Virtually *all* religions, not just Christian ones, think of the pentacle as a symbol of evil. There's got to be at least a dozen, maybe even a hundred, different religions in each of the states where the victims have been found."

Sam jumped in. "All of the recent victims have been discovered locally...perhaps Ohio is home t' the Angel, an' we'll find the answer somewhere in our state."

Right at that moment, Sam's phone started ringing. It was a number that he didn't recognize, so he answered with a gruff, "Sam McKay."

"Agent McKay? This is Mimi Smith, Lorraine Wyatt's grandmother."

Sam turned away from the others. "Yes, ma'am, wha' can I do fer ye?"

"You can come down to the entrance and tell these people to let me in to retrieve my granddaughter!" Sam could tell she was no longer talking directly to him by the way her voice had slightly lowered in volume. "No, I will not sit down! You get Agent McKay down here right now! Don't you—"

Sam hung up his phone and sighed. "Start searchin' fer incidents of religious cult activity in the state datin' back to...le's say the 1950s. I'll be back."

When Sam got to the reception desk, he almost didn't recognize Mimi: The older woman, who had a calm and reserved personality when he first met her, was raising quite a ruckus with the agents who were trying to get her to settle down. Things were starting to look ugly, so Sam rushed over and instructed everyone to back off.

"Thank goodness you're here! These brutes won't let me get Lorraine!"

"Ma'am, yer granddaughter's body cannnea be released yet. The DA is still buildin' a case against him, no' t' mention she was found only two days ago."

"So what? An officer told me that Trevor was arrested for her murder! That means you have everything, don't you?"

"Ma'am, i's no' tha' simple. There's still procedures t' be followed. An', t' be frank, everyone is backed up in processin'. It'll be some time before ye can give yer granddaughtar a proper burial."

By the way Mimi settled down, Sam could tell that he had gotten through to her. At least she would listen to him.

"Alright, thank you, agent." She turned away dejectedly.

Sam felt the familiar sensation that he had when he first met her: wonder and intimidation. Something about her commanded his humility and respect, and although he knew he should return to the third floor and help with the research, he couldn't stand seeing the old woman the way that she was.

"Mrs. Smith, do ye have a ride home? The roads are verra dangerous, bein' Christmas Eve an' all. Particularly when someone's upset, they shouldnea be drivin'."

"I had an Uber drop me off. I'll get another one."

Sam shook his head and, in one step, was at her side. "Ma'am, I'm verra sorry ye had t' come down here. May I give ye a ride as an apology fer my department's lack of communication?"

"Alright, thank you. I'd very much appreciate that."

Either everyone in the office was anxious to get rid of the old woman, or he got lucky, but a car was pulled up front almost instantly after Sam asked for one. The ride back to Mimi Smith's home was awkward, to say the very least; Not a word was spoken between Sam or Mimi. Not knowing what else to do, he turned on the radio and let the holiday music fill the silence.

Once he stopped in front of her house, Sam went around and opened the door for her. He noticed that the walkway was icy, so he took it upon himself to help her up to the door, despite her protests that she could manage. She had just gotten her key into the lock when she turned and said, very humbly, "I am sorry for all of the trouble I have caused you, Agent McKay. And I appreciate you taking the time to see me and...well, deal with my less-than-good behavior. I hope I haven't made things difficult for you."

Sam smiled. "Not a'tall, ma'am. Ye've been missin' yer granddaughtar fer five years. I's understandable tha' ye'd want t' lay her body t' rest as soon as possible."

Mimi smiled in appreciation and opened her door. "Would you like a cup of coffee or something before you leave? It's really the least I can do for how nice you've been to an old crazy like me."

He was just about to decline when he noticed something through the crack in her door: white flowers. He couldn't tell from the angle what kind they were, but his curiosity was piqued. "Um...yes, thank ye."

Mimi stepped through the door and ushered him in. "Please excuse the mess. I'm afraid I'm a terrible housekeeper. Just a moment, I'll go get that cup of coffee."

While she made her way to the kitchen, Sam walked into the living room and kept his focus on the flowers: They were white peonies, just like the ones left on the Christmas Angel's victims. He took a quick look around, and already he could tell that Mimi Smith was more than she seemed. While most women of her age collected cats or dolls or some such, Mimi seemed to collect plants and herbs. Her house was overrun with a cacophony of smells, a few of which he recognized instantly as rosemary, thyme, wild garlic, and so much more. But, other than the peonies, he couldn't see any other flowers. His suspicions grew.

"Ye seem t' have a verra talented green thumb, ma'am," he called.

"Thank you," she called back. "Did you know that herbs and spices hold as much medicinal value as pharmaceuticals do?"

Sam quietly continued to look around her house. Other than the plants, everything else was dusty or cluttered. "I know tha' cinnamon is good fer diabetes...garlic helps w' blood pressure..."

Near the back, underneath a small table, Sam noticed a rug that didn't have as much dust on it as the rest of the house. He had just enough time to pull up the corner and see a small cellar door sitting under it before Mimi entered the room holding a mug.

"I hope you're the adventurous type, Agent McKay. This brew has a special herb blend that I've made myself. Don't worry, nothing sinister. Just some things that are good for your overall wellbeing, including cinnamon," she smiled.

Sam took the cup from her, but he didn't drink. "The flowers are beautiful. Peonies, aye?"

"Yes, a rare beauty. And the flower makes a delicious and healthful tea as well."

"They're hard t' find, le' alone grow."

"Oh, I didn't grow these, Agent McKay. I'm afraid the peony is a little bit more advanced to care for than I am able to give it."

"So ye ordar them?"

"Yes, as a matter of fact I do."

Sam took one more look around him. He didn't want to think that the sweet, albeit peculiar, little old woman in front of him could be capable of such horrific murders, but the number of oddities that surrounded him couldn't be ignored, particularly the flowers. Carefully, he set the untouched coffee down on a nearby table and retrieved his cell phone. "Mrs. Smith, I'm afraid I'll need ye t' come back t' the office w' me. If ye'll have a seat, we'll wait until some of my friends arrive."

The look on Mimi Smiths face shifted from caring to worried almost instantly. Sam doubted a woman of her stature could do much to a big man such as himself, but he put his hand on the holster of his gun all the same. Thankfully, his hostess didn't make a sudden move. Quietly, she sat down on a couch and folded her hands in her lap. Relieved, Sam called Rivera.

Almost within minutes of the phone call, Rivera, Julie, and a team arrived at the house. Mimi was escorted back to the FBI office, along with Sam, while the house was searched from top to bottom. Sam made sure to point out the little door under the rug and emphasized the extreme care that was needed when whatever was under that door was investigated. Just as soon as they arrived back at headquarters and Mrs. Smith was led to the third floor for interrogation, Sam got a facetime from Rivera. He ducked into an empty room before he answered.

"Jesus, Mary, and Joseph, Sam," Rivera said, the disgust in his voice worrying Sam. "You are not going to believe the psycho shit we've got down here."

Before Sam could ask for further details, Rivera flipped his camera around. Sam's eyes widened as he looked at everything. The first thing Rivera showed him was a pentacle made of twigs hanging on a wall. Underneath it sat a wooden table with candles all along it. There was also a bowl that had multiple colored, smoothed out stones sitting before the candles, a large square board with the cycles of the moon was placed in the middle, and another large bowl filled with various dried herbs and greenery and flowers (including peonies) sat next to that. The camera shifted to another wall (which Sam assumed was directly behind Rivera) which showed a floor-length bookcase filled with bottles of different shapes, sizes, and colors. They all appeared to be filled with differing substances, either liquid or solid. And, finally, Rivera's camera shifted to the floor to show Sam a large chalk circle.

"Wha' the hell is all tha'?!"

"It's Wiccan, boss," Julie's voice rang through the phone. "Mimi Smith isn't a goodly Christian woman with a thing for natural medicine; she's a full-blown witch. And I think we just figured out what religious practice the Angel has been perverting."

Rivera scoffed. "I know Mimi Smith is 5'5" and probably a buck-nothing, but isn't it possible that *she* might have been the Christmas Angel at one point?"

"I don't know...maybe she knew the psycho doing this; hell, maybe she even taught him a thing or two."

"Or maybe we got the sex of the Angel wrong, and she's just passed along her knowledge to another witch," Rivera countered.

"You're forgetting the victims were raped, dummy. This is a startling revelation, but I doubt we're going to find a penis on Mrs. Smith."

"Don't rule it out, Jules. We've seen weird shit before. Besides, maybe she had a male accomplice. The possibilities are all there."

Sam heard all the banter, but he kept quiet while he tried to process it all. The interrogation was going to be one of the most interesting he'd ever done before. "Ye two keep lookin' around an' report back the minute ye're done. I'll have Simon work his magic on Mimi's past...an' I'll have Max join me on the interview."

"Are you sure that's a good idea? He's not cleared for interrogation."

"He'll observe. A' minimum, he migh' be able t' tell us if Mimi Smith is capable of murder or no'."

***

Sam stared at the old matriarch through the two-way mirror. Since confronting her at her house, she had been calm and compliant, and even now, she sat calmly at the table with her hands still folded together. Max stood beside him, observing her as well, and he appeared to be just as conflicted as Sam felt.

"You're absolutely positive she had white peonies?"

"I've tol' ye a hundred times, Max, yes. I wouldnea have thought anythin' of it, if it weren't fer how rare tha' flower is t' find. Then there's the mattar of wha' Rivera found in the basement of her house."

"I'm just having a hard time believing that skinny little old woman *could* be responsible for all of these murders."

"Well, we donnea know tha' yet. Bu' I know tha' she's hidin' somethin', an' i's no' jus' her basement shrine."

"Right, speaking of that—" Max pulled out a piece of paper from his pocket, unfolded it, and handed it over to Sam. "I finally figured out the significance to why these women's bodies have all been abandoned in winter. What do you see?"

Sam quickly scanned over what the doctor had written:

Dec 21, 1990
Dec 22, 2021
Dec 23, 2021
Dec 24, 2021
Dec 25, 1987
Jan 3, 2006
Jan 6, 1982
Jan 9, 1990
Jan 10, 2018
Jan 22, 2016

Feb 14, 1994
Feb 17, 1993
March 1, 2011
March 15, 2015
March 22, 2007

Sam was unfortunately confused. "Tha' all of the dates are out of yearly order. I assume ye're goin' somewhere w' this, Max."

"Do you know the approximate dates for the winter solstice, Sam? It's from December 21st to March 22. All the dates these women have been found are within the time frame of the winter solstices every year from 1982. This further proves that the Christmas Angel is someone familiar with pagan, Wiccan practices. Our suspect in there has a Wiccan shrine in her basement, and she had the exact same flowers as the ones found at the crime scenes. I don't want to believe it either, but what are the odds?"

The door to the observation room opened, and in pranced Simon, his laptop in hand and a giddy smile on his face.

"You guys are not even going to *believe* the dirt I have dug up on this lady! I mean, it's crazy! She's not only been leading a double life, she was *entirely* a witch up until forty years ago!" He opened his laptop and turned it around to show the two of them: On the screen were a few different pages of records and a couple photographs of naked women standing together in a circle or dancing.

Sam didn't want to waste his time reading through all the details. "Simon, give us the bottom line, if ye please."

Obviously very excited, Simon opened his mouth and words came out faster than he could stop them. "Okay, so first: I've been looking for any and all information to do with paganism, cults, and practices that have something to do with using a star—"

"It's called a pentagram," Max interrupted him.

"Right, yeah, the pentagram, and found *way* too many articles, police reports, and mentions. Then, once I narrowed it down to Ohio and the surrounding states, I got about a hundred different hits. So, I thought that maybe if I looked at the photos something might stick out." Simon then pointed to one photograph that he had enlarged. "Look at that necklace, boss."

Sam looked closer and started: It was a flower with an intricately carved band studded with jewels surrounding it, exactly like the one Mimi Smith was wearing when they first met her at her church, and she was still wearing now.

"Now, I know what you're both thinking: This pendant could have been very popular 40-50 years ago. So, I went searching for information on 50s vintage jewelry and found out that only a handful of these particular pendants were made by a no-named artist who claimed to have apprenticed under a huge jewelry designer that the British Crown favored. Anyways, not important, but what *is* important is that according to the claims, only four of these were made. Three of them have been accounted for through online registries and auctions, and Mimi Smith is wearing the last one."

Sam, and Max, were impressed. Then Sam took a closer look at the photograph and read the description below it: Mimi Smith's name was not listed among the women in the photo. Just as he opened his mouth to point this out, Simon continued:

"Hang on, boss, I'm getting there. Now, when I went looking into Mimi Smith's past, I couldn't find any record of her before 1981, which is when the article with this photo was released. But according to the records of the writer, the photograph was taken in 1957. Mimi Smith didn't exist until December 21st, 1972, but I can't find any connection to any of these necklaces to her. Mae Eygols, this woman with the same necklace dancing around in her birthday suit here, was reported missing by her parents January 13th earlier that year. Now, considering the necklace in this photograph is *exactly* like the one Mimi Smith is wearing, and the lack of records, I am positive that the woman sitting at the table in there is actually May Eyegols."

"Wow...nice job," Max said admiringly. "You guys really are good."

Simon widened his smile and puffed his chest out proudly. Turning his laptop around to face him, he added, "Okay, now according to this picture, Mae Eygols was a practicing member of a Wiccan sect calling themselves The Eclectic Chosen. Think about this: She was an actively practicing Wiccan who liked to dance around naked and then suddenly becomes a conservative pious believer in Christianity? There must be a good reason for why she went and changed her identity. Maybe even to throw off the trail of people hunting for the Angel."

Sam, more than impressed, had absolutely no problem in patting Simon on the back and nodding, "Well done, young man."

"1981..." Max mumbled. "The first victim, Gail Rodney, was found in 1982. I hate to say this, but that little old lady in there is looking more and more suspicious by the minute."

Sam nodded his agreement. "Simon, I want these photographs printed up fer the interrogation."

"Already done, boss." Retrieving a little manilla folder he held under his laptop, he handed it over. "The photos of the naked witch and all of your paper—" he said with a shudder "—evidence ready to go."

Max chuckled. "When we're done in there, I'd like to have a little discussion with you about why you hate paper so much."

"No getting inside *my* head, doc," Simon answered with a smile.

Sam nudged the doctor and, together they walked into the interrogation room.

Chapter Ten

Mimi/Mae didn't react much, other than turning her head down towards her hands and avoiding eye contact.

Once the two of them were seated comfortably, Sam started the discussion by laying out the photograph that Simon had found for them. "This is you, isn't it?"

"I'm sure I don't know what you're talking about."

"Mae Eyegols," he continued calmly, pointing to the woman with the necklace, "born April 17th, 1938, reported missin' in 1971, and never heard from again. Then, later tha' year, Mimi Smith surfaces. An' these—" he then began pulling out photographs of the victims they had found and laying them down one by one in front of her "—are victim's of a villain bein' called The Christmas Angel."

At the site of the bodies, Mimi recoiled in horror. "What is this? You think that *I* killed these poor girls? I would never!"

Sam pointed to the flower. "White peonies, ma'am. Difficult t' grow an' rare t' find, an' ye admitted t' me tha' ye ordar them. An' all of these women were found facin' a specific direction until, all togethar, they form this shape."

Sam adjusted the photographs until he had made the shape of a star for almost all of them; the newest victims were missing one more body to complete the shape. He stared hard at the old woman, whose eyes widened in horror...and yet, there seemed to be a realization behind them as well. Curious, he continued:

"Mimi...I donnea think ye're a murderer, bu' I know tha' ye know somethin'. Perhaps ye can help us catch whoever this man is. I need ye t' talk t' me an' tell me everythin', startin' w' wha' happened in January of 1981. Why'd ye run away an' change yer name?"

The old woman sighed, picked up the photo of her dancing, and clutched at the pendant still swinging from her neck. "This was so long ago...I had almost successfully forgotten about it."

Mae then broke away from the picture and stared at the photos of the girls long and hard before she said, "Do you have a pen and paper I could use?...Thank you...there are a few things that you need to understand: First, people always assume, when it comes to Wiccans, that the pentagram is a sign of evil, and that is not true—" on the paper, she wrote the points of a compass: North at the top, South at the bottom, East on the right, and West on the left, before she drew a leaning star on one side with the top point facing north, the left point North-West. "The pentagram in its true form is a sign of good, peace, love, and balance of the five elements: Spirit, Air, Earth, Water, and Fire. It has been for thousands of years. Even in Christianity, in the past, the five points represented the five wounds of Jesus Christ. Even deeper than that, it stood as a symbol of Jerusalem. It's even used on their flag today, different star but same implications. Second, thanks to modern Hollywood and other entertainment moguls, everyone believes that if the pentagram is upside down like this—" she proceeded to draw another star next to the first one, inverted so the two bottom stars were pointing up— "then it must mean the opposite: evil, which is also very much untrue."

Max interjected. "But the idea that it does represent evil was established from a supposed magician from France in the mid-19th century, who wrote a book explaining that if the pentagram is upside down, it means devil worship."

Mae nodded. "Yes, that's right. Unfortunately, thanks to events that happened in 1966 with a cult leader...I forget his name, but he started the Church of Satan. That church made things all the more difficult for Wiccans everywhere. Now, finally, Wicca is not witchcraft in the sense that you think it is: There are no animal sacrifices or casting of spells of misfortune on others. It's about the balance of the spirit with the elements, which is celebrated through rituals to honor the Holy Goddess of the Moon. Any spells cast have to do with healing and protection, *never* with the intent to harm others.

"But you see, throughout history, free thinking and strong women have been seen as evil because of men with inferiority complexes who labelled them Witches. The pentagram has been associated with Wicca from the beginning, so that's why it was deemed a sign of evil. The Church of Satan only reinforced the idea with their...actions and all the media coverage from it. You need to know this because what your killer has done...what he is doing… is similar to rituals that I've participated in, but what he's doing is not to celebrate the Goddess. This is something evil on its own and has absolutely nothing to do with Wicca."

Sam leaned forward and folded his hands together. "Alrigh', I understand. Now why donnea ye tell us the reason ye changed your whole identity in 1981?"

Taking a shaky breath, Mae leaned back in her chair and began her tale. "It was December 22nd, 1970. The coven—my sisters and I—had come together to celebrate the start of the Solstice—that's a holiday that celebrates the rebirth of the Horned God, the consort to the Goddess—" she chuckled suddenly "—it's also called Yule. As in Yule log? Well, anyway, the coven had come together for this celebration: We made wreaths of evergreen that we all wore on our heads, exchanged our gifts of nature with one another...I had brought beeswax candles for all my sisters. There was food, wine... honestly, anyone would have guessed it was a Christmas party if they happened to see us.

"Well, anyway...as the moon was rising to its peak, the leader of our coven, Lila was her name, made the announcement that it was time to cleanse our spirits of the clutter and strife that had been thrust upon us from the year. The way we chose to do that was through dance. ...Out on the grounds of the house we stayed at, an area deep in the woods where the snow could barely touch the ground, we made a bonfire of yule logs—specific wooden logs that each of us had specially chosen, that we felt connected to somehow. And once the fire was blazing, we danced for hours until we were exhausted."

"And that was part of the ritual of rebirth, right?" Max asked.

"Yes, exactly. Just as the Horned God was to be reborn, we would cleanse ourselves of everything and be reborn as well."

"And all you did was dance?"

"Sometimes we'd throw things into the fire to signify completely cleansing ourselves. Nothing important. Things like...our bras, a newspaper that deeply affected someone...one sister even threw in her wedding ring after divorcing her husband earlier that year."

"Tha' donnea sound like anythin' worth abandonin' yer life ovar."

Mae met Sam eye to eye and sternly answered, "If you'd let me finish, I can tell you exactly why that was the last night I ever participated in my coven's Winter Solstice celebration."

"...Forgive me, ma'am. Please continue."

"Between the wine and the dancing, most of the sisters would fall down in exhaustion. An observing member would help them up and lead them back to the house we shared during the season. I was the last to fall that night before Lila declared the ritual complete, and we all returned to the house. Later, I don't know what time, I woke up. I have no idea why, maybe I just couldn't sleep that night, maybe the Goddess was calling to me. All I know is I went to my window...I remember it overlooked the grounds perfectly...and I saw the fire still lit, and I thought I saw someone dancing around it. At first that didn't really concern me; I'd thought maybe one of our sisters who hadn't been chosen to dance wanted to do her own cleansing ritual. I was about to go back to bed when I thought I heard a scream. Not in the house, mind you, it was very distant. Well...I wanted to be sure there wasn't anything wrong, so, without waking anyone, I went back out into the woods towards the bonfire. And what I saw...changed everything for me that night..." The horror as the memory resurfaced shown in her eyes.

Very compassionately, Sam leaned forward and took her hand in his. "Wha' was it tha' ye saw, Mae?"

"Lila...the leader of our coven, was dancing around the fire...she was naked...but she was covered in blood." Mae's eyes suddenly filled with fear as she recalled the image. "And on the ground...staining the snow was more...I thought it looked like the points of the pentagram...Agents, our coven had never participated in bloodshed for any of our rituals, not even once. So, to see the woman I saw as our leader...doing that. ...There was a crazed look in her eyes, like she wasn't even there...it terrified me. And then that scream came again and I just...ran. I ran away from that place as fast as I could."

It was Max's turn to be compassionate. "Why did you disappear? And why did you wait until January to do it?"

"At first I wasn't sure I had actually seen what I'd seen. But the next morning when we were all having breakfast...Lila looked beyond exhausted—pale and shaky. I just knew it was real and not a dream after that. But unfortunately, I was curious about what she was doing, and my curiosity overtook my terror. It took some time, but eventually she admitted to me that she was trying to purge more than just clutter and anguish...she believed there was an evil entity in her midst, and she was trying to rid her family of it. She thought that by offering a blood sacrifice to the Holy Goddess and her consort during the rebirth ceremony, they might grant her request and purge the evil she was terrified of. It was...too extreme for me, so I left the coven. A month later, I received a message from Lila. She said that she needed my help, that the entity still had not left, and she would need help from everyone. I refused. I didn't know what kind of ritual she wanted to perform but... I just knew it wouldn't be a peaceful one. A few days later...one of the other sisters contacted me to tell me that a few members of the coven had disappeared, very unexpectedly. I...took it as a bad omen and, concerned for me and my daughter's safety, ran and changed my identity. My parents raised me a Christian...I don't know why, but I just took on the persona. But I've never stopped believing in the Goddess; she represents good and change. I cannot honestly tell you that I know anything about whatever evil Lila thought she was fighting; all I know is that it was enough to change her...perhaps even corrupt her."

"Did you ever find out who was screaming that night?" Max asked.

"No," she shook her head. "But I do remember thinking it sounded like a child's cry...I couldn't tell you for certain, though."

"Did Lila have any children that you know of?"

"One little boy...I think his name was Peter. But...you don't actually think..." Mae inhaled sharply. "Oh my God...the child I heard was her own son?"

"Aye, i's possible, but we donnea know if tha's a fact," Sam answered her. "Bu' perhaps we can find ou'. Wha' was Lila's last name?"

"I don't know; we only ever used our first names or our craft names. Hers was Ravenai."

"Wha' about the place tha' ye went t' for the solstice? Do ye remembar where i' is?"

Mae, obviously exhausted from her tale, nodded, "I remember it was in Pennsylvania...if you get me a map, I might be able to show you the whereabouts of the house."

Sam looked at Max and silently asked if he thought they had everything, and the doctor gave him a gentle (almost unnoticeable) nod. Turning back to Mae, Sam said, "Thank ye, Mae. Someone'll be righ' in w' tha' map."

The old woman nodded her head. "Agent McKay, I want you to know that I would never hurt anyone. I realize that must be silly to hear, especially because I don't expect you to completely understand what it is that I believe in. But I want you to know that I'm what's called a white witch; I prefer to use my powers to help people. That's why I have all of those herbs and plants around my house."

That reminded Sam of the flowers. "Why d' ye ordar the peonies? Especially in the wintar?"

"White peonies mean regret. I bought them to give to my Lorraine, to tell her I'm sorry that I couldn't protect her." For the first time since he had met her, Mimi/Mae let tears fall at the mention of her granddaughter.

Sam sighed. "We're gonna' need the name of the florist as well, ma'am."

Satisfied, the two men left the room, and a fellow agent walked in with a map. Sam and Max turned back into the observation room and weren't surprised to see the look of excitement on Simon's face had shifted to fear.

"Wow...I think I've got goosebumps all over me. The way she tells it, it's like she was part of a B-rated horror movie," the young man shivered.

"She obviously believes that her experience truly dealt with evil; otherwise, she wouldn't have done everything she did to change her whole identity," Max countered. "I think she's telling us the truth; she's not the Angel."

"Aye, I believe ye're righ'," Sam nodded. "Bu' I also think she helped us more than she knows. Ye said tha' the Angel suffered traumatic child abuse. Could i' be tha' the woman she mentioned, Lila, was the mother of the Angel himself?"

Max appeared more than relieved to finally have a name other than the Christmas Angel and nodded. "I think that little boy Peter is definitely worth looking into."

"But you heard her," Simon countered "they never told each other their last names. They only used their first names or...craft names?"

"I though' ye liked a challenge, Simon?" Sam countered.

"Okay, I'll get right on it."

The three of them headed back to their section of the office. Dana and Humbar had just finished contacting every precinct in Ohio and the surrounding states for information on known cults and pagan organizations and had a little list ready for Simon to run comparisons to. Julie and Rivera had also returned and updated everyone on their findings: While there was certainly proof of Wiccan and ritualistic practices, not a drop of blood was found on any inch of Mimi's property. Nor could they find any needles.

"Well, now I'm certain that little old woman isn't killing people," Max sighed. "But we've still got to find the location of her group; then maybe we'll be able to find the man who's converted these practices to evil."

Rivera scoffed. "This whole thing is evil: witches, rituals, devil worship—"

Julie interrupted him. "Hey! I know a lot of people who believe in non-Christian religions including paganism, and none of them are evil."

"At least not that you know of," Rivera mumbled, to which Julie answered with an angry stare.

"Agent Rivera," Max interceded, "there are in fact hundreds of religious offshoots that have stemmed from one main religion or another, just from the side of Christianity, and unfortunately someone somewhere who gets put in charge turns it into a cult through their own actions, which others might see as strange or sinister. Paganism, particularly Wicca, just happens to be a sect that very few actually understand. That does not, however, classify them as evil."

"But you do agree that pagan practices could be classified as a cult?" Rivera asked.

"I personally think *all* religion could be classified as a cult," Simon tried to say offhandedly. For a brief moment, everyone turned their perplexed attention towards him, and he followed up with, "Hey, I'm just saying, believing in something that you've never seen or felt or touched or even tasted seems weird to me. There's a reason I'm an atheist. And, besides, *your* church has more blood on its hands than most, Catholic choir boy."

Rivera opened his mouth to continue arguing, but Sam immediately silenced them all by grunting, "Enough, now i's no' the time t' be bickerin' over whether or no' there is one God, no God, or twenty! Simon, have ye found anythin', yet?"

"All I've really got to go on is the names Lila or Peter and Pennsylvania, but I haven't been able to find any hospital records or even birth certificates. At least not a narrow enough pool to wade through, yet. I'm working on it."

"That's where good old fashioned police work comes in handy, Boy Wonder," Humbar suddenly said, his phone at his ear. Sam turned his attention to his old friend, who was smiling brightly. "I figured it might be a long shot, but I made a call to a friend who worked at a Sheriff's office in Lawrence County, Pennsylvania in the fifties. He said he remembered a kid named Peter from New Castle, and he put me through to the old secretary, who's still working there. She used to work at the public school, and she remembers a family named Daverman living in New Castle. Lila Daverman was a widow with a son named Peter who got into a bit of trouble at school for fighting on the grounds: He knocked a kid's front teeth out, and a month later, that same kid went missing, body never found."

Simon said, "Wow, color me impressed! No pun intended."

"Me too," Max nodded. "That's lucky. So, what do we know about Peter Daverman?"

Simon, once again elated, began typing on his computer faster than anyone could breathe. "Okay... Peter Daverman, a venture capitalist who made millions from investing pennies into now huge name brands. Geeze, this guy has his hands in everything from McDonalds to Apple! No wonder he's rolling in dough! But he's also invested in quite a few of the smaller companies...get this, it looks like he has a thing for outdoor equipment merchants. The guy is in 60% of the RV market! ...I'm also seeing a juvenile record here, and thank you, Pennsylvania, for not sealing these things; you've made my job a whole lot easier. ...Damn...Peter Daverman was in a lot of school fights: Two kids walked away with broken arms."

Max stepped closer. "Has he ever served time?"

"No...but he got kicked out of school for starting a fire in the boys' locker room."

"That's a classic sign of a budding serial killer. What about illnesses?" Max pressed further. "Does he have any sort of condition that requires injectable medications?"

Again, Simon typed. "He's been diagnosed with Psoriatic Arthritis since 1979, but he didn't start taking injectable medicine for it until the early 2000s. Before then, it was always oral medicine or creams.”

“Maybe that’s really why he cleans his victims after he kills them. It’s not because of some obsessive-compulsive disorder; it’s because he has a skin condition!”

Sam, confused, turned to the doctor and asked, “Wha’? I though’ arthritis deals with muscle joint pain.”

“It does, but another symptom of Psoriatic Arthritis is legions and scaly shedding skin. The Ang—Peter Daverman—has a condition where that’s a possible symptom, which explains everything about how he treated the victims: He wanted to make sure nothing was left behind!”

“Wouldn’t that suggest he *has* had training in the forensics field, then?” Julie asked.

“I don’t think so,” Max shook his head. “Remember, DNA testing didn’t start being widely used until 1986, and he’s been killing since 1982—that we know of. More than likely, he would thoroughly clean his victims to send a message to his mother: She didn’t deserve to have any part of him.”

Sam stepped forward. “Wha’ abou’ travel? Isnea there some sort of trail he’s lef’ behind tha’ connects t’ the girls?”

“This guy definitely doesn’t stay in one place long, but I don’t see anything that matches up, boss,” Simon shook his head. “At best, he’s always been about 50-75 miles from where the girls were either taken or dumped. However, it does look like he went to a private spa and care facility near Ottawa from 2007 until 2016.”

“Which is when he started hunting in Canada instead of the US,” Humbar said, the excitement in his voice undeniable. “My God, we’ve found the son of a bitch!”

“No, we really haven’t,” Lieutenant Evanston said, which quickly earned a groan from everyone. “Any half-assed lawyer can tell you this is all circumstantial at best. We don’t have any physical evidence to connect to him, and I’ll bet anybody here $100 that he’ll have all of *his* needles accounted for, too.”

Rivera, still in a very foul mood from the discussion of religion, was the first to snap at her. “Lieutenant, were you born pessimistic, or did it come with time? This is enough to get a warrant to search his house. We’re *bound* to find something, if it’s really him.”

Sam nodded. "Aye. An' we can size Mr. Daverman up a' the same time."

"Hold on, Dana does have a point," Julie added. "If Daverman didn't start using injections for his condition until 2000, where'd he get the idea to use needles to kill his victims?"

Max answered her. "His rage is directed at his mother; what are the odds that she also had a medical condition requiring needles or maybe even used drugs?"

Simon's fingers flew. "Lila Daverman has a DUI record and was subsequently charged with possession. Considering what we know about our friend Mae in there, what are the odds that Lila cooked up her own version of Lucy in the Sky with Diamonds?"

"Which would also explain the crazed and erratic behavior Mae told us about," Max beamed. "She was an abusive user, and her son has been lashing out at her since!"

Sam smiled and nodded. "Somebody update Copper. Simon, where's Daverman now?"

"He's got a few places of residency all over Ohio, Indiana, and West Virginia, but the most recent address is in New Bedford, Pennsylvania. I bet that's his 'country home.'"

Sam looked at his watch; it was 3:30 p.m. "New Bedford's an hour an' a half from here. We've go' t' leave now if we're gonna' stop 'im!"

"That's assuming he's actually living there," Simon said nervously.

"No, that's assuming he's actually the Angel," Dana said pessimistically.

"He fits this profile better than Freddy Parinski did," Max said to the lady lieutenant defensively. "And more importantly, he's the best lead we've got."

Sam, who had already reached the elevator and was ready to get going, called to the bickering group, "Le's move!"

Chapter Eleven

It was already dark, the snow was once again falling, and Sam had his eyes glued to the road, as Rivera drove their SUV to Peter Daverman's house in New Bedford, Pennsylvania. A trail of cop cars and a forensics van were right behind them, and the night was lit up with the flashing red and blue lights. Despite the snow, the drive was less than two hours from Cleveland, but the hope that everyone was feeling practically made the trip fly by.

Even though Sam was relieved to have a viable suspect, he knew his feelings were nothing compared to Max's or even Humbar's. The Christmas Angel victims had haunted the police chief for nearly forty years. To be able to finally put a face to the terror was surely more than just a comforting thought. His old partner, Lieutenant Evanstan, kept up her outward façade of doubt. She continually told the others "Let's not count the chickens before they hatch; we're basing all of this on the assumption that we'll actually find something that connects Daverman to these crimes. And if we don't, then there's nothing that we can use to arrest the guy, let alone convict him." Everyone paid her no mind and kept gleaming at the possibility that the Christmas Angel was finally found. Before they knew it, they were driving down a long, quiet road completely surrounded by hooded trees and brush, and at the end of it was a large, elegant, red brick house that Sam ventured could have easily passed for a private school, rather than a private residence. There wasn't another home for miles; they were far out in the woods of New Bedford, and they had passed the closest semblance of a town at least twenty minutes ago. *A perfect place t' kidnap an' keep victims fer torture then kill,* Sam thought to himself. As soon as everyone had exited their vehicles, the seven of them walked up to the front door. Humbar lead the way, and he wasted no time in pounding his fists on the entrance.

"Easy, pal," Sam said. "We still donnea know fer sure i's him."

The door was opened by a short, young gentleman who appeared to be somewhere in his thirties. "Can I help you?"

"FBI, we have a warrant fer a DNA sample of Mr. Peter Daverman," Sam answered.

The young man, though visibly stunned by Sam's bluntness, stuttered, "H-he's resting. Can you call tomorrow?"

"I'm afraid not," Humbar answered him. The older officer didn't wait for an invitation before shoving his way into the house.

"Agents, he's in a very fragile state. You can't just barge into his room—"

"Fragile? Sonny-boy, we'd like to show him how fragile he really can be. Now where is he?"

"Up-upstairs."

"And who are you?"

"C-Colin Winkley, I'm his private care nurse. Agents, I really have to insist that you not disturb him."

"Well, our warrant says we can disturb him all we want," Julie answered sharply, thrusting the paperwork towards the bewildered Mr. Winkley.

The nurse barely opened the document before the others were racing up the stairs and looking inside every room, each of which appeared to have a theme or purpose, but no guest rooms. Rivera found an office, Dana found a small library that had its walls lined with books, Max and Sam discovered the trophy room that had all manner of taxidermized animals on display.

"Sam, come here!" Humbar's voice sounded from the next room.

Sam listened, and Max followed, and the minute that they walked in to what Humbar had found, they were convinced they had the right man: Humbar had found a second trophy room; only instead of more animals, it had on display different magazines and newspaper articles which featured 'The Christmas Angel.'

"Christ," Sam whispered to himself.

"Oh yes," Max nodded, the exhilaration in his voice unmistakable. "It's him. It's definitely him!"

Finally, in the last room at the end of the hallway, Rivera shouted to the others that he had found Peter Daverman.

Sam wasn't sure what to expect when he approached Peter Daverman's room, but his heart immediately sank when he saw a decrepit old man lying in a home hospice bed in the middle of it.

Peter Daverman was hooked up to an I.V. drip, an EKG, and a breathing apparatus that was continually feeding him oxygen. Sam stood at the doorway, surrounded by the others who appeared to be just as bewildered as he was.

The old man must have heard them because his eyes suddenly opened, and they flickered towards the doorway. He muttered something inaudible; the breathing machine's mask covered his mouth, and he could barely lift his hand to his face. Nurse Winkley suddenly shoved his way past the others and helped Mr. Daverman remove the mask. "What's the meaning of this?!"

As if his decrepit state wasn't enough to discourage them, the raspy, weak voice made the situation all the more embarrassing.

Finally, fed up with the uncomfortable air, Sam was the first to speak. "H-how long have ye been like this, Mr. Daverman?"

The sickly man tried to answer but coughed instead. Nurse Winkley replaced the mask and encouraged him to inhale deeply. He answered for him. "Mr. Daverman has acute Psoriatic Arthritis, agents. He's been unable to walk for nearly three years now, and last year he contracted Pneumonia. I told you that he was in a fragile state."

Sam, along with the others, turned to look at Simon, who cleared his throat, sheepishly. "Um...there's no record anywhere of Mr. Daverman's conditions being this severe."

The old man must have found a new source of strength as he aggressively pulled off the oxygen mask and, in between wheezy breaths, rasped out, "Do you idiots have any idea... who I am? And do you know what my competitors... would do, if... they were aware of how sick I was? They'd... circle my assets like sharks! Of course... you didn't find any record of my condition. I pay... more money than you could ever... dream of to keep that information quiet! Now... who the hell are you, and what... the hell are you doing in my house?!"

No one said a word; they were too in shock to believe what they were seeing. Could this man lying helpless and weak in a hospital bed really be responsible for the violation and death of the four women they had only just found? Sam certainly wasn't so sure anymore.

"Um...Mr. Daverman, sir, we have warrant here to search your premises," Rivera said. "And we need to ask you a few questions."

"All of you c-can go to hell!" the old man wheezed.

Humbar stepped forward. "Mr. Daverman, we can either make this easy and interview you here, where you'll be the most comfortable, or I will personally rip every one of those tubes—"

Sam quickly put his hand on his friend's shoulder and pulled him back. "Sir, we apologize fer the outburst, an' we'll take this time t' conduct our search, while ye ge' yerself prepared fer our interview."

Before Daverman could argue any further, Sam ushered everyone out and back down the stairs. "Spread ou' an' sweep, he's no' goin' anywhere fast, so we migh' as well continue lookin' around."

The only person who was unauthorized to conduct any searches was Max, so he stayed by the front door where he was out of the way. Sam kept looking at him out of the corner of his eye, however, and he could tell that he would have to keep the doctor away from Daverman at all times. While everyone else was visibly unsure of their conclusions, Max hadn't so much as flinched when he saw Daverman lying in the hospice bed. Sam couldn't help but wonder if Max had the same reaction when the officers in Canada arrested his suspect Freddy Parinski. He certainly understood Max's motivations, but the man had an unfortunate history of being unable to accept legal limits and concrete conclusions. Humbar, Sam could tell, wasn't faring any better. The man was looking through the house with a fervor Sam hadn't seen him possess in years. Sam wanted desperately for their conclusions to be right and prove that Daverman was in fact the elusive Christmas Angel, for both of his friends' sakes.

"You guys!" Julie called and everyone came rushing over. "You're not going to believe what this guy has out back: a greenhouse with all kinds of flowers, including white peonies."

Humbar's smile was beaming. "You did say it was possible that he grew his own flowers for his victims."

"Yes, but I didn't see any bushes that have any missing flowers or even shear marks," she followed up. "I'll have the guys process it anyway."

"And for an even bigger let-down," Simon added. "I found tons of cleaning chemicals under the sink—that kitchen is *massive* by the way—that all have lists of chemicals that match the poisons used."

"But, like Bicks pointed out, anybody could cook up that poison in their own kitchen," Rivera added sullenly. "Let's just hope that there's some blood residue around here..."

Sam made certain that not a speck of dust was missed during the search; he didn't know how long everyone there took to process the enormous house, but he had no doubts they would be more thorough than ever before. Eventually, he heard a throat clearing at the top of the stairs and he looked up.

"Mr. Daverman is ready to answer your questions," the nurse, Colin Winkley, said rather uncertainly. "But I have to insist that you not do or say anything that might upset him."

Sam started up the stairs. Max attempted to follow him, but Sam held up his hand. "No' this time, Max. Ye stay here, Julie'll be joinin' me."

The frustration in the man's eyes was evident, but eventually Dr. Darrel conceded with a nod and stepped back again.

Sam continued his ascent with Julie right behind him, Simon's laptop in his hands (with all the pictures he needed uploaded and ready to go for the interview). Julie would obviously do the clicking and showing, as Sam wasn't comfortable handling the computer the way the others were, but that didn't matter anyway, as Sam intended to keep his focus completely on the decrepit old man in the bed.

Nurse Winkley opened the door for them, and Sam was surprised to see Mr. Daverman sitting in an electric wheelchair next to the bed, dressed in a very nice dressing robe and comfortable slippers. A tank of oxygen was attached to the chair, and a line ran under his nose. There was also an IV right next to him which ran directly into his chest. Sam noticed all of these things, but he did his best not to let that sway his judgement as he looked into the man's eyes.

"Agents," Daverman said with a wheezy voice. His breathing was labored, but he didn't stop talking. "I apologize...for my...outburst earlier. You...caught me...in a state that...I don't let many...people see me... in."

"And we apologize for that, Mr. Daverman," Julie answered calmly. "Now, if you're ready, we'd like to show you a few photographs."

"Please...go right...ahead."

Sam knew what the first photograph would be: Gail Rodney, the very first victim that Humbar found. If Peter Daverman had ever been the serial killer they thought he was at one point, Gail Rodney would certainly be his victim. When Julie turned the laptop around and showed the old man the picture, Sam no longer had any doubt that Daverman was the Christmas Angel; his lips twitched, but his eyes were smilling.

"A white...peony," the old man rasped out. "Such a...beautiful...flower..."

Even with several short breaks in between, Sam and Julie spent close to five hours with Mr. Daverman. In all that time, they were unable to get anything that helped their case. Between his breaths of oxygen, he'd answer their questions with smugness and lewd remarks. Daverman admitted he knew all about the work of the Angel, citing that following the serial killer was a hobby of his, as seen from the room in his house. He even had an explanation for the peonies in his greenhouse: They were his mother's favorite flowers, and he had been growing them for years. But, not once, did he ever say anything that could implicate him. He denied ever seeing or knowing any of the girls who had been killed, and he provided an alibi for every date. Sam had the feeling that even after they traced down every witness corroborating Daverman's story, the alibis would be airtight. Sam hoped and prayed that forensics would have more luck than they were having. Then Daverman's attorney arrived at 10:30 p.m. and sternly instructed the two of them to continue their search, but the interview was over for the time being.

Not one person left the house until 2:00 a.m. According to nurse Winkley, Daverman was already asleep again. Winkley insisted that everyone leave as quietly as possible, for his patient's sake. As every cop, scientist, and agent was packing up, Rivera updated Sam on the search results:

"Forensics found some blood in the bathroom and a few needle disposal containers, but they don't look too optimistic about their findings."

"Well, i's unlikely he'd keep anythin' here. We'll go an' investigate his othar properties. Have Copper pu' surveillance on every one of 'em until we clear them."

"Right," Rivera nodded. The short man turned back to the house and shook his head, "I gotta' be honest...I think he's been smarter than that."

Sam nodded without hesitation. "Aye, bu' we've go' t' try. No mattar—"

"No matter how hard it gets, we have to try. I know," Rivera chuckled. "Hell of a way to spend Christmas, huh?"

Again, Sam nodded. "Aye."

Even though the team split up (and took at least one of their fellow compadres with them) for the searches, by the time that each and every warehouse, second home, apartment, and pleasurable rendezvous spot that Peter Daverman was associated with was searched and processed, it was already 11:00 a.m. the following day, Christmas Day. Sam refused to let anyone go home until he was absolutely certain that every inch was accounted for. When he finally called it quits, everyone was grateful to leave, including Humbar. But Max appeared to be just as awake as ever, and Sam had to practically order him to go back to his hotel and sleep.

As tired as he was, Sam didn't want to go to his apartment; it just didn't feel right when all he wanted at that moment was to be near Meredith and Oliver in some way. He still had his key; Meredith had insisted he keep it, when it was clear that he was a permanent resident of the USA again. The drive passed by in a blur, and before he knew it, Sam was pulling into the driveway of the big grey house where he had once lived with his little family. He wasn't the least bit surprised to see it dressed from roof to lawn with Christmas decorations. All manner of lights and figures shined gleefully amidst the cold grey snow, a large green wreath adorned with gold ribbon hung cheerfully on the bright red front door, and of course Meredith had stuck the electric candles in every visible window, and they were flickering away. He barely had a chance to touch the doorknob when it suddenly swung open.

"Dad!" Oliver exclaimed. "Mom, he's finally here!"

Meredith came out of the kitchen carrying a plate of more store-bought Christmas cookies. "Merry Christmas! ...You look awful."

Sam snickered. "I feel i', too."

"Well, come on in! We've been waiting for you."

"Yeah, we have," Oliver nodded emphatically. "She wouldn't even let me open *one* present."

"You know the drill: We celebrate Christmas as a family, and that includes opening presents."

At that moment, Sam wanted desperately to crawl into a bed and collapse, but he couldn't find it in him. Just knowing that his family had waited for him was enough to keep him awake just a little bit longer. He stepped inside, kicked off his boots at the door, and walked into the living room.

The inside of the house was trimmed just the same as the outside: A large and fully decorated pine tree sat in the middle of the living room, the deep and rich green pine needles only making the multi-colored baubles and lights that adorned it even brighter. Mountains of unopened presents sat underneath it with a light coating of dried-up pine needles resting on top of each one. With everything going on at work for the last five days, the Christmas tree was a welcome and warming sight for Sam. He plopped down on the couch and almost fell asleep then and there; it was so comfortable. Everything was so comfortable again.

"So, are we going to actually open these presents now, or should we just pack them up and wait for next year?" the young boy asked sarcastically.

"Well, I'm sure yer mother can find room somewhere t' store them," Sam smirked. The way Oliver's eyes widened in fear made him guffaw, "I'm kiddin'! Find a box fer everyone, le's open up these presents."

Meredith laughed at the whole affair before taking a seat on the couch next to him. Sam didn't hesitate to put his arm around her shoulder when she did; she clearly appreciated the gesture as she leaned into him, while the two of them watched their teenager turn into a young child right before their eyes again. For a few glorious moments, the house was filled with cheer as everyone ripped up the shiny wrapping paper and kept wishing each other a Merry Christmas over and over again. By the time they were finished, the entire living room floor had crumpled wrapping paper all over it. While Oliver was busy with the newest gaming system 'Santa' had gotten for him, Sam went to fetch a bag to start cleaning up, but Meredith stopped him.

"Let me do that; you're exhausted."

"Aye, I've go' t' go home an' ge' some sleep."

"Are you nuts? You're not driving like this. Come on, you can take a nap on my bed."

Meredith took his hand and pulled him up out of the couch; Sam was too exhausted to argue with her, not that he wanted to in the first place. As tired as he was, he couldn't get Oliver's comments about how he and Meredith flirted with each other out of his mind. He would never deny that, despite their recent history, he still loved Meredith very much. But he never allowed himself to entertain anything more than what they had. *Although,* he thought to himself, as she led him up the stairs to her bedroom, *ye havenea entertained the though' of things bein' less than wha' they are, either.*

Meredith's room, *their* room at one point, was just as Sam remembered it: A lovely four-poster bed sat in the middle with a cedar chest at the foot of it. To the left of the door was the walk-in closet, and a master bathroom on the other side of that. He sat down on the bed and groaned. Meredith had disappeared into the closet and suddenly returned with a set of pajamas for him. He looked at her mockingly.

"I knew you were going to be very late, so I swiped these from your drawer before we left yesterday," she answered with a smile. "And you're crazy if you think I'm going to let you sleep in my sheets with your clothes smelling like that."

Sam laughed and took the pajamas from her. "Thank ye, luv."

"You're welcome. Get some rest, and take as long as you need to, okay?" She leaned down and Sam didn't miss the opportunity to turn his head and catch the kiss she had meant for his cheek on the lips. He waggled his eyebrows at her, and she responded by playfully pushing his shoulder. "Okay, now I *know* you're tired. Change your clothes, you bampot. Merry Christmas."

"Merry Christmas," Sam replied as she shut the door. Although it took some effort, he did manage to get changed before he pulled back the covers and collapsed. Between the smell of Meredith's perfume (which smelled heavily of jasmine and sandalwood) in the pillows and the muffled Christmas music coming from below, the events from the night before were pushed completely out of his mind. Sam fell asleep faster than he had in so, so long.

Chapter Twelve

December 26th

Sam wandered over to his section of the third floor where Rivera, Julie, Simon, and of course, Humbar, Lieutenant Evanston, and their visitor Max Darrel were all starting to assemble. Despite everyone taking nearly a whole day off, they didn't look any better than he did. Everyone had bags under their eyes and was quieter than normal. They barely even acknowledged one another as they gathered around the white board and the dozens of crime scene photos still plastered on it. An asset from the forensics lab suddenly appeared, carrying some paperwork, which was undoubtedly the results for every fragment of the DNA, dirt samples, and trace evidence that had been collected. She handed it directly to Sam before disappearing again.

Sam opened the file and skimmed over the scientific babble until he found what he was looking for. His heart sank. While there were plenty of fingerprints, DNA, and other trace evidence to be found, none of it was a match to any of the recent four women. All the needles found were size 16 gauge with absolutely no blood evidence other than Daverman's, and the blood found near the needles all belonged to him as well. Sam closed his eyes and cursed under his breath before handing the results to Julie, who announced them to everyone else, while Sam turned to his usual habit of pacing the floor whenever he felt confused.

After another long, uncomfortable silence, Simon was the first to speak. "So, I'll go ahead and be Debbie-Downer here; it is possible that Peter Daverman isn't our guy."

"Men like him are smart, kid," Humbar insisted emphatically. "Just because we haven't found anything that ties him to these crimes yet, doesn't mean it doesn't exist."

Max, just as enthusiastically, added, "Psychologically, he fits all of the boxes: Crazy abusive mother, medical condition that gives him access to needles, money, travel, hell, even the timeline of Canada adds up!"

"Except that he's been paralyzed for three years," said Rivera. "That's why he was in Canada in the first place: for therapy. Physically, it would be impossible for him to have had anything to do with the murder of the four girls we've found this week."

"That, I completely accept," Max conceded. "But the rest of the timeline adds up, dating all the way back to 1982."

"We also don't know for sure that the voice that Mae Eyegols heard was in fact Peter Daverman's," Julie said quietly. "She said that she never saw the face of the person screaming. Look, I'll be the first to admit that Daverman gives me the creeps. But unless—"

"There is another answer here," Max interrupted her. "The Angel has been training a protégé. Think about it: My guys got close to him in Canada because of the cleaning chemical blunder. He is so set in his ways; he would have never made a mistake like that! What if these recent women are his victims by proxy?"

Sam stepped forward. "The footprints found a' a few of the scenes di' depict we're lookin' fer a short man weighin' abou' 130-160 tha' dumped the bodies. In his prime, Daverman stood abou' 5'11 an' weighed abou' 180. ...Wha' do we know abou' the nurse, Winkley?"

"No dice on that, Chief," Simon said sadly. "Colin Winkley has only been in Daverman's employ for the last six months, and I can't find any other connection between the two of them. Plus, he doesn't even have so much as a parking ticket, let alone a history of violence. If Daverman was training anybody, it probably isn't him."

"We could still bring him in for an interrogation," Julie countered. "Who knows? Maybe he saw something helpful."

Turning to Rivera, Sam grunted. "Do it. An' I want ye two—" he gestured to Julie and Dana "—t' go back ou' fer another interrogation with Daverman. If he's the Angel, then we know he hates women. Perhaps bein' 'ganged up on', so t' speak, will reveal a little more abou' our suspect. Humbar, go w' them an' poke around a little more, aye? An' Simon—"

"Get records for all of the private nurses that Daverman's had in his employ from the beginning?" The young man asked brightly.

Sam snickered and nodded.

"What about me?" Max asked, the anxiousness in his voice evident.

"You go back t' yer hotel an' cool off."

"What? You can't just kick me off this! We're so close—"

"No, we're not," Sam answered sternly. "Theoretically, everythin' suggests tha' Daverman is the Angel, yes. Bu' we cannea move on 'im w'out somethin' solid t' prove it. An' yer head's no' in the righ' place fer this, Max. Ye need t' le' us do our jobs."

"And what am I supposed to do in the meantime? Just sit around and wait? I can help!"

"No' until ye can be objective."

Tears were brimming in Max's eyes. "You just don't get it, do you? This man killed my wife!"

Sam couldn't take it anymore. Standing in front of Max, he stood up to his full height and stared down at the slightly shorter man. "I understand ye're still angry an' desperate. Bu' we have t' be careful. One wrong move, an' this whole thing'll be over before we can bring 'im t' justice. Go, Max. Now."

Sam stared Max down. Finally, the tired, disgraced man nodded and made his way for the elevators. With nothing else to do, Sam made his way to the conference room with another laptop. Simon had to help him set up everything to observe the interviews, and by the time he was done, the others were at Daverman's house. With a notebook at his side, Sam sat back and watched.

***

It had been three weeks since the searches of Peter Daverman's homes and businesses were conducted; per Sam's insistence, Bicks had double-checked all the recent victims for foreign DNA again, only to turn up nothing. The dirt sample underneath Chloe Hale's toenails wasn't even remotely a match to Daverman's house. What kept them digging for so long was everything they found that convinced them that Daverman was, at least at one point, the notorious Christmas Angel who had wreaked terror on women all across the north for the past forty years. Interrogating his nurse, Colin Winkley, proved to be just as much of a waste of time as Simon guessed it would be. He continually swore up and down that for as long as he had been working for Mr. Daverman, he's never seen anything remotely unusual and that his concern was purely for his patient's health. Simon did everything he could to find any sort of connection between Daverman and the victims from the past forty years, which also turned up empty. So, he tried to find any family members or acquaintances that the Angel might have decided to train in his image, and Sam, Humbar, and Rivera interviewed every one of them, only to be disappointed by solid alibis and no probable cause to search otherwise.

The only option left was interrogation, which was decided would be best if continually done by Lieutenant Evanston and Julie, given that they were both strong women and not nearly as hot-blooded about the case as everyone else was.

Sam watched the capable women interrogate Daverman again for what seemed to be the hundredth time; the more the man opened his mouth, the more Sam was convinced they were looking at the Christmas Angel. He was clearly enjoying toying with them.

Sam showed Max a few of the interviews to try and keep the doctor assured that they were sticking to Daverman like a bloodhound on a rabbit, but this proved to be a mistake. Max practically begged the team to arrest Daverman, saying he most definitely had the behaviors that a psychopathic murderer would possess. But, without proof, all Max's conclusions did was push Sam further in harassing the old man to confess to the crimes committed from 1982-2018. At this point, Sam was convinced that whoever had killed the four most recent women had copycatted Daverman before he disappeared, and yet no one in the old man's life could be pinpointed. He hoped that there might be a clue dropped in the interrogations, but Daverman kept his answers short and sweet. Everyone was growing weary, and Daverman's lawyers were pushing for all of them to back off, citing badgering of the disabled and whatever nonsense they could come up with.

In short, they had absolutely nothing that could empirically prove that Peter Daverman ever was the Angel, but every one of them could feel in their gut that they were looking at the notorious serial killer. Unfortunately, Sam knew that their time on this was running out.

"McKay?"

Sam didn't hear Copper come into the conference room, and her voice made him jump.

"Come with me, please." She gestured to the door for him to follow.

Sam knew what was coming. She was going to tell him it was time to cut this one loose, that they hadn't had another body turn up in weeks, everything that he already knew was coming. Begrudgingly, he followed her all the way to her office on the other side of the building (it was so late, Dower had already gone home). When he walked in, she encouraged him to sit down but he stood stark, waiting for the bad news.

"You already know what I'm going to say, McKay," she stated simply. "And it's the truth: It's time to put the Christmas Angel files back in the box. You have run this one as far as you can, and there are other perpetrators out there that I need you to catch after everyone takes a week of leave."

While Copper usually took this moment to take a seat behind her desk and turn her attention to something else in order to end the conversation, Sam was surprised to see her still standing before him, arms crossed, and unhesitant to look him in the eye. He figured she assumed he was going to fight for more time to crack Daverman and was prepared to shoot him down, but even Sam knew it was time to let these cold cases get even colder.

Sighing, he nodded his head in agreement. "Aye, alrigh'. Have ye tol' the others?"

"I've already informed Chief Humbar and Lieutenant Evanston, and Dr. Darrel will be going back to Toronto tomorrow afternoon. I trust that you will extend our gratitude for his help."

Then she took her seat, and Sam knew that was it; the conversation was over, and there was nothing more that could be said. He quietly left her office. When he got back to what was left of his team, it was obvious that they were already aware of the case's fate, as they were packing up everything they had without a word. Humbar and Dana had already left; the only person who was raising a fuss was Max, who was doing everything short of flipping tables over trying to convince everyone that they should keep working Daverman.

"Goddammit! We're so close to solving a forty-year-old string of murders! How can you all stop now?!"

"We have been looking and uncovering everything we possibly can, Dr. Darrel, and we still don't have a shred of evidence that can connect him to the girls," Rivera answered him shortly. "If we keep him here any longer, the department will be sued out of its toilet paper. And I can promise you that you will share a portion of that bill."

"I don't give a shit about a lawsuit!"

"It's not just that, we also have to consider the fact that there is no physical way that Daverman could have committed the murders of the four girls we've found this year."

"Which is all the more reason we should hang on to him! He had to have told somebody about his methods! If we find out who, we can turn them against each other and have an airtight case!"

"We all agree with you, Doc," Simon said next, but his quiet and quavering voice didn't do anything to lesson Dr. Darrel's anger. "But there's nothing more we can do that we haven't tried for the last month."

"You don't have to tell us how much this sucks, Doctor," Julie answered next. "But unfortunately, this happens. Sometimes, even we get ones that we can't solve."

The poor man was becoming more desperate in his pleas. "Daverman is guilty of rape and murder; we all know it!"

"Aye," Sam said sternly, yet compassionately. "An' I'd give me good arm fer a single piece of connective evidence t' prove it. Max, ye're no' familiar with regular law practice. Ye're a civilian. I promise ye tha' we'll do our best t' keep tabs on Daverman a' all times an' make sure he donnea harm anyone ever again–"

"And when he does? How good will your assurances be when another girl is kidnapped, raped, and poisoned because of his protege?"

"With us watching him, that won't happen," Rivera answered. "I can promise you that we'll be on him until the day he dies."

"Yeah, and when he does keel over, it'll be a peaceful death surrounded by luxury. Meanwhile, my wife's last moments were spent being brutalized and poisoned. And she won't get any justice for that! …That son of a bitch really is going to get away with it," Dr. Darrel hissed, the tears brimming in his eyes had already began making their marks down his cheeks. Turning to Sam, he spat out, "You bastards got my hopes up again, and now I'm right back to where I started when Angela died...you're all cowards."

He stormed off, but no one followed. Sam looked to the rest of his team, and the truth was plain on each of their faces. They all felt as though they had lost the war. This wasn't the first case they couldn't solve in all of their years together, but it certainly felt much more personal than the others. Not a word was spoken as Sam helped them finish packing up the case files, ready to be put back into storage. It was nearly 1:00 a.m. when they finished, and everyone was silent, as they left the office for their homes.

Sam knew there was absolutely no reasoning with Max in the moment, but he couldn't get his old friend Humbar off his mind. On a hunch, he drove to an old bar that he and the captain frequented together back in the day. He turned out to be right, as the older cop was sipping on a glass of Jim Beam without another soul around him.

"Hey, Sam!" The barkeep, a guy Sam recognized from back in the day named Dean, smiled at him. "Long time, no see."

"Hallo, Dean," he smiled. "Scotch—rocks."

"Anton had a feeling you'd show up; I'm all ready for you," the barkeep smiled and slid the half-filled glass down to him. Sam swallowed the whole thing in one gulp without an issue before he took a seat next to Humbar. He didn't say a word; there wasn't anything that he could say that would help. So, the two of them sat together in silence.

Finally, Humbar took another drink and cleared his throat. "You know...it doesn't matter how long it's been; I'll never be able to get the faces of those poor women out of my head. ...We have the son-of-a-bitch; it has to be him!"

Sam nodded. "I know, pal. I believe i', too."

"You know, there have been many times I've had to convince myself that the system may be flawed, but it works...I've been sitting here for the last two hours telling myself that over and over, but I can't seem to believe it. This time, the system is wrong..."

Sam turned and looked at his partner very seriously. "Wha' are ye thinkin'?"

"I'm thinking that I personally know the officers watching Daverman's house...I'm thinking about how easy it would be to send them home for the night..." Humbar took another drink.

Sam eyed Humbar carefully, "Listen t' me, pal, wha' ye're thinkin' abou' goes against everythin' we stand for as officers of the law. Can ye really live w' yerself if ye break tha' code?"

Humbar was about to take another drink, but Sam's words must have stopped him. He set his glass down, pulled out his wallet, and put some money on the bar.

"I'm sorry, Sam. I'm just...so tired of losing to this guy."

"Aye, anno, pal. We'll ge' him. Somehow, we'll ge' him."

Humbar stood up. "Yeah...sure we will." Not bothering to look at Sam, he walked out of the bar.

Sam knew he didn't want him to follow, and he wasn't sure that he could. Truthfully, his words felt like bile in his mouth, after what he had done to get a crack in the case. And while having Max around was certainly helpful, it wasn't enough. He tapped the bar for a refill before he finally went home.

***

Time went on, and more cases fell on Sam's desk. Before anyone knew it, it was May. Where there was once a thick blanket of snow alongside the roads, blooming flowers of different varieties of color had taken its place. Instead of the sky being grey or otherwise colorless, it had turned to a brilliant shade of blue (when it wasn't full of rain clouds). Aside from continually watching Peter Daverman's every move, the team had almost been able to put the horrible ordeal from the Christmas season out of their minds, with the exception of Sam.

Ever since their conversation in the bar, Sam had taken it upon himself to keep tabs on Humbar. He didn't think that his oldest and most trusted friend would ever really take the law into his own hands, but he couldn't shake the haunted look in the old man's eyes. But as time went on, Peter Daverman continued to grow richer and physically weaker, and Humbar kept himself buried in his duties as a captain. Every day, Sam had to tell himself to relax.

Then on a particularly beautiful, sunny spring day, just as Sam was sitting down at his desk and about to proceed with his case load, his phone started ringing. It was Humbar. Curious, he answered, "G'mornin'—"

"He's done it again," the old captain spat.

"W-wha'?"

"You heard me!"

123

Sam was stunned. "Jus' a moment." Pressing the speaker button, he motioned for the team to come over to his desk and listen. "Wha' di' ye find?"

"Three bodies were found early this morning on 68, north of Kenton: lying on their backs, squeaky clean, needle mark to the chests, and that damned white peony left on top of every one of them. You didn't really think I'd just let this go, did you? My office got the notification the second the details came through."

Julie was the first to step forward. "Three? In one spot? That's never happened before."

"Are...are you absolutely sure it's the Christmas Angel?" Simon asked very timidly.

"Oh, I'm sure, alright," Humbar seethed. "We never should have left this alone! ...I should have killed Daverman when I had the chance."

The old Captain hung up.

Everyone was bewildered; while Sam continued to stare at his phone, Rivera, Julie, and Simon began their usual repertoire of bickering with one another.

"Jesus...three bodies. That's an escalation."

Julie argued, "But we've been monitoring Daverman for months, now! There hasn't been a phone call we haven't listened to, an email we haven't read, he couldn't have cursed out a delivery boy without us knowing it! How could he have been in contact with the protégé?"

"The student has surpassed the teacher; he doesn't need advice anymore; he's making his teacher proud. Daverman is bound to hear about this on the news by tonight."

"But if he's trying to copy his teacher, why is he purposely going out of his way to change the timeline details? I thought we all agreed that the Angel did his killing in the wintertime for the...solstice, thing. It's spring, and there are flowers growing out there. And three bodies in one place at one time? That's extreme, even for an escalation, isn't it?"

Sam stood up from his desk and the three of them stopped bickering. Sighing, he nodded towards the elevators, "Come on, we're headin' t' Kenton."

Chapter Thirteen

It didn't matter that there wasn't any snow on the ground this time, the scene that Sam and the others arrived at was only too familiar. The road was lined with news vans while the officers were doing everything they could to keep them away from the scene. Forensics teams were combing every inch that surrounded the bodies, and deep into the brush, far away from the road was a tent. Underneath that tent, the coroner of Hardin County was carefully examining each of the bodies.

While Humbar wasn't there, Sam was surprised to see Dana on the scene He figured she would have heard about this a little later, but then again it was possible that Humbar had called her first.

"Agents," she nodded. "Here we are again. And this time it's the sign of three."

"How'd you know about this?" Simon asked, the curiosity in his tone genuine. "We only just heard about it when Humbar—"

"I had figured the day we dropped this that Ace wasn't going to let it go, so I've been having my own people keep watch on him. When they reported that he'd gone into a frenzy, I figured it had to be Christmas Angel related. It didn't take too long to get what I needed after that. Now," she turned her head back to the bodies under the tent, "What do you make of this change of MO?"

Sam scanned the positions of the bodies: While every other victim had been carefully positioned to represent a point on a pentacle, these victims were left lined up right next to each other.

Simon was the first to say something. "One of the victims is a boy? The Angel has never targeted men before."

"My first impression is obviously whoever's taken over for Daverman doesn't have the same motivations as his mentor, otherwise everything would have stayed inside of the winter solstice window, for one thing," Julie answered.

"And the bodies would have been positioned the right way instead of lined up," Rivera added. "But none of these details were ever released to the public, so are we certain this isn't another copycat? I mean, as Simon pointed out, that kid in the middle there is definitely different."

"The coroner has already confirmed that the hole in their hearts was made with a 16-gauge needle," Dana countered. "Right?"

"I can speak for myself," the man examining the bodies answered. "But yes, she's right. Definitely 16-gauge, I'm positive."

"And that detail wasn't released to the public either," the lady lieutenant added. "So, either this copycat got lucky on the needle size, or this is a message. Which do you think is more likely?"

While the three of them looked at one another and had their silent communication, Sam bent down to get a closer look at the faces belonging to each victim: one was a young woman, maybe in her early twenties. The boy lying next to her couldn't have been more than seventeen years old. But it was the last victim that really gave him a start: She looked almost exactly like Meredith; she might have even been her sister, if he didn't already know that Meredith was an only child.

"Boss? You okay?" Simon asked, shaking him out of his shocked moment.

Clearing his throat, Sam stood back up and addressed Dana. "Who found the bodies an' how?"

"That's the next best part: This was an anonymous tip to 911. The dispatcher said it was a man's voice, and he said, quote: 'there are three bodies on route 68 exactly three miles north of Kenton. You will find them 200 yards to the west.' He hung up after that."

While Sam took a moment to internalize the information, Simon retorted, "You know, lady, you could have started with that bit of info."

"Yeah, now we *know* this is a message," Julie nodded her agreement. "The protégé wants his work found, unlike Daverman did."

"Well, good news for us, his cocky attitude is ultimately what's going to bring him down." Rivera turned to look at Sam. "You've been pretty quiet since we got here, see something else that we don't see?"

"No. Le's ge' them back t' Bicks an' start identifyin' 'em, then we'll proceed w' interviewin' the families. Perhaps the protégé already made a mistake, an' somebody can identify 'im."

Sam turned on his heel and started back for the car; tried as he might, he couldn't shake the image of Meredith being the third victim out of his mind.

***

Bicks confirmed almost instantly that the poison ratios in the new victims' blood were exactly like the ones before. That, in turn, confirmed Dana's proposal that these new victims were intended to be a message. The only question that was unanswered was who was the message for? From the face of the third victim alone, Sam couldn't help the uncomfortable feeling that it was for him. He didn't voice that fear aloud. He even quietly reprimanded himself, *Ye're bein' ridiculous, ye bampot! Ye've nevar even heard of the Angel until Humbar brought ye the bloody files in Decembar. If anythin'*, he thought to himself, *he's probably tryin' t' ge' t' Humbar or maybe even Max. They've had vested interest in these cases fer years. Calm yerself, ye're overreactin'. The face is jus' a coincidence.* He really wanted to believe his own thoughts on this, but he still couldn't shrug the ridiculous thought off.

Once everyone, Dana included, was back in their little corner of the third floor again, Simon immediately set to work trying to identify the victims through his laptop.

"Okay, victim number one is Clara Gohurst, age 20. I found her in missing persons, reported by her parents three weeks ago in Cincinnati. According to the police report, Clara was a bit of a hellraiser, but they swear up and down that she changed her ways. Actually, it looks like she just got back to the US after a three month stay in the UK."

Sam could feel the hairs on the back of his neck stand up. "Wha' was she there for? School? A workin' visa?"

"No...the parents say she went to stay with her aunt, the mom's sister."

"That can't be cheap," Rivera said. "Does she come from a rich family?"

Simon's fingers flew across the keyboard. "Her parents' combined salary is roughly $70K a year, and she's got three other siblings still living at home. Maybe the aunt paid for everything. Anywho, I did find a fingerprint match to victim number three: Chelsea Aspen, age

41, had a DUI charge back in 2016. She went to rehab and got clean, hasn't had an issue since then. She worked for a pharmacy in Cambridge and went missing back in February. A coworker reported her."

"What about the boy?" Julie asked.

"There's nothing in missing persons about him, so either he hasn't been gone long enough, or his parents really don't care that he's gone. And if this kid has a social media account, he's very good about not putting his face on it."

Dana answered him. "Bicks found a skull tattoo on the kids' back, and he said he had pizza and beer in his stomach. He was probably at a party with some friends and got snatched when he was leaving. Kids like that usually come from broken families and take off for days at a time before they come home; we're most likely not going to hear about a missing person's report for some time."

"Considering how fast the Amber Alert system goes into play, I agree," Rivera nodded.

"Well, we're no' gonna' wai' around until somebody decides t' report 'im missin'. Start compilin' a list of every high school in the state, an' ge' on the phone w' all of the guidance counselors. We're sendin' this kid's photo t' all of 'em until we find out who he is."

"You really think this kid actually went to high school?" Dana asked doubtfully.

"Somebody somewhere had t' have seen 'im, an' I donnea want t' plaster his face all over the news an' give this protégé wha' he wants: attention. Fer now, we'll handle this the old-fashioned way, an' quietly."

"It's going to take me a while to get the email addresses of every guidance counsellor in the state," Simon said in a bit of a whiney voice, but one look from Sam, and he let his fingers fly across the keyboard again.

Meanwhile, the other three sat down at their desks and started calling out which areas of the state they would cover.

"I'm takin' the south," Sam stated plainly. "I'll start w' Cincinnati, an' I'll have the local PD speak t' the Gohursts an' tell them abou' their daughtar. Le's ge' t' work."

A few hours later, after at least a hundred high schools had been contacted, Sam stood up and went into the conference room with the case file of Clara Gohurst in his hand, feigning that he needed a minute to think before personally contacting the family. But that wasn't the truth. What he really wanted to do was ask the Gohursts what their daughter was doing in the UK. It seemed like such a silly thing to ask, but between the face of Chelsea Aspen and this little detail, Sam's gut was screaming at him for clarification that it was all entirely a coincidence. Mustering up the courage he needed, he dialed the number on the police report and waited.

Ring.... Ring.... Ring....

There was no answer, and it went to voicemail. Determined, Sam tried the number again.

Ring.... Ring.... Ring....

Again, there was no answer. Although he knew he should have left it alone, he just couldn't. *One las' time, please please answar...*

Ring.... Ring.... Ring.... "Hello?"

It was a woman's voice, and it was clear she had been crying. Sam sighed in relief to finally have someone on the line that might be able to answer him. "Mrs. Gohurst? Please donnea hang up, my name is Sam McKay. I'm an agent w' the FBI an' part of the team tha's investigatin' yer daughtar's death."

He heard a stifled sob. "W-what do you want?"

"I need t' ask ye a verra important question regardin' yer daughter's whereabouts."

The sadness in Mrs. Gohurst's voice quickly shifted to anger. "Do you have to do this right now? We just found out that our daughter is dead less than an hour ago!"

Although the pang of guilt was awful, Sam couldn't be deterred from the reason he had called her in the first place. "Yes, ma'am. I'm so sorry abou' yer loss, an' I understand this is a terrible time fer ye, bu' yer answer could be key t' the investigation."

"Fine, one question."

"Thank ye, ma'am. Please, wha' was yer daughter doin' in the UK, an' where was she stayin' a'?"

"She was staying with my sister. After she'd gotten in trouble, we thought sending her to live with her aunt might help her get her act together, that's all."

"Please, ma'am, where in England does yer sistar live?"

"My sister doesn't live in England; she lives in Scotland. Glasgow. Clara... Clara flew into England because my sister wanted to take her to the Royal London Theatre at the beginning of the trip before they went back to her—"

Sam didn't hear another word after Scotland; his palms were starting to sweat. When it sounded like Mrs. Gohurst had finished talking, he thanked the woman and hung up the phone before wandering back out of the conference room again. He knew he would have to tell his team his theory now, but the looks of worry on their faces immediately disarmed him.

Rivera stepped forward. "Sam, that kid's name is Phillip Browne...and he's a student at Lincoln West High."

Sam's blood went even colder. "Tha-tha's Oliver's school."

"Yeah, we know," Julie nodded. "You weren't the only one who suspected something was fishy when we got a look at Chelsea Aspen's face."

"Mrs. Gohurst jus' tol' me tha' her sistar lives in Scotland."

"Then that confirms it," Rivera nodded sullenly. "This was a message and, for whatever reason, the protégé has fixated on you."

"And somehow, he knows enough about your personal life to have been this specific," Simon added.

"We should really update Copper on all of this," Julie finished for them.

Sam was in a daze, but he nodded and led the way to his superior's office; he allowed his team to do the honors of explaining the new developments.

Copper, level as ever, was unfazed by the news and simply gestured for everyone to sit down.

"McKay, have you ever heard of The Christmas Angel before?"

Sam shook his head. "No, no' until Humbar told us abou' him."

"Have you ever seen anything remotely like these cases before? In victimology, M.O., anything?"

"No."

Rivera suddenly produced a piece of paper that had the names of the four women they found in December as well as the three newest victims. "Sam, are you familiar at all with any of these people?"

"No."

"Okay. Well, believe it or not, this is good news for us: The protégé told us something about himself."

"What?" Simon asked, his next comments dripping with sarcasm. "That he not only stalks his victims but the police investigating them, too? Yeah, that's comforting."

"Actually, it's more likely that he knows Sam," Julie answered him with a caring smile. "Which means that he's somewhere in Sam's past; we just need to find him."

"And it also adds weight to the theory that the protégé might have had law enforcement training." Rivera turned to the man himself and continued, "Can you think of anybody in your past that would want to get your attention like this?"

Sam had listened to the others go back and forth about the supposed 'good news', but he felt bewildered. He had already begun searching his memories for anyone that might have had a grudge against him. There were certainly a few throughout his career, even going back as far as his time in Scotland, but to copycat a serial killer he'd never heard of? And with women and one boy that he'd never met? What was the point?

"McKay?" Director Copper's voice shook him out of his thoughts, and he quickly looked up. "Calm down, don't let this man get inside of your head. Just take a deep breath and try to think. For the moment, let's assume that this protégé didn't meet you until you came to the states in 2008. Start there and spare no details."

Sam nodded and cleared his throat, "I was, um...I was workin' through the police academy shortly aftar me an' Meredith were married. I met Humbar a' the ceremony while he was there recruitin' graduates. He reached out t' me superiors in Scotland an' gave me a job. Shortly aftar tha', considerin' me pas' experience as an Inspector, I was made an IA Detective in February. Five years latar, I started workin' part time as a Hostage Negotiator fer SWAT, until I went private in May of 2017."

"And then the whole family came together," Simon beamed proudly. "Well, almost the whole family. Meat-sicle, here, didn't join us until August."

While Julie and Rivera chuckled at Simon's added narrative, Copper continued to grill Sam. "Is that everything?"

"Aye."

"There isn't anything else of interest that you can think of?"

"I donnea think so. I've met me fair share of disgruntled cops tha' dinnea like bein' investigated, bu' all of them were either cleared or relieved of duty. An' there's no' many suspects in SWAT cases tha' live t' tell the tale, le' alone target hostage negotiators."

"Are you absolutely sure you cannot think of *anyone* that would hold this bad of a grudge against you? I have absolutely no problem combing through every minute of your life for the last thirteen years, McKay, but I trust your instincts and would rather start with anyone that you might be able to think of."

Sam didn't immediately answer her; everyone's eyes fell on him. "... There is one man tha' we might want' look into, bu' I cannea believe he'd do somethin' this depraved...his name is Robert Grayers."

Within seconds of the name being revealed, Simon had his laptop open, and his fingers were flying across his keyboard. But Sam didn't wait for him to reveal anything.

"He was a cop tha' I arrested fer skimmin' drug money an' takin' bribes seven years ago...and he was also my partner."

Simon instantly stopped typing, and the air suddenly fell deathly silent; Sam could feel everyone's eyes on him at his admission, but he kept his head high and began his tale:

"Seargeant Robert Grayers was my senior an' took me under his wing when I was made an IA Detective in 2008. In 2014, we were put on the case of Officers Inez an' Felto fer police brutality accusations. I accidentally stumbled on a discrepancy in their patrol routes tha' had me curious. Grayers insisted I was wastin' my time an' t' stick t' the initial investigation, bu' I couldnea le' i' go. I learned tha' they'd been skimmin' 5% from a drug dealer, an' they'd had a meet up the day their patrol route seemed off. I found the dealer, an' he confirmed the officers had been skimmin', bu' he also le' slip there was a third party. ...Well, tha' third party was my senior an' mentor, Grayers."

Rivera was the first to speak, the shock in his voice undeniable. "You...you arrested your own partner?"

"Aye, an' I testified against him a' trial. He was fired and had all of his credentials stripped."

"No jail time?" Simon asked.

Sam didn't answer him.

"You joined SWAT around that time," Julie said in hushed tones. "I always wondered why you worked as a negotiator only part-time, on top of being an IA detective."

"Ye all know the golden rule among cops: Nevar, *evar* betray yer partners; they're the ones tha' go' yer back. An' I broke the rule. After the case was over, nobody would partner with me again, my case load slowly go' lighter, an' I was considerin' a change in positions anyway, when SWAT needed someone t' fill in. I'd been to a few seminars, so I applied. Humbar pulled a few strings fer me t' ge' it."

While everyone else remained quiet at his story, Copper began to issue orders. "Mr. Grayers would be an excellent place to start, then. Rivera, Russell, I want the two of you to pay him a visit and see what you might be able to learn. Mr. Abler, you will stay here and take notes while we look for anyone else in McKay's past."

Julie and Rivera, bewildered, stood up and left the director's office; Sam could feel their pointed stares at the back of his head, but he took a deep breath and shrugged it off. He knew Copper would do exactly as she promised and tear apart his whole past, if need be, to find whoever was targeting him, and that was assuming Sam had actually met the man once before. He knew he was in for a long afternoon.

***

Not twenty minutes later, Rivera was driving the SUV down 56th street in the Stockyards to ex-cop Robert Grayers' house at the end of the block. Simon was able to pull a current address (which was the same address as it had always been) as well as a police record for the two of them to look over. The drive itself from the office to Grayers' home wasn't very long, but Rivera had all the time in the world to think about the truth that Sam had revealed to all of them. His stewing, however, did not go unnoticed; when he parked on the corner of a tiny cul-de-sac, Julie quickly re-locked the doors before he could open his.

Confused (and a little annoyed), Rivera turned to her and sighed, "What?"

"You know he was in the right, don't you?" She said as-a-matter-of-factly. "He found out that a cop was accepting bribes; that's a third-degree felony."

"But you missed the part where he was a cop with twenty-three years of impeccable service under his belt. Grayers didn't even have so much as a misconduct charge filed against him."

"Yeah, because he was taking money from the people who would have filed it."

"You don't know that."

"I know that he broke the law when he promised to uphold it to the highest standard."

"Oh, and I suppose you never went five miles over the speed limit before you joined SWAT? That's against the law too, you know."

Rivera's jab hit where it was intended, as Julie crossed her arms in front of her chest and glared at him. "That's not the same thing as taking money from criminals, Rivera, come on. If nothing else, this goes way beyond irony; an Internal Affairs cop doing exactly what Internal Affairs is supposed to be stopping other cops from doing? He had a perfect setup, until Sam caught onto it."

Looking into the neighborhood of older, shabbier homes, Rivera pointed at their destination. "Look at Grayers' house, Jules: It's not exactly deep in the suburbs, and I don't see a pool through any of the chicken-wire. Five percent? That's a lot of money, yeah, but the real question is what did he do with it? It obviously wasn't going into home repair."

"Maybe he spent it on clothes, a new TV, took his wife to the Bahamas? Who cares how he spent the drug money?"

Rivera rolled his eyes and sighed. "I'm not saying what Grayers did was right; I'm only saying that men like him usually have more reasons than greed that drive them to do what they do. Sam obviously didn't want to hear what those reasons were. Honestly, that bothers me. I promise you this: When we go in to talk to Grayers, we'll see something that proves that I'm right." He unlocked the door and jumped out of the car before she could argue with him further.

Grayers' home very much fit in to the neighborhood. The house had peeling yellow paint all over it, and the front yard was unkempt and weedy. The house next to it had a large, mean-looking dog on a leash growling and barking at the two of them as they walked up the cracked pavement, but Rivera ignored it and knocked on the door; Julie was right behind him. A sturdy looking man with white hair answered.

"Yeah?" he asked in a gruff tone.

"Are you Robert Grayers?"

"Look, pal, the 'no solicitation' sign is right here next to my door."

"I'm Agent Rivera of the FBI, sir, and this is Agent Russell."

"Oh, I'm sorry about that. You'd be amazed how many salesmen we get around these parts. Please, come on in."

Grayers moved out of the way and beckoned them to come inside. Rivera could hear the flies buzzing when the door opened, but stepping inside of the house only made the sound intensify, and the smell certainly didn't help. Takeout cartons and pizza boxes were everywhere, along with various pieces of clothing tossed about. The walls had a few photographs of people that he assumed were Grayers' family, and he could also see a stack of notices sitting on a side table with the word OVERDUE printed in big red letters. Rivera had already guessed that things hadn't been easy for the discredited officer, and he instantly felt sorry for the man.

Grayers shut the door behind them and asked, "What can I do for you, agents?"

"Officer Grayers, we'd like to talk to you about an old partner of yours: Sampson McKay."

Grayers' disposition instantly changed from cordial to angry. "What about him?"

"Would you mind telling us a little about your partnership?"

"Hmph, some partnership," he grumbled and took a seat on the saggy couch behind him. "It's thanks to that limey jock that the only job I have now is as a janitor at the school up the street."

"You *were* convicted of taking bribes from a drug dealer, Mr. Grayers," Julie said coldly.

The old man snapped his head back up. Glaring, he pointed at a picture on the wall behind them; a pretty young girl in a graduation cap was smiling in it. "That's my daughter, Danielle, at her high school graduation a month before she went to the hospital and found out she had stage three colon cancer. Do you know how expensive treatment is, even after insurance, Agent?"

"That's no excuse for breaking the law."

"You don't have children, do you? Of course, you don't, otherwise you'd understand. But Sam...he has a son, I thought, of all people, he'd understand my position. Look at me, do I look like the kind of guy that buys toys, nice clothes, or petty things like that? Every penny went to my daughter. For all the good that it did. Thanks to that self-righteous bastard, I was fired and left without a pension, even with twenty-three years on the force under my belt. ...After Danielle died, my wife decided to slit her wrists."

Rivera, very gently, replied, "I'd be pretty upset if I were in your position, too."

"Anyone would be," Julie continued in a much less sympathetic tone. "Angry enough to get revenge, I should think."

The word revenge certainly got Grayers' attention as the man shot his eyes to Julie and glared, "Are you accusing me of something, missy?"

"Not yet," Julie answered. "But, just for the hell of it, can you tell us where you were December 20th to the 25th?"

"Cleaning shit off toilets at Stockyard Middle School and the local parks. I'll get you the names of the two other janitors who were working with me and can confirm my whereabouts."

"And what about last night?"

"Still at Stockyard. Why? Did McKay catch a bullet? As far as I'm concerned, he deserved whatever happened to him."

Rivera jumped in and quickly tried to diffuse the situation. "Officer Grayers, your anger is justifiable, sir, but you're not doing yourself any favors slinging about phrases like that."

"What have I got to lose, Agent? My wife has gone crazy and my child is dead because McKay couldn't just leave enough alone. I won't deny that if I had the chance to get revenge on him, I would. Now, unless you're here with an arrest warrant, get the hell out of my house."

The door had barely slammed behind them before Julie turned to Rivera and said, "Oh yeah, he's definitely a good candidate. Copper'll say yes to putting a tail on him, for sure."

Rivera didn't answer her; he made up his mind that as soon as they had a moment, he would pull Sam aside for a little chat. Disappointed didn't begin to describe how he felt. He knew Sam had been working in law enforcement long enough to know that there was always a reason why good people sometimes had to make bad decisions, but for him to completely throw his partner under the bus the way he did... Rivera was certain that wasn't like Sam at all. Under different circumstances, Rivera would have been the first to let a situation go and move on. But this time, he needed to know why his current partner had broken his own code, particularly with an old partner.

Chapter Fourteen

Sam rubbed his aching head; for what felt like an hour, Copper had been questioning and probing his memory, while Simon had been searching through everything he could on his laptop. Lieutenant Evanston had thrown in a peculiar question here and there, too. They had all but turned his life inside-out trying to see if in any way the seven recent victims were at all connected to him. Sam couldn't think of anything that connected them.

"Maybe you shopped at the same grocery store once?" Simon asked. "Maybe you helped one of these young ladies get something down from the top shelf, and the protégé got jealous."

Sam sighed. "Okay, sure, perhaps I did. Bu' I'm tellin' ye, I donnea recognize any of these women, so if I did, I cannea confirm tha'."

"What about banks?" Dana asked, "Did you ever have any accounts at any of the victims' banks?"

"Aye, I have a checkin' an' a savin's a' Chloe's, the firs' victim's, bank. Bu' the locations I use are a' least three blocks away from hers. This is ridiculous. If this is the best we can figure on how this protégé has developed his obsession with me, then the bampot's crazier than we thought."

"We've known that from the beginning," Dana said offhandedly.

"Please...I need a break." Sam stood up from his chair and left Copper's office without permission; ironically, he felt a little satisfaction that, for once, he got the last word instead of his superior. He bought a soda from the vending machine in the break room, but that didn't help. He tried to walk around the office, but that also didn't help. Before he knew it, he was back in his little corner on the third floor. With Julie and Rivera interviewing Grayers, and Simon stuck with Copper and Dana, at least it was quiet, and he could take a moment to breathe. Unfortunately, the photographs of the three people that had been found that morning were sitting on his desk, and he couldn't drag his eyes away from them, especially Chelsea Aspen. The resemblance between her and his ex-wife was positively uncanny, and it frightened him more to think that Meredith and Oliver might be in danger as well. He couldn't take any more that day; picking up his things, he left the office and headed straight to Lincoln West High.

Sam arrived just as the final bell rang; Oliver normally took the bus to and from Meredith's house, so he met the young man just outside of the doors to the bus yard to surprise him. When the fifteen-year-old emerged from the school, Sam smiled to see him holding the hand of a pretty girl; he knew that could only be Karliegh. He waved to the two of them and called out.

"Dad?" Oliver asked, the terror in his face more than amusing to Sam. "Wh-what are you doing here?"

"I go' off early an' though' I'd pick ye up, today. An' ye mus' be Karliegh?"

The young lady nervously smiled and nodded. "Hi, Mr. McKay."

Wondering just how much more he could embarrass Oliver, Sam bowed low and answered, "I's a pleasure t' meet ye a' last."

Karliegh giggled, but Oliver looked as though he might die from mortification.

"Dad!" Sam's son hissed at him. "Um... I guess I better go, I'll text you later tonight."

Karliegh, still giggling from Sam's antics, nodded and leaned up to kiss Oliver's cheek, before she said goodbye and boarded one of the waiting school buses.

"Oh my God, Dad! Did you really have to do that?!"

Sam couldn't hold back the need to laugh any longer. "Someday when ye're a parent, ye'll ge' t' enjoy the same privileges of embarrasin' yer children jus' fer fun."

"If she breaks up with me over this, I am holding you personally responsible!"

Still guffawing, Sam continued, "Aye, noted. Come on, le's ge' goin' t' the store. I want t' surprise yer mother w' a nice dinnar tonight."

Ignoring the curious look the teenager was giving him, Sam walked with his son back to the car.

Sam was just pulling the pan of potatoes au gratin out of Meredith's oven, when he heard the front door open and Meredith's voice calling, "Oliver? Sam? I'm home! Mmm...something smells good!"

He had just set the dish on the table, when she suddenly appeared in the kitchen. "I wasn't expecting you tonight. ...Are those potatoes au gratin?"

Chuckling, Sam nodded and returned to the stove to finish the rest of dinner. "Anno, I go' off work early. How was yer day?"

Smiling, Meredith set her things down on the counter and answered. "Good! I closed on three houses today."

"Well done! Dinnar'll be ready soon, then we can celebrate."

Oliver suddenly came bounding down the stairs and into the kitchen. "Hey, mom!"

"Hey, you," she answered by wrapping him in a hug and kissing his cheek. "How was school?"

"Fine...Dad picked me up."

"I figured that since his car's in the driveway."

"An' I me' Karliegh today," Sam added with a waggle to his eyebrows.

"Oooh, then you can tell me what this girl actually looks like. Hey, why don't you just invite her to dinner tonight? It looks like dad made enough to feed the neighborhood."

"God, you guys, don't make this weird!" Oliver groaned.

While both parents laughed at their son's discomfort, a timer went off, signaling that everything else was ready and Sam announced, "Dinnar is served."

Most of the meal was spent laughing. If Sam and Meredith weren't teasing Oliver about how he hadn't introduced them to his girlfriend yet, the three of them were talking about plans for the upcoming summer. Meredith was going to be extra busy with the way the housing market was looking, so Oliver would most likely spend most of his time at Sam's apartment. The boy argued that he was old enough to look after himself and that Sam's schedule was just as erratic as Meredith's. So, they continued to talk over how they would do things, but by the end of the meal a decision hadn't been made yet.

"Look, as long as I've got a key to both of your places and a phone, we can just play it by ear, right?"

Meredith and Sam looked at one another skeptically.

"At least think about it, okay? Look, I'm going upstairs to...do homework."

"Tell Karliegh I said hallo," Sam called after him knowingly. Again, the boy groaned, which earned another laugh from the two parents as they heard him run back up the stairs to his room.

Sam stood up and started to clear the table. He had barely set his and Meredith's plates in the sink when the woman herself stood right in front of him with her arms folded across her chest. "Alright, what's going on?"

He didn't break her piercing gaze, but he quickly tried to bluff with a casual, "Wha' do ye mean? We jus' had family dinnar, like we do every week."

"Sam, don't lie to me. We were married for twelve years. You really think I don't know when something's bothering you?"

He opened his mouth, but Meredith hadn't finished her deductions and instantly silenced him.

"In all that time, you have *never* told me anything about work. Not once. Then before Christmas, you ask me to carry a gun, even though you know I hate them. You come here very late on Christmas Day and kiss me. And, today, you left work early to pick up Oliver and make butter-thyme chicken and potatoes au gratin, which you *know* is my favorite. It doesn't take a genius to see that you're up to something. And you can either tell me what it is, or I can call Derrick and have him tell me."

Sam was completely stunned. It never failed to amaze him how easily Meredith could read him like an open book when she wanted to. He sat there, struggling to find an easy, non-threatening way to explain the situation, but from the intensity of her stare, he already knew it was pointless to try. Finally, he gave up.

Wiping his hands on a nearby towel, he sighed. "Alrigh', there's a possibility a serial killer has targeted me."

The shock and worry that flashed across Meredith's eyes was unmistakable, but she remained quiet and waited for him to continue.

"Christ, I shouldnea be tellin' ye any of this...Jus' before Christmas, we found four women brutalized an' murdered in a verra' specific way. We had a suspect, bu'...i's complicated. Then this mornin', three more victims were found w' the same specific MO; tha' means modus—"

"Modus operandi, a serial killer's signature. I know," Meredith smiled.

"Right," he nodded. "Well, the problem w' these three is tha'...they were sort of...addressed t' me, an' I cannea say more than' tha'."

The smile on Meredith's face slowly disappeared. "Alright. Do you think we're in danger?"

"I donnea know... my team an' I are tryin' t' figure ou' why he's been fixatin' on me, an' my superior is havin' us keep tabs on Robert Grayers. Ye remember me ol' partner from AI?"

"Yeah, I do. ...I also remember how things were pretty crappy around here near the end of your partnership with him."

Sam shifted very uncomfortably.

"Your boss thinks that sweet man is really capable of doing those things you said?"

He sighed, "I's a' start, otherwise we've go' nothin' else t' go on."

"Okay, so what does that mean for me and Oliver? Are we going into...what is it, witness protection?"

Sam chuckled at the suggestion. "I donnea think so, no."

"But you're obviously scared of something happening, otherwise you wouldn't be doing all of...this."

"...I suppose I jus' needed t' be reassured tha' everythin's alrigh' here. I donnea want anythin' t' happen t' the two of ye." Leaning forward, he took Meredith's hand in his and gently squeezed it.

Meredith's eyes softened at his confession. "Sam, we're fine. If I even thought that somebody was doing something fishy around me or Oliver, you would be the first person I'd call, and you know that. You don't need to do stuff like this just to check on us."

Sam narrowed his eyes at her. "This man's a rapist, Meredith. An' a killer. He donnea stop—"

"I know all about rapists, Sam," Meredith interrupted a little loudly. She quickly lowered her voice again. "And I know all about walking in the dark with a buddy, staying in the lamplight, keeping my car keys in my hand, checking the peephole, and even carrying pepper spray. Just because it's been sixteen years since I was raped, doesn't mean I've forgotten about it, so don't patronize me."

He wanted to argue back, but the urge to bellow caused him to stop himself; there was no need to bring Oliver into the middle of this discussion. Taking a deep breath, he continued calmly, "I'm no' patronizin' ye; I'm tryin' t' keep ye safe."

"And I am telling you that I can handle myself and our son just fine."

Sam didn't want to fight with Meredith, but the mix of his and her stubbornness often led to an explosive result. He shut his eyes and shook his head. "Fine, then I won't do this anymore."

He tried to go back to the table to get more dishes, but Meredith's hand on his arm stopped him. Curious, he looked back up; her features had softened, and her tone had lowered. "Sam, I'm not saying that I don't appreciate these surprise visits. I'm not trying to fight with you."

"Then why are ye?"

Meredith's outward façade of bravery wavered; vulnerability was never her strongest attribute, even after her assault, and Sam knew it. He couldn't help but take her hand again, doing his best to encourage her. Finally, she closed her eyes and took a deep breath, before she admitted the truth. "You've been in hundreds of dangerous situations, but I can't think of one that has scared you so much that you would just...do things that you don't normally do, like leaving work early and picking up Oliver. And, honestly, that's what scares me."

Sam didn't waste a moment in pulling her into his arms. "I tol' ye Meredith, I'll no' le' anythin' happen t' Oliver or t' you."

"I know you won't. But...Sam, let's be honest here: By everyone's standards, you shouldn't be this concerned about us."

That comment made his eyebrows furrow. "Wha' are ye talkin' abou'?"

"I'm just stating the obvious: Because of my infidelity, we're divorced. And Oliver isn't biologically yours. So why are you doing all this?"

Sam, stunned, rubbed his face. "Christ, Meredith, ye really wanna' do this now?"

"Yes, as a matter of fact, I do."

"Why didnea ye wanna' talk abou' this a' family counselin'?"

She narrowed her eyes, "You know why: because of Oliver. I'm not ready to tell him the whole truth. Now, answer my question: Why are you doing this?"

"I's because I love the two of you. Tha' biological shite has naught t' do with anythin'; Oliver is my son. And you were my wife."

"But *why?*" Meredith pressed again, and Sam began to feel very uncomfortable. "I mean, let's look at the facts: Fifteen years ago, I went to Scotland with some friends, and you stopped a conman from robbing me of all my money. I thought that was the end of it, but then the next day you show up to ask me out for a cup of tea. I tell you that I'm not a local; you say you don't care. Somehow, you convince me to let you write to me, which I honestly never expected to happen, but I get letters from you. ...And then I tell you about Oliver, thinking that will really drive you away, and instead you ask if you could come to the USA to meet him. Sam, the moment you saw him, you wanted to stay. I've been ignoring this question for fifteen years, and I think now I deserve to know why. Why would you automatically decide to take a kid that's not yours as your own son, and why would you want to marry a damaged woman?"

Her choice of words had Sam's curiosity piqued. "Is tha' wha's botherin' you? You think I pity ye?"

Meredith sucked in a ragged breath. "I think I don't understand how your mind works when it comes to us. And I can't tell if you're still around because of pity or some misguided sense of responsibility, and I don't like either answer."

"So wha' are ye sayin'? Ye want me t' leave ye alone? Cut all ties w' Oliver an' never return?"

"Of course not!" Tears were brimming at the corner of Meredith's eyes, but she quickly wiped them away. "Sam...just this once, I want you to tell me the whole, and completely honest, truth. Did you ever really love me? Or is Oliver the only reason you've stuck around?"

And there it was: The ever-constant elephant in the room when it came to Sam's insistence of his presence. It wasn't the first time the question had been asked, but Sam had always responded with a quick "Of course, I love ye" and would move on to a different subject. But this time, under these circumstances, he knew Meredith wasn't going to accept that. His intimate thoughts and feelings were not the easiest things for him to talk about. With everything that was going on, he didn't know whether or not he had the strength to answer her.

Sam turned away from her and stared at the sink, doing his best to piece together what he wanted to say, so it wouldn't come out incorrectly. Meredith waited, but he could feel her eyes on him while he thought. Finally, he mumbled, "Ye know my mum left when I was a wee lad...When ye firs' tol' me abou' Oliver, I knew I needed t' meet him. And...I saw myself in tha' boy: growin' up fer years wonderin' why his parent nevar wanted him. Ye made clear ye dinnea want t' tell him the truth abou' his father, an' I cannae blame ye for it. Bu' he donnea know tha', Meredith, an' all I could think was tha' I'll no' le' this boy grow up without a da. Aye, i's true tha' Oliver had my heart from tha' moment—" Sam turned back to Meredith and, gently, placed his hand on her cheek "—Bu' you had it since I met you in Glasgow, lass. Tha', I promise ye, is the truth."

Meredith's bottom lip was trembling, but the relief on her face was clear. A small smile pulled at the corners of her lips, and she gently nodded. "Thank you...I know that 'talkin' abou' our feelin's an' shite' is not easy for you to do."

Sam snorted at her poor imitation of him. He pulled her to his chest and wrapped his arms around her before he kissed the top of her head. "Meredith, I donnea think ye're damaged. I think ye're an incredibly strong woman...I jus' donnea want ye t' ge' hurt again. An' unless I catch this man, tha' may verra well be a possibility."

Her head turned on his chest, but he felt her nod against him. "Okay...just this once, I will do whatever it is that you need."

Sam didn't know if it was an attempt to ease the situation or his discomfort from being so exposed, but Meredith's comment made him ask, "Will ye, now?"

Whatever his reasons, he got the reaction he was hoping for as Meredith smacked his chest and snickered. "Shut up."

The two of them stood there in the kitchen, chuckling, and neither one wanted to move out of the warm embrace they were in. It wasn't until Meredith lifted her head from his chest that Sam finally looked back down at her and was pleasantly surprised that she had leaned up to give him a gentle kiss on the lips that time.

He didn't want her to just yet, but she pulled back far enough to say, "I love you, Sam. And you'll catch this guy, I know you will."

Her faith and her admission both disarmed and calmed him. He nodded his head. "Aye, I'll do me' best."

Chapter Fifteen

The following day, after a stern lecture from Copper regarding leaving the office with no concern for his safety, it was right back to poking and prodding into every corner of Sam's life, and he was quickly growing weary.

"Can we really be absolutely positive that nobody from Scotland is a suspect?" Julie asked honestly.

"That's highly unlikely, Jules," Rivera answered her. "The Christmas Angel has only been seen in the US and Canada, so how on earth could any of this information have gotten back to Sam's little village?"

"Internet," Simon pointed out.

Dana had been sitting at a nearby desk reviewing as many of Sam's old case files as she could. "From what I can tell, we've got a decent list of potential suspects, aside from your first IA partner, that could have held a grudge enough to do this."

"Speaking of Grayers," Simon chimed in. "His work schedule checked out: He punched in perfectly on time in and out every day that he said he did. And the report from CSU says there is not a trace of any of the girls DNA on his property anywhere, and not one needle could be found."

"What about orders to a florist?" Julie proded.

"Not a one, but I can tell you that he's a regular with his local takeout crew."

"I still think he's our best suspect; you should have *seen* the way he went on about how much he hated Sam. Plus, he's a cop! If anybody would have had access to the information of *exactly* how Daverman killed his victims, it would have been him!"

"How? He was stripped of all his credentials and access codes when he fired, remember?"

Julie eyed Simon with amusement. "Twenty-three years of impeccable service well before we used computers for everything, egg-head. He would have made friends that, I have no doubt, would have been only too happy to help him out."

"But why copy the Christmas Angel?" Dana asked pointedly. "I agree that he's good for this, but of all of the serial killers to copycat and scare this big guy, here, why pick one that he'd never even heard of before? There's easier ways for an ex-cop to get revenge."

Sam had heard enough about Grayers; he didn't deny that his old partner still hated him enough to try and get revenge, but turning into a copycat serial killer? He couldn't fathom it.

"Enough!" He bellowed. "While ye lot are still sittin' here theorizin' abou' every man, woman, an' child I've pissed off, this protégé is still a' large. Le's ge' down t' some real investigatin', aye?"

"What do you think we've been doing all this time, Sam?" Rivera asked, perturbed. "There isn't anyone in Daverman's known circles that we could even try to search for this, and unless you can think of anybody else that is crazy enough to—"

"We go back t' basics an' search the areas where these three—" he pointed to the newest photographs of victims "—were las' seen."

"Except that we, and every cop in those counties, has already done that," Dana pointed out. "And everybody was struck down with a case of see-no-evil, remember?"

Julie walked up and placed her hand on Sam's shoulder. "I know you're sick of this, boss, but combing through your life really is going to be the best thing we can do."

Letting out a frustrated sigh, Sam headed for the elevator. "Then go ahead an' do tha': every inch of me life is in those files. I'm headin' t' Detroit Avenue."

"What's at Detroit Avenue?" Simon asked.

"Christ! I's the las' spot where Chelsea Aspen was seen, ye nance! Read the damn reports!"

***

The bright, warm sunshine made the spring thaw glisten like crystal, but it didn't lessen the chill Sam felt as he walked up and down Detroit Avenue in front of the bar Jukebox, where it was assumed that the victim who looked exactly like his wife was kidnapped from. Instead, he stood silently at the nearest corner and observed his

147

surroundings: The street was lined with parked cars and many people were walking up and down on the sidewalks. There was a nearby gym and a restaurant right next to the bar. *No' a verra secluded place t' kidnap someone,* he thought to himself. He turned the corner and started walking down the next street, which wasn't as populated with businesses and the like, but there were much more secluded spots that Sam could see: a corner parking lot, an outdoor eating area for a restaurant that had been closed because of the weather, and even a garage door with hardly any security system. Sam couldn't see anywhere that looked like a decent kidnapping point for the Angel.

"She would've had t' go with him willingly," he whispered to himself. "Tha's definitely no' his usual trick. So...he's friendly an' charmin' enough fer her t' leave with him bu' doesnea stand out enough t' be recognizable..."

Sam turned around to walk back towards the bar when a familiar, bothersome figure suddenly caught his eye: Across the street, sitting in a dented red car, was none other than the annoying young blogger, Cole Terry. Sam didn't know how long the young man had been sitting there, but it was clear to him that he had been watching Sam's every move. He suddenly started scrambling to get to the driver's seat. Sam's desperate curiosity fueled him, and he didn't waste a moment to leap across the road, yank the door open, and grab Terry firmly by the coat collar. The young man barely had his feet on the ground before Sam shoved him up against the side of the car and growled, "Wha' the hell are ye doin' here, Terry? There's nothin' t' see here, so ye mus' know somethin' abou' wha' we're investigatin'."

"Hey! Hey! Take it easy! I was just...leaving the gym, I swear!"

Even a child could see through the bald-faced lie just from the smell of Terry: not a hint of sweat, rather a cologne that the mildly chilly air intensified.

Not in the mood for his games, Sam growled again. "Donnea play dumb with me today, Terry. I'm no' in the mood. Now I'll ask ye again, wha' the hell are ye doin' here, an' wha' do ye know tha' made ye follow me out here?"

Other than the visible gulp, Cole Terry didn't say anything for a good moment. Sam was just about ready to slam him up against the car again when Terry threw up his hands and spilled his guts. "Okay, okay! You're right! I followed you from the FBI, okay?"

"Why?"

"I, um, saw you talking to my boss at *The Daily*."

Sam raised his eyebrows. "Varnce? Ye work fer Jake Varnce?"

"Yeah...kinda," Terry answered with a shrug.

"I *knew* I saw somebody familiar tha' day. So ye saw me talkin' t' Varnce, an' ye decided t' stalk me an' my team again, is tha' it?"

"No, actually. Well, that is not until Varnce sent Heather Yates out to cover a story that he said was on 71."

"Who's Heather Yates, an' wha' does tha' have t' do with anythin'?"

"She's the on-scene reporter that I get coffee for," Terry answered, the pout in his voice unmistakable. "I've been working for *The Daily* for two years now, and I'm still just the errand boy to a prissy trust fund kid. Well, what was weird about this particular story was that we arrived literally moments after the police did."

"So? Donnea ye reporters have informants an' spies all over the place t' tell ye where t' ge' the next story from?"

"Yeah, but we usually don't arrive until a good while after the cops do. At first, I didn't think too much about it, until I heard through the breakroom gossip that he sent out another reporter to another scene yesterday just like during Christmas. The staff were saying how lucky they were to get the first scoop on the story before our competition did, and they even got there just as the police started pulling up. It just seemed a little weird to me that my boss knew where the juicy stories were before anyone else did. And after I saw you storming out of his office...well, I figured if there was something nuts happening, then you would know about it."

Sam wanted to argue with him that he'd thought wrong and give him a stern warning, but he stopped himself. Route 71 was where Chloe Hale, the first protégé victim, was found. If what Terry was telling him was true, then it was possible that Jake Varnce was getting insider tips to (what he thought) was the Christmas Angel's victims, which meant that Varnce hadn't told Sam the whole truth about anything. Cole Terry, normally a nuisance and an annoying stalking blogger, was suddenly useful to Sam.

"How friendly are ye w' Varnce?"

"Not very. I doubt he even knows my name."

"Bu' ye do know a lot about him?"

"Well, yeah. Any would-be reporter knows about Varnce."

"Wha' abou' his personal habits? Where he goes, wha' he does, who he has lunch with?"

Cole Terry's eyes started to widen in understanding. A thin smile began to form, and he looked around himself before answering, "I think I can find out. But what do I get?"

Sam, finally letting go of Terry's coat lapels, stepped back and answered, "Tha' depends on wha' ye give me."

"I can give you whatever you want, Sam. You know I'm annoying enough." Terry chuckled at his own joke, but quickly cleared his throat when he saw the look on Sam's face. The big man was not amused. "Look, if I know what to look for, I can find it. For example, who it is that you're chasing this time?"

Sam noticed a couple walking along the main road together, hand in hand, eyeing him and Terry suspiciously. Motioning to get inside the car, he followed suit and didn't answer Terry until he was certain that the two of them were truly alone.

"Wha' do ye know abou' Varnce's articles abou' The Christmas Angel?"

"I knew it!" Terry answered excitedly. "I *knew* with how excited Varnce was about these murders, it had to be related to his big story! That's who you're going after now?"

"Aye."

The blogger suddenly furrowed his eyebrows. "Wait a minute...you think Varnce knows about these murders ahead of time because the Angel is telling him?"

"Tha's my hunch."

"Then why hasn't he let the Angel's name be released in the press? He's the expert; he'd know his signature anywhere."

"Because then we'd know t' look closer a' him. He's waitin' till the right time, like when somebody can ge' a detail from the officers."

"Okay, okay, well, if you think he knows the Angel personally, then why don't you go arrest him?"

"Nevar mind tha'; wha' I need from you is t' figure out *how* the Angel an' Varnce are in contact. Ye're gonna' help me, Terry." Sam stared directly at the young man and lowered his voice. "I want ye t' ge' in Varnce's graces; I donnea care how. Follow him, learn everythin' abou' his habits, figure out how he ge's his information, anythin' a' all and then ye report directly t' me an' *only* me. Do ye understand?"

"Yeah, yeah sure. You got it. But...you still didn't answer my question: What'll you give me?"

Sam smirked. "A chance t' never be the coffee boy evar again."

Terry smiled excitedly. "An exclusive? You mean it?"

"Only if ye delivar', an' we catch 'im, understand?"

"Yeah, yeah absolutely! Don't worry, Sam, you can count on me!"

Sam snorted. Exiting the car, he walked away without another thought of Varnce, as he heard Terry drive away. *Well, a' leas' now I have someone on the inside,* he thought to himself. It wasn't much of a lead, but it was something to get started with. That was assuming his hunch was right, and the Christmas Angel was telling Varnce about his victims directly. Which made Sam wonder, *Why would he be callin' attention' t' his murdars jus' t' ge' t' me? He's go' my attention...so why does he want worldwide attention?* The more he thought about what the protégé's motives could be, the more nothing made sense. Shaking himself out of his thoughts, he tried to turn his focus back to anything he could make from the recent abduction site.

Looking all around again, Sam went back to assessing the street: There weren't any traffic cameras or ATMs around, so no chance of getting a direct picture of a car or vehicle. The best he could hope for was an eyewitness hiding somewhere unseen. He started tapping on some windows and doors, but that proved to be just as useless as Simon said it would be: Every single person he talked to insisted that they never saw anything. Well, except for the neighborhood 'psychic' who insisted he could see the ghost of the person Sam was looking for and to tell him she was at peace. It was a maddening search that he kept up for at least three hours, determined to question every living, breathing *thing* he could find.

In a last-ditch attempt for a decent lead, Sam stepped into the bar called Jukebox and started questioning the bartender. Luckily enough, he did recognize Chelsea Aspen, but he told Sam the exact same story he had told the other investigators: It was a busy night, and he poured at least 250 drinks for a couple hundred different patrons. He couldn't remember if he saw her with anybody or not.

Sam was just about to leave when the bartender offered him a free drink for his trouble. With how stressed Sam felt, he wasn't in the mood to say no, and he didn't care that it was only two o'clock in the afternoon.

He asked for one Scotch Whiskey. Then one became two. Then three. Then he'd stopped counting. It took a lot of alcohol for a big and burly man like Sam to get drunk, and he was just starting to feel the enticing waves of warmth coupled with drowsiness he usually felt, when a slightly blurry figure sat down next to him.

Rivera's voice came clearly through the haziness as he said to the bartender, "No more for him."

"I'm amazed he's still sitting upright," the bartender grunted. "He's had six of those in the last hour."

"Yes, thank you," Rivera replied briskly. "Can we have some water, please?"

The bartender put a tall glass of clear liquid in front of Sam and left him alone with Rivera. Sam didn't need to turn his head to know that his young partner was waiting for him to say something; he could feel his eyes boring into him. When it became clear that he would have to make the first move, Sam swallowed the dryness in his throat and said in a hoarse voice, "Nobody saw anythin'. No' the girl, the man with her, no' even a car or van."

"Yeah, Evanston had already told you that before you took off. And now you're getting drunk on the job." Rivera leaned forward onto the bar, pushed the glass of water closer to Sam, and folded his hands together. "I know this case is rattling your cage harder than most, Sam, but you can't let him get inside your head like this. That's what he wants."

"An' how do ye know tha'?"

"Because that's what every serial killer who fixates on somebody wants: to bring the hero down to their level."

Finally, Sam accepted the glass of water and nearly drained it in two swallows. "I'm no' a hero, Rivera."

"You know what I mean."

"Aye, anno wha' ye mean, bu' tha's jus' wha's botherin' me: I cannea think of any reason why the Angel would want t' come aftar me. There has t' be one, an' I'm jus' no' seein' it..."

"Sam, take it from me, you're going to make yourself sick if you spend all of your time fixating on finding a reason why. The reality is, sometimes there isn't any why."

"Aye, anno tha' too... i's jus' convincin' meself tha's the case is the problem." Swallowing the last of the water, he set the glass down and rubbed his temples. He could still feel Rivera staring at him, so he grunted, "If ye have somethin' t' ask me then go ahead an' do it."

"Actually, I have been meaning to catch you alone to ask you this...it's about Robert Grayers."

Sam bristled at the mention of his old IA partner. "Wha' abou' him?"

"Sam...for as long as I've known you, you've always given the impression that your moral judgement trumped that of the legal system...Grayers told me and Julie what he'd done...and I just can't believe that you would turn on your own partner for trying to save his daughter."

Sam, breathing heavily, closed his eyes. "I's complicated."

"When isn't it? ...Look, you turned on your partner for something that you would have done if you had to. You do see why I'm concerned, right?"

Sam scrubbed his face with his hands, but he didn't answer him.

Rivera scoffed. "Come on, I'm your partner. I got your back, so did Grayers. I think I deserve to know the reasons why you'd ignore your own moral code."

"An' I wish I had a good answer for ye, Rivera. Bu' I don't."

"What did he do? Make a pass at Meredith? Say something you didn't like about Oliver? I never pegged you as the type to want petty revenge."

Finally, Sam turned to face his partner and growled, "If ye know wha' good fer ye, drop it an' leave it alone *now*. Now unless ye're here t' tell me ye found somethin', ye bettar go."

The mood in the air instantly shifted; Rivera, in a low and curt voice, said, "If you had your phone turned on, you'd know that another body was found in the Rocky River Reservation. Everyone's in the car, are you coming or not?"

He was buzzed and angry, but the minute Rivera said the word 'body', he was instantly alert. He dropped enough cash on the bar before storming out to the waiting SUV.

Unlike the other victims that were dumped on the side of roads and therefore easy to get to by car, the team had to walk the public trail for about twenty minutes before they got near the crime scene. Despite his early drinking, Sam's senses were on alert as he took in his surroundings. There weren't any security cameras to speak of, other than the ones at the docks where some boats had just been de-winterized and open for public rental, but that was a distance from where the body was found.

There weren't many onlookers this time, given the difficult access of the dump site. First responders were taking witness statements from a young couple who found the body under the trees while they were out for a run through the trail together. Sam did see a small camera crew belonging to *The Daily*, but his earlier informant Cole Terry couldn't be seen among them. Still, he made sure to point them out to the police and told them to get their statements of what they were doing clear out here in the first place. Finally, they came to the body itself, which was left a little more unceremoniously than the others: The victim was still lying on her back, but her arms weren't carefully laid by her side like the others, and the white peony had almost been tossed on top of her. Not to mention there was a very clear shoe impression next to her, which the forensics teams had already set to work making a cast of for tread comparison analysis. Sam, Rivera, Julie, Simon, and Lieutenant Evanston stood out of the way but kept analyzing everything they could see.

"Could this be another copycat of the copycat?" Simon asked first. "I mean, it is pretty sloppy, compared to the other bodies we found."

"More likely he was in a hurry this time," Dana answered. "This may not be a route or highway, but a passing car is less likely to ID you vs. anyone on a walking trail."

"Considering the flower and the size of the needle mark, I agree with the Lieutenant," Julie said next. "It just doesn't make sense why he would leave her here, where he's more likely to get caught. Deep in the woods, I can understand. But right next to a trail where everyone can see? That's ballsy, even for this guy."

"This is still good news for us," Rivera added, the shortness to his tone not unnoticed by anyone. "If he's getting cocky, then he's more likely to make a mistake. First things first: Sam, do you recognize this girl?"

The victim looked like she was in her mid-twenties to her early thirties and completely unfamiliar. Sam shook his head' "No, I don't."

"Then maybe something in her history will stand out. How long has she been dead?"

"With the state of her rigor, I'd say 12-15 hours," the coroner answered. "And you guys should know, I see a tiny bit of dirt under her toenails. I'll make sure some scrapings are taken for you."

Satisfied that, at the moment, there was nothing else to learn about the victim, Sam turned his attention back to the footprints next to it: There were only handful, and they originated from the paved trail, so there was no way to track them and find out where her killer had brought her from. "How'd he ge' her here? The river's too shallow here fer any boat t' come up, an' somebody would've noticed someone carryin' somethin' big enough t' be a body."

"This could be an opportunity kill," Dana answered. "Maybe she was walking or jogging around here and was in the wrong place at the wrong time with the wrong guy."

"That goes completely against Daverman—the Christmas Angel's methods of stalking his victims... maybe the protégé doesn't have as much control as his predecessor did," Julie added. "Rivera's right; this could be a break for us."

Sam nodded, but he took no comfort in everyone's assessments: Another person was dead, and Daverman's protégé was still at large.

Chapter Sixteen

With the discovery of the newest victim, the team were unable to get results from the crime scene for at least three days. The team did everything within their power to ID the woman, but her fingerprints were not in the system, and, after an extensive search of the park, there wasn't any tossed clothing or ID that seemed to belong to her. They were forced to wait for something concrete, and it was driving everyone up the wall. Then the morning came when a tech finally delivered the results of everything: the autopsy, the rape kit, and the rather abundant forensic evidence.

"Bicks confirmed the poison ratios are an exact match the others, but here's a surprise: no signs of sexual assault." Rivera tossed the file on Sam's desk.

"He didn't rape her this time? What does that mean?" Simon asked, perplexed by the news.

"That he couldn't get it up, and that's probably because the scenario was too different," Julie answered. "This was the first body that we found in a park; it probably threw off his game."

Dana, who had been on her phone the whole time while the rest of them talked, barely hung up and joined the conversation. "Officers got an ID while canvassing the pedestrians: Her name is Jeanette Conders. Her friend, Brett Sholby, was supposed to meet her for a run; he ID'd her."

"Did he say if Jeanette usually runs the trail alone?"

"Often, she was preparing for a 5k. The police are going to check out her neighborhood now; hopefully, they'll turn over a bit more and corroborate the friend."

"And in the meantime, I can at least try to see if she's got a connection to our fearless leader," Simon smirked.

While their young companion's fingers flew across his keyboard, Sam kept his focus on the forensics report. Specifically, the shoeprint information. "Accordin' t' the expert, whoever made the shoe impressions is abou' 5'8" an' weighs abou' 130-140 pounds."

"That's about the same description of the impressions found near...Chloe Hale's body," Julie said excitedly. "Well, at least we know for sure that this is the same guy."

Simon stopped typing. "Okay, Jeanette Conders: She's a kindergarten teacher at Westpark Community, and she lives about a block away from the school. Hey, maybe she taught Oliver when he was in kindergarten?"

Sam shook his head. "Olivar went t' Miles Park."

"Okay, um...her spending habits were pretty frugal; but sometimes she went to the Greater Cleveland Aquarium."

"Probably for school trips with the kids," Julie countered. "Next."

"Okay, then, moving on to banks, grocery stores, hair parlors...nothing anywhere close to where you've been, boss."

"I tol' ye; I donnea know the woman. This was a random, convenient attack fer the protégé."

"What's bothering me is why he changed his kill zone in the first place," Dana said. "I mean, he kinda had a good thing going following the Christmas Angel's routine, so what made him switch it up?"

"Considering this was a crime of convenience, it's highly likely that something triggered him, and he just lashed out," Rivera answered her.

"And he happened to be carrying a 16-gauge needle full of cleaning chemicals with him at the time? I'm sorry, Agent, but I don't agree with you; I really think this was done on purpose."

Julie nodded her agreement. "Carrying his weapon of choice *does* signify premeditation...could we be looking at both scenarios together? He went to the park intending to kill someone, and he just waited until the right girl came along, so he could do his thing uninterrupted."

"The lack of sexual activity to the victim suggests that he wasn't in control this time," Rivera countered.

Before Dana or Julie could counter again, Sam's phone started ringing, which earned everyone's attention. It was a number he didn't recognize, so his tone was more gruff than usual when he answered, "Sam McKay."

"It's Cole Terry," said the familiar voice. "And something's up."

Knowing full well why he had given the annoying young reporter his number, Sam felt his blood begin to turn cold as he feared the worst. "Wha' is it?"

"Varnce ordered us out to a house in Pennsylvania on a tip, and we got here just before the cops did and found the body of a really old man. It's really freaky; he's all spread out and there are tons of cut marks on him. Obviously, he didn't do this to himself."

"Where are ye?"

"I saw that we passed a town called New Bedford, the house is deep in the woods, though."

Sam started. "W-where are ye?"

"At a house near a town called New Bedford."

Sam jumped out of his chair and thrust his phone to Simon. "Trace this call, now!"

Simon was startled but acted immediately: He hooked up Sam's phone to his computer and worked his fingers across the board faster than lightening. Within seconds, a familiar address popped up and everyone stared at the screen.

"That's...that's Peter Daverman's house," Julie said.

"Yeah, that's the name we got, too," Terry's voice sounded from the phone. "This guy is really Peter Daverman? The billionaire?"

"You and your crew stay right where you are, Terry," Rivera barked into the phone. "We'll be there as fast as we can, and we're going to have some questions for all of you."

The five of them rushed to the nearest vehicle and, with Rivera driving, sped for New Bedford, Pennsylvania. While the others were going back and forth about how anyone could have gotten near Daverman with the surveillance they've been keeping on him, Sam remained quiet with his thoughts. *Wha' the hell is goin' on? ... Di' Max or Humbar... no, they wouldnea have done this... could they? Maybe this is another message from the protégé.* As they drove, he hoped with all his might that the answer was the latter. Because if it wasn't, then that meant that either his oldest or his newest friend was going to be charged with murder, and there was absolutely nothing he could do about it.

Rivera had barely pulled off the main road towards Peter Daverman's house when the sight of news vans filled everyone's view. Eventually, they made it to the front of the house where the local beat cops were guarding the yellow tape, doing their best to keep the press and a few bystanders away from the scene. All it took was a flash of their badges, and the team was let through, where they were immediately met by a few of New Bedford's Deputies, led by a rather young but sturdy looking man that they could only assume was the Sheriff.

"I'm Sheriff Dan Breecham, can I help you?"

Sam flashed his badge first, and the rest of the team followed suit. "I'm Agent Sam McKay of Ohio's FBI; this is the rest of my team: Rivera, Julie Russell, Simon Abler, an' Lieutenant Dana Evanston of Columbus PD. We're here t' speak t' the first witnesses on the scene, the reporters tha' called in the body."

"Well, my deputies have already taken their statements if you'd like to look those over and save yourselves the trouble of—"

"If ye donnea mind, Sheriff, we'd like t' ge' their accounts ourselves."

"Okay, they're over there away from the rest of the circus. Excuse me, Agents, but is there a reason for the FBI's appearance here? Have you guys seen something like this before?"

"Have you?" Julie asked carelessly.

"Well...no, not in New Bedford. Anyways, I'll take you right over to them."

"Thank you, Sheriff," Rivera answered. "And make sure nobody touches the body; we're going to want to take a look at that, too."

"No problem, my guys are a little too rattled to have done more than look at it for a few seconds before losing their dinner. It hasn't been moved."

"Sam! Guys! Wow, you got here fast!"

While his team groaned to hear the familiar voice of Cole Terry, Sam was more than anxious to speak to him and the rest of his cohorts, who turned out to be a young, pretty woman dressed very smartly and a few guys in jeans and sweatshirts who were obviously camera crew. After directing the others to take everyone aside for an interview, Sam personally handled Cole Terry's statement.

"Alrigh', tell me exactly wha' happened from the moment Varnce tol' ye abou' the lead."

"Okay...I was fetching a smoothie for Madame Yates over there when Varnce came out of his office and said, 'Tip about suspicious crap going down at a billionaire's home in New Bedford; I'll text you the address. Get going before somebody else catches wind of this!' And the next thing I knew, we were piling into the van and driving like maniacs to wherever this place is. Jeb, the camera guy, rang the doorbell, but nobody answered. We had no idea what we were supposed to find, so we just started poking around. About that time, I noticed there wasn't even so much as another car hiding in the bushes near this guy's house. If there was some sort of crazy story going on here, well, you'd at least see some freelance reporters poking around for a lead; my spidey-senses started tingling at that point. Then I heard Heather scream, and we all came running and found this old guy..." Terry's demeanor suddenly shifted; his excited, confident act was immediately replaced by a glossed-over eyes that had Sam more than curious. "He was hanging by his wrists in between two trees, behind the house a little way. Look, I know that's not the Christmas Angel's M.O., I've read every single article by Varnce...I guess I just panicked. I-I'm sorry if I brought you out here for nothing. I just thought...you know, since Varnce heard about it first..."

"Who called 911?"

"I don't know, maybe Scott did. I just thought I better call you, so I moved away so nobody could hear me."

"Di' ye notice anythin' else while ye were pokin' abou'? Any footprints? Tire marks? Anythin' a' all?"

"Um...actually, I did see some footprints over there—" He pointed to the woods.

Sam nodded and patted the young man's shoulder. "Alrigh', we'll take a look. Donnea tell anybody else, aye?"

"Yeah, yeah. I got it."

Not bothering to wait for the others, Sam started wandering the direction Terry had pointed him in. The Sherriff's office had done a good job mucking up the grounds closest to the house, but thankfully they didn't wander too far off, as he was able to find a lone set of footprints near some bushes, just as the young reporter had described to him. With no other footprints surrounding them, it was easy to assume they were made by somebody not a part of the current crowd. He was quickly disappointed to find that these shoe impressions didn't even look remotely close to the ones found near Jeanette's body. His heart sank a little bit: More and more, he suspected that either Humbar or Max might have done this. After calling over a CSU tech to take photos and make plasters, Sam followed the footprints as far as he could find them, which eventually led back to the main road before the path to the house. Unfortunately, with the surrounding locals and news vans, he couldn't search any more without attracting attention. On his way back to the house, he instructed the Sherriff to move the search grid out for another 600 yards (as the footprint path couldn't have been more than 300). While local law enforcement troubled themselves with that task, Sam met up with the rest of the team—time to look at the body of the Christmas Angel.

Careful to not disturb any evidence, everyone walked behind the house and towards the woods. They didn't have to walk very far before they saw more yellow tape surrounding a small patch of trees. Right in the middle of it all was the old, decrepit body of Peter Daverman. He was just as Terry had described to Sam: hanging from his wrists in between two of the closest trees, the lowest branches holding him up, despite his knobby feet still touching the ground below him. Naked from head to toe, the only thing covering up his rawboned body was the congealed blood dripping from the many cuts that were covering him.

"Well, considering his skin is practically blue, I think it's safe to say that he's been out here for a while," Julie said first.

"Look at the cuts on his body," Simon said next. "They look pretty deep."

"And done while he was alive, too," Dana nodded. "Obviously an autopsy will confirm it, but I think we can safely guess that the cause of death was stabbing and bleeding out. Somebody was making a statement, and considering our very short list of people who knew where Daverman lived, I think we can all guess who suspect number one is: the good Doctor Max Darrel."

"And Chief Anthony Humbar," Rivera added.

Dana snapped her attention to Sam's Latino partner, and he felt a curdling in his stomach.

"You really think those guys are capable of something like this?" Simon argued.

"Ace isn't," Dana said very defensively. "He would never shoot a man in cold blood; forget stringing him up and stabbing him to death."

"You all remember how pissed the two of them were when we couldn't do anything else about Daverman? Humbar's a seasoned cop; he could get creative. And let's not forget the fact that Max has a history of getting physical with potential suspects."

Simon, sheepishly, argued, "I dunno man. I don't doubt Dr. Darrel would go rogue and get revenge, but Humbar? Would either of them really go this far to torture a guy living in hospice care?"

"Daverman probably pushed all the buttons the right way; we all know how careful he was with words."

"Yeah...I guess that's possible."

"For Dr. Darrel, maybe. But not Anton," Dana said angrily.

"Hold on guys...look at Daverman's face," Julie noted with an air of disconcert. "Is it just me, or does it look like he's smiling?"

Everyone stopped talking and took a closer look at the dead man's face.

"Oh, that's definitely a creepy-ass smile," Simon shivered. "I'm not sure I want to know the answer to this, but why would he be smiling while somebody is stabbing him to death?"

Rivera answered first. "Because the guy who killed him did him a favor: He was trapped in his own body and unable to keep terrorizing women, but he didn't want to die like an old decrepit man, either. He probably felt this was the death he deserved—one filled with attention—instead of slipping away quietly."

"Or he knew his reign of terror dinnea stop with him," Sam mumbled to himself.

"What was that?"

Sam sighed. "Tha' day I went pokin' around a' the bar where Chelsea Aspen was las' seen, Cole Terry was there. He tol' me Varnce had been gettin' some fishy tips abou' these murdars, an' their trucks were always the firs' on the scene, so I tol' him t' call me if tha' happens again. Tha's why he called me tonight: Varnce go' another fishy tip."

"Okay, so what does this have to do with anything?"

"I'm jus' thinkin' abou' the fact tha' Varnce heard abou' this first, much like the protégé murdars. I cannea help wonderin' if this body is meant fer us."

"Darrel probably called him."

"Bu' why?"

Julie answered, "Well, he did reach out to Varnce before, in order to bring more attention to the Christmas Angel. Maybe he did it again as a poetic ending to the killer."

"Anyways, none of this matters," Rivera said shortly. "This is completely out of our jurisdiction, and I have no doubt that Toronto's police will find Darrel at home with the knife he used to kill the bastard, or Humbar's already burned his clothes. Let's tell the Sherriff what we know and go home."

Angry at how callously Rivera could just throw their friend's names at the local authorities like that, Sam shook his head. "No, I donnea think Humbar or Darrel would do somethin' like this."

"You mean you don't want to admit they're capable of doing something like this."

"Tha's no' it. I wanna be sure of who killed Daverman an' why, an' somethin' abou' this isnea right."

"And you're basing all of this on the fact that Terry called us before the rest of the press knew about it?"

"My gut is tellin' me—"

"To hell with your gut, Sam. What was done to this man was revenge, pure and simple. There isn't any pattern or MO that even *remotely* suggests otherwise. Since nobody else around here has the balls to do it, I'll tell the sheriff who to look at myself." Rivera marched off.

Sam followed him with his eyes and clenched his fists together in rage. Finally, he turned back to Julie and Simon, who were standing in front of him quietly.

"An' you?" He growled, "Ye think this is jus' revenge?"

Simon shifted uncomfortably, but Julie nodded apprehensively. "We've been over every case related to the Christmas Angel; we know the methods he and his protégé used. If there's even a hint of their M.O. here, I don't see it."

"Me neither, boss," Simon agreed. "This whole thing looks pretty sloppy, filled with rage. Everything about the Angel's victims was so meticulous and careful, right down to the last detail. Well, obviously excusing the one we found three days ago. But the point is...yeah, we think Rivera might be right, and the yokels better look into Dr. Darrel... and the Chief. We should go home."

Sam couldn't say a word. Eventually, the other two walked away from the scene and towards the waiting deputies, leaving him and Dana alone with the dead body of Peter Daverman. He looked over. Dana appeared to be as bewildered as he felt: no doubt torn between her loyalty to their old, mutual friend and her duty to bring everyone to justice, no matter how righteous the kill might have been. Eventually, she shook her head in defeat and turned to follow the others. A little nagging voice inside said Sam should be relieved that this heinous serial killer was dead, but it couldn't drown out the other voice that was desperately pleading with him to take over the case. As much as he wanted to, Sam knew that what Rivera said about jurisdiction and lack of clear and present evidence was right. He couldn't touch this murder, no matter how badly he wanted to. Dejectedly, he turned around and started towards the car, just as Rivera finished telling the Sheriff where they should start for Jake Varnce, Daverman's last known nurse Colin Winkley, Chief Anthony Humbar, and Dr. Max Darrel.

The drive back to the office was tense; no one said a word, not even Simon tried to lighten the mood with his sarcastic quips. When the car was parked in the garage, Sam practically ripped his door off the hinges as he got out, anxious to be away from everybody else. Rivera and Dana appeared to share the same attitude, while Julie and Simon just kept their mouths shut. While the four of them headed for the elevators, Sam took a detour and began looking for a place to pace, which ended up being on the other side of the garage in front of the doors to the morgue. Back and forth he stomped, completely unaware of a van backing its way near him. His mind was buzzing with thousands of intangible thoughts that he couldn't begin to piece together, and yet they always came back to the phone call from Cole Terry. He didn't hear the doors to the morgue open, but when he turned on his heel and ran into Bicks, he was finally brought back to the present.

"Christ, Bicks! Cannea a man pace in private?"

"You're the one lurking outside of *my* doors, McKay," the pompous, callous man answered.

Sam immediately took note of the gurney with a zipped-up bag and asked, "Wha's this? Another relative demandin' t' bury their loved one?"

"For once, I'm calling the shots on when to move around the bodies. This is the homeless girl from Pennsylvania; she's been sitting in our freezer for months now. I had to call in a favor with a judge in Pittsburg to order her parents to pick her up before they did anything. They've finally made arrangements to have her moved to Pittsburg."

Sam sighed; he didn't know why, but he stepped forward and pulled down the zipper to take one last look at her.

"You got a thing for dead bodies, McKay? Because Burt here charges the city by the hour."

"Jus'... give me a mo'," Sam retorted and looked at the face of poor Lily Vanderguard. for a moment, he was able to let go of his rage, as he looked over her young face outlined by the body bag: Two parents who were so caught up in their own messes, they didn't care if she was in a morgue with other murderers, let alone one of the Christmas Angel victims. He could already tell the poor thing never had a chance in life. "Well... a' leas' now ye can rest, darlin'. I'm sorry."

Quietly and gently, he zipped the bag back up and watched Bicks and the other man, Burt, load the young teenager's body into the unmarked van. Bicks had already turned around to go back into his morgue, but Sam kept his eyes on the van until the last possible moment, before he went right back to pacing.

Chapter Seventeen

Weeks went by since the night Daverman's body was discovered, and to everyone's surprise, the protégé didn't leave behind another victim. Or, if he did, the body hadn't been discovered yet.

Sam, the team, and the Lieutenant spent all that time focusing their energy on everything that was found with Jeanette Conders: the lack of sexual assault, the footprints, and the obvious change in the attacking grounds. The shoe impressions were the best lead they had. Simon scanned the treads and was able to match them to three different brands of tennis shoes, which the team tried to trace, starting from the manufacturer all the way to the stores where they were distributed. Unfortunately for them, there wasn't anything particularly unique about the shoes, so that proved to be a dead end more than a lead.

Next, they focused on the crime scene: They wandered north and south, east and west for roughly 600 yards from where Jeanette's body was found, trying to find any whisper of a hint as to why the protégé would lash out the way he had, or why he broke his routine. This also turned out to be a dead end.

Finally, they turned to the information about Jeanette Conders herself: They re-interviewed her neighbors, peers, and coworkers. They asked the same questions and got the same answers: She didn't have anyone special in her life; her passions were her students and running. The neighbors said she was a nice, quiet lady who always said hello whenever they saw her, and they never had an issue with her. Every one of the kids she taught, and their parents, absolutely loved her. In fact, the entire kindergarten class was devastated to learn that Miss Jeannie wasn't going to teach them anymore.

The more they found out about the park victim, the less they understood about the protégé. In a desperate attempt to find an answer, everyone started to wonder if the protégé was planning on completely changing his methods and finding his own signature, one that the Christmas Angel hadn't taught him. One that he could make his very own.

During all this time, Sam was unable to get the site of Daverman's body out of his mind; every day that he tried to do his job, at least twice he would think about why the original Christmas Angel was killed. Every time he did, his gut would nag him that there was a piece of information there that could be helpful. Finally, he couldn't stand the nagging anymore. One morning, he arrived early to work and made for the morgue, intent on asking Bicks for his help.

Sam walked through the doors to the ice-cold room and saw the lead coroner had a fresh body on the table, obviously with the intent to begin a new autopsy. Before the man could pick up his scalpel, Sam cleared his throat to make his presence known.

Bicks looked over his shoulder. "Agent McKay. Whatever it is that you want, it'll have to wait."

Sam smirked. "Ye mentioned three weeks ago tha' ye called in a favor w' a judge in Pittsburg, so ye've go' ties in Pennsylvania?"

"Yes," Bicks nodded, the scalpel in his hand.

"The autopsy results fer a corpse tha' was discovered three weeks ago should be in the system by now, right?"

"That depends entirely on how backlogged the county where the body was found is. If it was found somewhere, say like New York, I wouldn't be surprised if an autopsy hasn't even been thought of yet. For Pennsylvania, they typically take 8-12 weeks before the report is finalized, depending on how backlogged they are. Of course, you would know all of this, so why don't we get directly to the point, and you just tell me what you want? Because, obviously, you're not going to let me do my job until your curiosity is satisfied."

"The body I'm interested in was found in Lawrence County, an' I cannea wait five more weeks fer a result."

Bicks sighed in frustration; setting down his scalpel, he ripped off his gloves and retrieved a cell phone from his pocket. Sam watched as he pressed a few buttons and held the phone to his ear. "Jaimie, It's Judd Bicks. ...Yes, it has been a while. ...Well, I've got a pushy agent here who wants to know where you're at with—" he looked at Sam for a name, if he had one.

"Peter Daverman," he supplied.

"The corpse of Peter Daverman. ...Really? Okay, I'm sending him your way. ...Agent Sam McKay. Don't worry, he'll be sure to bring his ID. ...Thank you, best to Harry." Bicks hung up. "Peter Daverman's autopsy is scheduled in two hours at the Lawrence County coroner's office. If you hurry, you might just make it."

Sam smiled. Rushing out the door, he called back, "Thank ye, Bicks, ye're pure dead brilliant!"

"Uh-huh," the coroner mumbled after him.

Sam had his lights flashing the entire way to the Pennsylvania coroner's office. He knew that Copper, and no doubt Rivera, would give him hell for his sudden and completely unsanctioned departure, but he couldn't let this go until he was absolutely certain that Daverman had nothing more to tell them, no matter what it was. And what better way for him to be absolutely sure there wasn't anything else than to witness the actual autopsy? But he knew he couldn't press his advantage anymore after this. So, for the entire drive, he kept telling himself over and over, "If there's nothin' fishy abou' Daverman's body, then ye le' this go once an' fer all. Tha's it, tha's the end of it."

He pulled into the parking lot of the Lawrence County coroner's office with just enough time to flash his badge and get to the basement. On the autopsy table was the old, decrepit body of Peter Daverman, and a tall, middle-aged woman with dark, curly red hair and a scalpel in her hand stood over him.

"You must be Agent Sam McKay," she said rather cheerily, with a heavy southern drawl. "I'm Dr. Jaimie Heath. You made it just in time for the big show."

"Hallo, Dr. Heath," Sam nodded, taking a seat on a nearby chair and catching his breath. "Thank ye fer allowin' me t' come, I know this is completely against protocol."

"Boy, you're a *long* way from home, aren't you, sweetheart? Anywho, it's no trouble at all. Actually, this is kinda exciting for me. I've performed plenty of autopsies before, but I can't say I remember anyone having a special interest in one the way you do. You'll have to tell me the whole story. If you legally can, of course. Well, here we go!"

Sam watched with awe as the good doctor began her work, and he had to admit that he was impressed with how skillfully and gracefully she moved with her knife. While more than once he had to turn away from the sight of her removing certain organs and sawing through bone, he did his best to keep a careful watch of everything that she did and documented. Even though he kept his phone on silent, he could feel the vibrations in his pocket as it was, no doubt, somebody from the team calling him, demanding to know where he was. He had no doubt that Simon would track his location and inform the others that he was in Pennsylvania, so he just let it keep going to voicemail.

It only took a half hour before Dr. Heath set down her scalpel and looked up at Sam. "Well, sweetheart, I'm in the nitty-gritty. You wanna' come over and take a look?"

"I'm good, thanks," Sam nodded. "I would appreciate the quick version."

"Then I assume you're not too interested in exactly which stab wound killed him," she smiled. "Just the side notes, you got it. Well, it was a six-inch serrated knife that killed him. And I'm willing to bet from what I found in his stomach it was most likely a steak knife."

Sam furrowed his eyebrows. "Wha' makes ye say tha'?"

"Oh, this poor devil had a good last meal: I found steak, potatoes, string beans, and red wine."

Sam nearly fell off his chair. "Wha'? Are ye positive of that?"

"Oh, absolutely. He was killed right after dinner, nothing had time to digest yet. And I've raised five babies, Agent McKay, I know what chewed up food looks like better than most."

Sam laughed. Searching his brain, he knew he heard those exact same stomach contents before very recently. Standing up, he paced the room back and forth as he went over each and every victim they had come across in the past six months. He stopped pacing, and his head snapped back up: He remembered that Lorraine Wyatt had eaten that exact meal before she was killed. "Christ! …Ma'am, I know ye're no' supposed t' release anythin' until the report is finalized, bu' would ye mind printin' me a copy of yer initial findin's? I need t' show these t' my superior, if I'm gonna' be able t' move forward in my investigation."

"No problem, sugar," Dr. Heath smiled. Ripping off her gloves, she walked over to a computer on a nearby desk, tapped a few keystrokes, and Sam heard a printer warming up. There were only four pages, but the lady coroner signed the bottom of every page, and even went as far as to highlight the stomach contents, "Since this part is so important to you," she said airily.

"Thank ye!" Sam exclaimed. "Ma'am, ye jus' cracked open my case. May I give ye a hug?"

"I'm from the south, honey, you better!"

Again, Sam laughed, gave the funny woman a quick embrace, and took off like a shot. Just as he had raced the whole way to Lawrence County, he raced the whole way back to Cleveland. A quick look at his phone showed him that he had at least six missed calls, and at least one came from every member of his team. Exhilarated, he called the first number on the list back, which happened to be Julie.

"Jesus, Sam! Where have you been?!" The young lady practically shouted, though the relief in her voice was evident. "We've been trying to get a hold of you all morning; hell; we were just about to go break into your apartment and make sure you weren't dead, before Simon said you're in Pennsylvania?! What are you—"

Interrupting her, Sam exclaimed, "We need t' reopen Lorraine Wyatt's case! Her husband dinnea kill her!"

***

The minute he was back on the third floor at headquarters, Sam wasted absolutely no time in marching straight past everyone and practically ripping down all the photographs of the protégé's victims from the board, but he left the segment of the protégé on the far right alone. His team, Lieutenant Evanston, and even Copper (who had come over after Sam called Julie) either protested or watched with curiosity at his movements, but he didn't stop until he had finished: Lorraine Wyatt's photograph was back up on the board, along with the important pieces of information they knew about her case. Next to her mini-profile, in the middle, was written "Peter Daverman," and what they knew about him was listed underneath as well.

"Does anybody want to explain to me what the hell this giant lug is getting at?" Dana asked in annoyance.

Pointing to the far-left side of the board at the picture of Lorraine Wyatt, Sam began his onslaught of a theory. "Lorraine Wyatt's murder was staged. Because of the differences in MO, she appeared t' be a copycat of the Christmas Angel: a white rose instead of a peony, the wrong sized needle t' the heart, an' even the poison ratios were all wrong. Further, the other victims were nearly starved t' death, makin' them easy t' rape an' inject the poison into their

170

hearts. Lorraine Wyatt's las' meal was steak, potatoes, green beans, an' red wine. She was also eight weeks pregnant when she was killed, an' she was kept in a freezer fer five years before we found her, staged t' look exactly like the victims of the Angel."

"No offense here, boss, but didn't we already know all of that?" Simon asked first.

Ignoring him, Sam then pointed to the middle of the board. "Peter Daverman: psychologically, he's a textbook example of a serial killar, an' every single thing we know abou' him proves tha' he's the Christmas Angel: the use of needles, his usin' an' abusive mothar, the greenhouse full of white peonies, an' even the travel timelines indicate he was somewhere *near* the deaths or disappearances of the victims from 1982-2018 in the US an' in Canada. Bu', we know tha' he's physically incapable of committin' the murdars of the las' seven victims we've found in Ohio."

"Because somebody else was copycatting Daverman," Julie said plainly. "A protégé took over his work for him, so he's still been killing by proxy."

"Then we find ou' Daverman was killed in wha' appears t' be an act of revenge: He was tortured an' eventually died from multiple stab wounds. Bu', accordin' t' the initial findin's of Lawrence County's coroner, Dr. Jaimie Heath, he had an' excellent meal before he died: steak, potatoes, green beans, an' red wine." Sam handed the coroner report over to Copper, who had been sitting quietly while listening to his explanation. "I witnessed the autopsy meself, as ye all were able t' guess."

"So, both of them ate at the same steakhouse before they died?" Dana asked, rather annoyed. "What does that have to do with anything?"

Finally, Sam pointed to the last part of the board where was written 'The Protégé.' Picking up an eraser, he erased the name and wrote in its place, 'Enemy of Daverman.'

"The girls in December were no' proxy killin's; they were messages. This man, this enemy, has replicated every part of the Christmas Angel's signature w'out missin' a single detail, right down t' the way Daverman would position the bodies t' represent the points of a pentagram, an' all within the dates of the winter solstice. These were perfect copycats: absolutely no' feelin' t' them the way Daverman would have enjoyed wha' he was doin'. If this was truly the work of a protégé, he would have left *something* of his own signature behind. No, he was tryin t' tell Daverman tha' he was comin' for him. An' tha's why he would drop a tip w' the reporter tha' named him, because he knew he would run the story an' Daverman would hear abou' It."

"Boss, Daverman has a list of enemies at least a mile long, and we've already looked into every single one of them. There's absolutely nothing that suggests any of them are capable of foul play. Well, at least none of them seem to be as smart as you think this guy could be."

Sam went back to the picture of Lorraine Wyatt. "Tha's because we're no' gonna' find 'im in Daverman's known circles. No, Lorraine holds the key t' findin' this man. Think abou' it, if ye wanted t' make sure nobody could find ye, bu' there's one person in yer life tha' knows ye verra well, ye'd have t' ge' rid of them. How? Ye'd dispose of a body somewhere or *some way* tha' couldnea or wouldnea be traced back t' ye. Now, ye could jus' dispose of the body where nobody could ask any questions, bu' ye run the risk of eventually somebody findin' it. So, the next step is through a patsy, an' in this case, the patsy is Trevor Wyatt.

"Lorraine's ex-husband is the perfect candidate for her murder: He's cold, calculating, an' a complete arsehole. The end of the marriage was messy; Lorraine had signs of marital abuse, an' she was sleepin' w' somebody else an' go' pregnant. Surely, tha' would've made her husband angry enough t' kill 'er, an' no' knowin' w' t' do w' her body, he holds her in a freezer until the right time t' ge' rid of her. Considerin' the media hype abou' the return of the Christmas Angel, wha' bettar way t' ge' rid of her than make her look like a victim of a serial killar still a' large!"

Sam stepped away from the board. "Bu', if ye're the enemy of a serial killer, an' ye've been clevar enough t' no' be caught yet, then ye'd revel in yer pride an' take it a step further w' an ingenious plan: Ye'd stage the murder of somebody ye'd want t' ge' rid of t' look like an' obvious copycat, even plantin' the righ' evidence in the righ' places, an' therefore the police would go aftar the person who obviously wanted Lorraine gone: the abusive ex-husband."

Rivera, Julie, Simon, and Dana stood there completely dumbfounded. Sam looked over to Copper, who appeared to have finished looking over the autopsy report of Peter Daverman, and was seriously considering everything Sam had to say.

"You got all of this just because they had the same last meal?" Rivera asked skeptically.

Sam shook his head. "No' jus' tha': Lorraine Wyatt's grandmother, Mae, helped us uncover who the real Angel was because of her history. Wha' are the odds tha' Daverman's enemy dinnea use her granddaughtar fer the same reason? An' when she was no longar useful, he killed her an' saved her body fer a rainy day, when his plan was ready."

"But if his plan was just to kill Daverman, why didn't he go after him first?" Simon asked.

"To scare the shit out of him," Julie answered.

"Aye," Sam nodded. "Perhaps. Daverman targeted his victims for the specific purpose of completin' his ritual. The women we found in December were targeted t' le' Daverman know tha' he was bein' hunted. An' now tha' we know this, I think we'll find a deepar connection than we have before. An' by goin' deepar into Lorraine's life, we'll find the man behind I' all."

"Do you think he's the one that got her pregnant multiple times?"

"Aye," Sam answered quickly.

"Then what was with the three lined up bodies and the park girl?" Simon asked next.

"To throw us off the scent," Rivera answered quickly; there was still some malice in his voice, but Sam was relieved that he believed his theory.

"An' because we interrupted the final point of his ritual: killin' Daverman. We found four girls, only four points t' the pentacle. Daverman was intended t' be the fifth, an' we stopped i' from happenin' when we go' involved. Bu' when we were convinced tha' he was targetin' me, we took our eyes off Daverman, an' tha' gave his enemy time t' go in an' finish wha' he started. An' the fourth body, Jeanette Conders, was jus' another false trail."

Everyone turned their attention to the director. The fact that Copper had yet to say one word during his entire explanation worried Sam a little: Quiet and reserved as she was, he could tell that she was angry with him for going this far out on a limb without going through proper channels. He didn't think it would influence her decision. He knew that she trusted his instincts, but he was definitely going to hear something about this, and that wasn't a comforting thought.

When the director set the paperwork on the table and nodded her permission, Sam thought he might pass out from relief.

"Reopen the investigation of Lorraine Wyatt; I will inform Mr. Wyatt's lawyer that he may, or may not, be exonerated from a murder charge. McKay, my office. Now."

Sam knew the reprimand of his career was coming, but he didn't really care at this point. Finally, they were on the right trail to catching the real serial killer; he could feel it in his gut. He followed Copper all the way back to her side of the building without a word. Her right-hand man, Evan Dower, looked as though he wanted to say hello, but he quickly stopped himself before he could. Sam could tell Copper must have been *really* angry to have stopped her bubbly assistant from saying anything to him.

Sam barely stepped inside of her office before the doors behind him were closed.

"I didn't think I would ever have to explain to you of all people why there are protocols in place: First of all for your safety, and for the safety of your family. Do you realize that what you did not only—"

"Copper, I only—"

"I am the one talking here, *Agent*," Copper said sternly, uncharacteristically reminding him that she was his superior. Even Sam had to admit that he felt a twinge of fear by the way the matriarch held herself. "You are listening. What you did is not only a reflection of me; it reflects on this entire office. I shouldn't have to remind you that you are not the only person here that has heinous cases fall on their desks. *Everyone* in this building is trying to catch one son of a bitch or another. And stunts like yours give the Attorney General a reason to have us investigated, possibly even shut down. Law enforcement is shorthanded enough. And have you considered what would have happened if something had happened to you on the way to Lawrence County? What if you are still the target of this man, and he stopped you on the way? How the hell would your team know where to look for you? What would I have to tell your wife and kid if we couldn't find you? Did you even stop for one moment to consider these things before you just took off this morning?"

Sam couldn't speak; Copper's words hit exactly where they were meant to hit, and he was very quickly cut to the core by them.

"I didn't think so. And, what's more, I recently found out that this isn't the first time in this investigation that you've broken the rules. Obviously, nothing too dangerous that would merit punishment, otherwise I would have heard about it before now, but your behavior since taking over these cases has been nothing short of abominable. On top of all that, you should know that every protocol you broke this morning is grounds for suspension. ...However, true to your tenacious nature, you were able to find what everyone else was unable to see. And, true to *my* nature, you know that is the very thing I value about you as an asset to this office. But I cannot in good conscience believe that you won't do something this reckless again, Sam. At least not without your word that you won't." Copper stood directly in front of him and waited.

Ashamed, he nodded. "Aye, Belinda, I promise: Ye have my word tha' I'll nevar follow up on a dangerous lead without followin' protocol again."

She crossed her arms and maintained eye contact, seemingly weighing his words on their validity. Finally, she said, "You may move forward with re-opening Lorraine Wyatt's case, and I will have the body of Peter Daverman and all information pertaining to his murder transferred to us. Find the man that killed them and these other victims, and we will *all* work together to stop him. Understood?"

Sam nodded, "Yes, ma'am."

"Good. You are dismissed."

Sighing in relief, he turned to go when Copper stopped him once more.

"Sam? ...Take it from a person with experience, do not give a killer access to your head, or they will consume you."

Her strange comment made him stop for more than a moment, curious to push for a reason why she would say something like that to him. But between the harsh words she had railed on him and the way she had turned back to her usual pile of paperwork, he knew he wasn't welcome to ask any questions. He kept his curiosity to himself and headed back to the third floor, where his team was working harder than ever. Although his pride was wounded, that didn't stop him from working with just as much zeal as the others.

Chapter Eighteen

The entire team split up to tackle different angles of proving Sam's theory: finding a connection between the four girls and Daverman. Simon dug deeper into all their digital fingerprints while Sam, Julie, and Rivera split up to personally re-interview the families again. The investigation was long, arduous, and even absurd at some points, but the results were worth the effort with every victim:

1) Chloe Hale's connection was through her brother Mitch, who admitted that his biological mother Gillian Usgord had been harassing him for needles, and that was what the fights the neighbors heard were about. He had assumed they were for her fixes, but the junkie mother admitted she had been selling the needles to 'some old guy' for years. When they showed her the picture of Peter Daverman, she confirmed that was him.

2) Lily Vanderguard, the teenaged runaway's connection was through her father. Mr. Vanderguard not only worked for the company Peter Daverman was using to handle his investments, he was his direct stockbroker.

3) Catherine Simms was Peter Daverman's attorney's old secretary, but she had left the firm four years prior.

And finally, victim 4) Rachel Wiley was harder to pinpoint, but she was a cashier from one of the dozens of companies that Peter Daverman invested in. Upon further digging, Simon was able to uncover that Daverman visited the particular store where Rachel worked frequently when he was able to walk without hospice assistance.

Every girl was connected to Peter Daverman in obscure and difficult-to-see ways, and the only person who would have really known it was Daverman himself. Sam's theory was correct: Peter Daverman was the real target; the four victims before him were warning shots. And this added more weight to his deduction that

Lorraine Wyatt would help uncover the identity of who murdered the serial killer.

From the moment they were positive that Lorraine was the key, the entire team set their sights on uncovering her past: Simon obviously working his magic on the computer to try and uncover her movements from five years ago, Sam had declared that he would re-interview the grandmother for more detailed information about Lorraine's social life, and Julie and Rivera were given the task of talking to her old boss at the mom-and-pop hardware store.

The owner, a pot-bellied old man with a thick grey mustache, remembered Lorraine very well and wasted absolutely no time in unleashing his gripes he'd been holding onto for five years.

"That girl was one of the laziest employees I have ever made the mistake of hiring."

"So why did you?" Julie asked.

"Her grandmother is an old friend of mine; she's the one who convinced me to give Lorraine a job. I figured I'd have her stock a few shelves, maybe greet people at the door; it couldn't hurt. But she'd always be on her phone when she was supposed to be working. Heck, she quit the day I threatened to fire her."

"Really? Did she say why?"

"Something about a man who really loves her and will take care of her; she didn't need this job anyway. Some crap like that."

Rivera and Julie looked at one another before Rivera turned back to the owner and asked, "Please, Mr. Gordy, try to think and be as specific as possible."

The owner sighed and shrugged his shoulders. "Um...she was standing over there, near the table saws. She was supposed to be stocking the aisle...I caught her on her phone, told her I'd had enough of the screwing around on the job and that I didn't care if her grandmother begged. If she couldn't do her job, then I was going to fire her. Hey, I don't need lazy employees, agents. And I've never had to give any of the people who worked for me more than one warning. That girl looked up from her phone and said...I think she said that she didn't want this stupid job anyway, that while I'm still peddling power tools, she'll be traveling across Europe with her wonderful boyfriend. Then she threw her name badge on the floor and walked out."

"Did she ever give any specifics about this boyfriend? Maybe there was somebody here she liked to talk to?"

"I don't think I ever saw her looking at anything but her stupid phone... but I think I did see her chatting with a girl... Fiona sometimes. She was a cashier for me, but she left a few years back when she started taking college courses full-time."

"We're going to need her last known address, please," Julie asked.

Fortunately, Mr. Gordy was a hoarder of tax records, dating back as far as 20 years, so tracking down Fiona Sharpe was easy. Unfortunately, Fiona's memory of Lorraine was virtually the same as his: The girl was always on her phone, and Fiona never actually saw the guy; she'd only ever heard of him. Considering there didn't appear to be anyone else in Lorraine's life who knew much of anything, Julie and Rivera decided it would be best to go back to the office.

Sam returned just as empty-handed as they did: As far as Mae was concerned, her granddaughter was perfect and couldn't do anything wrong. But, neither did she know of any friends or boyfriends that her granddaughter associated with, other than her 'horrible ex-husband Trevor.' She did, however, confirm that Lorraine loved to spend almost every second of her life on her phone. So, any hope of tracking down her movements was left to Simon, whose only comment was it wouldn't be much of a challenge.

"Thankfully this was only five years ago, so her thumbprint in the dataverse shouldn't be too hard to find," the young, lanky man said giddily, his fingers flying across his keyboard.

"If this guy really is as smart as we think he is, he's probably already destroyed her phone," Rivera said, the doubt in his voice clear. "Hell, maybe he even wiped it."

"After all this time, meat-sicle, you still think I need the phone to do my thing? Don't you pay attention? I can get enough from her phone number just fine. And I highly doubt that we'll run up against any encryption problems. Any time she used her phone, it had to ping off a nearby cell tower. So, I can, at the very least, triangulate her movements during those times."

"Can ye tell us where she was when she used i' the verra las' time?"

"Please, that's child's play. ...Okay the very last call I've got from her is November 23rd, 2016, and it looks like it was to her grandmother."

"That's consistent with what Mae's told the authorities," Julie said.

"Yeah, and the call bounced off cell-towers in...Youngstown. Give me a minute to narrow down...I think she was going across McKelvey Lake when she made the call. I can only narrow the area down to half a mile, and most of it is the water."

Rivera sighed. "Well, at least there won't be a ton of ground we need to cover...we just might need to go swimming today, too."

"What do you mean?" Simon asked.

Sam answered him. "If tha's Lorraine's las' known spot, then perhaps tha's nearby where she was murdared."

"And if it wasn't, maybe we'll be able to find the cell phone," Julie added up. Turning to Simon, she nudged him. "You can't get *everything* from the dataverse, the phone might be able to give you a little more than you can get your hands on."

"Finding an intact phone after five years? I hope you came back clean on the last drug test, Jules," Simon teased her back. "But, if you do happen to find even a piece of the phone, then yeah I could do something with it."

"Then ye know exactly wha' t' look fer," Sam smiled. "So ye're comin' w' us."

Everyone but Simon smiled and headed for the elevators. The young man didn't hesitate to whine, "More field work? I'm not the field work guy! I'm the computer guy!" but nobody paid him any mind as they made their way to the garage.

An hour and a half later, the team was walking all along Jacobs Road through McKelvey Lake looking for anything that could resemble a crime scene, or a piece of an old cellphone. The bridge through the lake was nearly a mile long, and there was plenty of evidence to be had: cigarette butts, bottles, and various trash had been tossed by litterbugs a-plenty and could be easily found on both sides before even getting to the water. Sam and the others didn't dare to write off a piece of it, just in case there was at least one hint of DNA belonging to their killer on something. Once they finished with the actual road, they moved on to the bits of land connecting the bridge on either side: Sam and Julie on the north end and Rivera and

Simon on the south end. They searched and searched for hours, and Sam was starting to worry that the killer might have been smart enough to take the phone with him after all, if he didn't throw it in the lake itself, then it certainly would have been long gone.

"Guys! Northwest of the bridge, I've found a phone!" Julie's voice rang loud and clear through the walkie.

While the other two would have to drive back over, Sam ran to the other side where Julie was and practically shouted with relief: It was half-buried in rocks and dirt and cracked completely beyond usability, but Julie had found an old iPhone 6. Sam didn't want to convince himself that it was Lorraine's phone, but considering the age, he was more than hopeful. The two of them had just finished taking all the pictures they needed to document the find, just as Rivera and Simon pulled up.

"Huh, what do you know!" Simon said first.

"I'll be damned," Rivera nodded his agreement.

Gloves on, Sam gingerly lifted the phone from its long resting place and placed it in an open evidence collection bag. "Simon, I want ye t' handle the processin' of this phone personally: If ye even smell Lorraine Wyatt on here, ye le' me know. Understood?"

"Of course, boss," he smiled. "I'll start with the photos. If we were this lucky to find a five-year-old phone, maybe we'll be even luckier, and Lorraine took a picture of this mystery boyfriend."

***

Anything that Simon could get from the cracked, weather-worn, and otherwise completely destroyed phone was going to take time. And, considering it was the end of the day, and there weren't any other leads to follow-up on, Sam declared that everyone else could go home. Simon was the only one to complain that he had more work to do, but with one stern look from Sam, he quickly went back to pulling everything that he could from the damaged SIM card.

Since the night Sam and Meredith had a true heart-to-heart, the family dinners were becoming more and more frequent. Since Sam was off work on time, he invited Meredith to his apartment, for a change. Oliver was just getting settled in as the school year was starting to come to a close. She stated that she would be a little late but agreed all the same.

Sam decided to do something simple that night for dinner and made shepherd's pie, one of his and Oliver's favorites. Sam knew it would take some time to cool, which would give Meredith enough time to get there. Sure enough, twenty minutes after he pulled the casserole out of his oven, Meredith came through the door and immediately commented on how good everything smelled. As their arrangement for whoever wasn't making dinner, she had dessert in hand: a small strawberry shortcake from the local grocer. Oliver was more than happy to start digging in the moment his mother walked through the door, and Sam had to remind the young man to wait until everyone was at the table.

The evening was calm and relaxed. Sam and Meredith kept prodding Oliver about when he would finally bring Karliegh over for dinner or games so they could at least meet her, but the teenager would do everything that he could to avoid answering the question.

Suddenly, Sam's phone pinged with a text from Simon which read:

The SIM card was too badly damaged to get much, but it's definitely Lorraine's phone.

Sam sighed and texted back:

Did you get any pictures or something useful?

(...) Most of the pictures are selfies, no boytoy. There is a couple of a house. I'll send the best one to you.

A few seconds later, a picture of an old house that had obviously lacked care came through on Sam's phone. It didn't look particularly special; he could think of a few neighborhoods with houses similar to this one, even in the same condition. It was a clue, but he had no idea where to even start looking for more information on it.

Meredith nudged his rubs with her elbow. "Hey! You're the one that put the 'no texting during family dinner' rule in place, hypocrite! Put your phone down!"

He chuckled. "Aye, sorry abou' tha'. I's work stuff."

"Doesn't matter; no texting during family dinner, Dad!" Oliver followed up, the sarcasm thick in his voice.

Sam quickly texted Simon back a thank you, told him to go home, and that they'd figure out what to do next in the morning before putting the phone back in his pocket.

Once dinner was over, it was Oliver's turn to clean up, and Sam was free to keep staring at his phone while Meredith picked a movie to watch. He couldn't see any defining landmarks or shrubbery; it was just a house that Lorraine had chosen to take a selfie in front of. It was obvious the house was important by the way she framed the selfie to include more of the house than herself, but for the life of him, Sam couldn't think of a reason why she would do that. They already ran down the apartment she was supposed to be renting with a friend when she moved out from her grandmother's house. Not only was it a false story; it was deep in the city with hardly any forested areas nearby. This house had a yard and was surrounded by tons of trees, and from what he could tell, there was plenty of space between this house and any neighbors, assuming it was in a neighborhood.

He had started to formulate a plan that he and the team would search the area where the apartment was for this house, just in case it was nearby, when Meredith leaned over his shoulder, surprising him.

"Work will still be there in the morning, Sam. Come on, I've picked an old Cary Grant film tonight."

"Awe, Mom! Come on!" Oliver whined. "Do you really have to pick the old stuff?"

"Oh, be quiet; it would do you some good to see classic cinema for a change."

Sam tried to put the case from his mind, but he just kept thinking about it. It was bizarre; what could be so special about a house that the victim would purposely take a photograph of it? If it was meant to be a gift, Lorraine's personality seemed like the type to appreciate new things, not run-down old ones. But what was even more troubling was the fact that he didn't even know where to start looking for it. Looking back at Meredith, he ventured, "Darlin', can ye tell me if ye recognize any areas where a house like this would be?"

She mocked an annoyed sigh. "If I look, will you promise to put the phone away for the rest of the night?"

"Aye, ye have my word," he smiled.

She rolled her eyes in return and took the phone from his hand, studying the photo. After a few moments, the relaxed look in her face suddenly shifted to slightly panicked. Sam noticed.

"What? Wha' is it?"

"I...I know this house..." she said quietly. "I...Oliver, honey, I need you to go to your room for a few minutes, please?"

"Why? What's going on?"

"Now, Oliver," Meredith answered sternly. "And turn on your music or something. Please don't argue with me."

The young man, thankfully, sensed the panic in his mother's voice and did as he was instructed, making sure to close the door behind him with an audible click. Meredith, her hands shaking, took a seat in the chair next to Sam. Her eyes never left the phone.

Sam watched her intently, his worry intensifying. He could only think of one moment in his ex-wife's life that had her this worried, and he feared the worst. Doing his best not to jump to conclusions, nor jump all over her for an answer, he waited until she looked settled enough to answer his questions before he gently probed, "Meredith?"

Her head snapped up at his voice. "Sam...this house...I was...I was attacked at this house."

"Ye mean—"

"Yes," she nodded almost violently. "This is where I was raped 16 years ago."

Sam felt as though the rug had been pulled out from under him.

"Ye—are ye absolutely sure?"

Tears were brimming in her eyes. "Yes, Sam, I'm sure. Trust me, you never forget where the most...horrible moment of your life happened."

Sam gulped. "Alrigh', I believe ye."

"How did you find this? Are you investigating this place? What happened here? Is this girl another victim? Oh my god, does this have to do with that guy that you think is targeting us?!"

Before she could get too carried away, Sam took her hands in his and clutched them tightly. "Meredith, ye know I cannea tell ye anythin' in the middle of an investigation. I donnea want ye t' worry...bu' I need ye t' tell me everythin' ye know abou' this house."

The alarm in her face intensified, but Sam kept going.

"We havenea been able t' find any leads, an' I donnea know the firs' thing abou' this place or why i's so important. Perhaps ye migh' be able t' help."

She was shaking now, her breathing erratic. "Sam, I can't—"

"I'm no' askin' ye abou' the nigh' ye were attacked, luv...I donnea think it'll come t' tha'. I jus' need ye t' think abou' the house..."

It took a moment, but she straightened her shoulders and nodded, taking a deep breath to calm herself. "Okay, okay...I don't know how helpful I'll be, here, though. All I did was conduct the open house before I...I think it was the first time the house was being shown."

"Wha' abou' the owner?"

"I never met the owner; the house was owned by the firm I worked for...Bennel and Fitz, out of Youngstown."

Something in the way she said their names had Sam's attention, like she blamed her old bosses for what happened to her. Not that he blamed her for the correlation, but he made a mental note of the peculiarity before he pushed further.

"Okay, bu' ye must've had a chance t' look around before the open house. Di' ye notice anythin' peculiar? Anythin' a' all tha' looked like i' dinnea belong?"

She shook her head emphatically, her hands wrapping around her middle. Between her body language and the hazed look in her eyes, Sam could tell that she was starting to spiral out of control, and he wouldn't get any more out of her at the moment. He immediately pulled Meredith in for a tight hug. Eventually, she relaxed in his arms before her body began to shake, the sobs against his shoulder soaking through his clothes. Sam didn't feel any more in control than she did, but he kept a firm and gentle hold on her while he soothed, "i's alrigh', luv... i's alrigh'..."

***

Everyone was already at the office and, from what Sam could see, they were scrolling through photographs of old houses in the entire state of Ohio trying to find a match to the one on Lorraine's phone. He mentally prepped himself for the onslaught of questions that was to come before he announced that the house they were looking for was at one point being sold through a realty company known as Bennel and Fitz, but he didn't know where it was and who bought it.

"How'd you figure that out?" Julie, genuinely curious, asked.

"Meredith recognized it," he answered.

"Oh, good, so the house is local," Rivera said.

Simon's fingers suddenly stopped typing. "No, Bennel and Fitz Realty is based in Youngstown, where Lorraine's last known

185

location was. So, it's more than likely that this house is somewhere around there."

"I thought Meredith's been selling homes in Cleveland for the last ten years?"

"She has been," Sam confirmed. "She recognized l' from 16 years ago."

"How could she recognize one house out of hundreds that she's bought and sold?" Julie asked next. "Unless something happened to her?"

Sam nodded. Taking a deep breath, he steeled himself before he answered. "Meredith donnea want anyone t' know wha' happened tha' donnea have to. So ye lot have t' promise me tha' this stays between us, understood?"

"Yeah, of course," Rivera answered. The other two agreed as well.

"Alrigh'...In January of 2006, Meredith was conductin' an' open house of this property. Later tha' night, she was attacked."

"Attacked? …You mean she was raped?" Julie asked first.

Sam nodded.

"Did she report it?" Rivera asked next.

"Tha' I donnea know. …We've nevar really talked abou' wha' happened."

"Wait a second," Simon piped up next. "She was raped in 2006...you didn't come to the US until 2007, but Oliver's almost sixteen, isn't he?"

Sam could see the wheels turning in all their heads, and they were all looking to him for a definitive answer. Taking a deep breath, he screwed his eyes shut and said, "Aye, Oliver was born September 13th, 2006, exactly nine months aftar Meredith was attacked. Bu' I dinnea even meet her until the summer of the followin' year."

"Oliver's not your kid?" Rivera asked in astonishment, then his tone shifted to anger. "Man, we really don't know you at all, do we?"

"The details abou' my family are nobody's business bu' mine," Sam growled. "An' now ye all know the truth, bu' Oliver is still my son, an' I'll no' be hearin' any of ye say any differently, understood?"

"Of course, boss," Simon nodded emphatically.

"Absolutely," Julie nodded her agreement. "Does Oliver know about this?"

"No," Sam answered sternly.

"Okay. But what does any of this mean for us? Unless you think her rape had something to do with this, and this psycho is mad because she moved on and had her kid without him knowing?"

"No, I donnea think tha's it...a' leas' I hope i's not. Bu', all the same, we can a' leas' ge' an address from her case file. Simon?"

"Right," the young man nodded and began typing again. It took him maybe ten seconds to stop, but the perplexed look on his face had Sam curious. "Um...there isn't a location on the police report, in fact the notes from the officers say, 'victim unable to remember area of attack' and there's another note that says, 'victim refuses to cooperate.' Maybe she was in shock and couldn't answer them?"

"Even if she was, eventually she would have remembered where she was attacked and told the police long before now," Julie countered.

"That's right," Rivera nodded. "The detectives on her case would have at least narrowed down a location to start searching. If they think she was being uncooperative, then she purposely didn't tell them where it happened."

Sam furrowed his eyebrows at this curious detail before he turned back to Simon. "Alrigh', she was workin fer Bennel an' Fitz a' the time. Can ye find ou' if it's still in their inventory?"

"Of course, I love it when I get to do a good hacking job," Simon smiled and let his fingers fly across his keyboard faster than lightening. "Just let me...Okay, from January to April 2006, Bennel and Fitz had twelve houses in Youngstown listed with them. Just give me a minute to sift through the ownership history...bingo, I've got it right here! The house we're looking for is on Beachwood Drive, that's just south of McKelvey Lake where we found Lorraine's phone. It's still in their inventory, alright, and according to public record, nobody's been living in it since 1999, when the original owner just up and disappeared one day."

Sam looked over Simon's shoulder at the report. "Who was the owner?"

"A guy named Gideon Cauldmor."

"Anythin' particularly interestin' abou' him?"

Simon's fingers flew across his laptop. "No marriages or kids, if that's what you mean. The only relation I can find is a sister that passed away a few years after he disappeared. According to the records, it was from accidental drug overdose. Hey, here's something: According to his financial records, he was an investor in Bennel and Fitz."

"Maybe that's why Meredith wouldn't say where she was raped," Rivera said. "The Realty company kept her quiet, so she couldn't slander their friend and partner, even though he was dead."

"That and crime rates can have an effect on the equity of a house and neighborhood," Julie nodded her agreement. "No doubt they wanted to keep the whole thing quiet so they could still try to make a sale; they made sure she would leave that detail out when she went to the police."

"Well, tha' certainly explains why she donnea like them: Meredith nevar could be around people who treated her like baggage."

"Hold on here, guys," Simon jumped in. "The bank reclaimed the property for lack of payments in 2000, but I'm finding tons of probate applications and disputes for this property made, and not just by our buddies B and F, from 2001-2005. There's everything from land conservation nuts to long-lost relatives claiming the house was to go to them. Gideon Cauldmor didn't have a reputable will, so every one of them had to be investigated. Even though Bennel and Fitz eventually won the bid, the firm couldn't move forward with listing the house until all the other claims were resolved. Meredith was literally the first person to show it to anyone, once the final dispute was closed. But after her assault, it wasn't ever shown again. It's still listed in Bennel and Fitz's business assets, but they've made absolutely no move on trying to sell it again. It's almost like it was just...dropped."

While everyone stood there quietly, processing the information Simon had given them, Julie was the first to ask, "Does anybody else feel like Meredith's assault was a threat?"

"Considering the shadiness surrounding this place, I think you might be right," Rivera nodded.

"What could be so important about a house that somebody would literally threaten a company to leave it alone?"

Simon leaned away from his laptop and smirked. "Well, I think we all know the obvious answer to that one: buried treasure."

Everyone gave an uneasy chuckle except for Sam, who leaned back from Simon. The room went quiet; the obvious thought was floating around in the air, but Sam didn't want to say it.

Julie was the one to make the hard declaration. "Maybe we're wrong, and Meredith's rape really does have something to do with this. We should at least find out everything that happened to be sure."

"Not to be an asshole or anything, but we could also get some DNA from Oliver for comparison," Simon said offhandedly, earning an angry glance from Sam. "What? You know that's the next step. If you're right, and Lorraine's baby and the sperm supplier that made Oliver are the same person, we could easily get proof for that right now."

"Only one problem with that: Bicks never took a fetal sample from Lorraine Wyatt," Rivera said. "There wasn't any reason to at the time. So, considering we tore Mimi/Mae's secret life apart the last time we talked to her, it looks like we're going to have to be doing a little bit of schmoozing to unbury her granddaughter."

Closing his eyes, Sam nodded. "Aye...I'll see wha' I can do t' ge' a sample. In the meantime, ye two go talk t' the detectives on her case...I'll be askin' Meredith meself wha' happened tha' night."

Chapter Nineteen

Sam set off for the home of Mimi Smith, a.k.a. Mae Eyegols. Although the matriarch didn't appear surprised to see him, she wasn't very friendly either. And when Sam asked for her permission to dig Lorraine back up for another examination, she did the strangest thing and invited him inside for a cup of tea.

Taking a seat on her couch with a mug in her hands, Mae took a sip of the steaming drink before she spoke. "If you want to re-examine my granddaughter, Agent McKay, then that must mean that you missed something. Am I right?"

"Aye, ye could say tha', ma'am."

"And you're so certain that you'll find whatever the answer is on Lorraine?"

"Aye, ma'am, I certainly hope so."

The older woman set her mug on the wooden coffee table before her. "Agent, my granddaughter had a life full of pain and anguish, and her last moments were in fear. Her body is finally at peace, and you're asking me to disturb it."

Taking a seat on the other side of the couch, Sam leaned his arms onto his knees and folded his hands together, "Aye, I am."

"I'm afraid you're going to have to give me a really good reason why you need to do this. But I can't promise you that I will say yes."

Sam tried to think how he could answer her delicately. "Mae, wha' I said t' ye when we firs' met abou' Lorraine no' bein' in any pain wasnea the truth. I lied because I though' I was sparin' ye unnecessary hurt. I'm bein' honest w' ye now: Lorraine was subjected t' terrible things by a cruel, cruel man tha' left somethin' behind w' her...t'was a baby. I dinnea think it important before because I was lookin' fer the wrong man. Bu' now I'm positive I'm chasin' the righ' one, an' she's holdin' the key tha' I need t' prove it."

The old woman gave him a faint smile. "You misunderstood me, Agent McKay, I said I need a good reason why *you* need to do this. I can tell that this is personal to you. And, considering the lengths you've gone to for this case, including invading my personal life, I feel I deserve to know your reasons."

The way Mae kept her eyes on him made Sam shift uncomfortably, but it wasn't nearly as uncomfortable as he felt from how easily she could read his emotions. He swallowed the painful lump in his throat and clenched his fists before answering. "This man...he may have a connection t' me wife an' son, ma'am. I need t' find him before he hurts them."

Her faint, wrinkled smile stretched into a larger, kinder one. "Although I suspect you never really needed it in the first place, you have my permission to exhume Lorraine's body."

Sam sighed in relief. "Thank ye, ma'am. Ye've been verra helpful, an' ye've helped a lo' of people."

Mae shook her head sadly. "I wouldn't say that...I've been unable to sleep since your people called me in to talk about Lila Daverman...all I can think is, if I had said something instead of hidden away all those years ago, perhaps I could have saved those poor women from the monster I let that poor boy become. ...Who knows? Maybe Lorraine would still be alive today."

"Ye're no' responsible fer Peter Daverman's actions any more than ye're responsible fer wha' happened t' Lorraine."

"Aren't I, though?"

"No."

Mae Eyegols wiped a lone tear away from her eye, straightened herself up, and replied. "Thank you for your kindness, but I'm afraid it will be some time before I will believe you. If ever."

Sam, smiling gently, produced the piece of paper she needed to sign and a pen. As he made his way to the door with the paperwork in his pocket, he stopped when Mae called out, "Good luck, Agent McKay. And thank you for your honesty. If there's anything else that you need, you know where to find me."

Although he appreciated her offer, Sam hoped this would be the last time he would have to bother the mysterious Mae Eyegols. He took her offering of luck to heart, though. Something told him that he would need all the help he could get.

****

Tracking down the officers who handled Meredith's assault was an easy enough process for Julie and Rivera and, after a little bit of a refresher over a couple of chili dogs, Detectives Sydney and Wellis were more than cooperative.

"Yeah, I remember that case," Detective Sydney, a middle-aged woman with strands of grey hair, answered first. "Dispatch sent us out to a house in Campbell where a few officers were waiting. Ms. Staton was the renter. We took her to the hospital for a complete examination, and the staff confirmed that she had indeed been raped."

"To be honest, the medical examination was the only thing that kept us believing that she had in fact been raped," Detective Wellis said next. He appeared to be a little younger than his partner and had a gaunt build to him.

"What do you mean?" Rivera asked.

"Well, it's not unusual for victims of sexual assault to be...not very forthcoming, you might say, about the details of the experience. But this woman, there were times during the interview I genuinely wondered why she had called the police at all, if she wasn't at least going to help us find the man that raped her."

"It could have been that the experience was too traumatic for her," Julie answered much more defensively.

Detective Sydney must have sensed her anger, as she quickly took over the conversation. "Yes, but with some help and counseling, sometimes even hypnotic therapy, the victims usually warm up a little more to the officers of the case, and a few details shake loose. Meredith Staton remained very tight-lipped for most of the questions. For example, when we asked her where the last place she was before her assault, she insisted she couldn't remember. Eventually she told us she had been drinking with a friend, and that's why nothing came to mind, but when we interviewed all of her associates, they insisted that 1) she was never with any of them the night of the incident, and 2) she never drank that much in the first place."

"Like I said," Detective Wellis continued. "Not very helpful."

"So, you dropped the case?" Rivera asked.

"What else could we do? Without any leads and the lack of cooperation, we could only do so much poking about."

"Well, when you were poking about, did you find anything interesting?"

"Nothing as far as the assault case was concerned," Detective Sydney answered him. "Believe me, agents, we talked to everybody in Ms. Staton's circle: Her friends and coworkers, her bosses, the people at her bank, even her landlord, and they all sang the same tune. Meredith Staton was a very trustworthy and level-headed person, never late for payments, and finished all her work on time. Her boss told us that she sometimes stayed late at the office to help finish filing closing reports and whatnot. We got a warrant to search Mr. Bennel and Mr. Fitz's office and for their DNA, but when the results of the kit came back negative for DNA and positive for spermicide, there wasn't any point in making the comparison. Nothing out of place turned up from the search warrant, either."

"What made you decide to get a warrant for those two in the first place?" Julie asked.

Detective Wellis answered her. "When we were interviewing them, the two of them seemed pretty...shady."

"Shady as in uncooperative?"

"Oh, they answered our questions and were cooperative, alright. It was just something in their movements that made them a little suspicious. It was like they were a little...too cooperative, you know what I mean? But, like my partner said, nothing even remotely weird turned up when we searched their office and their homes. But to be truthful, we didn't get a look into their business dealings. Our warrant specified we could only do a non-invasive search for physical evidence in relation to the rape, and we turned up squat there."

"I wish we could be more helpful to you," Detective Sydney added. "I really do, but sexual assault cases without a suspect are difficult to solve, and even more difficult when the victims can't find it in them to go through it all again."

"We understand," Rivera answered. Standing up from the table, he offered a handshake. "Thank you both for your time."

Julie said her quick goodbye as well, and the two of them didn't speak again until they were back in their vehicle and the doors were shut. Rivera was the first to speak. "Well, the theory about Gideon Cauldmor's business associates' loyalty has more weight to it now.

If Bennel and Fitz had nothing to hide, why else would they go to the trouble of keeping Meredith quiet?"

"Yeah, which makes you wonder what they wanted to hide so badly if Cauldmor was only missing," she answered him. Rivera had had just put the key in the ignition when a thought occurred to her. "Unless..."

"Unless what?"

"What if they knew that Cauldmor was dead?"

"What are you talking about?"

"What if Bennel and Fitz stopped pursuing selling the house, not because of Meredith, but because of something much more sinister? Like, for example, proof that their friend and colleague was dead? What if they are more afraid of: Meredith's attacker or jail time? The Detectives did say they never looked into their business dealings because they had no reason to...what if this goes much deeper than just the *where* Meredith was attacked?"

Rivera listened to her and sat quietly, thinking very intently, before he nodded, "It's possible, but unless we have a real reason to believe that's true, I doubt we'll even find anything to prove it."

Julie gave him an annoyed look. "Do you have to be so... so..."

"Right?" He provided for her. "Somebody has to be. And, sometimes, it can't be Sam."

He saw her pointed stare out of the corner of his eye, but he ignored her as he put the car in drive.

***

Meredith stood in the middle of the most comfortable conference room in their building, clutching her hands so tightly her knuckles were almost white. Sam was standing on the opposite side of the room with his arms crossed over his chest, while Simon was in the other room working his computer magic. Sam himself looked down at the floor with commiseration; he already knew this wasn't going to go over well, but he was ready to do whatever he had to help Meredith if she started to lose it.

"Y-you can't be serious," she stammered. "You really think this has to do with..."

When she couldn't finish, Sam stepped forward and took her hands in his. "I's only a theory, darlin', an' we donnea have much t'

194

go on from our victim. The only other person who knows anythin' abou' tha' house is you...an' we've nevar talked abou' wha' happened t' ye before now, anyways. Perhaps somethin'll stick out t' ye."

"Sam...I can't...I can't go through that night again!"

"I know, luv, I know this is hard. Bu' I'm here w' ye this time, I'll help ye through this."

"But if you're right...Oliver...he can't know about this!"

"An' he won't. The team is undar strict orders no' t' say a word abou' it. As far as he knows, ye're here t' give me some advice on real estate."

Meredith choked on the chuckle; Sam continued to hold her hands while she took deep breaths to try and steady herself. Finally, she nodded her head. "Okay...I'll try..."

Sitting down on the nearest couch together, Sam took out his phone and pulled up a recording app. Once it was running, he set it down on the table nearest Meredith. "Alrigh', jus' take yer time an' try t' speak clearly. Donnea leave anythin' out, anythin' is important."

"Right, okay...I was working for Bennel and Fitz Real Estate as a junior agent at the time, and I was conducting an open house...there were a lot of people coming and going."

"Where?"

"Um...I was living in Campbell at the time...the house was in Youngstown...honestly, I've tried so hard to just forget everything..."

"Were ye in the house alone?"

"Yes. I do remember Mr. Bennel had an important meeting that he couldn't miss, and he said I could handle a simple open house without him."

Meredith started to shake; Sam didn't know what else to do except hold her hands and give them a gentle squeeze. "I's alrigh', darlin'; I'm here. Go on."

"...The open house was wrapping up; I was handing out business cards to the last few people. It was getting very late, so as soon as I thought everyone had left, I shut the doors and started walking through to turn off the lights, pick up solo cups and plates from the hors d'oeuvres, and then..." Meredith took a shuddering breath; tears started forming at the bottom of her eyes. "I was in the basement; there was a beautiful wine cellar down there which was a major selling point...I-I walked forward to clean up when somebody grabbed me from behind...I tried to fight, I screamed for help but...he put something over my mouth and nose...oh, God."

The tears fell; Meredith wrapped her arms around herself and sobbed. Sam clenched his fists; the short version of this story had horrified him enough in the past, but seeing her carry this much pain around not only angered him, it broke his heart more than he thought possible. He wanted so desperately to lean over and hold her, take some of the anguish away, but he had to help her finish her statement. With great restraint, he slowly placed his hand around her shoulders in the most comforting way he could muster.

"I'm here, Meredith. Ye're no' alone."

Meredith took a few more moments to get herself under control before she looked back up at Sam again. Sniffling, she continued. "I woke up on the floor...my clothes were...I tried to cover myself as best as I could before they—I went home...I ached everywhere..."

Her slip made him furrow his brows. "Who di' ye see firs', Meredith? Tell me."

"... Bennel and Fitz." She gasped. "They...they came and got me...took me home..."

Sam's anger flared: Her bosses really did try to cover her assault up.

"I's okay, sweetheart. They cannea hurt ye again; I'll make sure they pay fer downplayin' this. Wha' happened after ye go' home?"

Meredith stopped shaking. "I called the police after they left."

"An' the police performed an examination?"

"Yes...there was a lady officer that held my hand through the whole thing...I told them they could keep my clothes; I never wanted to see them again. ...I left Bennel and Fitz shortly after."

"Okay, now this is verra' important, Meredith: Was there anythin' peculiar abou' the house tha' ye noticed when ye firs' saw it? Anythin' a' all?"

"The wine cellar...it's different from other wine cellars...whenever I went down the stairs, I thought I could feel somebody breathing down my neck..."

Sam nodded; he could tell she was shutting down, and he wouldn't get anything more out of her in that moment. Leaning over to stop the app, he gently pulled her closer and held her. "Ye did good, luv... ye did verra good."

She remained icy and still in his arms; he didn't let her go.

Almost an hour had gone by, but Sam didn't care that he and Meredith stayed in the room on the couch for all that time, and he didn't care that Julie and Rivera had returned. He refused to just get up and leave the woman he loved when she had gone through such a terrible ordeal all over again. It wasn't until she had finally physically relaxed that he was willing to loosen his embrace. But even after she insisted that she was alright, he wouldn't let her leave until she promised that she would go straight home and rest for the remainder of the day. When he was about to call an agent to drive her home, she smacked his arm and told him to stop being silly. She was a grown woman who could drive herself home. Only then was he convinced that she was doing better, and he escorted her to her car. It was then that he remembered they still needed physical proof that the man who fathered Oliver was in fact involved with Lorraine, and he asked Meredith if she could (inconspicuously) get something for him. She said she would try.

When Sam got back to the third floor, he found Julie and Rivera (Dana had announced that she needed to get back to her own house and left earlier) gathered around Simon, who had a giddy smile on his face.

"I am happy to report that I found...the...report."

The others snickered at Simon's blundered quip, but Sam didn't even crack a smile; even though he was able to get a lot from Meredith regarding her attack, the whole interview was still wearing on him.

Bringing them back to the present moment, Simon muttered a quick 'shut up' before he dove right into expelling the information to everyone.

"Okay, so the police interviewed everyone from Meredith's work and neighborhood, and they all willingly gave up DNA samples. The problem was the rape kit didn't find any semen, but they did find a few hairs that didn't belong to Meredith. Every DNA sample they collected tested out, though. Bottom line: They had absolutely no leads to even start going on, let alone a suspect."

Julie was the first to start poking holes. "How is it possible that this guy didn't leave behind any semen? He had to have left *some*; Oliver is living proof of that."

"According to the results of the kit, there were trace amounts of spermicide: The guy used a condom; guess he just picked a faulty one that night."

"Yeah, and I bet Meredith found that very comforting when she found out she was pregnant six weeks later," Rivera said. His bluntness earned him a dirty look from everyone except Sam, but that didn't stop him from continuing to run his mouth. "Is she absolutely certain the guy that raped her is Oliver's father?"

That questioned made Sam glare at him. "She wouldnea lie abou' tha'; yes she's certain."

"And she didn't have a boyfriend or—"

Julie elbowed Rivera in the ribs hard enough to make him double over and cough. "Will you stop being an asshole, for once? He says she's certain, so she is!"

Simon tried to divert everyone's attention. "Anyways, getting back to the subject at hand, the examining officers were very official, right down to taking dirt samples from under her fingernails. But, again, nothing was very conclusive, so eventually the case went cold."

Sam finally spoke. "Simon, I want ye t' call the precinct an' have them send over all the physical evidence, then have forensics run a comparison t' everythin' we found from the five copycat victims, Lorraine, an' Daverman. An' tell Bicks t' re-examine Daverman's body when i' ge's here."

"Okay, but what are you hoping he'll find, boss?"

"I dunno, bu' tell him t' indulge me." He turned to Rivera and Julie next. "I want the two of ye t' track down Bennel an' Fitz an' tell 'em we know they're involved w' coverin' up Meredith's assault, an' unless they tell us wha' the hell is goin' on, you'll arrest 'em right there."

"You're forgetting that the statute of limitations for Meredith's rape has run out," Rivera answered. "We might be able to get them for conspiracy, or even aiding and abetting, but I doubt they'll cave, if that's the only ammo we have to throw at them."

Sam knew he was right; but he didn't want to admit it. Taking a moment to pace back and forth, he went over everything Meredith had told him. "They had an' important meetin' they couldnea miss the night she was attacked. Wha' if the meetin' was abou' the house?"

"I thought the same thing!" Julie shouted, elbowing Rivera in the ribs again much more gently this time. "Why else would they just not show up to an open house for the building they fought so hard to get?"

"Um...we're assuming that the guy who threatened them is the same guy that attacked Meredith, right?" Simon asked doubtfully. "So how could he be in two places at once?"

"With how smart this guy has been about hiding from people, I highly doubt Bennel and Fitz met him in person," Julie answered.

"Either way, there's a connection here somewhere; I can feel it!" Sam insisted. "The two of ye go shake loose wha' ye can from them."

"And what are you going to do?" Rivera asked.

Sam had already started for the elevator. "I'm goin' t' see this goddamn house for meself."

***

Julie and Rivera called ahead and learned that the two head honchos of Bennel and Fitz were still at their office. When they arrived, they wasted absolutely no time in marching past everyone with a quick flash of their badges to anyone that tried to stop them. They found two men who looked to be the ones in charge having lunch together in the main office. When Julie and Rivera burst through the door, both of them looked up in surprise.

"Can we help you?" asked the one with a cocoa-colored complexion.

"Which of you is Bennel, and which of you is Fitz?" Julie demanded.

Both men looked at each other in question before introducing themselves.

The other gentleman, white with a salt and pepper mustache, answered, "I'm Raymond Bennel."

"And I'm Joe Fitz," answered the darker one. "And you two are?"

"Agents Rivera and Russell," Rivera answered with a flash of his badge. "We need to talk to both of you about a house on Beachwood Drive in Youngstown."

Julie didn't miss the brief look of fear that flashed across both of their eyes when they looked at one another. But, very quickly, Mr.

Fitz answered, "I'm afraid you'll have to be more specific, as we have a whole neighborhood development on Beachwood—"

"You know exactly which house we're talking about," Julie interrupted him. "The house that belonged to your old friend and investor, Gideon Cauldmor. In January 2006, you had a junior agent named Meredith Staton conduct an open house on it. That same night, she was assaulted. Conveniently enough, when she went to the police to report her assault, she was sure to leave out the details of where she was earlier that night."

"She told us everything; we know she was assaulted at that house, and we know that you two picked her up after the fact," Rivera added. "We also know that you, Mr. Bennel, were supposed to accompany her to the open house that night but had to miss it due to a 'very important meeting.'"

"You're both looking at obstruction and conspiracy," Julie finished. "So, should we go ahead and very publicly arrest the both of you? Or do you want to explain what was so important about that cover-up while we're feeling forgiving?"

Mr. Bennel suddenly stood up from the table and walked behind the two of them to close the door. When he turned back around, he cleared his throat. "Agents...where to begin?"

"How about at the beginning? With the truth, if you please," Rivera said.

"And you can start by confirming that you threatened or bribed Meredith," Julie added.

"Yes, we did," Fitz answered. "But listen agents, you have to understand something. That meeting that you know about...it was more than just a meeting."

"It was a threat," Bennel finished for him.

"On your precious business?" Julie asked, sure to make her tone obviously accusatory.

"Not just that, on our very lives."

Julie and Rivera shared a look before taking a seat across from the businessmen. "Alright, we're listening."

Bennel started talking first. "I was preparing to leave the office with Meredith for the open house, when Joe called me and said I had to stay behind. We were waiting for hours when, finally, a messenger arrived with a package."

"What was in it?" Rivera asked.

"Evidence of...less reputable business doings. And pictures."

"You'll have to be more specific if you expect us to believe you," Julie snarled.

Again, the two men looked at one another for a moment before Fitz answered, "For a brief time...we were helping some clients with some funding problems."

"Oh, for God's sake, the word is embezzlement! Look, fellas, you're already persons of interest; the best thing you can do is just be completely honest!"

Rivera put his hand on Julie's shoulder. "What my colleague *means* to say is that it's in your best interest to come completely clean with us. We don't have interest in your business doings—"

"At the moment," Julie said in hushed tones, which earned a glare from Rivera before he continued.

"We're after a different fish. So do yourselves a favor, guys, okay?"

"...Alright, yes, we were embezzling money for a select group of clients. Somehow, this man got a hold of that information. Not just about one client, but all of them."

"Okay, you mentioned he had pictures in there as well. What were they of?"

"...Something that would ruin our professional and personal lives."

"Hookers?" Julie asked bluntly.

The two men looked at one another again before Fitz answered. "If only it were that simple."

"The pictures were of us, agents," Bennel hissed under his breath. "It was the early 2000s; there was extensive media coverage over the bakers who refused to bake a wedding cake for a gay couple. What do you suppose would have happened if word got out about the two of us being involved with one another?"

"Not to mention, both of our wives would have taken us to the cleaners in the divorce settlements," Fitz added. "We were up against a wall, we had no choice but to comply to his demands."

"And what were those demands?" Rivera asked, the note of discomfort in his voice evident. "Did he leave a list with those pictures?"

"He left a burner phone in the package. He called at midnight on the dot; I remember because my wife called just before to ask when I'd be on my way home."

"He told us that we could keep the house in our inventory, but if we ever tried to sell it again, he'd release the copies of the photos to our wives and to the media.... Then he said if we didn't want Meredith's blood on our hands, we should listen. Then he hung up. Naturally, we immediately went out to the house. We had just finished remodeling it for a resale, but the walls had been scratched and torn, and everything was practically destroyed. And we found Meredith on the floor in the wine cellar...her clothes were disheveled and...it was obvious what had happened. If he could do that to poor Meredith, what was he capable of doing to us? To our children?"

"So yes, we drove her home. We begged and pleaded and, yes, threatened to have her real estate license revoked, if she revealed where she was attacked. I wanted to drive her to the police station myself, but she insisted that we leave."

"We know it was wrong, agents, but what choice did we have?"

"The right one," Julie snarled at them. "The police could have protected your families; you were more concerned about your reputations and your money."

"Tell us about Gideon Cauldmor," Rivera quickly interjected. "What was your relationship with him?"

"Nothing particularly special, he was just an old friend who invested in our firm."

"We've seen his financial records, fellas, we know he didn't exactly have a lot of money to spend, let alone 'invest' anywhere. So, stop lying."

Again, the two men looked at one another. "Alright, he helped us get in contact with a few of our other less-honorable clients, and he got a small cut from the profits. It was very odd when he went missing; he wasn't the type to just go missing."

"Did the police question you about his disappearance?"

"Yes, of course, but we didn't have any useful information for them."

"You mean other than him being your embezzlement partner," Julie snarled.

"Honestly, when the police first came to investigate, it was the first we had heard about it," Fitz insisted. "And as we've already told you, we had to keep that detail quiet."

"Alright, we're going to need a list of all of the 'clients' he provided you with," Rivera said.

"And one more thing," Julie interjected. "Are either of you acquainted with Peter Daverman?"

Bennel and Fitz looked at each other once more. "As a matter of fact, he was one of the 'clients' that Cauldmor sent our way. We heard about his murder on the news...do you think there's a connection?"

Finally, it was Julie and Rivera's turn to look at one another. A silent agreement not to say anything passed between the two of them, and Julie turned to the two men and said, "We can get a warrant, but that'll just waste time. So, the two of you are going to give us permission to tear that house apart, understood?"

Both nodded dumbly, and Julie and Rivera left before they could ask any more questions. Back in the car, Julie turned to Rivera and asked, "So Daverman was involved in money laundering as well, huh? How come Simon couldn't find the connection between these two before now?"

"You know as well as I do that money launderers are very careful about who sees their records, Jules. But at least we know that there really is a bigger connection to Daverman than just Sam's obsession."

Rivera started driving, but the silence in the air only made Julie's thoughts scream louder until she finally just came outright and said them. "What the hell did we walk into here?"

"I'm not sure anymore," Rivera shook his head. "But I do know whoever's behind this—the guy that Sam is determined to catch— he's not just some bum criminal. He's smart. And that makes him even more dangerous."

Chapter Twenty

Sam pulled onto Beachwood Drive in Youngstown quietly; driving slowly down the little one-way road, he took note of the surrounding houses. Most of them looked relatively new, no more than ten years old and obviously part of a development, judging by their modern fashion. There were a few small cul-de-sacs along the drive, but the blissfully ignorant neighbors sitting and the children playing seemed innocuous enough. Eventually the houses started thinning out, and he came to the end of the road. It stopped abruptly before some very tall and lush trees. Just before the trees sat a house that was clearly much older than its neighbors. While the other houses had levels and defined separate rooms in the outside architecture, this one was a solid two-story block with a roof. It was made of red brick that had signs of fading from years of sunlight exposure, and every window was boarded up. The path of overgrown weeds cracking through the pavers leading up to it was also a clear sign of its lack of life, as the remainder of the neighborhood had fresh and clean concrete walkways and drives. With the forest of trees behind it, the mysterious house had an ominous air to it. If Sam didn't know any better, he'd almost believe that it was haunted.

Shaking the goosebumps off, Sam left his car in the front and trekked toward the house. The door, surprisingly, was unlocked. The little voice in the back of Sam's mind reminded him that he didn't have a warrant, but his need for something solid that pointed towards the identity of Meredith's attacker very quickly told that voice to shut up, and he turned the handle. The door was a little sticky, but with a good shoulder shove, it opened. The inside of the house only reaffirmed his feelings of haunting: Despite the sun shining brightly outside, the inside was dark. Only a few lucky rays of sunlight managed to break through the boards and illuminate the dust particles floating through the air, which only added to the stale smell. Sam turned on his flashlight app and looked around: There wasn't any furniture, but the few indentations in the dusty carpet suggested that at one point it had been furnished. It was really the walls that got his attention: They had obviously been painted to sell, but there were multiple scratches all along the surfaces that exposed the old wallpaper underneath. He shined his light on the ones closest to him and squinted for a better look. It was almost as though somebody was trying to uncover the past, not cover it up. With nothing else standing out on the first floor, Sam turned his attention to the staircase directly to the left: One set led to the upstairs, and another, directly underneath and adjacent to it, led to the downstairs. *The wine cellar was where Meredith was attacked,* Sam thought to himself. Deciding that would be the next best place to poke around, he walked over and made his descent, crouching and ducking to avoid hitting his head.

The wine cellar was more of a small empty basement with shelves than a spirits storage facility. Every wall was lined from the ceiling to the floor with wooden brackets like bookcases. There were a sparse number of bottles coated with an inch of dust here and there, and it was smaller than the rest of the house upstairs, but otherwise, nothing out of the ordinary stood out to Sam. *...Meredith though' somebody was breathin' on the back of her neck...where?* Slowly and quietly, he walked the 20x12ft room around its perimeter. It wasn't until he was almost back to the staircase again when a very faint smell caught his attention. He looked all around him: the shelves, the ceiling, then the floor, and noticed some vague markings next to the base of the shelves, barely concealed by the layer of dust. Leaning his flashlight closer, they looked like skid or scratch marks, as if something was moved with great difficulty. Sam leaned in for an even closer look: The marks went directly under the shelf with no break in the pattern. On a hunch, he looked even closer at the shelving bracket and noticed a hairline separation in between the cases. *...There's somethin' behind this wall!* He dropped his phone on the ground and started feeling around for a button or anything that would move the shelf but couldn't find one. He was just about to lift the whole shelf out, when he stopped and reminded himself of the rules of evidence collection: He was in the house without a warrant, and without the proper equipment for evidence collection. If he opened that wall now and found something, it couldn't be used later. Taking a deep breath, Sam stepped away from the wall, picked up his phone, and made for the upstairs.

The second floor was just as eerie the rest of the house: The hardwood floors had been stained and updated, but the continual coating of dust didn't make them appealing. There were only two bedrooms, along with a bathroom, and Sam discovered much of the same treatment to their walls as he had seen on the first floor. The second and farthest bedroom, however, provided something even more interesting: Not only were there scratches and evidence of paint being chipped away by someone, that same person had also ripped up the furthest corner of the carpet away from the baseboards. Sam didn't touch the ripped-up corner, but he did lean closer for a look at the wood underneath and found the start of a stain. It was obviously old, but it didn't look like blood. It was more like rot from water damage. Sam couldn't tell without further inspection, but he was definitely going to keep a special note in his mind about this particular spot in the house. Since he had no legal reason to tear the house apart yet, he left before his overwhelming curiosity got the better of his common sense.

Next Sam investigated the surrounding yard and forest. Carefully, he walked the perimeter and kept his eyes glued to the ground for footprints, tire treads, a dropped key, anything at all, but the further he walked, the more disappointed he became. It wasn't until he was at least a hundred yards into the trees that he finally got a stroke of luck: Embedded in the ground were some curious drag marks that looked too purposeful to be caused by an animal or even a fallen branch. Giving them a wide berth, he kept his eyes glued to the curious tracks until they led him another fifty yards deeper, then they stopped. ...*Someone tried t' hide their footprints,* he concluded. Obviously without a footprint for comparison, there was nothing to gain from the tracks, but it did give Sam all the more reason to think that he was on the trail of something. Why else would anyone go to the trouble of hiding their footprints? More importantly, could this person be of value since they were so close to the condemned house? His gut told him yes, and he desperately began looking around the ending marks for something else more useful when he saw it: a few feet away, barely covered with some sticks and leaves, was a cigarette butt poking out of the ground. Sam almost cried with joy: This was *much* better than a footprint! It was DNA!

He practically smashed the icon to dial Simon and started barking orders the moment the young man answered. "Ge' forensics ou' here immediately! I want the entire house an' a 500-yard perimeter processed before the end of the day!"

"They'll be there before you can sneeze, boss. I'm glad you called; I can update you."

"On wha'?"

"Bennel and Fitz were threatened, and that's why they kept Meredith silent about the site of her attack. Plus, they admitted to doing some embezzling on the side. So, I figured they might have only been telling half the truth, and I did a little hacking and—"

"Ge' t' the point, Simon."

"Mr. Bennel and Mr. Fitz have made themselves pretty rich from selling houses full-time while sporting the embezzlement scheme up until January 2006. So, naturally, I've been chasing down every single dime spent by these guys since then, and I've found multiple transactions made every month through different banks and accounts, but they all go to one place in the end: an untraceable offshore account."

"How much were they sendin'?"

"Roughly $10,000 a month."

"Meredith's attacker has been blackmailin' them all this time?"

"Bingo," the young man answered excitedly, and Sam smiled to himself. "But here's the bad news: All the accounts are listed under different names. I'm running down every one of them; maybe we'll get lucky."

"Okay, bu' ge' forensics ou' here first." Sam was just about to hang up when he heard a pinging noise in the background, and Simon's demeanor instantly shifted to somber.

"Boss… I think you better head over to Ridgeville."

"Why?"

"The lady Lieutenant just texted me: She's found our old buddy, Max Darrel: His body was found in the bathroom of a Motel 6. ...Captain Humbar is already en route."

Sam's brief moment of elation was quickly replaced with bewilderment; he couldn't answer Simon, but he vaguely heard the young man say that he would let Dana know he was on the way as well before hanging up. Sam would have liked to stay until CSU had arrived, but he had to be absolutely sure that it was his friend Max Darrel who was dead. And if it was, maybe he had one last piece of help to give them. Taking one last look at the cigarette butt half buried in the ground, he turned and started back towards the car.

Pulling into the parking lot of the Motel 6, Sam wasn't the least bit surprised to see the entire block swarming with police cars and bystanders. With a flash of his badge, he was let through the blockade and immediately greeted by Dana.

The Lieutenant held out her hand. "Hey, Sam. Long time no see."

"Hey," he nodded with a returned handshake. "Wha' room is he in?"

"Fifteen; it's over there. You better brace yourself, though. Poor Max didn't have a peaceful ending."

As the two of them made their way over to the crime scene, Sam began to probe. "Who identified the body? Simon couldnea find 'im, so he must've paid cash fer this place."

"Somebody complained about the loud noise coming from his room, and management found him and the TV on. So, he called the police. The wallet is still here, but cash and credit cards are missing. My officers called in to give an initial report about a brutal robbery, and when I heard Max Darrel, I drove out here myself. I called Simon first then I called Ace."

"So, he's been cleared as a suspect, then?"

"Yeah, but he's not happy about being thrown under the bus by you guys," Dana answered bluntly. "Considering he and Max were both passionate about catching the Angel, I had to let him know."

Only a few more steps until the motel room, and Sam already had to cover his nose from the stench. Sam recognized the doctor and colleague instantly just from his face. The sight of Darrel's body was gruesome: His eyes were wide open and glossed over, and there were numerous cuts and lacerations all along Max that had been left to bleed out. Some of them were oozing, causing Sam to look closer and notice a few bugs had made a meal for themselves.

"Christ," Sam hissed to himself.

"That's exactly what I thought when I saw him," Dana nodded her agreement. "The poor man spent the better part of his life trying to solve his wife's murder, only to be killed in a robbery."

"I'm not so sure this is a robbery," came a familiar voice behind the two of them. Sam turned to see Humbar there, and the portly police chief barely glanced at him before he continued. "Although it's been staged to look like one from the state of this entire room, it looks like Darrel was tortured."

"He was a doctor and a respected psychologist at one point, Ace," Dana countered. "Maybe this robber felt like taking his time."

By the way Humbar refused to look at him, Sam could tell he was still very angry at him, and he turned back to look at the body of their former friend. Humbar's keen observation on Darrel's state didn't escape Sam's attention. In fact, he was inclined to agree with him, though he was careful not to let on to that. "He's been here a while. Do ye have any clues on who killed 'im?"

"None of the other renters saw anyone else besides Darrel coming and going, and CSU is still sweeping."

Lieutenant Evanston grimaced and swept off her blazer. "I'd like to be positive and say maybe the bugs will tell us something, but given the state of this motel, it's more than likely that they were hiding under this mattress waiting for a suitable meal. I'm going to need to have a lice check when we're done here."

Sam took a closer look at the wounds with bugs on them: They didn't look particularly out of the ordinary, at least not to him, as he wasn't a bug expert. But his gut told him that they might tell them something. Looking closer at the wounds, he noticed how cleanly cut they were: Obviously whoever killed Max wasn't without practice. "Well, make sure the labs run somethin' on these bugs anyway. If ye wouldnea mind, Dana, I'd like ye t' send everythin' over t' me when yer men are done."

"I can do that. But, honestly, what for? Unless you think Ace is right, and Max was tortured?"

"Aye, I do. Though I donnea know why. I' could be a brutal robbery, bu' I'd like t' be sure. Aftar all, we knew 'im; he deserves a thorough investigation." Sam hated lying to his friends: He had a very good idea who might have tortured Max, but he couldn't be sure. Other than Max's involvement with the Christmas Angel cases, there wasn't anything that connected him to the man he was chasing now. Not even his death appeared to be connected, and Sam highly doubted an autopsy would say that he had steak and potatoes before he died. It was only his gut that told him to look deeper, but Sam didn't see the point in concerning either of them about the bigger angle of everything. At least, not yet. Besides, at minimum, the DNA could be crossed with the corpse of Daverman, and they would know whether or not Max had anything to do with the Christmas Angel's death. "Thank ye fer lettin' me come out."

"You bet," Dana nodded.

Humbar didn't speak; he just brushed past Sam and walked back towards his own car.

Sam didn't say anything about it, and Dana was nice enough not to ask. He started walking and had barely made it back to his car when his phone started ringing. It was Simon.

"Wha's up?"

"First things first, was it Max? Is Dr. Darrel really dead?"

"Aye, he is."

By the way the young man sighed into the phone, Sam could tell there had been a friendship between the two. He wanted to urge Simon to tell him what he had called for, but he let the young man have a minute instead.

"...Was it our guy?" he asked.

"I donnea know; it doesnea look like it. Bu' Dana's promised t' send over everything they find."

"Okay...that's good..."

"Di' ye have somethin ye wanted t' tell me, Abler?"

"Yes! Right. Sorry. CSU is still processing the house of hell, and they've already found some pretty sick stuff, including a body behind one of the walls in the basement."

I knew it! Sam nodded to himself, glad that he was able to curb his overwhelming curiosity, and so quickly for once.

"But that's not what I wanted to tell you about," Simon continued. "They also found a cigarette butt in the little forest behind it, and there was plenty of saliva on it. The DNA was in the system, and they got a match instantly! You'll never guess who it belongs to."

"Jus' tell me, Simon. I've had enough surprises today."

"Well then, brace yourself for this one, boss: The saliva on it belongs to Robert Grayers, your old IA partner."

Sam's blood froze. "Are they positive?"

"One hundred percent. There wasn't another bit of human DNA on that cigarette. So, here's the million dollar question: Why would Grayers be out there—"

"Unless he knows somethin' abou' our killar," Sam breathed into the phone.

"Exactly. Julie and Rivera are on their way to pick him up, so you better get back to the office fast, if you don't want to miss the interrogation."

"Tell 'em t' le' him sweat until I ge' there," Sam said shakilly. "…I'm leadin' this interrogation."

***

Sam looked through the two-way mirror into the interrogation room at Robert Grayers; it had been nearly ten years since he'd last seen his Internal Affairs partner and mentor, and his stomach was churning at so many thoughts. Could Grayers really be involved with something as gruesome as these murders? But there was no denying he was involved in some way: Why would he be smoking a cigarette in a neighborhood so far away from him? And a better question: Why was he hiding in the grove of trees to do it? It was possible that someone had placed his cigarette there, but Sam didn't think that likely. Robert Grayers was a clever man, and a really good cop. If he smelled something fishy then he would follow his nose. Not to mention, there was the reason for Grayers' ultimate hatred of Sam: the reason for his betrayal. Sam already knew this was going to get ugly, but he stood up straight and proceeded towards the interrogation room.

The moment Sam opened the door, the air in the room shifted: Grayers, who had been sitting peacefully enough behind the table, clenched his fists together so tightly his knuckles started to turn white.

"You," the disgraced office snarled. "You limey son of a bitch."

Sam couldn't find it in himself to react to the offensive insult. Instead, he took a seat across from Grayers and began laying out photographs of the condemned house. Grayers didn't even bother to look at them. He continued to glare daggers at Sam; if looks could kill, Sam knew that Grayers had already fileted him alive a dozen times over. Although it took a beat, Sam tapped on the middle photograph on the table and asked, very quietly, "Wha' d' ye know abou' this house?"

Grayers responded by spitting in his face.

Sam calmly wiped it away before producing the photo of the cigarette butt. "Robert, this was found no' too far from the house,

211

an' i' has yer DNA all over it. I jus' wanna' know why ye were there."

Grayers leaned back into his chair and folded his arms together. "I was having dinner with some friends in the neighborhood, then I wanted a smoke, so I went for a walk to go have one."

"Ye know tha' my people have already canvassed the entire neighborhood, askin' if anybody knows ye. If ye're gonna' lie t' me, a' leas' try t' be creative abou' it."

"Fine, I was doing a little late-night rabbit hunting."

Sam sighed. "Robert, this house is the site of an' assault, an' possibly a murdar. Ye've go' t' tell me the truth. You bein' there doesnea look good, an' ye know tha', yer record'll—"

"My record?! I had a perfect service record! I killed myself taking down bad cops who abused their badges! I served the public faithfully for 32 years! But, thanks to you, none of that matters. Thanks to you, I lost everything! My pension, my daughter; my wife has to be monitored 24/7 because of you!"

Sam could feel the tears brimming at the corner of his eyes. "Robert, ye can still be a good cop. I jus' want t' know—"

"Go to hell!" Grayers bellowed in his face. Picking up the corner of the interrogation table, he flipped it and all the photographs scattered along the floor.

Sam didn't flinch at the outburst, but within mere seconds, the door opened and Rivera, Julie, Simon, and, surprisingly, Copper entered.

"Mr. Grayers," Copper said firmly. "Sit down and calm yourself. Now."

The staring contest between the two didn't last long, and Sam's old partner did as he was told. While the rest of the team set to work cleaning up everything, Copper continued speaking. "McKay, I'd like a word with you, please."

With a devastated look at the resentful man, Sam quietly rose from the chair and left the room. He could tell Julie and Rivera were planning to take over the interview while he was gone, but he already knew that they wouldn't get much out of Grayers. Numbly, he followed his boss back to her office. Her assistant, Evan Dower, with his friendly 'Hello,' barely registered as he took a seat across from her desk while Copper closed the door behind them. Sam didn't know what she wanted to talk to him about, but he guessed it was probably going to be a pep-talk or a reassignment, something to get him away from the case. Then she laid a photograph on her desk directly in front of him, and Sam's blood froze: It was of Danielle Grayers, Robert's daughter.

Sam instantly returned to his angry and gruff demeanor. "Wha' the hell is this abou'?"

Chapter Twenty-one

As if it was a perfectly normal conversation, Copper answered, "Robert Grayers didn't have so much as a complaint against him in his 32 years of service, and yet he was fired for skimming drug money, which was to help pay for his daughter's cancer treatment. Even for a cop, the sentence for skimming should have been five years of jail time plus a fine. But his old partner agreed to testify on the condition that Grayers receive absolutely no jail time and no fines, merely the pension revocation. Grayers walked away from 32 years of service completely scot-free with absolutely no money. Sampson Angus McKay has a habit of deciding, in certain circumstances, when his morality trumps the law; I would like to believe that he would simply look the other way, until Grayers daughter had made a full recovery, before encouraging his partner to drop his bad habits before he became reliant on them."

Sam started to sweat; she was interrogating him.

"Danielle Grayers: A straight-A student with a very high IQ, head of the cheerleading team and the student council at Avon Lake High and considered highly popular. A perfect record and a model student. Beloved by all her teachers, but according to her friends, whom I interviewed personally, she could be manipulative, vengeful, even terrifying at times. According to one young woman, Danielle was responsible for the suicide of a young man in their graduation class. Her exact words were: 'It's hard to put it into words; it's just that Danielle always seemed to know things, personal things, about people. Things that you didn't really want other people to know, especially in high school. Whenever she wanted something, she would tell you that she needed a favor. And if you tried to refuse, she would sort of off-handedly mention your secret and the fear of somebody else hearing about it.' She couldn't tell me what the secret of that young man was, but she did tell me that he used to follow Danielle Grayers around like a puppy, doing everything she asked him to do."

Copper leaned forward on her desk and folded her hands together before continuing, "A law enforcement father breaks his personal code in an effort to save his dying daughter, who, most likely unbeknownst to him, is not as angelic as she appears to be. Knowing all of this, there's the glaring question of why Sam McKay would go against his nature and get his partner and friend into trouble, and yet make it as harmless as possible? The answer: It must have something to do with the daughter. Am I wrong?"

Sam was completely flabbergasted. " H-how di' ye find ou' all tha'?"

"You're not the only one who gets curious, Sam," she answered in a kinder voice. "When you first mentioned his name, you acted as if you were ashamed. You let him have control of that interrogation just now. And when I read Rivera and Russell's interview notes, I could tell that there was a story no-one knew about. You can be a forgiving, if sometimes naïve, person, McKay. Finally, you of all people would understand doing anything for your child, no matter the cost. So, for you to decide that this one should not be saved, there must be an excellent reason for that."

While Sam sat still with his stomach still churning, Copper stood up from her desk and turned to the bookcase behind her. She retrieved two glass tumblers and her favorite bottle of cognac, Hennessy XO, before coming to join him in the other chair next to him. She filled one of the tumblers halfway and handed it to him before making her own drink. Setting the teardrop bottle on the desk in front of the two of them, she leaned back, took a sip, and waited.

Sam stared at the drink; Copper hadn't directly ordered him to give an explanation, but rather, she was asking for one. He couldn't understand why she would be so curious: She had made a point in the past to never delve too deeply into other people's affairs. He couldn't deny her assessment of him when it came to Grayers: The shame that he felt was overwhelming. He downed the cognac in one gulp, hoping that the dark amber liquid would help to loosen his tongue more than his will could.

"Meredith an' I had a figh' the mornin' i' happened, an' a' the end of the day, she tol' me t' find a couch fer the nigh'. Robert heard me callin' some nearby inns an' insisted I stay a' his place. ... I'd me' Danielle before, a' a Fourth of July barbeque earlier tha' year. ...Tha' night, aftar dinnar, Robert, his wife Lisa, an' I went t' the sittin' room, an' Danielle claimed she had homework t' do. A' some point, I go' up t' refill everyone's drinks. The girl was sittin' a' the kitchen table, an' when I asked Robert where I could find somethin', she go' up t' help me." Sam clenched his eyes together painfully, and his brogue grew stronger without thinking. "I think she must've slipped me somethin' when I wasnea lookin', because i' takes more than' two glasses of whiskey t' ge' me drunk. Bu' I only took a few sips of my second bourbon, an' I started feelin' tired. Lisa go' me a blanket an' a pillow, I wished everyone goodnight, an' the next thing I knew, I was out. Bu' when I woke, i' wasnea even sunrise yet..."

Sam started breathing heavily; memories of that horrid night were flooding back, and every emotion he had tried to ignore for so long was plaguing him. He turned to Copper; she hadn't moved. She just sat quietly and kept eye contact with him, encouraging him to get it all out. He needed another cognac before he could, and he didn't hesitate to reach over and pour himself another glass. He downed it in one gulp, too.

"Danielle was on top of me...doin' things no fifteen-year-ol' girl should be doin' w' a thirty-five-year-ol' man. I wanted her t' stop. I tried t' tell her, push her offa' me, bu' me arms were so heavy, I couldnea do anythin'...an' I'm ashamed t' say my body reacted to it without any problem. ...When i' was over, she peeled the condom off, an' I watched her put it in a plastic baggie. She covered me w' a blanket again. She dinnea say a thing...she jus' smiled a' me. I passed ou' again. The next mornin' a' breakfast, I though' I had a nightmare abou' the whole thing. Hell, I hoped an' prayed tha' I did. Bu' when tha' girl came t' the table...she looked a' me an' smiled again, and I knew i' wasnea a nightmare." Sam inhaled deeply: The tears that were resting at the corners of his eyes had finally broken the dam, but he quickly wiped them away. "I waited fer a few days before I tried t' talk t' her...I couldnea understand wha' had happened or why she di' tha'. I tried t' convince myself tha' i' was a girlish crush tha' she'd taken too far, an' I intended t' stop her. ...Wha' I dinnea know was tha' Danielle was no girl w' a crush...I caught her after school one day when she was walkin' home...an' she tol' me tha' no' only does she still have the condom w' both of our DNA on it, bu' she'd taken pictures. She showed me her phone an' said she had copies. ...She tol' me tha' if I said anythin', she'd claim tha' I forced her t' have sex w' me... I asked wha' she wanted t' make all of this go away, an' she tol' me she'd call me if she evar needed a favor."

Sam expected Copper to have a look of complete disgust on her face at his admission, but when he turned to look at her again, she was still completely neutral: no judgement, no anger, no disgust. Only the barest hint of sympathy. Sam felt completely exposed, and the rest of his explanation came pouring out of his mouth.

"I was cornered, I couldnea do anythin'! Who was gonna' believe tha' a 6'6" Scotsman was raped by a fifteen-year-ol' girl? If she tol' anybody, losin' my job was the least of my problems: statutory rape charges would have been only the beginnin'! ... Every time I go' a phone call, I though' t'was her callin' t' 'cash in' tha' favor, or t' tell me tha' she'd tol' her da' abou' tha' night...it ate me alive!"

"And then she got colon cancer," Copper pressed.

"Aye, I almos' cried fer joy when I found out. It felt like God had given me justice. Robert was killin' himself t' try an' pay for her treatment...an' then I discovered wha' he was willin' t' do t' save her...All I could think t' myself was, if this little girl could take advantage of a big man like me as a teenager, wha' was she really capable of in the future?"

Sam reached forward for the bottle of cognac again, but this time Copper stopped him by pulling the bottle away.

"So, you turned your partner in, making sure that he would get the lightest sentence possible," she pressed again.

Sam pulled his hand back. "...Aye, I did. T'was the only way out of this. I tried so hard fer so long t' find another one. I even tried t' convince meself tha' the cancer could take her anyway, even with the treatment, bu'... I couldnea leave tha' up t' chance. I... had t' ruin' Robert's life t' stop her..." Sam leaned back in his chair and brought his hands to his face.

"Have you ever told anyone about this?" Copper asked. "A therapist? Maybe your wife?"

"How could I tell my wife? She's a rape victim too, an' she still hasnea dealt with her own assault. How could I tell her abou' mine? An' worse, why would she believe me tha' a teenaged girl did it on the night we had a fight? No... ye're the only one tha' knows this, Belinda."

"You have nothing to be ashamed of, McKay. That girl was a budding psychopath."

"Tha's wha' I tol' myself over an' over: If I dinnea stop her now, she would have gone on t' destroy so many more lives...bu' tha' dinnea lessen the pain when Robert was stripped of his credentials...An' shortly aftar his daughter died, Lisa attempted t' kill herself. Several times. I offered t' help him find her somewhere tha' she could ge' help, bu' Robert wouldnea speak t' me. An' anytime tha' he did, t'was with verra angry an' colorful language tha' I wouldnea repeat in front of a lady. I dinnea blame him then, an' I still don't... bu' Christ, the shame an' guilt of wha' I've done—"

"You did nothing wrong, McKay," Copper interrupted him firmly. "You did the only thing that you could do. There will always be some that will never see it like that, but you did."

"Then tell me: How do I finally convince meself tha's true? How can I justify killin' a young girl an' ruinin' two other people's lives like I did?"

"By accepting everything that happened, first. Second, by getting the proper help for the rest." Copper walked around her desk and opened a drawer for a blank piece of paper. Sam watched as she wrote down a number with a name over it. "When you call, and you will call, tell him Belinda Copper sent you."

Sam, reluctantly, took the piece of paper and placed it in his pocket. "Wha' do I do abou' Robert? He knows somethin'."

"For now, we'll keep him on ice. In the meantime, have Simon run another check on his financial records."

"Wha' for?"

"You said that you offered to help with his wife, and he said that she has to be monitored 24/7. So where is she, and how is he paying for the help?"

The fog in Sam's mind suddenly cleared; these were good questions. "Ye think tha' whoever attacked Meredith is payin' for her treatment?"

"I think Robert Grayers knows a lot more than he's telling us, and this would be an excellent piece of leverage to use, since we can't appeal to his nature as a former cop. Grayers has gotten desperate, McKay, and we'll use that against him."

"Bu—"

"This is my call, not yours." Copper grabbed one of the many stacks of paperwork on her desk and placed it in front of her, but instead of focusing her attention on it and ending the conversation like she usually did, she maintained her eye contact with Sam. Much more softly, she said, "Your friend isn't there anymore, Sam. He's an accomplice in some way, and we need to break him to find the real bad guy. Can you do that?"

Her words both scared and, strangely, empowered Sam: She was willing to make the hard choice so that he wouldn't have to again. "Aye, I can."

***

Knowing that he needed to take a break, Sam left the interrogation floor and made for the morgue; he didn't know whether Bicks would have anything useful for him yet. At least a little walk would help get his thoughts straight before he could continue with the investigation, let alone the interrogation. He walked into the freezing cold room and found the doctor bent over the decrepit body of Peter Daverman. Bicks heard him enter and turned to look at him.

"Agent, you're just in time for my report: Jaimie did her job beautifully, and nothing was out of place in the autopsy. Peter Daverman was hung by his wrists in the woods anti-mortem and stabbed repeatedly with a short-serrated blade, like a steak knife."

"Anythin' else?"

"As a matter of fact, there is: He had a very good dinner just before his death. Prime rib, potatoes, string beans, and red wine."

"Aye, anno tha' part. I meant were ye able t' find anythin' suspicious? Or perhaps somethin' similar t' the other bodies?"

"Not a thing," Bicks shook his head. "Nothing in his tox screen, nor can I find any defensive wounds. Though I highly doubt Mr. Daverman was able to put up much of a fight for the last few years, anyway. His medical history of arthritis, combined with the pneumonia—it's amazing he's held on to life for as long as he has."

Although disappointed, Sam nodded his head in agreement. "Alrigh', keep 'im on ice, please."

Next, Sam made for the third floor where he found his team sitting close together: Simon was typing frantically, his fingers flying across the laptop keyboard. "You're just in time to answer the million-dollar question, boss: How is a part-time janitor, making less than $25K a year, able to pay $3,500 a month for an addiction and

219

recovery center in Pittsburg, which is *not* government funded and approved, I might add, for the last six months?"

"I'm assumin' ye're no' gonna tell me outstandin' credit card debt has anythin t' do w' it."

"Correct," Julie answered. "Grayers has been receiving monthly payments of $3,500 into a bank account made in his wife's maiden name since the beginning of the year."

"The transaction ID's say it's ACH mumbo jumbo, but Simon was able to break down the transaction's codes and trace it back to another credit agency that's completely bogus," Rivera added.

"So ye have no idea where this money's comin' from?"

"Not exactly," Simon balked, "I do know that it's coming from another 'untraceable' offshore account. But, surprise surprise, the name on the account is *another* stolen identity. I'm sorry, boss. This guy is just...really good."

Sam sighed. "Alrigh'...well, a' leas' we can freeze the account, an' tha'll stop the payments t' the rehab centar. Perhaps tha'll give us some leverage w' Grayers." Sam continued looking at Simon's computer, but his mind was on everything that Bicks had told him about Daverman. Considering how briefly they were there just to look at the body, they never really got a good look at the entire grounds. "Pull up a copy of Daverman's case file, will ye?"

The young man looked at him completely confused. "Um, how did we get there from offshore accounts?"

"Jus' do it...an' open up Max Darrel's case file, too. I's on me desk jus' there."

Julie went for the physical file. Simon shrugged his shoulders and began typing again while Sam walked over to their whiteboard, pushed all of the other victims' pictures aside, and started writing everything he remembered about the night Daverman was killed: He was at his home; it was brutal; and it was definitely not like the Christmas Angel MO he had used in his prime.

Simon stopped typing. "Okay... according to the New Bedford Sherriff's department, there were absolutely no signs of a struggle in the entire house, and no signs of forced entry. They concluded that Daverman knew his attacker, and, given his state of physical health, the murderer had their work cut out for them."

"Wha' abou' the footprints I found a' the scene? ...look a' the report on Max, his shoes should be in there."

Julie was already flipping through the contents of Max's case file until she found what she was looking for and handed the photograph to Simon. After he scanned the photograph of Max's shoe treads into his computer, he started typing again, and Sam waited.

"Max was there," Simon said quietly. "The shoe treads are a perfect match. ...Does this mean—"

"No. The footprints were far away from the house, an' they were no' verra old. Bu' i' does mean tha' Max saw wha' happened, an' I'm willin' t' bet tha's wha' really go' him killed." Shaking his head, Sam turned back to the board. "Wha' abou' the nurse? Di' they find 'im?"

"Daverman fired Colin Winkley two months before he was killed, but the Sheriff hasn't been able to find him," Julie answered. "And according to the notes, Winkley's apartment was cleaned out, and it looks like he hadn't been living there for months."

Rivera spoke up. "Even a live-in needs to have a place to go...did Winkley have any financial problems? Or any problems?"

Simon typed. "I'm seeing some credit card debt, but not much."

"What about family? Maybe he's taking care of somebody."

"He's got a brother serving time for drug charges in Parkersburg Correctional. Give me a second, let me see if I can...got it! Okay, Colin Winkley's brother, Phillip seemed to be a regular at Parkersburg's Medical facility until two years ago, right after Colin went to work for Daverman."

Rivera turned to Sam. "I didn't get the mastermind genius vibe from Winkley; he's got to be an accomplice."

"I agree. Why else would he jus' disappear? Somebody came along, offered t' ge' his brothar out of general population, an' moved t' a more secure part of the prison, in exchange fer keepin' track of Daverman. Tha's why there wasnea any signs of forced entry; Winkley gave the murderer everythin' he needed t' know t' ge' in."

"Then he's most likely already dead: He's not useful anymore."

Sam made his notes under Daverman's photo before he stepped back. Crossing his arms across his chest, he huffed in frustration. "This man...he manipulates an' uses people as a resource fer information. An' somehow, he manages t' stay completely hidden while he does it. How? He has t' have a life, friends, *somebody* he confides in."

"Maybe he doesn't, boss, and that's how he does it," Simon offered.

Sam's phone suddenly started ringing. It was the officer in charge of the forensics team at the abandoned house. Knowing it had to be something interesting, he answered with a clear, "McKay."

"Agent McKay, it's Jayda Riggs from the lab. I'm calling to give you the initial findings. First of all, you were right about the basement: There was a body hiding behind the wall next to the stairs. Even though there's not much left, it's been decently preserved from some plastic wrap. Judging by the state of the decay and some of the enthusiastic mice that have been nibbling, he has to have been dead for at least twenty years."

"He?"

"Coroner is positive it's a male, judging by the bones, but we'll be sure to confirm that before the report. Don't you worry. But what I really wanted to talk to you about is that stain under the carpet on the second floor."

"I's no' blood, is it?"

"No, freakier than that: It's amniotic fluid."

Sam wasn't sure if he heard her right. "Wha'?"

"Amniotic fluid. Very old amniotic fluid, at least forty years. We tested a small sample of wood in the middle of the stain and got two different but similar DNA signatures: Some poor woman gave birth in that room, and nobody bothered to clean it up."

"Bring back another sample t' run against fetal tissue."

"Will do," CSI Riggs confirmed before hanging up on him.

Sam lowered his phone in shock.

"What?" Rivera asked, bringing him back to the moment. "What did they find?"

"I think they found the body of Gideon Cauldmor, an' I think they also found the birthplace of our killar. Tha' house has more history than we though'."

Chapter Twenty-two

"So, the guy wants to keep the house off the market because it's the site of his first kill? Or the site of his birth?" Julie asked.

"Maybe both, maybe it's something else that we haven't found yet," Rivera answered her. "The bigger problem is that we still have no idea who this guy is."

"You're not kidding on that, brutha," Simon agreed. "I've scoured every record possible, and the only people living in that house were Gideon Cauldmor and his sister Hannah. I can't find a marriage license for either of them. If, assuming it was her, Hannah was the one to give birth, but she didn't report it or even go to the hospital. Maybe the kid died in childbirth, and that's why there's not a record?"

"Or the kid was shut in and raised by Uncle and Mama Cauldmor, who made sure he was never in the system for their own twisted reasons," Julie countered.

Everyone shrugged in agreement. Sam heard them, but he had turned his attention to Lorraine Wyatt's photo.

Rivera nudged him, "Sam? What are your thoughts on this?"

"I donnea know...Tha' house is obviously a major piece of his past, bu' unless we find somethin' more concrete, i' donnea tell us anythin' more than i's close t' him fer some reason. I' could be his birthplace, or i' could be the first site of revenge. Perhaps i's both. Bu' tha' house existed long before Bennel an' Fitz built the surroundin' neighborhood. Hell, a' one point i' must've been more like a cabin in the woods. There's absolutely no witnesses tha' we can talk to fer information, so we'll have t' wait on the forensics report. An' whoever tha' child is, *if* he's the maniac behind all of this, we donnea have anythin' tha' proves he exists...I think the house is no' our primary concern yet—" Sam turned the picture of Lorraine around to the others "—bu' she is."

"And you're so certain that Lorraine was sleeping with this maniac?" Rivera asked.

"Aye, I am. She go' involved w' this man somehow, someway, an' if we can' find tha' out, then we might be able t' find him. So, we start from the beginnin' since her firs' miscarriage six years ago; a few months before then, she had enrolled in Cuyahoga CC then she suddenly dropped out. Perhaps tha's where she met our killer. Simon, ge' a list of every class she took an' the professors' names, an' a class list. We'll track them down one by one an' ask."

"I'm already on it, boss," Simon nodded enthusiastically. "There were thirty-one other students enrolled in that specific night course; I'm fetching current addresses and numbers right now."

Rivera looked more than skeptical. "From six years ago? She hardly made an appearance in class. What makes you think anybody will remember her?"

"Somebody's bound to."

By the end of the day, the team tracked down everyone on the list to ask about Lorraine, only to be disappointed at every turn. No one seemed to even remember someone named Lorraine, let alone recognize her picture. Their last hope was a philosophy professor who had retired a year after Lorraine's disappearance and was living in a nursing home in Broadview Heights. Sam sent Julie to speak with him, but she quickly learned that the man was suffering from dementia, and the interview took quite some time. But thankfully, he recognized Lorraine and was able to pass along some helpful information.

"Teach says he knew that Lorraine was one of those students who wouldn't last very long in the course," Julie explained to everybody over dinner. "He said at the beginning of every semester, he'd have thirty students, but by the end there's usually only twelve. Students usually drop the course for one of two reasons: It wasn't what they thought it would be like or because it proved to be too tough. According to him, Lorraine was the latter. But he did give her credit for trying her best at first: She asked him for extra credit to help with her grades, so he sent her to the campus library with a list of books to read to help understand the material. So, I went to the library and asked the librarians if anybody who had been working at least six years before was still there, and there are two little old ladies that have been there for ten plus years. One of them recognized Lorraine and said she spent a couple of nights in the library studying until closing time. She also said that she remembered seeing Lorraine meet somebody outside of the library sometimes, and they looked like they were friends, but she never got a good look at the man."

"Please tell me the campus had some security cameras in place that I could try to hack?" Simon asked hopefully.

"Sorry, no. Cameras got installed three years ago."

"Considering the rest of her classmates didn't even know Lorraine existed, we can rule out asking about a boyfriend," Rivera commented.

"Di' the professor evar see her w' anyone?"

"I went back to ask him, but he swears up and down he never saw Lorraine socializing with anybody."

"Wha' the hell attracted this man t' Lorraine in the firs' place? He's been so careful abou' bein' unseen, why would he go ou' of his way t' mee' her at a crowded college campus? Nothin' abou' this man's movements makes any sense!"

"Personally, I've been feeling like we're chasing a new Zodiac killer," Simon commented, "a guy who just kills randomly for no apparent reason and is impossible to catch. All we're missing is the list of demands to the press."

Sam ignored him and started pacing the floor. "Le's take a closer look a' Lorraine's work a' the hardware store. The man loved tyin' his victims up, maybe he bough' wha'ever he used to tie them up from Lorraine."

Rivera stood up from his seat. "Well, they've already closed for the day. We'll have to check it out tomorrow."

"Does this mean we get to go home and sleep now?" Simon yawned.

Julie snickered and nudged him. "Come on, Simon, I'll drop you off."

Everyone started getting ready to go home for the night, but Sam was still sitting in front of the whiteboard staring at everything they knew about Lorraine.

"Sam, it's time to call it a night," Rivera said.

He heard them, but he waved them off and continued to stare. The same questions kept circling around in his mind: Why would this man pick Lorraine? Could Lorraine have been more than a victim? What drove him to kill her? What drove him to target Daverman in the first place? And the most important question of all: What did he want?

Sam's phone started ringing, interrupting his thoughts. He looked down and wasn't surprised to see Meredith was calling him. "Hey."

"Hey, I got that sample that you wanted: I swiped the glass Oliver had been drinking from when he wasn't looking. Do you want me to bring it to you or...?"

"No, no, I'll ge' i' meself. Jus' put it somewhere Oliver cannea see it. Are ye alrigh'?"

"Yes, just going a little stir crazy being shut up in the house all the time. Oliver's the same way. Actually, I think it's worse for him."

"Wha' do ye mean?"

"He and Karliegh had a fight, and now she's not answering his texts. Apparently, she even unfriended him."

Sam couldn't help but chuckle, relieved that his son had regular teenage problems. "Tell 'im t' give i' time. If i's meant t' be, she'll come 'round."

"You know it would be better if you told him that yourself," Meredith said pointedly. A brief moment of silence passed before she followed up with, "Would you mind spending the night here? We're both a little on edge, and I'd feel a lot safer knowing you were on my couch."

"Aye, I can do tha'," Sam smiled. He glanced at the clock, which read 12:06 a.m. With everyone else gone for the night, there wasn't anything more he could do with the case. "Actually, I'm on me way now. Go ahead an' go t' bed, Meredith."

"Alright. I've left some dinner in the microwave for you. Stroganoff."

Sam smiled. "Thanks, darlin'. Ge' some sleep." He heard her snicker her agreement before she hung up. Taking one last look at the picture on the board, Sam mumbled to himself, "Wha's yer story, Lorraine? How di' ye fall in w' a man like this?"

When he couldn't hold back a yawn himself, Sam grabbed his things and made for the elevator.

***

The next morning, while the rest of his team were busy collecting surveillance records from Mr. Gordy, Sam took the DNA sample belonging to Oliver and the fetal remains that Bicks had collected directly to the forensic lab. The labs worked tirelessly, promising that they would get to the DNA comparison as soon as possible. Finally, after a few minutes of just sitting and making the lab techs nervous, Sam left them alone and made for the third floor. His team arrived shortly after him with very little hope in their eyes: Simon had determined that the store owner's computer wasn't sophisticated enough, nor did it have nearly enough storage, to contain more than a year's worth of camera footage, and he added a snarky "If that" at the end of his report. But he did notice they had an Apple account, and they might get lucky there. So, while he was working on sifting through years of invoices and saved footage, the team was back to staring at Lorraine's gathered details and trying to piece together exactly what happened in her life, right up until the moment she was killed. Eventually, Rivera decided to take a break from the thinking and try to put another rush on the release papers for Trevor Wyatt, Lorraine's ex-husband.

"Bingo!" Simon said triumphantly, his fingers finally taking a rest from the lightening-speed clacking he'd been doing for the last hour.

"Tell us what you found, egg-head," Rivera said indifferently. "Quickly, before the prison guards holding Wyatt pick up, and I can't hear anymore."

"Five-year-old security-cam footage with Lorraine Wyatt talking to a few customers, you're welcome."

Julie was impressed. "They still have all the footage from the last five years because of Apple?"

"I told you that I noticed that they have a cloud account, and *nothing* can be deleted from the cloud. Didn't anybody else here see the movie with Cameran Diaz and—"

"Ge' to the point, Simon," Sam growled over his third cup of coffee.

"Yeah, sorry boss. The owners of the store must have very tech-savvy kids 'cause they uploaded everything that gets recorded on the security cameras to a cloud storage system. Since only Apple or the account holders can access it—"

"Did you hack their private cloud account?!" Julie asked, completely appalled.

Simon turned and, in mocked pain, answered, "You wound me, Jules. I only do that to the really bad homies we chase. No, I called the owners back and asked if I could remote access their cloud account through my laptop, so I could run my facial recognition software and save myself hours of searching for Lorraine's face. This is where I'm pretty sure they've got a tech-savvy kid somewhere on the side helping them, because I'm pretty sure they didn't even know what I was talking about, let alone—"

"Abler!" Sam growled.

"They gave me their permission, and I walked them through how to do the remote connect. And now that the facial recognition software is done doing its thing, I've got an approximate total of two hours of footage of Lorraine Wyatt here for the viewing."

"Fantastic," Sam nodded, "Watch it all an' make note if anyone in particular pays special attention t' Lorraine."

"Yes, sir. I'll get right on it."

Sam turned around to face the whiteboard behind him. While Rivera was still on the phone, Julie had her eyes glued to what little details surrounded the strange victim. Curious, Sam nudged her.

"Wha' are ye thinkin'?"

"That this guy has been so careful to cover his tracks since the day he came into the world that I don't think that even Simon will be able to find more than a disguised face. ...But maybe Lorraine wasn't as careful in her movements."

Right at that moment, a messenger from the lab walked over to Sam and handed him some papers. "I'm sorry these took a while, Agent, but we've been backlogged for over a week now."

Sam began glancing over the results of the DNA comparison. "Can ye give me the short answer of the results?"

"The DNA sample you gave me, and the fetal tissue are biologically related."

Sam closed his eyes with a sigh. Nodding, he mumbled "thank you" as the tech turned and left.

"Then your hunch was right: Lorraine was sleeping with the guy that attacked Meredith."

Rubbing his eyes, he nodded in agreement. "Aye, bu' wha' I cannea figure out is why he'd kill her."

"Maybe she saw something that she wasn't supposed to, like that house. The more we learn about this guy, the more I am convinced of just how cold and smart he is. He didn't care about Lorraine; she was just a toy for him to play with until he got bored."

"An' she would've been more than happy t' ge' any ounce of affection from him in the firs' place..."

"What do you mean?"

Sam looked back up at the board but not at the picture of Lorraine. Instead, he turned his attention to the photographs of Bennel and Fitz and Daverman. "This man has made a point of findin' out everythin' he can abou' someone tha' he wants t' exploit. Why would he settle on a serial killer an' a pair of real estate salesmen? ...Perhaps there's more people out there tha' he's blackmailin'."

"Okay, I can buy that theory. But what does that have to do with Lorraine?"

"Lorraine quit her job abou' six months before she went missin'. Her grandmother tol' us tha' she was preparin' t' move out again. ...Mae wouldnea jus' le' her abused granddaughter out of her sight, unless she was convinced she had the means t' take care of herself. Mae had t' have known she had some money. Bu' she has no job history aftar the hardware store, so how was she goin' t' afford livin' on her own, unless someone else was payin' her a small sum?"

"She did make cash deposits into her bank account every week right up until she went missing," Julie nodded. "But what could she have been doing for this guy that made him pay her? Unless he was paying for the sex, and she resorted to prostitution."

Sam shook his head. "Remember tha' Bennel an' Fitz said a messenger gave them the box w' the phone an' copies of the paperwork sixteen years ago? Well...wha' if Lorraine was the next messenger? She's so in love w' this man, sleepin' w' him an' havin' his babies, wha's runnin' t' another business t' make a delivery? Especially if she'll ge' paid fer it?"

Julie snapped her fingers. "When Derrick and I went through the missing persons call list, there was a guy who said that he saw her in the lobby of the company he worked for, but that was months before she went missing! Hang on a second, it's still got to be in the file...here it is! The caller identified himself as a security guard for a jewelry store in Lakewood."

Sam, smiling, nodded more enthusiastically. "How much d' ye think they're payin' a month fer blackmail?"

Julie smiled in turn, but it quickly faded. "But how does this help us? Sure, he might have used Lorraine as his errand runner, but he also used Colin Winkley, and who knows how many others? And they've got to be all dead."

"Aye, anno. Bu' this tells us tha' he's no' only cautious, he's methodical. If Lorraine was playin' deliverywoman, then tha' means she hasnea been the firs' one he's taken advantage of. Look a' everythin' he's done—" Sam gestured to the board "—this man has stalked every one of the people he's used an' victimized: He learns their habits an' weaknesses, an' exploits them all fer his gain, whether i's financial or usefulness. He has no physical type; i's all been completely random."

"Like he's picked them out of a supermarket, which makes him even more dangerous and harder to catch."

"Exactly, bu' he's never been seen by the people he targets, only by the people he uses do the dirty work. We know tha' he used Colin Winkley because his brother needed t' be moved, an' he used Lorraine because she was malleable. She was in a loveless marriage t' a cold, workaholic husband, depressed, an' mentally unstable. This man is a mastar manipulator; tha' made Lorraine an easy target fer him t' use. An' this time, he dinnea have t' blackmail her...he jus' had t' have sex w' her now an' then t' make her feel loved."

Julie shook her head in disappointment. "The more I learn about this girl, the less I feel sorry for her. She could have done so much more with her life. Okay, but how are we supposed to find the new errand boy?"

A small shiver went up Sam's spine, but he quickly pushed it back down. "I think we already have 'im—me ol' partner Robert Grayers."

Julie furrowed her eyebrows. "I know he was a dirty cop, but you really think he would willingly participate in killing people?"

"Somebody's been payin' fer his wife's treatments fer six months, which means tha' *somebody* came t' talk t' him abou' movin' her t' a bettar facility. If he's no' the new errand boy, then I think he might know who is."

"But, considering this guy seems to use people like tissue paper, what are the odds that he'd be using the same errand boy that talked to Grayers?"

"We'll nevar know unless we ask...I think i's time me ol' partner an' I have another chat."

Rivera had just hung up the phone. "Lorraine Wyatt's husband has finally been exonerated and released from prison. Whoa—where are we going?"

"To warm up ex-cop Grayers," Julie answered as she grabbed him by the shirt sleeve and made for the elevator. "Sam is going to break him, *today.*"

Sam smirked; he admired Julie's faith in him, but he wasn't sure he had any faith in himself.

***

Sam stared through the two-way mirror into the interrogation room at Grayers; he'd been brought out of his jail cell about an hour before, but Sam hadn't entered the room yet. Not even once. Whether it was to let his old partner sweat a little bit or because he himself was feeling nervous, he wasn't certain. *He knows somethin', an' this time ye've go' t' ge' i' out of him. No mattar what...*Finally, with a heave of a sigh, Sam stiffened himself upright and walked into the interrogation room.

The familiar icy glare returned to Grayers' face the second Sam opened the door.

"Get out of here! I've made it pretty damn clear that I'm not talking to you!"

Sam paid him no mind as he opened the little manilla folder he was carrying and laid out the financial records Simon had dug up. "I know tha' ye're no' payin' fer yer wife's institute, Robert. Someone else is."

"Have you gone deaf, McKay?! I said I'm not talking to your limey ass!"

"As of twenty-four hours ago, this account has been frozen. So have all yer accounts. An', accordin' t' my man, the next payment fer the center is tomorrow."

The rage in Grayers' eyes quickly disappeared, as he started to make sense of what Sam was telling him. "You wouldn't."

"Lisa's bein' released this afternoon."

"You can't do that!"

"How long di' she last outside of a mental care facility the las' time she was released?"

231

Grayers jumped out of his seat faster than Sam saw the table flip again. He wasn't surprised that Grayers lept towards him, making for his throat, but he was prepared for it. Just as quickly as his old partner tried to attack him, Sam was quicker and jumped to the side, sending Grayers to the ground. Sam jumped on top of him and held his thrashing body as still as he could. When Julie and Rivera burst in and attempted to help, he waved them off. He knew this had to be between him and Grayers. Sam had him pinned to the ground.

"Yer wife'll try t' kill herself by the end of the day, Robert!"

"Let go of me, you bastard! You stupid bastard! I'll kill you!"

"I know tha' ye were contacted six months ago by a man tha' knew everythin' abou' you! He knew abou' Lisa, Danielle, how much ye hate me, an' he also knew tha' ye've still go' friends on the force!"

Grayers didn't completely stop thrashing, but he slowly stopped struggling.

"He's been killin' innocent women, Robert! I know ye can help me find 'im!"

"I'll burn in hell before I ever help you!"

Finally, Sam's last bit of painful restraint was gone. Just as quickly as Grayers had sent them both to the floor, Sam got them both up from the floor and slammed Grayers back against the wall. Picking up a few of the photographs of the dead girls in their crime scenes, Sam shoved them in the former cop's face.

"You helped 'im do this! These women are dead because of yer petty need fer revenge! Ye want t' burn in hell?! Tha's exactly where ye'll be goin'! Ye spent thirty-two years on the force, Robert! Ye saved countless lives as a detective alone! Ye're really gonna' le' all tha' go an' pretend ye donnea know wha's happenin'? Well, take a good look." Sam pulled him away from the wall and bent the man over with a shove, forcing him to look at the other toppled photographs of the dead women. "Do ye really think tha' the lives tha' ye've saved will make up fer wha' you helped this man do? Do ye, Robert?"

Grayers had stopped struggling; his eyes were glued to the photographs on the floor. When his muscles started to relax, Sam could tell that the little piece of his partner that was left was getting to him. Grayers suddenly dropped to his knees, and Sam joined him at his side.

"What can you do for Lisa?" he mumbled.

Sam sighed in relief. "I'll personally make sure she's picked up before she's taken two steps away from the facility."

"How can I know that for sure?"

"If the information ye give me is good, I'll have ye released. Then ye can personally oversee everythin'."

Grayers looked up from the ground and directly into Sam's eyes. The anger was still there, but the desperate need to help his wife, Sam could tell, made him much more willing to cooperate.

"...You're right... about six months ago, some guy came to my door and had a package for me. There was a burner phone inside, and a few minutes later it started ringing..."

On a hunch, Sam took out the photo of Colin Winkley. "Is this the man tha' came t' ye?"

"... Yeah, that's the guy."

"Alrigh', wha' di' he say t' ye over the phone?"

"Just that he knew about my wife's condition and that in exchange for a little information, he could get her into a much better facility. ...I didn't say yes right away; I'm still a cop deep down. But then he said he only wanted some information about you...that he hated you as much as I do...I said I would think about it, and he said I'd be receiving something else in the mail in a few days and to call him back then. Well, a few days later, I got a notice of an open bank balance in Lisa's maiden name and a letter of admission to the care home...I knew that's what he was talking about, so I called the number again and told him I'd tell him anything he wanted to know."

"An' wha' di' he want t' know?"

"Everything," Robert growled. "Where you came from, who your family is, any complaints... absolutely everything."

Sam leaned forward and folded his hands together. "Di' he ask ye specifically abou' Oliver? Meredith? Di' he seem particularly interested in them?"

"Not really, he just seemed to want to know anything about everything; he wasn't too concerned about any particular detail."

Sam felt a surge of relief. *Then perhaps he donnea know abou' Oliver after all!* "Alrigh', wha' were ye doin' ou' a' tha' house? How di' ye know t' look there?"

"A couple months ago, a different guy came back with another package and another burner phone, this time there was a note saying he'd be in touch...I followed him."

"Why?"

"I don't know...a hunch. I thought that maybe he could lead me to whoever I had made the deal with...I just wanted to know who it was I was accepting a bribe from."

Sam's eyes opened wide. "An' he went straight t' tha' house?"

"He seemed more interested in a random spot of ground behind it."

"Wha' do ye mean?"

"I mean he walked a couple hundred yards behind the house and just stood there. He didn't seem to be looking at anything in particular, just the ground. I watched him for maybe an hour, waiting for him to leave before I went to check it out, just in case, he'd dropped something there, but the only thing I could find was a rock."

Could it be? "Wha' di' this messanger look like?"

"He was older, like in his forties, dark hair."

"An' di' anyone evar make contact on tha' burner phone?"

"No."

"Bu' ye still have it?"

"Yeah, it's at my house. It's in the drawer of the side table next to my bed."

Then we've go' it in evidence, Sam thought desperately. "I'm havin' a sketch artist come in; I want ye t' describe the man tha' gave ye the las' phone." He practically jumped away from the table and left the interrogation room. Rivera and Julie were already outside the door.

"If that messenger went to the Caulmore house, then maybe Grayers actually met the killer!" Rivera exclaimed.

"And there's something buried underneath that rock!" Julie added with the same enthusiasm. "It has to be another body...but who's and why the hell is it out there?"

"Aye," Sam nodded. "We've go' t' go back out there. Bu' first, we need t' ge' Simon tha' phone!"

Chapter Twenty-three

The forensics team was still processing the Cauldmor house; all Sam and the other two had to do was find the rock that Grayers had found, which was exactly 200 yards in the back and just before the tree line. The three of them stood on the sidelines and watched as the experts drew a grid of at least 20x20 feet before they began to dig. In no time at all, one of the scientists uncovered the bones of an adult. While the coroner was taking a quick assessment, Sam walked over to listen to his initial findings.

"Well...the only thing I can tell you for sure is that the victim here is a female."

Only a few feet away, another scientist called out, "I've got more bones here!"

"Me too!" yelled another.

Sam went to one, Julie and Rivera went to another, but what they saw in the holes horrified them all: The bones found were so tiny; they belonged to infants. Sam didn't need to wait for forensics to tell him what the black stuff was surrounding the bones. He recognized a plastic bag when he saw it. Within the next hour, four more infant bones were discovered. Six children were buried with one woman.

"Jesus Christ...Wha' the hell happened in this house?" Sam whispered to himself in horror. He didn't know what to think anymore. His phone buzzed with a text from Simon, who had sent him the completed sketch from Grayers: dark, short and receding hair, a pointed nose, and small eyes. As happy as he was to have a face to the mystery, the man in the sketch was so average looking, he could have been anyone, and Sam didn't feel confident enough to let this go public yet.

Sam, Julie, and Rivera watched as the grid got wider; now that everyone knew they were standing on an unofficial graveyard, the entire grounds were going to be dug up to make sure every single burial was discovered. It took nearly twelve hours, but the bones of the woman and five children were all that were buried behind that

God-forsaken house. But that didn't bring anyone much comfort, particularly Sam. He didn't want to leave as the burial site was still being processed, but Rivera reminded him that he had made a promise to Robert Grayers, and that needed to be upheld. Reluctantly, he left the scene. Mrs. Grayers was being supervised in her home by a fellow agent, and before Sam could park the car, Robert jumped out of the back seat and ran to her. As the poor, distraught couple walked into the house without a backwards glance, Sam was already making his way to Meredith's house.

***

Two Days Later

Sam was sitting at his desk just staring at the whiteboard; the rest of the team knew better than to interrupt him while he was thinking, so they kept out of his way and did their part to hound the lab for results. Lorraine's photograph was still on the whiteboard, but Sam's focus had turned to Peter Daverman's photograph, the house, and the picture of whom he could only assume was the body of Gideon Cauldmor. Over and over again, he asked himself: *Wha' is the connection? Cauldmor connected Daverman t' his embezzlin' friends...could they have crossed the wrong man? ...The bodies...wha's so important abou' those bodies tha' would drive a man t' copycat a serial killar? There's easier ways t' kill somebody...*

His thoughts were interrupted by Rivera, who was holding a stack of papers and flipping through them. "Okay, it took dental records combined with facial reconstruction, but the body in the basement is in fact Gideon Cauldmor. He died of multiple stab wounds with what looks like a kitchen knife, and the best that he can figure is he's been dead for twenty-two years."

Sam snapped his head up. "A kitchen knife? Tha's exactly how Daverman was killed."

"Yeah, which tells me that our guy went back to his comfort zone in his MO."

"If that was Gideon Cauldmor they found, then the backyard bones have to be Hannah Cauldmor, right?" Simon asked.

236

"She died of a drug overdose remember?" Rivera flipped through the files. "The DNA on the bones doesn't even come close to Cauldmor's. They're not related."

"What about the kids?" Julie pressed. "He had to have been raping that poor girl and just killing the children over and over."

"Again, no. Five of the fetal remains do have a biological match to the mother, but only one matches Gideon Cauldmor and not the mother."

"What? That can't be right. Why the hell would he be holding a girl hostage, if he wasn't raping her and killing the babies?"

"According to the ME's report, two of those kids were stillborn, and the other four died shortly after they were born. He examined each and every set of bones carefully, and there wasn't anything out of the ordinary, other than the trauma of birth. The two stillbirths' bones were too small to have been fully to term; he estimates they were about 30-34 weeks. The Cauldmor baby was also a stillbirth."

"That poor, poor woman," Simon sighed. "You'd think they'd take her to a hospital or something."

"Was he able to at least identify her?"

"He's put her factors into the system, but nothing's turned up yet."

Sam finally stood up from his desk and looked at Simon; the young man nodded and said, "Right, I'll do better. I'm on it."

Sam took the reports from Rivera's hands and read over them himself. "Says here she's between 25-28, an' buried fer forty-eight years...an' she died of multiple stab wounds as well...Christ, he estimates tha' she firs' gave birth as a teenager." He turned back to the whiteboard. "Have the lab compare the DNA of Peter Daverman t' the five othar fetal remains."

"I already thought of that Sam, and no dice. Those reports are the ones in the back."

"Then run the remains against Lorraine's baby an' Oliver's sample...then compare Daverman's DNA t' the baby an' Oliver."

"What?" Rivera barked, but Julie went ahead and made the call.

Sam turned back to Simon. "Look up cases involvin' men stabbed repeatedly w' somethin' resemblin' a steak knife...go back twenty-two years."

Simon looked up in surprise. "But, what about—"

"Jus' do it," Sam barked.

Simon jumped but his fingers flew across the laptop. "Okay...not including the ones where the killers were apprehended, there's thirty-seven."

"That's got to be too much," Julie countered. "Can you cross-reference them to Cauldmor? Try the schools he went to, what he did for work—"

"Got it... that narrows it down to nineteen. That's not an impossible number, right?"

"No... but it certainly doesn't feel right, either" Rivera answered. "...Did Cauldmor ever practice a religion?"

"I didn't see anything in his file that said he did. Hang on, I'll double check...sorry, the section asking about religious preferences is clean, and there's nothing in the notes from his disappearance."

"What about the sister?"

"Bingo! According to the investigating detective's interview notes, Hannah constantly mentioned God and the Bible...she proclaimed herself a member of The Gathering to Jehovah church."

"I've never even heard of that," Julie said.

"Me neither. Hang on, let me see if I can find something about them... damn..."

Everyone gathered around Simon's computer for a better look, and what they saw was more than disturbing: There were many articles surrounding the 'religion.' Everything from its beliefs to its practices was made available for reading, but one look at the website name was enough for Sam to turn away in disgust: man.inhisimage.com.

"Well, this doesn't surprise me," Simon continued. "Considering y'all found a backyard full of bodies, it makes sense that the Cauldmors were a part of a cult—"

Interrupting him, Julie turned to Rivera and demanded, "How did you know to look for that?"

"This is where my Catholic upbringing comes in handy: Didn't any of you notice that the Cauldmors and Daverman's first names are bible names? Peter Daverman, Gideon Cauldmor, and Hannah Cauldmor."

"But why the hell would Daverman be a part of *any* religion? Didn't we establish that he despised religion because of his mother?"

"He despised his mother and perverted *her* religious beliefs. Remember what Max said: Daverman's whole purpose for doing what he did was to get revenge on his mother. Mae Eyegols told us that Wicca is all about celebrating the Goddess, a female diety. It makes perfect sense to me that he'd choose to be a part of a cult that worships men; it fueled his superiority."

"Cross reference the Gatherin' of Jehovah's dealin's t' the victims ye found," Sam pressed.

Again, Simon's fingers flew. "...Five, and all of them were found within roughly 300 miles of each other from Indianapolis to New Bedford, where Daverman was killed."

Everyone was quiet; the four of them looked back and forth at each other, trying to understand what it was they had walked into. Finally, Sam stepped back to the whiteboard and started writing. "Alrigh', here's wha' we know: There's an unnamed woman, un-related t' the Cauldmors, tha's given birth a' leas' five times. There're six children buried behind tha' house, bu' only one is no' hers."

Julie was next to add, "The Cauldmors were cult practitioners, and judging from the website name alone, the hierarchy was made entirely of men. I know we should wait on the DNA tests to prove it, but I think it's safe to say that every one of those men raped the woman we found in the ground."

"So, the theory is that the guy we're chasing hunted every one of them down and stabbed them to death? Why? And where does Daverman fit into all of this? He didn't father any of those babies...Could the guy we're looking for be the girl's boyfriend or something?" Simon offered. "She was kidnapped and somehow the man that really loved her found out, and he's been spending all this time getting revenge on everyone involved. We know that Daverman was very good about luring women during his Christmas Angel days; maybe he's the one that provided her for the Cauldmors."

"Even if we assume the boyfriend was 16 at the time she first disappeared, he'd have to be like...75 by now." Julie's phone pinged with a text, and everyone fell silent while she looked at it. "It's the lab... I think the boss has a theory that's not too far off from yours, Simon."

Sam could tell by the way she opened her eyes that what he was thinking was right. "Daverman's related t' Lorraine's baby an' my son, isn't he?"

"Yeah, he's the grandfather."

Sam inhaled sharply: All he could think of in that moment was Meredith. He had to tell her all of this, but he knew it would destroy her.

Rivera interrupted his thoughts. "So, just to be clear here, we think what happened is that Cauldmor, his buddies, and his sister started a chauvinistic cult that objectified and used a specific woman for the purpose of breeding. Five other babies died, the Cauldmore baby died, but Daverman's child survived, and then they 'sacrificed' her when she gave them a healthy child. So, that child has been hunting down every member of this cult to brutally murder them the way they did his mother, and he saved his biological father for last. And, because his father was the one he hated the most, he copycatted his MO and killed women that were indirect enough for any of us to miss the connection, but clear enough for Daverman to know that he was being hunted. That's the theory?"

"Yup," Julie nodded. "And because Sam stopped him before he could finish his 22-year plan, he sent a warning shot across the bow to throw us off the trail of Daverman."

"Considering how this entire investigation has gone since Captain Humbar first came to us, I buy it," Simon answered.

Rivera was obviously stunned, but he didn't argue. "Okay, so what are we going to do to catch him?"

Everyone looked to Sam, who was still bewildered as everything came together. "...I donnea know."

A tense moment of silence followed; nobody had anything helpful to offer. They had walked into the middle of a well-thought-out, nearly flawless plan for revenge. It was obvious that the killer would never make a mistake, and any time he did, he quickly cleaned it up before anyone could notice it.

Sam turned back to the board; he loathed the idea of dropping this until another clue, or worse another body, turned up, but no matter how much he went over these cases with a fine-toothed comb, he couldn't find so much as a piece of a needle in this enormous haystack of crime. The best any of them could do would be to reopen the cases involving the other five cult members to look for clues, but Sam wasn't feeling too optimistic about that. He was so caught up in his thoughts, he didn't even hear his phone start ringing.

"Um, boss?" Simon nudged him. "Aren't you going to get that?"

Shaking himself out of daze, Sam answered it without bothering to look at the number. "McKay."

"Oliver's gone!"

He practically jumped from his seat. "Wha'? Wha' happened, Meredith?!"

She was in hysterics, but in between the sobs, she was able to talk clearly enough. "K-Karliegh texted him that she wanted to meet up and talk. He asked me if he could go, and I—oh God, I said yes! I drove him to Fun 'N Stuff, Sam! I wouldn't let him go alone! I was doing everything I could to be careful! I—" Sam put his phone on speaker "—I told him I'd be around the corner, and I'd meet him at the concessions later! That was two hours ago! When he didn't show, I tried to call him, bu-but he's not answering! I had security call him! They can't find him!"

Sam turned to Simon and barked, "Trace his phone! Now!"

"Already on it, but it's dead," Simon looked up in horror. "Even if he turned it off, I'd still be able to get a read on—"

Sam had already started running towards the stairs; the entire team was right behind him. "We're comin' Meredith; stay righ' where ye are! Donnea leave the security guard's sight!"

After sending Rivera and Julie to Karliegh Branders' house, Sam drove like a maniac to the small amusement park; there was a traffic jam on the way, and Sam was about ready to barrel through it with the SUV, but thankfully the cars managed to move just enough out of the way that he could squeeze through. The trip itself was only fifteen minutes with the lights blaring the entire way, but every second that passed felt like an age to Sam. The longer it took to find Oliver was more time for the kidnapper to get away with him. *Or both of 'em,* he remembered. It wasn't just his son that was in danger; if Karliegh really had contacted him, then it was more than likely that she had been kidnapped, too.

The local PD was already on the scene and scouring every inch of the building, the outside amusements, and the massive parking lot. There were some officers interviewing every single person that was inside the center, as well as the businesses that surrounded it. Sam noticed that Humbar was on the scene and leading them, but he wasted absolutely no time in marching straight past everyone with the barest flash of his badge. He was going to Meredith first. He found her still talking to the manager with another officer there, and the moment they saw one another, she ran straight to him and sobbed. "Oh my God, he's done it, hasn't he? He's come after Oliver!"

Sam had been wondering that for the entirety of the trip to the Fun N' Stuff, but he hoped and prayed with all of his heart that he was wrong. He did his best to soothe Meredith as she cried onto his shirt, but not even he could mask the fear that he was feeling. "I's gonna be alrigh', darlin'. We'll find 'im, I promise. Simon!"

His young companion grabbed the manager of the amusement park by the sleeve. "You, me, security camera central, *now!*"

While the manager led Simon away, Humbar was walking towards Sam and his frightened ex-wife. "My guys are going over every inch of the premises and talking to absolutely everyone. I promise you, if anybody saw anything remotely suspicious, you'll be the first to know."

"Chief!"

Humbar turned to one of his officers who ran up with a broken phone in a bag.

"Is this your son's?"

"Oh my God!" Meredith wailed.

Sam's heart was pounding. Shakily, he nodded, "Aye—yes, it is. My man ran t' the manager's office, ge' i' to him now. He migh' be able t' find somethin' on it."

The officer nodded and followed the direction that Sam pointed.

Humbar filled Sam in on everything they knew so far, but he wasn't listening. He was too busy looking around the warehouse filled with different toys and arcade games. Everyone who was there was between the ages of 5-17, and the only adults were the ones who were holding on to the younger kids they had obviously brought out. Anyone not there with a kid would have been easy to notice out of the crowd, even for untrained eyes. Sam's blood grew colder: This was definitely a planned kidnapping.

Rivera called, interrupting Sam's thoughts and Humbar's report.

"Where's Karliegh?" Sam demanded.

"She's not here, her parents said she left with some friends for the Fun 'N Stuff and said she'd be back by dinnertime. We already tracked the friends down, and they said they were with Karliegh, but they took off for some lunch around noonish, and Karliegh stayed at the amusement park."

"Di' she text Oliver?"

"One of the friends says she was talking about it, and that's why they left her at the park, so she and Oliver could have a little private time to talk. They came back at one o'clock but couldn't find Karliegh. They said they figured she'd gone with him to do something else and went home."

"Di' any of them notice anyone peculiar aroun' here when they left her? Anyone tha' looked like they dinnea belong?"

"…They all say no, nobody looked out-of-place or weird."

Sam scrubbed his face, wiping away the beads of sweat that were starting to appear on his forehead. "Keep on 'em; somebody had t' have seen somethin'!"

"I'll call you back," Rivera confirmed and hung up on him.

"Boss! I think I found the guy!"

Sam, Humbar, and Meredith turned to see Simon running back with his laptop open. The picture on the screen was mildly pixelated, but clear enough to make out a young-looking man that was talking to Oliver and Karliegh. From the looks of things, it appeared that he was trying to get past Oliver to talk only with Karliegh, and Oliver wasn't having any of it. Then he left. Simon then fast-forwarded the video to see Oliver and Karliegh walking out of the amusement park for the parking lot, and in the parking lot they continued to walk, hand in hand, until they were out of the security camera's sight.

"I looked all up and down for weird, creepy looking dudes and couldn't find one," Simon said. "This guy was the only one who had contact with Oliver and the girl."

"Can ye tell us who he is?"

"Only if he's in the system for something. Hang on, let me get a good shot of his face...his name's Ried Humphries, and...oh, shit. Sorry, Mrs. McKay. Sam, this kid is in the sex offender registry."

"Ge' the address t' Rivera an' tell 'im we're on our way!" Sam shouted, and Simon was already running back to the car. "Humbar, have yer officers circulate this picture aroun' an' see if anybody saw this man sittin' in the parkin' lot. Meredith, I want ye t' stay here until Humbar's done an' can drive ye home."

She was still shaking, but she nodded emphatically. Sam leaned in and kissed her forehead before he turned and ran after Simon.

Sam was driving once again, but he didn't stop grilling Simon for information. "Wha' was he arrested for?"

"He was caught molesting a thirteen-year-old boy when he was twenty; apparently he was the babysitter. That was only two years ago."

"Wha' the hell is he doin' out of prison?!"

"He was a first-time offender and a model prisoner, and because of the pandemic, they needed to clear out the prison. He was a good candidate."

Sam furrowed his eyebrows in rage before his thoughts cleared: He molested a boy, but he seemed to be harassing Karliegh in the video. "…Check his financial records, has he received any payments lately?"

Simon had to hold the laptop still, but that didn't stop him from typing as fast as lightening with only one hand. "I'll be damned, he deposited $5,000 in cash two days ago!"

"Which is when we discovered tha' God-forsaken house an' started tearin' i' apart," Sam shuddered. "Oliver was his real target! How much further until we're a' his apartment?!"

"Six miles, boss. Rivera and Julie are right behind us."

"Wha' kinda car is registered t' him?"

"A white cargo van."

Sam practically smashed the gas pedal into the floor. The first thing he noticed in the apartment parking lot was a white cargo van. Even though he knew better, Sam didn't wait for confirmation from Simon before he ripped the doors off their hinges: Oliver and Karliegh weren't there. He drew his gun and raced to Humphries' apartment with Simon barely keeping up with him. His only priority was finding Oliver and Karliegh, and he wasn't about to waste a second with protocol. He didn't bother to knock or announce himself when he kicked the door in; he stormed through the apartment, ready to shoot anyone that was in his way. But what he found in the living room made him stop cold: Reid Humphries was already dead.

"Oliver! I's dad! Oliver! Where are ye?! Karliegh?! Karliegh Branders!" No one replied. There wasn't even a muffled sound, but that didn't stop Sam from searching every corner of the one-bedroom apartment. He'd even gone as far as to flip over furniture, though that was more to satisfy his rage than to search. "They're no' here…"

He came back to find Simon bent over the body checking for a pulse, but he knew there wasn't much point in finding one:

Humphries body looked exactly like Max's did in the motel room, stabbed repeatedly and in the right places to cause the most pain before death.

"He's gone, boss," Simon confirmed. "But not for long, his body's still warm."

"Goddammit! We jus' missed 'em!"

Julie and Rivera burst through the door.

"Shit!" Julie exclaimed.

"Everybody take a minute to breathe, okay?" Rivera said calmly. "We're not too far behind him; I'll get an amber alert out ASAP."

"I noticed security cameras in the hall; I'm gonna go talk to management and get working on it," Simon added before he raced out the door.

"I'll get forensics out here to start processing Humphries' apartment," Julie nodded. "In the meantime, I'll start snooping around the van for clues: The kids *had* to have put up a fight when they got moved."

While everyone else raced to get to work, Sam stood there staring at the body of Reid Humphries. while seeing Max in this state was horrific, Sam didn't feel nearly as much compassion for the pedophile on the floor. Enraged, he kicked the dead body with everything he had. But it wasn't enough to quell the sick feeling in his stomach: Oliver was at the mercy of a serial killer, the man who fathered him.

Chapter Twenty-Four

Within minutes of the team splitting up, the entire apartment complex was swarming with police, FBI, and bystanders wondering what in the world was going on. While everyone was able to do their jobs to the best of their ability, Sam's emotions had control of him, and he couldn't think. Rivera noticed and very compassionately asked him to sit in the SUV. Of course, Sam argued, but eventually relented. All he could do was stand out of the way while everyone else processed the scene. Just sitting and waiting for some speck of an answer was maddening, but everyone was constantly updating him the moment they learned anything. Sam was grateful for that much, but he still couldn't get his head in the game enough to help, and that was crippling. Eventually, he was driven back to Meredith's house where he was told to just sit and wait.

A witness saw a man with a black sedan near the white van in question but couldn't recall the license plate. Thankfully it was enough for the amber alert, and Rivera had the information sent out within seconds. Not a moment later, the tips came pouring in: A black sedan was heading east on 82; a four-door sedan was going south on 480; a family in Twinsburg Heights saw a black sedan in their neighbor's driveway, and dozens more like that came through on the line. For the next six hours, Sam's team tracked down every one of the leads, and all of them turned out to be legitimate misunderstandings except for one: A black sedan was heading south on 271 and was discovered abandoned on the side of the road. A piece of a red and grey striped shirt was stuck to the door hinges, which Meredith confirmed was what Oliver was wearing that day. Even after tracing the car, it turned out to be a stolen vehicle from an elderly gentleman three towns away.

The search for Oliver and Karliegh went on for hours, but without a description of the new car, nobody had any idea what to look for. Rivera assured Sam that forensics was taking extra care in the tire track molds and that nothing would be left unturned, but that didn't ease the overwhelming fear that sabotaged Sam's ability to think. His and Meredith's greatest fear had come true, and there was nothing either of them could do about it.

Sam, dejectedly, sat on the living room couch with Meredith; while his team was out in the field scouring every possible lead they could get their hands on, other agents from the office were at Meredith's house setting up their equipment. In the likelihood that the kidnapper might call them, they would be ready to perform a trace. Sam would have felt more comfortable if Simon was there setting things up, as he knew the young man could narrow anything down within milliseconds if he needed to, but the agents that were there were almost as good as him, and Sam knew that Simon would be of more use to the others.

In the twenty-five years he had been doing this job, from the time he was a constable in Scotland to his actions now as an asset of the FBI, Sam had never experienced anything like the paralyzing fear and impotence of not being useful that he was faced with now. He was a victim, forced to step away and let others do their jobs. His job. It was his child who couldn't be found, and there was absolutely nothing he could do about it. It wasn't just maddening, it was debilitating. And watching as the other agents he barely talked to set up or otherwise ignore him and Meredith, it wasn't helping the overwhelming guilt that wracked his mind. He was responsible for this.

For what had to have been the dozenth time, an agent walked right past the two of them without so much as a kind word. And, yet again, Sam asked, "Isnea there somethin' else I can do? Le' me talk t' my team, maybe they've found—"

"McKay," an Agent named Shawn Harlin insisted sternly. "We are doing everything we can, I promise. Please, just sit down, comfort your wife, and wait."

Sam snapped.

"T' hell w' jus' waitin'!" he bellowed. He stood up from the couch so fast he knocked the coffee table over. He knew that poor Meredith needed him to be strong for both of them, but he couldn't take it anymore. He marched past everyone, straight to the kitchen where he knew Meredith had a bottle of his favorite whiskey waiting. He'd normally get a glass and pour one, maybe two fingers, of the alcohol when he was feeling particularly stressed, but this time he drank straight from the bottle without care. The warm and intense buzz wasn't helping him. He didn't expect it to, and he really didn't expect to feel tears brimming at the corner of his eyes. He drank more, and the tears started falling freely. Before he knew it, he was crumpled on the kitchen floor and sobbing into his arm. He didn't hear the door open, but he felt a gentle hand on his wrist, and his head snapped up.

Meredith was in front of him; her eyes were just as red as his from crying, if not more. Gingerly, she took the bottle away from Sam and placed it on the ground next to them both before taking his hands in hers.

"M-Meredith...I'm so sorry," Sam cried. "Th-this is all my fault."

"What are you talking about?" Her voice cracked. "You didn't make anyone kidnap our son."

"Bu' I did," Sam wailed. Scrubbing his face with his hands, he covered his eyes before he could continue. "I should've known tha' the bodies we found were warnin' shots... if I'd've jus' stayed away, if I'd jus' stopped pushin' so goddamned hard! This man... he knows everythin' abou' anyone he wants t' hurt. I should've realized tha' he'd find a way t' ge' t' ye an' Oliver! Bu' I was too...blinded by my need t' catch 'im tha'...This man took our son because I couldnea jus' leave 'im alone...Christ! I'm sorry, luv... I'm so sorry..."

Meredith pried his hands away from his face and fell into his arms, holding him tightly and crying just as hard. Burying his face in the crook of her neck, Sam held her tighter than he had in years, as the two of them sobbed together on the kitchen floor.

"Ahem, Mr. And Mrs. McKay?"

Meredith was the first to let go, and Sam reluctantly did the same as they looked up to see Agent Harlin at the kitchen door.

"Director Copper is here."

Sam rubbed the crying out of his face before he stood up, pulling Meredith up with him. The two of them, hand in hand, went back into the living room and saw Sam's superior there with a young woman whom Sam didn't recognize. She was dressed casually and wore too much makeup. Sam got the feeling she wasn't anybody he would have known from police circles.

"McKay," Copper said in her usual stern yet level manner "This young lady has important information for you."

"Are you Sam McKay?" she asked.

"Aye," he nodded. "Do I know ye?"

"No, but a couple weeks back some guy came into the restaurant I worked at and gave me $300 to find you and give you this," she handed over a cell phone.

Sam furrowed his eyebrows: This obviously wasn't a burner phone; it was a personal phone. "Wha' di' this man look like?"

"Older guy, kinda messy looking like he just rolled out of bed... made me think of a high school teacher I had."

"Max? Was his name Max Darrel?"

"I don't know, I never asked. He came in, ordered a sandwich, paid in cash, and when I was cleaning up the table, he left his phone there with the money and a note asking me to find you at the Cleveland, Ohio FBI office. Here, see?" The waitress handed over a napkin with ink on it that was definitely Max's handwriting. "I thought it was just a joke, but when I saw the video he left you...I figured you really needed this. Sorry it took me a while to find you, but he left specific instructions to not call and to speak to you face to face."

Sam read the note:

I did not forget my phone, please take it to Sampson McKay of the Cleveland FBI office. DO NOT CALL THE POLICE, ONLY SAM MCKAY. This is urgent. Here's $300 for your trouble. Please. 091598.

Sam guessed that the digits were meant to be the code to unlock the phone and they did just that. Going to the photographs, the last thing on them was two thirty-second videos of Max. He didn't recognize the room behind him, but the waitress did.

"That's the men's room," she said firmly.

Starting with the first video, Sam pressed play.

"Sam, God I hope you're the one watching this. Look, I...I didn't do what you told me. I just couldn't leave Daverman alone. I was stalking him...I'm ashamed to admit that more than once I came close to breaking in and killing him myself. One night, I had made up my mind that I would do it, but somebody else was already inside with the old bastard. I never saw his face, only the back of him. He's average height and on the skinny side, black hair. He took Daverman out through the garden and kept pointing to the peonies, saying how hard they were to get a hold of, but he was determined to make his father proud. If I know you, I'm sure you've already figured that part out by now. He hung the old man up by his wrists and held some sort of kitchen knife to his throat. The next part is very disturbing, he said—hold on!"

The video ended. Sam scrolled to the next one. Max was looking around him at the slightest noise.

"He blamed Daverman for leaving him with somebody named Cauldmor. I didn't find out who he was talking about, but he did say in great detail that Cauldmor liked to touch him inappropriately, and his sister would regularly beat him." Max stopped looking around erratically and focused on the camera, looking directly at Sam. "There wasn't any emotion in his voice, Sam. You know that when people kill for revenge, it's an emotional release of sorts. This man was experiencing...rapture. He scared the hell out of me. I ran back to my car after that. I wanted to call you, but my battery was already dead. So, I followed him. I don't think he saw me, but he went east onto the route 208 and headed north, then 376, then on 18 for almost two hours before he got off on...Wassle... West bridge? Something like that, then he turned left for another thirty minutes or so, and then he turned left again and then one more time. I have no idea where we were, but it did look like a hunting lodge that he was pulling into. A lot of trees. I made a mistake, Sam, I got too close and when he started to turn around, I took off. I don't know where he is now... but I have this pending sense of doom that I can't shake. I know that he'll be coming for me. My battery's dying, good lu—"

The video cut off.

Sam looked up at the waitress. "Ye've ha' this fer three weeks?! Why the hell di' ye wait until now t' find me?!"

"Hey, man, I don't own a car! It's not exactly easy to get all the way here from Churchill! And like I told you, I thought it was just some stupid prank. The damn phone was dead anyway, took a while to get it charged up, and then I forgot. Be happy I remembered it at all."

Sam wanted to argue, but Director Copper stepped in between the two of them. Gesturing to another agent, she said, "Thank you for getting this to us, Miss Feener. My people will drive you home, and you will be compensated for the trip."

"Damn right, you'll compensate me," she nodded, "that $300 barely got me here!"

Copper turned back to Sam. "Get this back to the office and start narrowing down where Max was. I'll have your team meet you there."

"Yes, ma'am," Sam nodded. He squeezed Meredith's hand before running out the door.

***

By the time Simon, Julie, and Rivera had walked through the elevator onto the third floor, Sam was almost finished triangulating the directions that Dr. Darrel had given in his videos.

"Copper filled us in," Simon said rather excitedly. "I *knew* the good doctor wasn't a murderer! Boy's straight up James Bond!"

"That's why he was tortured before he died," Rivera said next. "This guy had to have figured he'd left something on his phone, and Max wouldn't give up where it was."

"Wasser Bridge Road, tha's wha' he had t' have meant," Sam muttered to himself. His finger on the map, he continued to follow Max's directions until he could only be sure of a small radius which he circled. "Simon, look up this area an' see wha's around it, an' if anybody owns any property ou' there. Give i' a twenty-mile radius."

Ever quick with his laptop, Simon typed away.

"It's mostly farmland in that region," Julie answered. "But, from what I saw at Daverman's house, the trees in that area are so thick, anybody could have a little shack down those dirt roads."

"A few people do," Simon confirmed. "I'm showing three different property claims in that area, but one guy died a year ago."

"Doesnea matter, we'll search the entire area. Call the locals an' have them start; we'll meet 'em there!"

It was nearly three in the morning by the time they arrived to find the Sheriff and a large group of volunteers on dirt bikes and four-wheelers ready to help. The Sheriff had announced that the civilians were to search the forest and not to enter any premises they come across, but radio those in for law enforcement to check out. They had only gotten roughly two miles covered. Sam didn't care; he was more than grateful for the local help and told them to carry on while he and his team checked out the homes.

One by one, they entered each premises and searched them from top to bottom. The first two had local couples living in them, but the men didn't resemble the description Max left him. The last shack was a way deeper to the west, and everyone gagged the minute they opened the door: The smell of a decomposing body that had been there for some time was overwhelming. Sam took a good look at his face and started: It was Colln Winkley, Daverman's old nurse. But there were no signs of Oliver or Karliegh. An hour had passed, and Sam was starting to panic again, until a call came in from a radio.

"This is Volunteer Micculs, I've found a girl here tied up! I am ten minutes west of the road."

"Send up yer flare!" Sam barked into the radio.

Not long after, a faint red light was shining in the night, and everyone started running towards it.

"Is she alive?!" Rivera asked next.

"Yes, she's alive and crying."

"Okay, do not touch her. I repeat, do not touch her until we arrive."

"Officers, you should know that she's naked. I'm not going to touch her, but I am going to cover her with my jacket."

"That's fine, but do not touch her and do not try to untie her. Wait for the sheriff's department. Volunteers, continue your search. Repeat: Continue your search; do not go towards the flare. There is still one more child missing."

Sam and the others weren't the closest people to the flare; the Sheriff arrived first. Sam recognized Karliegh from that day at Oliver's school and sighed in relief: Max had given them one final gift. The poor girl was terrified and had bruises all over her body, but she was alive. Sam watched as the first responders attended to her, waiting for his chance to ask her about Oliver; he knew that she had to be checked out first, but Oliver was still missing, and the clock was still ticking. Finally, the EMT nodded, and Sam stepped forward.

"Karliegh, do ye remember me?"

The young girl looked up at him completely bewildered at first. "You're Oliver's dad."

"Aye, tha's right. Where is Oliver now? Is he still ou' here?"

"I don't know," she cried, her voice hoarse.

"Alrigh', sweetheart, tell me wha' happened when ye an' Oliver left the Fun 'N Stuff. Where'd ye go? Why di' ye leave?"

"We...we wanted to go for a walk...the arcade was too loud."

"Wha' abou' tha' man tha' was tryin' t' talk t' ye? Di' he say' wha' he wanted?"

"Sam, take it easy," Rivera reminded him. "Give her a minute to answer you."

"…I'm sorry, darlin'. Le's start again, tell me abou' the man tha' was talkin' t' ye."

"He...he said I was really pretty..." she cried. "He wanted to buy me a pop...I told him no thanks, I was waiting for somebody. But he wouldn't leave me alone. Then Oliver...Oliver came over and pushed him away...then he left..."

"Alrigh', then wha' happened?"

"...I wanted to talk to Oliver... we had a fight... we walked out to the parking lot... that guy hit Oliver on the head, and somebody grabbed me... I tried to fight him, I really tried! But he put something over my mouth... and then I woke up here... it hurts..." Karliegh started crying again, and the EMT put his hand on her shoulder.

"That's enough, guys. We're taking her to the hospital; you can continue your questions there."

But Sam had heard all that he needed to hear: There were two in the kidnapping, and after the killer murdered the pedophile, he took off with both kids. He turned to the Sheriff, who had already made sure to carefully preserve the rope that was binding Karliegh for them, and barked, "We're no' done searchin' ye'; I want every inch of this forest covered before anyone leaves!"

"You've got it, agent."

Sam lifted his flashlight and started scouring the ground for tracks, but it was impossible to make out anything with how badly the ground had been mucked up by everyone. Forensics would perform elimination comparisons, but he continued to look for a trail or anything out of the ordinary. Nothing stood out. Once he had given up the hope of finding anything useful, he returned to searching the forest with the others.

All through the night, the forest was scoured by Sam and the team, the Sheriff's department, and the volunteers. Sometime around 4:30 a.m., search dogs were brought onto the scene, but they couldn't find a scent to track from the ropes on Karliegh. Daylight was starting to peek through the trees; the volunteers were exhausted, and a few had left. Sam didn't want to give up, but the further they got away from where Karliegh was found, the horrible feeling that Oliver wouldn't be anywhere in the woods was growing. Eventually, the Sheriff had to declare it was time to dismiss everyone for some rest, and they would keep looking later. Sam and the others had no choice but to agree, so they made their way to the hospital where Karllegh was being treated. Her parents, Karen and Victor Branders, were already there and at their daughter's side while the young lady was sleeping.

Once they found the attending doctor, he gave them the facts: He performed a rape kit with the consent of Karliegh's parents and was unfortunately able to confirm that she had been assaulted. What was worse, she was a virgin before. There wasn't any sperm to be found, but he expected there would be spermicide from the use of a condom. She also had bruises on her thighs as well as the remainder of her body, but there was no internal bleeding or sprained bones. The doctor's exact words were: "He roughed her up a little, but aside from raping her, nothing too damaging." He was then paged over the loudspeakers and left Sam and his team alone.

Rivera was the first to speak. "Why would he leave Karliegh alive? She might be able to ID him."

"No, she won't," Sam shook his head. "She was passed ou' when he assaulted her; he knows his identity wasnea in any danger."

"She was just a bonus for him," Julie nodded her agreement. "Oliver was his real target. And we're not going to find him in those woods, Sam."

His companions looked at him with more than just pity; behind the sympathy, there was the steeled coldness they had to have whenever they delivered bad news to a victim's family. Sam knew it well; he had to do it enough in his line of work. He didn't want to believe them, but he knew the statistics of recovering a kidnapped child just as well as they did. And considering how the man they had been chasing for the last eight months had dodged them at every turn and was always three steps ahead of them, the chances of finding Oliver again were even lower than normal. Sam clenched his fists together, but it wasn't enough. To his left was a vending machine, and he punched it with enough force that the glass cracked. He wanted to keep punching it, but Julie and Rivera were already doing everything they could to hold him back. Even though Rivera was a whole foot shorter than Sam, he had a good grip on his arms, while Julie helped push him into a nearby chair to settle down.

The commotion Sam had caused drew the attention of staff and patients; while Rivera and Julie explained that the damages caused would be paid for, Sam sat there helplessly staring at his damaged hand: He'd broken a knuckle this time; he could already feel it. But that pain was nothing next to the knowledge that he and Meredith might never see their son ever again. Right at that moment, his ex-wife was calling him. He stared at her picture, trying to will himself to answer the phone and lie to her, tell her that they were still searching and not to give up hope. But he couldn't do it. He put the phone back in his pocket and ignored the way it buzzed against his hip.

***

When Karliegh woke up an hour later, Rivera and Julie conducted the delicate interview while Sam had his hand looked at. The poor girl couldn't give them any useful information, as the doctor confirmed that she was drugged and had been assaulted while unconscious. She never even got a look at her attacker's face; she only saw the face of the man who was first harassing her the day before, and he was already dead. Her traumatized parents swore up and down that they never saw anyone suspicious in their neighborhood, and certainly not a white cargo van or a black car. Eventually, the team realized that the Branders wouldn't be any more helpful than the other victims, so they gave them their contact information and left.

The three-hour drive back to Cleveland was quiet, unbearable. Rivera had told Sam that he would need to take time off, and he would personally make sure that Copper got a detailed report of why. Julie, although not nearly as enthusiastically, agreed that the best thing for him and Meredith would be to be together. They insisted up and down that they, and Simon, wouldn't stop searching for Oliver.

"I've got a friend in missing persons that's better than the best," Rivera insisted. "I'll bring him in and make sure this is his top priority."

"And you know Simon with his kick-ass facial recognition program; if Oliver or that maniac's face shows up in so much as a gas station parking lot, he'll find them," Julie agreed.

Sam heard them, but he wasn't really listening. He continued to stare out of the window as Rivera drove. He wasn't looking at anything in particular, just staring off into space. He was exhausted, hungry, and his hand hurt, but all of this was nothing compared to the feeling of the terrible, harrowing numbness that was engulfing him. He felt his phone buzzing in his pocket with a text message but couldn't bring himself to look at it. The others had gotten a text at the same time, and Sam could guess it was Simon sending them all something. He didn't care anymore, any fight that he had left was extinguished.

"Sam, Simon was able to pull a little more off of Lorraine's phone," Julie said encouragingly. "He got some of the guy's face. He's wearing a hoodie and glasses, so he had to do a facial comparison to the sketch, but it's definitely the same guy Grayers gave us. We know what he looks like now, this is good."

He was only doing it to appease her, but Sam pulled out his phone and looked at the half photo Simon had found. Sure enough, he was covered too well for a clear shot of his face, but he could tell from the nose that it was definitely the same man from the sketch. That still didn't give him any hope.

"I' doesnea mattar," he mumbled.

"Yes, it does," Rivera said encouragingly. "He may kill everyone who sees his face, but he can't kill every computer in the world."

Sam's mind suddenly cleared. "…Say tha' again?"

"What? That he can't kill a computer?"

"No, no, before tha'."

"He's killed everybody who's ever seen him," Julie said, "So what?"

Sam sat up straight, the mind hazing numbness combined with no hope was gone. "He's killed everyone who's ever seen him, bu' Grayers go' a look a' him an' was able t' give us a sketch?"

His companions realized what he was saying just as suddenly as he did.

"So why did he leave Grayers alive?" Rivera asked.

"Forget that, Grayers and his wife are in danger!" Julie shouted. "If he hasn't killed them already, he might be on his way there now!"

"An' he migh' have Oliver w' him, or I'll beat i' out of him if I have to," Sam snarled.

Rivera slammed his foot on the gas pedal and turned on his siren. Julie called Copper, and Sam called Humbar: They needed to get to Robert Grayers' house now.

Chapter Twenty-Five

Rivera didn't even park the car before Sam jumped out of his seat and started running towards Grayers' front door. Humbar and Copper had arrived only just after them, but he wasn't about to wait for backup. His gun drawn, he ignored the throbbing in his hand as he pounded on the front door of the Grayers home.

"Robert! Lisa! Open up!" He continued to pound, but nobody answered. He kicked the door in with ease and stormed in, the others right behind him. But they were too late: The living room was in complete disarray, no doubt from a struggle. In the midst of it all, Robert Grayers lay on the ground face-down. Sam rolled him over and saw the multiple stab wounds and knew he was already dead. He searched for a pulse anyway. It wasn't there, but his body was only barely warm, which meant that he'd been murdered only a few hours ago.

Everyone else had already started searching the rest of the house, and an officer from above yelled he'd found the wife in the upstairs bedroom in the same condition as her husband. That didn't deter Sam: He remembered the layout of this house and knew that Robert had a few nooks and crannies they could investigate. The killer had moved in such a rush the last 24 hours, he *had* to have left something behind this time: a hair, a fingerprint, a footprint, anything at all that might lead them to Oliver. His hope was back, and he wasn't going to give up again, not now when he was right on the killer's tail.

Sam moved through the house quickly before going to the shed outside. An officer had to use bolt cutters to get past the lock, and Sam practically shoved him out of the way once he had finished. Ripping the door open, Sam's heart nearly stopped: Oliver was inside the shed. He was tied up and unconscious, and a bead of blood had traveled down the side of his face. Holstering his gun, Sam rushed to his side and checked the boy for a pulse: He was still alive.

Sam cried out in relief. "Oh, Christ!"

"He's here!" The officer with the bolt cutters yelled through the radio.

Within minutes, the entire force was swarming to the shed: Everyone stayed out of the way while the EMTs rushed to Oliver. Sam let everyone do their jobs, but not once did he let his son out of his sight.

"I's alrigh', son, we've found ye. Ye're alrigh', now."

Oliver was loaded into an ambulance; Sam was right next to him the whole drive to the hospital, and the first thing he did was call Meredith once they got moving. After the ambulance stopped, Sam was practically pushed out of the way as Oliver's gurney was lowered and rushed inside. Because of the Covid pandemic, he wasn't allowed to keep watch while they tended to him. Impatiently, his nerves throbbing, he paced in front of the hospital.

"Sam!"

He turned to see Meredith running towards him, tears streaming down her face. "Is he alright?! Where is he?!"

"Aye, he's alrigh', luv."

"But you said that he's unconscious! How can we know what that—that monster did to him if he's—"

Sam pulled her into his arms. "He's alive, darlin'. The doctors are takin' good care of him, an' we'll be able t' see him soon. Everythin's alrigh', now. I promise."

Meredith relaxed, but the panic in her voice was still evident. "I need to see my baby."

"Anno, and ye will," he whispered soothingly.

The two of them didn't stop holding one another; as much as Sam tried to just be there for his wife and their son, his mind kept going back to the details of the crime scene, and so many questions were running through his mind: Did Oliver witness the man kill Grayers and his wife? Did he ever figure out the truth about Oliver? Is that why he left him behind? But the one that plagued him most of all was the one that he dreaded: What exactly did he do or say to the boy? Part of him hoped and prayed that Oliver had remained knocked out for the entirety of his ordeal, but the other part of him couldn't help but wonder if Oliver might have another clue for them. The mixed feelings going through Sam made him sick: Just once, he wanted to be a father first and a cop second, but now more than ever he wanted to catch this man. *I's me rage,* he rationalized with himself, *Tha's why I'm still lookin' fer him. Oliver migh' help—*

"I have to tell him, Sam," Meredith mumbled against his chest, interrupting his inner conflict. "I have to tell Oliver the truth... but he probably already knows, doesn't he?"

He held her strongly and firmly, but he couldn't lie to her. "...I think he might."

She was trembling.

"D-do ye want me t' leave ye two alone when ye—"

"No...I don't think I can do this without you...I don't even know how I'm going to tell him..."

Sam placed his hands on her shoulders and gently pushed her away until she was looking at him. "We'll figure i' out, an' we'll do i' togethar."

Her lips trembled, but a small smile pulled at the corner of them.

"Are you the parents of Oliver McKay?"

Meredith broke away from Sam and rushed to the doctor. "Yes, we are. Is he okay?"

"He has mild a concussion, and it would appear that he was drugged, but yes he's okay. We've got him on an IV, and we've administered Naloxone; it's an antidote for overdoses. His vitals are stable, and we're keeping a close watch on him, but he will be alright."

"When d' ye think he'll wake up?"

"Most likely in a few hours."

"Can I see him?" Meredith pleaded.

"Yes, ma'am. Nurse Moran will take you to his room."

While Meredith walked to the awaiting nurse, Sam cleared his throat to get the doctor's attention and quietly showed him his badge. "Doctor, my son was kidnapped fer nearly eighteen hours. Now, I need ye t' tell me...di' ye see any signs of sexual abuse when ye examined him?"

The doctor's eyes opened wide. "Um...I didn't see anything that suggested sexual trauma, the bruises we found on him were consistent with being bound and held captive."

Sam looked over the doctor's shoulder to make sure that Meredith was gone. "Alrigh'...ye may have t' perform a rape kit. Here is my superior's numbar an' my badge number; ye can' confirm w' her tha' this is part of an ongoin' investigation."

"Yes sir," the doctor nodded. "I promise I will get on this. But, for now, I have to insist that you go be with your wife and son."

Sam sighed. "Aye, thank ye."

After donning a face mask, Sam was led by another nurse to Oliver's room. Wires and tubes were coming out of everywhere and connected to various medical equipment, but it was the headdress that was wrapped around the boy's temple that made Sam's heart ache. The pedophile must have hit him harder than he'd thought to need that kind of attention. Meredith was by his side, his hand in hers. The look of relief mixed with worry on her face was unbearable for Sam to see, and the exhaustion that both felt from being up all night only made it worse. He came around the bed and pulled up a chair next to her. He wanted to suggest that she try to catch some sleep for a few hours, but he could already tell that would have been a futile argument: She wasn't going anywhere until their son was awake. There wasn't anything more to be said. He wrapped one hand around her shoulders while the other rested on his son's leg, and the two of them sat together and waited.

Two hours had passed, and Oliver was still sleeping, but Julie was calling Sam's phone. After assuring Meredith that he would only be a few minutes, he got up and left the room before answering.

"Tell me ye found somethin'."

"Robert put up a hell of a fight before he went down, and he managed to get some hair and skin epithelial cells in the process. I'll make sure the lab does a comparison to Oliver's DNA first to make sure it's actually him we're dealing with."

"Wha' abou' Lisa?"

"She struggled a little, though not nearly as much as her husband did. The ME thinks he saw blood under her fingernails and forensics took a sample, but it's probably her husband's blood from the killer's hands."

Sam sighed in relief. "Well, a' leas' we have *somethin'* t' work w' this time. He was obviously in a hurry."

"Yeah, no kidding: Forensics is still working on the shed, but they found a lot of good prints all over the door alone. It'll be some time before they're finished with the elimination process, but I think we've finally gotten lucky, and this man got sloppy."

"Wha' abou' the neighbors? Robert put up a hell of a fight, surely somebody heard somethin'."

"The only other resident in this neighborhood had enough weed on him to send the whole precinct to Mars. Nobody saw or heard anything....How's Oliver?"

"Still unconscious, bu' he's stable."

"And Meredith?"

Sam looked back at her through the small window to the patient room: The dark circles under her eyes were so pronounced, it was almost impossible to determine the last time she'd slept soundly. "Barely keepin' i' togethar."

Julie didn't say anything, but Sam could almost hear her nodding over the phone. "We're almost done here, I'll let you know the minute anything else comes up."

"Aye, thank ye, Jules." Sam hung up and went back into the room. He'd barely sat back down when Oliver's left hand jerked, and his eyes fluttered open.

"It's okay, honey," Meredith said softly, but the tears of joy were streaming down her face. "We're here, and you're safe now."

Oliver looked at her first, then his attention turned to Sam, who could already tell that something was definitely wrong. He recognized the look of confusion, shock, and betrayal in the boy's eyes, and his hope that Oliver had been unaware of his ordeal was immediately gone: Something awful had happened in the eighteen hours he'd been held captive.

"Oliver?" Sam pressed gently.

"The man that took me...he called me son." His voice gave away what Sam could already see in his eyes, and Meredith took in a shuddered breath. "He...told me things...a—and then he made me watch..."

"Oh my God," Meredith sobbed.

Oliver turned his focus to her. "Mom?"

"I...I should have talked to you about this long before now..." She had started to hyperventilate; Sam took her hand in his. "Honey...the man that took you...he at—attacked me..."

Sam watched Oliver with bated breath; the boy's expression was so hard for him to read, and he kept his eyes fixed on Meredith. She took a ragged breath before slowly, and painfully, recounting every excruciating detail for him of the night it had happened, including that she was forced to keep the real location a secret because of her bosses. It was long and intense for the three of them, and Sam had to squeeze her hand more than once to help her continue.

"Six weeks after it happened, I learned that you were coming. At first, I—I was scared. I didn't know if I could be a single mother. And because of who fathered you, I...I didn't know if I could give you the life that you deserved...love you the way that you deserved..." She stopped trembling and met Oliver's eyes; a small smile pulled at the corner of her lips. "But the first time I saw your heart beating...I knew then and there that no other mother could love you as much as I did. How you came to be...that didn't matter anymore. Right there and then, you were my son. Not his."

Tears had started to pool at the corners of Oliver's eyes. He turned to look at Sam. "H—he told me that you had figured out who my gran— who his father was...He said I'm destined to be like them."

All the pain and anguish that had engulfed Sam in the last eighteen hours was immediately replaced with rage.

"Ye're not," he insisted.

"My father is a rapist...a killer... and my grandfather—"

"You are not one of them," Meredith interrupted. "Oliver, honey...what he's done, what he did to you, there isn't some grand design that says you'll be like that. You have always been our child; you're nothing like him."

"Yer mother is exactly righ'. Ye're no' them, an' ye nevar will be."

"Then why did he make me...why did he show me..." Oliver turned away from them both. In the quietest, most hurt filled voice Sam had ever heard come from his son, he asked, "Could you guys please leave me alone?"

Meredith sucked in another ragged breath; Sam didn't know what more they could do. It had to be enough that he was awake, and he would make sure that the hospital kept a close watch on him. Gently, he placed his hands on Meredith's shoulders and pulled her, very reluctantly, away from the young boy.

Not a word was spoken as they drove back to Meredith's house; Sam had all but made up his mind that he would be finishing the bottle of whiskey when they walked in, but he had the feeling that Meredith would want to try something similar, and that was the only thing stopping him from drinking this problem temporarily away. He parked in the driveway and had barely gotten the key in the door when Meredith collapsed onto him, crying uncontrollably. Once the door was opened, he held her tight as they walked to the kitchen together.

"This is all my fault!" She wailed. "I should never have kept this a secret from him!"

"Ye had yer reasons, darlin'."

"That's no excuse, and you know it; you told me so hundreds of times!"

Sitting her down at the kitchen table, Sam went to the cabinet and retrieved two glasses, along with the bottle he'd thought of earlier. Careful to only pour a half glass each and leave the bottle out of reach, he walked back and handed her one. She accepted it without question and took a big drink, wincing at the burn.

"Nobody could make ye do anythin' ye weren't ready for, luv'. Includin' me. Tellin' Oliver the truth abou' this man has always been yer choice—"

"And any hope of him understanding why I couldn't talk about this for so long is gone now!"

"Because yer choice was taken away from ye again," Sam insisted. "If ye need t' blame someone, darlin', i's me ye should be blamin'. I should have stopped lookin' for 'im the second I knew wha—"

"No!" Meredith, muffled by the hands that covered her face, said emphatically. "No... no, you're right... the only person to blame for all of this is that son of a bitch! ... It's like he's raping, not only me again... but all of us this time... Oh my God! How will any of us get through this?!"

"We will, Meredith. I promise ye tha' we will."

Finally, she dropped her hands from her face and took another drink. Followed by another wince, she faced him directly and said the last thing he thought he'd hear her say in this moment: "I want you to move back in."

Sam nearly choked on his whiskey. "Wha'?"

"What we're facing now...I won't be able to do this on my own. We all need help, and you and I need to be there for Oliver. You're his father, Sam, not that sick bastard. And, now more than ever, he's going to need both of his parents. I know it, and you know it."

Speechless didn't begin to cover how Sam felt. "I.. I donnea know tha' now is the time t' be makin' such a rash—"

"Stop it," Meredith insisted. "Just stop it. Sam... Oliver isn't the only one that needs you; I need you too. I know the last time I asked you to do this was right after we got divorced when he'd gotten into trouble—"

"An' wha' makes this time any different?"

She was just about to retort back but quickly stopped herself; Sam felt guilty for being so quick to jump to an argument.

"You're right, this is just like the last time. But the truth is, I've been wanting to talk to you about this since Christmas. I just...I didn't know how to...Never mind. You're right; now isn't the time to talk about this." Meredith drank the last of her whiskey and practically slammed the glass back on the table. "Just... can you please forget that I said anything about it?"

Sam nodded, but it was only to appease her. It wasn't that he didn't want to come back home again; it was what she said before that scared him more than the idea: that they would all need help. There were things he hadn't told Meredith that would need to come out, most notably what had happened with Grayers' daughter. And he wasn't sure if he was strong enough to face that again, especially now.

***

Copper had told Sam that he wasn't to return to the office for at least two weeks, but after 17 hours of sleep he was on his way back to the third floor. None of his team, including Rivera, tried to say otherwise, and he was grateful. The initial forensics reports from Grayers' house was just coming in.

"Grayers may have been a dirty cop, but he did us a favor and didn't go down easy," Julie commented. "Blood, skin, and hair on him are all paternal DNA matches to Oliver."

"He wasnea a dirty cop," Sam said firmly, earning a curious look from everyone (particularly Rivera). Ignoring them, he continued. "Wha' abou' the samples found on Lisa's body? Are they the same?"

Rivera was holding those results. "No... it says here it's a completely different DNA sample from Grayers, and it's female."

"Oh, great," Julie shook her hea, "He's already found another toy to use until he's outgrown her."

265

"Di' any of the prints on the shed come back w' somebody?"

"Yup, and you're not going to like the answer," Simon confirmed. "The only set of prints that shouldn't have been there belong to a woman named Kimber Raisley. She's got a couple of possession charges and DUIs, did a nickel in Warren Correctional back in 2013. The last time she checked in with her parole officer was six months ago. He probably assumed she'd OD'd behind a dumpster somewhere."

"Wha' was she usin'?"

"Her drug of choice was crystal meth."

"Which is probably what they gave Oliver," Julie added. "This guy knows he's going to have to move quickly, so he brings along his newest throwaway girl to open all the doors and whatnot, so nobody will be able to get anything on him."

"But Grayers put up just enough of a fight to get a tiny piece of him," Rivera nodded. "Unfortunately, this guy has never existed since birth. For the first time in the 45-50 years he's existed, we're only just now getting his DNA."

"Which is the first time he's ever left any behind," Simon added sullenly. "I went ahead and checked all of the FBI's databases and then some for a DNA match to *any* open or closed cases, and I've got squat. There isn't even anything on the other five stabbing cases that we know about."

"And the police chalked those murders up to random acts of violence from homeless nutjobs," Julie said, throwing the files down on her desk. "This guy is so damn meticulous...just *one* fingerprint off the shed would have been great!"

Sam listened to all of them, but there was still one glaring question that he couldn't understand. Finally, he voiced it. "Why di' they leave Oliver behind? An' why a' Grayers house?"

"Because it's all a game to him," Rivera answered. "His twenty-two-year plan of revenge has finally come to an end, and now he's found a new playmate. He left Oliver behind just to screw with you, Sam. Don't let him."

"Wha' abou' the phone?"

"What phone?"

"The one that he hand delivered to Grayers?" Sam turned back to Simon. "Have ye had a chance t' examine i' yet?"

"Yeah, but there's nothing on it: no outgoing calls and no incoming."

"Wha' abou' physically? Was there anythin' hidden inside it?"

"The lab guys have taken the thing apart piece by piece, boss," Julie shook her head, "It's just a regular burner phone, paid for in cash, and not even used. Not once."

Fortunately, the box of evidence pertaining to Grayers was still in their possession, and Sam rooted through it until he retrieved the burner. Taking it out of the evidence bag, he turned it on and kept twisting it around in his hands, as if hoping he'd see some tiny, microscopic detail that would give him something to go on.

"There has t' be a reason he lef' this w' Grayers... i's like he knew we'd find it."

"Or it could be that he wants you to fixate on this, and he's just trying to throw us all off the trail again," Rivera countered. "If he really wanted to contact us, wouldn't he have done it before we figured out he'd go after Grayers? What more could he possibly want to say to you, Sam?"

"McKay, you're on leave."

Sam closed his eyes and sighed when he heard Copper's voice coming behind him. Setting the phone down on the desk, he turned to see his superior (figuratively) glaring him down, her arms crossed.

"You, your son, and your ex-wife have been through a traumatic event and need proper time to recover from it."

"Copper, I cannea spend three weeks doin' nothin'."

"Resting and taking care of your family is not nothing, McKay," the director answered. "If I remember correctly, you have a thing for boats. So, when your son is released from the hospital, go fishing. And to make sure that you won't do anything foolish during that time, you will surrender your badge and your service weapon for the duration of your leave. That is a direct order."

Normally, this was the time that Copper would walk away under the assumption that her orders were going to be carried out. But by the way she continued to stare down Sam and the others, ever unflappable and not moving, Sam could tell that wouldn't be the case this time. Reluctantly, he removed his gun from its holster and his badge from his pocket and handed them to Copper. She gestured towards the elevators where her faithful assistant, Evan Dower, was waiting to escort Sam out of the building. But before he left, he turned back to the team and said, "Keep tha' phone on."

Chapter Twenty-six

The first place Sam tried to go was back to the hospital, but as soon as he got to the right floor, the nurse informed him that Oliver did not want any visitors. Not even his own parents. Meredith had also tried to see him earlier (after learning that she too needed to take time off from work), and had informed Sam as much, but he still wanted to see for himself. Sam thought about going back to Meredith's house and commiserating with her some more, but the brief conversation they'd had about him moving back in kept replaying through his mind and stopped him from doing so. He thought about doing as Copper suggested and going fishing, but that would mean he'd have to go to Meredith's house anyway for the boat, and he knew he'd never make it to the lake. He went for a drive instead, but that did nothing to help sort out the complicated thoughts and emotions he was feeling. He knew that Meredith was right, and Oliver would need both of them and their support as he was helped through the trauma of his kidnapping experience. The fact that he and Meredith were closer than ever made him want to say yes to her offer. He could already see the future: He'd move back in, Oliver would get the right help that he needed, and the three of them would be a 'happy family' once again. But, just like before, something would happen that would drive the two of them apart again. Sam didn't know if he had the strength for that, but keeping the woman he loved and raised a child with at arm's length wasn't, he knew, fair to either of them either. Without a case to turn his concentration to, he was forced to face this and ask himself the hard question: Was he willing to do what he had to, if he wanted to get back together with Meredith? It wasn't just a difficult question; it was a painful one.

Eventually, Sam found himself in front of Mae Eyegol's house. He didn't understand why he valued her insights, but in that moment, she felt like the only person who might understand how he was feeling. He, hesitantly, knocked on her door.

"Just a minute!" She called.

He could hear the old matriarch shuffling to the door, and he stuffed his hands in his pockets while he waited. The surprised look on her face when she opened up didn't come as any shock to him; she probably figured that he was there to ask another question related to her granddaughter again.

"Agent McKay? Was there something else that you needed for your case?"

"Actually, I'm no' workin' righ' now. I...I wondered if I migh' ask ye a question."

She blinked at him through her half-moon glasses curiously, but eventually she stepped out of the way. "Please, come on in. Can I make you some tea?"

Sam chuckled. "Aye, tha'd be nice."

While she walked back to her kitchen, Sam made his way to the living room and took a seat on the antique couch. He was so busy trying to put the questions scrambling around in his mind into a clear context, he didn't even see her come back in with the mug. She had to hold it in front of him before he knew she was there. Smirking, he asked, "Wha' mystical brew di' ye make me today?"

"Chamomile," she answered calmly, a small smile pulling at the corners of her lips. "But there's also some rose hip extract and raw honey in there."

Sam blew on the steaming liquid before taking a sip: It was very good, and the floral aroma did calm him somewhat.

"You seem upset," Mae said casually, taking a seat on the chair across the coffee table.

He didn't know where to begin; looking around her home at the blooming herbs that were practically growing on the walls, he was reminded that he wasn't the only person who had been keeping a secret that, at one point or another, ate the bearer alive.

"When I firs' me' ye, ye were leadin' a meetin' t' a group of Christians. ...Ye talked abou' forgivin' the people tha' wronged ye, abou' how God is a daily antidote...somethin' like tha'."

Mae cocked her head to the side, obviously curious about his declaration. "Are you here to ask me about forgiveness, Agent McKay? Or did you want to talk about God instead?"

"No, no. I's jus' tha'...Ye tol' me ye nevar stopped believin' in Wicca, bu' the persona of Mimi Smith was a devout Christian woman. Fer a practicin' witch, tha' had t' have been hard t' keep such a secret fer so long. Di' ye ever tell anybody abou' yer past?"

Without much hesitation, she shook her head. "No, I did not...but there have been many times in the last five years that I wished I had."

"Why?"

"Because it is a part of me. I'm not ashamed of my beliefs, Agent. ...For so long, I believed that I was hiding this part of me because I was protecting the people I loved: my daughter, and then my granddaughter..."

"Because of wha' happened w' Daverman?"

"It did start out that way, but I never really told you the whole truth. ...Eventually, when I started to really believe that I had nothing to fear anymore, I seriously thought about telling my daughter...Aurora was her name. But...Aurora had her own problems in life that she had a hard time coping with. Finding out that her mother is a practicing witch in the middle of Christian-land—she wasn't capable of handling that. And I didn't want to make her suffer the consequences for a lie that I had already cultivated for so long... my daughter didn't handle things well, Agent. She hung herself when Lorraine was two, after she found out that her husband had been cheating on her since the day they met. I just couldn't tell her about this."

"Bu' wha' abou' Lorraine? Ye could've tol' her."

"I suppose I had kept this to myself for so long, I was used to it staying out of the light. It was only after Lorraine had been missing for six months that I started entertaining the thought of how things might have turned out differently for her, if I had let her share in this secret with me...No matter how different a parent can be from another, they always end up making the same mistakes: thinking they must hide whatever truth they're hiding from their children in order to protect them. ...I don't suppose you would do me the courtesy of telling me why you're asking these things?"

Sam shifted uncomfortably in his seat. "Ye're... no' the only one w' a secret."

The sympathy in Mae's eyes unsettled him, but he kept his eye contact.

"I'm an old woman, Agent McKay. There are few things in my life that I regret. Keeping my true self from my girls is the biggest regret of all. So, please take it from me when I tell you: Keeping a secret from the people you love for so long...it's not worth it."

"Except there's a difference: Yer secret was abou' who ye are. Mine...is no' as simple as tha'."

"Yes, it is. It's obviously something that has an impact on you, for good or evil. That part doesn't matter. What does matter is whether or not you can live your life the way you want to if you keep it to yourself. Because if the answer is no, well, then you have a choice."

"An' wha's tha'?"

"Either A) Continue keeping your secret to yourself and risk your decision hurting the people you love someday, or B) do the brave thing and let them in and trust them to accept you with it."

Sam snickered. "If only everythin' were as black an' white as ye think."

"Young man, I'm 85 years old. I can assure you; things really are that black and white. Not easy, or quick, but black and white they are." Standing up, Mae took the empty mug from Sam's hands. "I'm going to go ahead and tell you the cliché thing, agent: Don't make the same mistakes that I did."

Sam laughed and nodded. "Aye... alrigh', I'll do me best."

"Good," she smiled.

He stood up from the couch. "I donnea want t' take up anymore of yer time. Thank ye fer the tea."

"Agent McKay, you may come back any time for tea."

Sam left Mae's house still feeling conflicted, and yet calmer than he had in some time. He knew he could trust her wisdom; now it was just the matter of working up enough courage to act on it. He couldn't help but scoff at the ironic situation of his predicament: His philosophy has always been that no matter how hard anything gets, you have to try. And yet, in quite possibly the hardest situation of his entire life, he wasn't sure if he could try. Sitting in the driver's seat of his car, squeezing the steering wheel until his knuckles were white, he wrestled with himself on his options: either let Meredith go and keep this to himself, or let her in and trust to hope. Both choices would be painful, but only one provided a chance. He made up his mind: He would try. He put the car in drive and went directly to Meredith's house.

It didn't matter that he'd practically been living there for the last couple of months anyway, Sam still knocked on the front door.

Waiting for an answer, he was trembling. Part of him was practically screaming that this was a horrible time to discuss this when their son was still in the hospital, but the other part of him was saying there would never *be* a good time to tell her the truth, and he would just have to do it. If he thought talking to Mae was difficult, this was going to be even harder, and he didn't even know where to begin.

Meredith opened the door wearing her pajamas and a bathrobe; from the dark circles under her eyes, Sam could tell she hadn't been faring any better than he had, even with sleep. "Hey, forgot your key?"

"Hey...may I come in?"

He could already see the concern and confusion brewing in her eyes, but she stood to the side and answered, "Of course you can. What's going on?"

"Meredith, I... Christ, I donnea even know where t' start..."

"It's that serious, huh? Come on." Meredith took his arm and pulled him to the living room. Taking a seat on one end of the couch, Sam sat on the opposite end and leaned onto his knees, his hands folded together, unable to look her in the eye.

He tried to find the right way to talk to her, tell her what had been haunting him for so long, but he couldn't find the words. Meredith didn't push him; she sat patiently, the concern etched in her features was very clear, but she didn't press him. When she leaned over and took one of his hands in hers, Sam relaxed a little. "I...I've been thinkin' abou' wha' we talked abou'...the truth is I...Christ..." he scrubbed his face with his hands and let out a deep breath. "Do ye really want me t' move back in?"

"You know I do," she nodded. "But, Sam, I don't want you to feel like you have to just because I want you to. Obviously, this bothers you—"

"No, no, tha's no' it, luv. I do, I really do want t' move back in."

The obvious joy that made her glow was quickly replaced with fear. "But?"

"But... there's somethin' I have t' tell ye before I can do tha'..." Sam could feel his hands shaking worse than ever; he closed his eyes and tried to find the right words. "Ye're...the reason we...I'm jus' as responsible fer our divorce as you are. I nevar cheated on ye, tha's no' why. Bu'...I donnea blame ye fer runnin' t' Ryan like ye did...I left ye lonely; I know tha' now."

"Sam, you're starting to scare me. Whatever it is you're trying to tell me, please just come out and say it."

He stood up and paced the room; he was just about to ask her for a glass of whiskey, thinking the burn might help him finally get the truth about what Danielle Grayers did to him out in the open. But he quickly shut the idea down: He knew that would have been the cowardly thing to do, and she deserved to hear it straight from him.

"Alrigh', alrigh'... d-do ye remember three years before the divorce...things had...we were fightin' more, I started buryin' meself in work—"

"Yes," she nodded, "that time is pretty hard to forget."

"Aye... before it'all, we'd had a fight...an' I dinnea sleep a' home that night. Remember tha'?"

Meredith furrowed her eyebrows, searching her memory for the specific moment he was talking about. "I think I remember that."

"Right... somethin' happened—"

Meredith's phone started ringing; Sam groaned. *Of all the possible times*—but by the way she looked at her phone, he immediately snapped to attention.

"It's the hospital!" Meredith said, the panic in her voice evident. When she answered, she put it on speaker so he could hear too. "Hello?"

"Is this Meredith McKay? Oliver McKay's mother?" said an unfamiliar female voice.

"Yes, and Oliver's father is here with me too."

"Mr. And Mrs. McKay, my name is Gwen. I'm the nurse who's been attending your son today."

"Is he alrigh'?" Sam asked.

"I'm...not able to say over the phone. I need to ask the two of you to come down to the hospital right away. It will be better to tell you in person. Please don't panic; we have your son on our monitors, and he's stable."

"Wha' the hell happened?!" Sam demanded.

"I'm sorry, Mr. McKay, but I am not at liberty to tell you anything over the phone. Please, listen carefully: Oliver has been moved from the recovery ward to the psychiatric ward, so when you come through the front doors—"

Sam wasn't listening anymore; grabbing Meredith by the hand, the two of them raced to the car and Sam used his siren the whole way to the hospital. Oliver being moved into psychiatric care wasn't good; he had a very good idea what had happened, but he didn't want to admit it to himself or to Meredith.

Once they were at the hospital, it took a few minutes to get through the hallways to the psychiatric ward, but Nurse Gwen was already waiting for them at the double doors.

"Tell us what happened!" Meredith demanded.

"Mr. And Mrs. McKay, Oliver attempted suicide this morning."

Sam closed his eyes as his fears were confirmed.

Meredith sucked in a ragged breath. "What? H-how?"

"He was getting a shower and...he tried to hang himself with the towels. When I went in to check on him, he was already passed out, but we were able to revive him and stabilize him. Once we were certain that we had him back, he was moved, and I called you."

"Bu' he is alrigh'?" Sam pressed. "He's no' in any danger of... brain damage or anythin'?"

"He hasn't woken up yet, but yes, we're certain that there won't be any lasting effects. We got to him in time. He's been moved to the care of Dr. Susan Wai. She's one of the best psychiatric physicians in the nation. I promise you; your son is in the best possible hands." Nurse Gwen scanned her keycard and led the two of them through the hallway to the psychiatric ward's desk, where a young, Asian woman was waiting.

"Hi, Mr. And Mrs. McKay, I'm Dr. Wai."

"Why?!" Meredith wailed. "Why would he try to kill himself?!"

Sam wrapped his arms around her and held her; in a soft, soothing voice, he answered, "He's been through the worst possible trauma of his life, luv... i's alo' fer anyone t' process."

The young lady doctor nodded sympathetically. "Your husband is right, Mrs. McKay. Unfortunately, suicide is not uncommon for kids in Oliver's situation, but it's also not always predicted. Because of the nature of Oliver's injuries, he was being seen daily by the hospital's on-call psychologist, and his last report, which was yesterday afternoon, stated that Oliver was coping as well as could be expected. There weren't any red flags that he might attempt to harm himself. But what is important, is that he was found before he suffered serious damage, and I can assure you that in my ward, he will be monitored 24/7 and will not have the opportunity to try again."

Slowly, Meredith nodded. "Okay...okay. Can we see him?"

"I can only let you see him for a moment; there are other patients in our ward that are high-risk individuals. Follow me, please."

Sam's arms were still wrapped around Meredith as they followed Dr. Wai through the hallway until they came to a large room with three other people on gurneys. All of them were hooked up to monitors, and their wrists and ankles were constrained; Oliver wasn't any different. Sam shuddered when he saw the nasty, large, purple bruise forming around his neck. Like every patient there, he was unconscious and had his own attendant monitoring him closely. While Meredith rushed to the boy's side, Sam stood stark-still in complete shock; he didn't think the bastard who kidnapped Oliver could have done any worse damage, but he was wrong. Sam knew this was his fault, and nobody could convince him otherwise: Oliver was paying a horrible price for his unwillingness to stop looking for that killer.

"Danny, could you keep Mrs. McKay company for a moment?" Dr. Wai said to the attending nurse. "Thank you. Mr. McKay, would you mind stepping outside with me, please?"

The doctor had to tug on Sam's elbow before he knew what was going on, but he followed her back out to the hallway though his eyes were still on Oliver.

"Mr. McKay...may I call you Sam? Or would you prefer Agent?"

"—Um, Sam is fine."

"Sam, I'm afraid the admitting staff didn't record a very thorough account of your son's state when he was found. I do understand that it had something to do with your job, and Oliver was a victim of it. If you wouldn't mind, I'd like you to recount to me the exact details of his experience, as you know it."

"Why?"

"I'd like to have a complete picture of what Oliver experienced, so that I may be able to help him better. Recovery from trauma this severe, combined with a suicide attempt, is very delicate and, to be frank, not always successful, if the full situation isn't disclosed. Obviously, it will be some time before Oliver tells me or my staff the truth about what happened during his experience, so perhaps you could fill in a few blanks for me."

"Yeah...alrigh', I can do tha'..." for the next fifteen or so minutes, Sam did his best to describe in detail about the day Oliver was kidnapped right up to the minute he was found: Every clue, every place they searched, he was careful not to leave anything out that he could legally disclose. Dr. Wai listened very patiently and, occasionally, made notes in the chart she was holding. "An' then he was discovered in the shed, which I'm sure the admittin' staff has all written down fer ye."

"Thank you, this will be very helpful," she nodded. "I did say it will be some time before Oliver is able to truly talk about what happened, but in the meantime, I can recommend a very good family therapist who would be able to help you and your wife at this time. He's here on site, and I can try to arrange a visitation with Oliver after your sessions if you'd like."

Sam's phone started ringing; Rivera was calling him. "Um...I'm sorry, I have t' go. Talk t' me wife, please."

Sam turned around and looked for another quiet spot before he answered. "Wha's up?"

"You need to get back to the office ASAP."

"Wha'? Copper said I'm on leave—"

"You were right, Sam: he did call the burner, and he was looking for you. We tried to leave you out of this and trace him, but his only words were, 'I won't speak to anyone but Agent Sampson McKay. I'll call back in fifteen minutes.' Copper knows, and she's letting you back for this. I'll meet you at the front door."

Rivera hung up. With one last look down the hall at Oliver, Sam ran through the hallways and back out to the parking lot. Using his siren again, he raced through the streets until he was back at the office where, as promised, Rivera was at the front door waiting to check him in.

"We've got two minutes until he calls; Simon is all set up and ready for the trace."

Sam nodded as they ran up the stairs to the third floor; channeling all the pain and rage of watching Oliver suffer, he steeled himself. He had this man's DNA, had a good idea of what he looked like, and now he would finally hear from the man himself. And he was determined to get a name. Sam had been playing his game long enough; he wasn't going to let him get another win if he could help it.

The two of them burst through the doors to the third floor: Simon and Julie were waiting for them with the burner phone sitting on the desk all alone. Copper was also there, her arms folded across her chest, and she nodded a quick greeting to Sam. Her stoic presence didn't do anything to help Sam, but he appreciated her taking the time to be there, in case he needed it, even though he suspected she would personally escort him off the grounds the moment the phone call was over. He didn't have time to worry about that, though, as he tried to steady his breathing while Simon went over everything he had ready.

"I've got this phone wired, boss: The minute he says 'hello,' I'll get a bead on him in fifteen seconds flat."

Before Sam could answer, the burner started vibrating on the desk. The number was unknown, but Julie nodded that it was the same one from before. Taking another deep breath, Sam lifted it to his ear. "Hallo?"

"How is my son?"

He had a tenor voice that wasn't unpleasant, but his first words already had Sam's blood boiling.

"He's no' yer son."

He chuckled first before replying. "Yes, I'm sure that you feel that way, given you helped Meredith raise him. Very well, how is *our* son?"

"You are no' any par' of him in any way, ye sonnoffabitch!"

"You've run the DNA tests, Sam, and you know that DNA doesn't lie. Oliver's blood is my blood and, as you've figured out by now, Peter's as well."

Sam wanted to scream into the phone, but one look at his team reminded him that he needed to stay calm. "Then why di' ye leave 'im behind? Why are ye callin' me now?"

Simon started waiving his hand frantically, mouthing 'I've got him!' Rivera and Julie ran out the door.

"First question: as a gift. Second question: because you've managed to do something that no one has ever done before, Sam. You figured out my plans before I could finish them. Admittedly, it was very frustrating having to put everything on hold for you. But, after taking the time to consider all, I'd be lying if I didn't say that your abilities are impressive. Congratulations, Agent Sampson McKay, I'm a fan of your work."

"If ye're such a fan, then ye know tha' I'll find ye eventually."

"Oh, I'm sure that you will try, which brings me back to my gift. Now that you know exactly what I'm capable of, I'd like to extend a professional courtesy and give you a warning: Don't get in my way again."

A chill ran up Sam's spine as he said it. "…Wha' is yer name?"

Again, he chuckled. "Normally I wouldn't ever give that information out to anyone, but since it's you: My name is Seth."

"An' wha' makes ye think I'll listen t' yer 'warnin', Seth?"

The light, tenor voice suddenly got deeper and menacing. "Because, if you cross me again, I will not only take away everything that you love, but you'll never get it back."

Sam clenched his fist. "If ye evar touch Meredith or Oliver ever again, no' even my duty t' the law will stop me from makin' ye bleed."

A moment of silence passed before he heard Seth snicker. "We'll see."

He hung up.

Sam turned to Simon, who was already typing away on his laptop. "The signal's gone, but Julie and Rivera are close...they're right on top of him!"

A heavy moment of silence passed as Sam, Simon, and Copper waited for a report from the others. Finally, Simon's phone rang. It was Julie.

"The bastard played us again!" She shouted. "There's nobody here, just an elaborate setup of computers. He re-routed the entire phone call."

Simon stood up, his laptop in hand, and approached Director Copper. "Ma'am, request permission to meet Julie and Rivera at the site to try and crack the code so I can pinpoint—"

Copper interrupted him with a wave of her hand. "Get going."

"Thank you, ma'am." Simon ran off.

Sam hadn't moved; the burner was still in his hand. He wanted to crush it into tiny pieces. He was about to when Copper, very gently, removed it from him. "Agent McKay, you are still on leave. I want you to stay away from this office until your son is well enough to be released from the psych ward."

He turned to look at her directly. "How di' ye know abou' tha'?"

"It's my job to know," she answered simply. "Evan will walk you out."

Her right-hand man suddenly appeared with a smile. Reluctant to leave the burner behind, Sam did as instructed and followed the young man back down to the entrance. Evan Dower, in his usual way, kept trying to talk to Sam and say happy and encouraging things, but Sam didn't hear any of it. Every word of that phone call was replaying through his mind; undoubtedly, Simon had made a copy. The first second he could, Sam would have a copy of the conversation sent to him; he was determined to become so familiar with that voice, he would know it better than his own. Because, right then and there, Sam had already decided one thing: He would hunt Seth Daverman down, and he would kill him.

To Be Continued.
Sam's Team will return.

Cited References

Colossians 3:13
"Bear with each other and forgive one another if any of you has a grievance against someone. Forgive as the Lord forgave you."

PENTAGRAM
https://en.wikipedia.org/wiki/Pentagram
https://www.alchemyengland.com/site/index.php/2020/03/baphomet
-and-the-inverted-pentagram/

YULE-Winter Solstice
https://en.wikipedia.org/wiki/Yule#:~:text=In%20most%20forms%2
0of%20Wicca,do%20so%20with%20their%20covens.
https://www.learnreligions.com/about-yule-rituals-2562970

WICCA NAME
https://en.wikipedia.org/wiki/Craft_name

About the Author

K.M. Hardy has held an interest in solving crimes since childhood. Graduating with a degree in Criminal Justice in the top ten percent of her class, she went on to work for the government for ten years. Her experience in Law Enforcement and Corrections has given her invaluable insight to the world of crime and politics, which had earned her a finalist spot in a ghost writing competition for the renowned James Patterson. She currently resides in the mountains of Utah with her husband, their three children, and their faithful German Shepherd.